Peter Tremayne is the fiction pseudonym of a well-known authority on the ancient Celts, who utilises his knowledge of the Brehon law system and seventh-century Irish society to create a new concept in detective fiction.

Peter Tremayne's ten previous Sister Fidelma novels, most recently *Act of Mercy*, *Our Lady of Darkness* and *Smoke in the Wind*, are also available from Headline, as is a Sister Fidelma short story collection, *Hemlock at Vespers*.

An International Sister Fidelma Society has been established with a journal entitled *The Brehon* appearing three times yearly. Details can be obtained either by writing to the Society at PO Box 1899, Little Rock, Arkansas 72203-1899, USA, or by logging onto the Society website at www.sisterfidelma.com.

'The Sister Fidelma books give the readers a rattling good yarn. But more than that, they bring vividly and viscerally to life the fascinating lost world of the Celtic Irish. I put down *The Spider's Web* with a sense of satisfaction at a good story well told, but also speculating on what modern life might have been like had that civilisation survived' Ronan Bennett

'An Ellis Peters competitor . . . the background detail is marvellous' *Evening Standard*

'A brilliant and beguiling heroine. Immensely appealing' *Publishers Weekly*

The Haunted Abbot

Peter Tremayne

headline

First published in 2002 by
HEADLINE BOOK PUBLISHING

First published in paperback in 2003
by HEADLINE BOOK PUBLISHING

10 9 8 7 6 5 4 3 2

ISBN 0 7472 6435 X

Typeset by Palimpsest Book Production Limited,
Polmont, Stirlingshire
Printed and bound in Great Britain by
Mackays of Chatham Ltd, Chatham, Kent

HEADLINE BOOK PUBLISHING
A division of Hodder Headline
338 Euston Road
London NW1 3BH

www.headline.co.uk
www.hodderheadline.com

In memory of Moira Evans
(22 September 1951 – 4 August 2001)
a great friend, who offered support
and encouragement and
believed in Sister Fidelma

Do not stand at my grave and weep.
I am not there, I do not sleep.
I am a thousand winds that blow,
I am the diamond glints on snow.
I am the sunlight on ripened grain,
I am the gentle autumn's rain.
When you awaken in the morning's hush,
I am the swift uplifting rush
Of quiet birds in circled flight.
I am the stars that shine at night.
Do not stand at my grave and cry,
I am not there, I did not die . . .

Anon.

Even when there is no law, there is conscience.

Publilius Syrus
First century BC

Historical Note

The Sister Fidelma mysteries are set mainly in Ireland during the mid-seventh century. This story, however, takes place while Fidelma and her companion in adventure, the Saxon Brother Eadulf, are en route to Eadulf's birthplace of Seaxmund's Ham, in the land of the South Folk (modern Saxmundham, Suffolk), in the kingdom of the East Angles (East Anglia) in what was to become England.

It should be remembered that East Anglia and the kingdom of the East Saxons (Essex) to the south had only been converted to Christianity by Irish missionaries a few decades before Fidelma's visit, which takes place in December, AD 666.

In AD 653 King Sigebert of the East Saxons was baptised by the Irish Bishop of Lindisfarne, Finan. Finan sent one of his brethren, Cedd, to work among the East Saxons. Cedd was to attend the famous Synod of Whitby in AD 664 as an advocate of the Celtic Church. He built a church at Lastingham and died there soon after of the Yellow Plague. King Sigebert and his East Saxons returned to their pagan worship but Eata, the new Bishop of Lindisfarne, sent another Irish missionary to reconvert them.

Some years earlier, in the East Anglian kingdom, a prince of the royal house, also named Sigebert, had to flee to Gaul to escape being killed by an ambitious cousin who claimed the kingship. In Gaul, about 610–12, he met the famous Irish missionary Columbanus (c. 540–615), who had founded monastic centres at Annegray, Luxeuil and Fontaine and went on to establish the monastery of Bobbio, in Italy, which is said to have been the model for the abbey in Umberto Eco's *Name of the Rose*.

Sigebert eventually returned to East Anglia having been converted by Columbanus to Christianity. Between 631 and 634 he brought missionaries into his kingdom. Among them was a Burgundian named Felix (d. AD 648), who set up his abbey at Dunwich, while a group of Irish missionaries, led by Fursa (known to the Angles as Fursey – 575–648), established their abbey at Burghcastle. Fursa was accompanied by his brothers, Foillan and Ultan, and by many other Irish religious. Among them were Gobban and Diciul, the latter leading the first Christian mission to the South Saxons (Sussex) and establishing his church at Bosham (AD 645).

Fidelma's companion, Eadulf, had been an hereditary *gerefa*, a magistrate, in Seaxmund's Ham before being converted by these Irish missionaries and receiving his religious training in an Irish foundation.

After the decision taken at the famous Council of Whitby in AD 664 (see *Absolution by Murder*), most Saxon kingdoms accepted Roman influence as being in the ascendant over the original Celtic Christian concepts. But in December 666, at the time this story is set, Christianity was still very new and the old pagan ways were dying hard. The East Angles and East Saxons were not even a generation away from their initial conversion from worship of their gods and goddesses – Tiw, Woden, Thunor, and Frig. The power of the old deities was such that even today, in the English language, the days of the week are still named after them – Tuesday, Wednesday, Thursday, and Friday – while the Easter festival takes its name from the fertility goddess Eostre. Christmas coincided with the pagan Saxon feast of Yuletide.

Sister Fidelma is not simply a religieuse, a former member of the community of St Brigid of Kildare. She is also a qualified *dálaigh*, or advocate of the ancient law courts of Ireland.

The Ireland of Fidelma's day consisted of five main provincial kingdoms; indeed, the modern Irish word for a province is still *cúige*, literally 'a fifth'. Four provincial kings – of Ulaidh (Ulster), of Connacht, of Muman (Munster) and of Laigin (Leinster) – gave their qualified allegiance to the Ard Rí or High King, who ruled from Tara, in the 'royal' fifth province of Midhe (Meath), which means the 'middle province'. Even among the provincial kingdoms, there was a decentralisation of power to petty kingdoms and clan territories.

This cohesion was not yet reflected among the warring kingdoms of the Anglo-Saxons. At the time of Fidelma's visit there were around ten or eleven such kingdoms, including petty kingdoms. Of these there were three main contenders for power – Northumbria, Mercia and Wessex. Each was fighting to establish its king as the Bretwalda – 'ruler of Britain'. A cohesive unit which could be recognised as England was not to emerge for another three centuries after Fidelma's time.

We should remind ourselves of the cultural perspective from which Fidelma views the Anglo-Saxon kingdoms, and discover how she could be an advocate in her country's legal system – a thing impossible in Brother Eadulf's native land.

The law of primogeniture, inheritance by the eldest son or daughter, was an alien concept in Ireland. Kingship, from the lowliest clan chieftain to the High King, was only partially hereditary and mainly electoral. Each ruler had to prove himself or herself worthy of office and was elected by the *derbhfine* of their family – a minimum of three generations from a common ancestor gathered in conclave. If a ruler did not pursue the commonwealth of the people, they were impeached and removed from office.

The monarchical system of ancient Ireland had more in common with a modern-day republic than with the feudal monarchies which developed in medieval Europe.

Seventh-century Ireland was governed by a system of sophisticated laws called the Laws of the Fénechus, or land-tillers, which became more popularly known as the Brehon Laws, deriving from the word *breaitheamh* – a judge. Tradition has it that these laws were first gathered in 714 BC by order of the High King, Ollamh Fódhla. Over a thousand years later, in AD 438, the High King Laoghaire appointed a commission of nine learned people to study and revise the laws, and commit them to the new writing in Latin characters. One of those serving on the commission was Patrick, eventually to become patron saint of Ireland. After three years, the commission produced a written text of the laws, which is the first known codification.

The first complete surviving texts of the ancient laws of Ireland are preserved in an eleventh-century manuscript book in the Royal Irish Academy, Dublin. It was not until the seventeenth century that the English colonial administration in Ireland finally suppressed the use of the Brehon law system. To even possess a copy of the Irish laws books was punishable often by death or transportation.

The law system was not static and every three years, at the Féis Temhach (Festival of Tara), the lawyers and administrators gathered to consider and revise the laws in the light of changing society and its needs.

Under these laws, women occupied a unique place. The Irish laws gave more rights and protection to women than any other western law code until recent times. Women could, and did, aspire to all offices and professions as the co-equals of men. They could be political leaders, command their people in battle as warriors, be physicians, local magistrates, poets, artisans, lawyers and judges. We know the names of many female judges of Fidelma's period –

Bríg Briugaid and Aine Ingine Iugare, for example, and Dari, who was not only a judge but the author of a noted law text written in the sixth century.

Women were protected by law against sexual harassment, against discrimination, against rape. They had the right of divorce on equal terms from their husbands, with equitable separation laws, and could demand part of their husband's property as a divorce settlement; they had the right to inherit personal property and the right of sickness benefits when ill or hospitalised. Ancient Ireland had Europe's oldest recorded system of hospitals. Seen from today's perspective, the Brehon Laws seemed to enshrine an almost ideal society.

This background, and its strong contrast to Ireland's neighbours, should be understood in order to appreciate Fidelma's role in these stories. Fidelma went to study laws at the bardic school of the Brehon Morann of Tara and, after eight years of study, she obtained the degree of *anruth*, only one degree below the highest offered in either bardic or ecclesiastical universities in ancient Ireland. The highest degree was *ollamh*, which is still the modern Irish word for a professor. Fidelma's studies were in both the criminal code of the Senechus Mór and the civil code of Leabhar Acaill. Thereby she became a *dálaigh* or advocate of the law courts.

Her main role could be compared to that of a modern Scottish sheriff-substitute whose job is to gather and assess the evidence, independent of the police, to see if there is a case to be answered. The modern French *juge d'instruction* holds a similar role. However, sometimes Fidelma is faced with the task of prosecuting or defending in the courts or even rendering judgments in minor cases when a Brehon was not available.

In those days most of the professional or intellectual classes were members of the new Christian religious houses, just as, in previous centuries, all intellectuals and members of the professions had been Druids. Fidelma became a member of the religious community of Kildare, established in the late fifth century by St Brigid. But by the time the action in this story takes place, Fidelma has left Kildare in disillusionment. The reason why may be found in the title story of the Fidelma short story collection *Hemlock at Vespers*.

While the seventh century is considered part of the European Dark Ages, for Ireland it was a period of Golden Enlightenment. Students from every corner of Europe flocked to the Irish universities to receive their education, including the sons of many of the Anglo-Saxon kings. At the great ecclesiastical university of Durrow at this time, it is recorded that no fewer than eighteen different nations were represented among the students. At the same time, Irish male and female missionaries were setting out to return a pagan Europe to Christianity, establishing churches, monasteries, and centres of learning throughout Europe as far east as Kiev, in the Ukraine, as far north as the Faeroes, and as far south as Taranto in southern Italy. Ireland was a byword for literacy and learning.

However, what we now call the Celtic Church was in constant dispute with Rome on matters of liturgy and ritual. Rome had begun to reform itself in the fourth century, changing its dating of Easter and aspects of its liturgy. The Celtic Church and the Eastern Orthodox Church maintained their independence from Rome in such matters. The Celtic Church of Ireland, during Fidelma's time, was much concerned with this conflict so that it is impossible to write on church matters without referring to the philosophical warfare between them.

One thing that was shared by both the Celtic Church and Rome in the seventh century was that the concept of celibacy was not universal. However, there were always ascetics in the Church who sublimated physical love in a dedication to the deity, and at the Council of Nice in AD 325 clerical marriages had been condemned (but not banned) by the Western Church. The concept of celibacy arose in Rome mainly from the customs practised by the pagan priestesses of Vesta and the priests of Diana.

By the fifth century, Rome had forbidden its clerics from the rank of abbot and bishop to sleep with their wives and, shortly after, even to marry at all. The general clergy were discouraged from marrying by Rome but not forbidden to do so. Indeed, it was not until the reforming papacy of Leo IX (1049–54) that a serious attempt was made to force the Western clergy to accept universal celibacy. The Celtic Church took centuries to give up its anti-celibacy attitude and fall into line with Rome, while in the Eastern Orthodox Church priests below the rank of abbot and bishop have retained their right to marry to this day.

An awareness of these facts concerning the liberal attitudes towards sexual relationships in the Celtic Church is essential towards understanding the background to the Fidelma stories. The condemnation of the 'sin of the flesh' remained alien to the Celtic Church for a long time after Rome's attitude became a dogma. In Fidelma's world, both sexes inhabited abbeys and monastic foundations, which were known as *conhospitae*, or double houses, where men and women lived raising their children in Christ's service.

Fidelma's own house of St Brigid was one such community of both sexes during her time. When Brigid established her community at Kildare (Cill Dara – church of the oaks) she invited a bishop named Conláed to join her. Her first surviving biography, completed fifty years after her death in AD 650, during Fidelma's lifetime, was written by a monk of Kildare named Cogitosus, who makes it clear that it continued to be a mixed community after her death.

It should also be pointed out that, demonstrating their co-equal role with men, women were priests of the Celtic Church in this period. Brigid herself was ordained a bishop by Patrick's nephew, Mel, and her case was not unique. In the sixth century, Rome actually wrote a protest at the Celtic practice of allowing women to celebrate the divine sacrifice of Mass.

Unlike the Roman Church, the Irish Church did not have a system of 'confessors' where 'sins' had to be confessed to clerics who then had the authority to absolve those sins in Christ's name. Instead, people chose an *anam chara* – a 'soul friend' – clerical or lay, with whom they discussed matters of emotional and spiritual well-being.

To help readers more readily identify personal names, a list of principal characters is given. And in response to the numerous readers who have asked for help in pronouncing the Irish names and words, I have included a pronunciation guide. Thus armed, we may now enter Fidelma's world. The events of this story take place in December 666. It was the new Irish Christian month of Nollaig, named from the Latin *natalicia* – birth festival – which only a few years before, the Irish had called Medónach Gemrid or 'Middle Winter'.

How to Pronounce Irish
Names and Words

As the Fidelma series has become increasingly popular, many English-speaking fans have written wanting assurance about the way to pronounce the Irish names and words.

Irish belongs to the Celtic branch of the Indo-European family of languages. It is closely related to Manx and Scottish Gaelic and a cousin of Welsh, Cornish and Breton. It is a very old European literary language. Professor Calvert Watkins of Harvard maintained it contains Europe's oldest *vernacular* literature, Greek and Latin being a *lingua franca*. Surviving texts date from the seventh century.

The Irish of Fidelma's period is classed as Old Irish. After AD 950, the language entered a period known as Middle Irish. Therefore, in the Fidelma books, Old Irish forms are generally adhered to, whenever possible, in both names and words. This is like using Chaucer's English compared to modern English. For example, a word such as *aidche* ('night') in Old Irish is now rendered *oiche* in Modern Irish.

There are only eighteen letters in the Irish alphabet. From earliest times there has been a literary standard but today four distinct spoken dialects are recognised. For our purposes, we will keep to Fidelma's dialect of Munster.

It is a general rule that stress is placed on the first syllable but, as in all languages, there are exceptions. In

Munster there are three exceptions to the rule of initial stress. If the second syllable is long then it bears the stress; if the first two syllables are short and the third is long then the third syllable is stressed (for example *amadán* – 'fool' – is pronounced amad-*awn*); and where the second syllable contains *ach* and there is no long syllable, the second syllable bears the stress.

There are five short vowels – **a, e, i, o, u** and five long vowels – **á, é, í, ó, ú**. On the long vowels note the accent, like the French acute, which is called a *fada* (literally, 'long'), and this is the only accent in Irish. It occurs on capitals as well as lower case.

The accent is important for, depending on where it is placed, it changes the entire word. *Seán* (Shawn) = John. But *sean* (shan) = old and *séan* (she-an) = an omen. By leaving out the accent on the name of the famous film actor, Sean Connery, he has become 'Old' Connery!

These short and long vowels are either 'broad' or 'slender'. The six broad vowels are:

a pronounced 'o' as in cot	**á** pronounced 'aw' as in law
o pronounced 'u' as in cut	**ó** pronounced 'o' as in low
u pronounced 'u' as in run	**ú** pronounced 'u' as in rule

The four slender vowels are:

i pronounced 'i' as in hit	**í** pronounced 'ee' as in see
e pronounced 'e' as in let	**é** pronounced 'ay' as in say

There are double vowels, some of which are fairly easy because they compare to English pronunciation – such as **ae** as in say or **ui** as in quit. However, some double and even triple vowels in Irish need to be learnt.

ái	pronounced like the 'aw' in law
ia	pronounced like the 'ea' in near

io	pronounced like the 'o' in come
éa	pronounced like the 'ea' in bear
ei	pronounced like the 'e' in let
aoi	pronounced like the 'ea' in mean
uai	pronounced like the 'ue' in blue
eoi	pronounced like the 'eo' in yeoman
iai	pronounced like the 'ee' in see

Hidden vowels

Most people will have noticed that many Irish people pronounce the word film as fil'um. This is actually a transference of Irish pronunciation rules. When **1**, **n** or **r** is followed by **b**, **bh**, **ch**, **g** (not after **n**), **m**, or **mh**, and is preceded by a short stressed vowel, an additional vowel is heard between them. For example, *bolg* (stomach) is pronounced bol'ag; *garbh* (rough) is gar'ev; *dorcha* (dark) is dor'acha; *gorm* (blue) is gor'um and *ainm* (name) is an'im.

The consonants

b, **d**, **f**, **h**, **l**, **m**, **n**, **p**, **r**, and **t** are said more or less as in English.

g is always hard like the 'g' in gate.
c is always hard like the 'c' in cat.
s is pronounced like the 's' in said except before a slender vowel when it is pronounced 'sh' as in shin.

In Irish the letters **j**, **k**, **q**, **w**, **x**, **y** or **z** do not exist and **v** is formed by the combination of **bh**.

Consonants can change their sound by aspiration or eclipse. Aspiration is indicated by using the letter 'h' after them.

bh	is pronounced 'v' as in voice.
ch	is a soft breath as in loch (not pronounced lock!) or Bach.
dh	before a broad vowel is like the 'g' in gap.
dh	before a slender vowel is like the 'y' in year.
fh	is totally silent.
gh	before a slender vowel can sound like 'y' as in yet.
mh	is pronounced like the 'w' in wall.
ph	is like the 'f' in fall.
th	is like the 'h' in ham.
sh	is also like the 'h' in ham.

Consonants can also change their sound by being eclipsed, or silenced, by another consonant placed before them. For example *na mBan* (of women) is pronounced nah m'on; or *i bpaipéar* (in the paper) i b'ap'er or *i gcathair* (in the city) i g'a'har.

p can be eclipsed by **b**, **t**; **t** by **d**, **c** by **g**, **f** by **bh**, **b** by **m**, and **d** and **g** by **n**.

For those interested in learning more about the language, it is worth remembering that, after centuries of suppression during the colonial period, Irish became the first official language of the Irish state on independence in 1922. The last published census of 1991 showed one third of the population returning themselves as Irish-speaking. In Northern Ireland, where the language continued to be openly discouraged after Partition in 1922, only 10.5 per cent of the population were able to speak the language in 1991, the first time an enumeration of speakers was allowed since Partition.

Language courses are now available on video and audiocassette from a range of producers from Linguaphone to

RTÉ and BBC. There are some sixty summer schools and special intensive courses available. The television station Teilifís na Gaeilge broadcasts entirely in Irish and there are several Irish language radio stations and newspapers. Information can be obtained from Comhdháil Náisiúnta na Gaeilge, 46 Sráid Chill Dara, Baile Atha Cliath 2, Éire.

Readers might also like to know that *Valley of the Shadow*, in the Fidelma series, was produced on audiocassette, read by Marie McCarthy, from Magna Story Sound (SS391 – ISBN 1-85903-313-X).

Principal Characters

Sister Fidelma, of Cashel, a *dálaigh*, or advocate of the law courts of seventh-century Ireland
Brother Eadulf, of Seaxmund's Ham, a Saxon monk from the land of the South Folk

At Cynric's inn

Cynric, the innkeeper
'Mad' Mul, a farmer

At Aldred's Abbey

Abbot Cild
Brother Botulf, a friend of Eadulf
Brother Willibrod, the *dominus*
Brother Osred, the smith
Brother Higbald, the apothecary
Brother Redwald, a youthful religieux
Brother Wigstan
Brother Beornwulf

In the marshlands

Aldhere, an outlaw
Bertha, a Frank, his woman
Wiglaf, one of his band
Lioba, a local peasant girl

On the road

Dagobert, a Frankish merchant
Dado, his companion

At Tunstall

Brother Laisre
Brother Tola
Gadra, chieftain of Maigh Eo
Garb, his son

Sigeric, high steward to Ealdwulf, King of East Anglia
Werferth, commander of his bodyguard

Chapter One

'Please close the door, Brother. The wind is blowing the snow in here and it is already cold enough.'

Brother Eadulf turned from where he had been peering in disgust through the half-open door of the inn, out into the dusk at the whirling snowstorm. He reluctantly pushed the door shut and fastened the wooden latch before facing the small, stocky innkeeper. The man, with balding head and cheeks so red that they seemed polished, was regarding him with some sympathy.

'Are you absolutely sure that there is no available transport to Aldred's Abbey?' Eadulf had asked the question several times before. What was the innkeeper's name? Cynric? Yes, that was it.

The innkeeper stood, wiping his hands against the leather apron that covered his corpulent form.

'As I have already told you, Brother, you and your companion were lucky to have made it this far before the storm started in earnest. If you had missed this tavern, there is no shelter between here and the River Alde.'

'The snow was nowhere near as bad as this when we left the river at Mael's Tun and began to walk here,' Eadulf agreed, moving away from the door into the warmer interior of the inn.

'So you came up to Mael's Tun by the river then?' the innkeeper asked with that interest all hosts have in the comings and goings of their guests.

1

'Aye. We came by barge from the mouth of the Deben. Only after we had left Mael's Tun did the wind get up and the snow start to fall like a white sheet. It was so dense that you could scarcely see a hand in front of your eyes. By then we were far enough away from the settlement not to contemplate turning back.'

'Well, you were lucky to strike on my little tavern,' the innkeeper repeated. 'The marshlands to the north and east of here are no place to be wandering unless you can see the path before you.'

'But the abbey is no more than four or five miles from here,' Brother Eadulf pointed out. 'We'd be there easily enough if we had a horse.'

'*If* you had a horse,' the innkeeper replied with emphasis. 'I have one mule and that I need, Brother. And you'd be very lucky to find the abbey even if you had such an animal to transport you. There is no one else on the roads this evening. Look at the snow outside. It is drifting in the valleys and against the hedgerows. The wind is bitter and from the east. No one in their right minds would attempt to travel these roads on such a night.'

Brother Eadulf made a clicking sound with his tongue to express his irritation. The innkeeper continued to regard him with sympathy.

'Why not seat yourself by the fire? Your companion should join you shortly and I will bring you some refreshment,' he suggested cheerfully.

Brother Eadulf still hesitated.

'Tomorrow, the storm may abate and the roads to the abbey may be easier to negotiate,' the innkeeper added persuasively.

'I need to be at the abbey this evening because . . .' Brother Eadulf hesitated and then shook his head. Why should he explain his reasons to the innkeeper? 'It is essential that I reach the abbey before midnight.'

'Well, Brother, you will never make it on foot, even if you knew the roads. What could be so important that the difference of a day might count?'

Brother Eadulf's brows came together in annoyance.

'I have my reasons,' he said stubbornly.

Cynric shook his head sadly. 'You outlanders are all the same. Hurry, hurry, hurry. Well, you will have to bend before the wind this night for you have no other option.'

'I am not a stranger in this land, my friend,' protested Eadulf, irritated at the other's use of the word 'outlander'. 'I am Eadulf of Seaxmund's Ham and was the hereditary *gerefa* of that place before I took the tonsure of St Peter.'

The innkeeper's eyes widened. A *gerefa* was a man of local importance, holding the rank of a magistrate.

'Forgive me, Brother. I thought that you spoke our language too well. But I had assumed, as you travelled in the company of an Irish religieuse, that you were of that nation.'

Eadulf was defensive. 'I have been in foreign lands for a while. But, *Deo adiuvante*, with God's help, I will see Seaxmund's Ham, my native place, in time for Christ's Mass.'

'Four days to go then, Brother. But why stop at Aldred's Abbey? Why not wait until the storm clears and then go straight on to Seaxmund's Ham which is only a little distance beyond?'

'Because . . . because I have my reasons for doing so,' Eadulf replied tersely.

The innkeeper pursed his lips at Eadulf's agitated reticence. He shrugged and went to the fire. The inn was deserted. No one else had managed to make their way to the snowbound crossroads where it was situated. The innkeeper bent to a pile of logs and lifted one, balancing it in his arms for a moment before dumping it on the fire.

'You will find many things altered in this land, Brother,' he said as he turned from the hearth. 'In fact, you have been lucky to reach here in safety.'

'I've seen snows before and travelled through blizzards that would put this' – Eadulf gestured with his hand towards the door – 'to shame. What threat in that?'

'I was not thinking so much of the weather. Man is often more cruel than nature's elements, my friend. In many places now, the Christian communities are under siege and attack. There is much animosity towards the new faith.'

'Under siege and attack? From whom?' demanded Eadulf, reluctantly taking a seat at the side of the fire, while the innkeeper went to draw a tankard of cider from a wooden barrel.

'From those who have returned to the worship of Woden, who else? In the kingdom of the East Saxons there is civil war between Sigehere, the King, and his own cousin, the Prince Sebbi. Not only do they fight for the kingship, but each represents one of the two beliefs. Surely you must have travelled through the land of the East Saxons to get here? You must have seen something of the conflict?'

Eadulf shook his head and reached forward to take the tankard from Cynric's hand. He sipped at it cautiously. It was sweet and strong.

'I did not know that there were such divisions which had caused actual warfare,' he said, after he had taken another sip. 'Sigehere and Sebbi were both firmly on the path of Christ when I left this kingdom and there was no animosity between them.'

'As you say, they were both Christians. But when the Yellow Plague struck among the East Saxons two years ago, Sigehere came to the belief that it was a punishment of the old gods on those who had renounced them and so he turned his back on the new faith and reopened the pagan temples. His cousin, Sebbi, has remained true to the new faith. Both have followers who ravage the countryside, burning the sacred sites of the other's religion and killing the religious who fall into their hands, whether they be of Christ or of Woden and the old gods.'

Eadulf was shocked. In Canterbury, he had heard some talk about the dissensions among the East Saxons but no one had spoken of actual violence or warfare. He shivered slightly, remembering that he had almost decided to journey from Kent through the kingdom of the East Saxons to get to the land of the South Folk. As the innkeeper had assumed, it would have been the normal route for wayfarers into this land. It was by chance that, having left Canterbury and gone north to join the road at the small port of Hwita's Staple, Eadulf had encountered an old acquaintance. Stuf, a sea-captain who ran his vessel along the coast of the Saxon kingdoms, had persuaded him to take passage directly to the land of the South Folk. This had cut several days from the journey. Stuf's vessel had landed Eadulf at the township called St Felix's Stowe, where the blessed missionary had established an abbey some twenty years before. Thanks to the chance meeting with Stuf, Eadulf had bypassed the volatile kingdom of the East Saxons.

'It was lucky then, innkeeper, that we came here by way of the sea from the kingdom of Kent,' he reflected.

'Ah, so you did not come through the lands of Sigehere and Sebbi?' Cynric's puzzled face lightened a little. 'You were blessed in your choice of route. But even here among the South Folk there is some friction between Christian and pagan. The conflict has spilt over the border and

Sigehere is trying to stir up the dissension so that he might find allies among us. Outlaws prowl the marshlands and, of course, we also have to contend with threats of war from our western neighbour, Mercia. They mount constant raids against us.'

'When was Mercia not a threat to the kingdom of the East Anglians?' Eadulf smiled with grim cynicism. All through his life, he could remember little else but the continued warfare between the East Anglian kingdom and the Mercians.

'Our King, Ealdwulf, has recently rejected the King of Mercia's demands that East Anglia pay him tribute. Since Ealdwulf's mother, Hereswith, is a princess of the Northumbrian royal house, we can expect an alliance to keep the Mercian threat in check. We have good prospects before us if King Ealdwulf can keep the internal conflict between pagan and Christian from spreading here. And this is what I warn you of, Eadulf of Seaxmund's Ham. Do not assume that everyone will greet you and your companion as friends and respect your cloth. There is much bitterness abroad in our land. Some thanes have even threatened to declare allegiance to Sigehere of the East Saxons unless King Ealdwulf renounces Christianity. There is much trouble brewing, Brother. You have chosen a dangerous time to return home.'

Brother Eadulf sighed deeply. 'So it seems.'

Cynric placed another log on the fire. At that moment the door on the far side of the room opened, and a tall, red-haired religieuse entered. She smiled quickly at Eadulf.

'My robes are dry now and I am warmer than when we arrived.' She spoke in Irish which was the common language between them. 'I think that I would like some mulled wine to give warmth to the inner body.'

Eadulf returned her smile warmly and gestured to a chair by the fire near him.

'I doubt that a Saxon inn will have wine, but there is good cider, or mead if you wish.'

'Cider before mead if there is no wine,' she replied.

The innkeeper stood patiently during this exchange, not understanding.

'I don't suppose you have wine, innkeeper?' Eadulf asked.

'You would be wrong if you had supposed it, Brother. Where would I be able to purchase wine, and if I did so who would buy it? The shipments of wine that are landed at Felix's Stowe go mainly to the abbey there or to some of the other monasteries along the coast. You'll find wine at Aldred's Abbey but not here.'

'Then serve my companion some of your best cider.'

The innkeeper looked at the religieuse and asked Eadulf: 'Your companion does not speak Saxon, then?' He was surprised when the tall religieuse turned and spoke to him in a halting fashion.

'Enough to follow the conversation in general terms, innkeeper. But my knowledge is not good enough to understand all the nuances of your tongue.'

The innkeeper bowed his head a moment in reflection. 'I've heard it said that the people of Ireland are versed in all the languages of the world.'

'You flatter my people. Our missionaries certainly try to achieve proficiency in several tongues to accomplish their task. Latin, Greek, a little Hebrew, and the languages of our neighbours. But our ability is neither greater nor less than that of others given the same circumstances and opportunities.'

Eadulf nodded approvingly, overlooking one or two small lapses in grammar.

The innkeeper filled another tankard and handed it to

her. While Fidelma sipped appreciatively, Eadulf ordered a meat pie, which Cynric told him was a speciality of the inn, for their supper.

'This innkeeper says that we will not reach Aldred's Abbey this night,' Eadulf began, when Cynric had vanished to prepare the meal.

'I don't doubt it,' replied Fidelma solemnly with a glance towards the tiny, snow-blocked window. 'I have never felt it so cold, or seen snow so like little flecks of ice.'

'Yet Brother Botulf was specific. He wanted me to arrive at the abbey before midnight tonight. The message he sent to me at Canterbury was underlined at that point.'

'He must make allowances for the weather,' rejoined Fidelma, with a shrug. 'This storm puts the matter entirely out of your hands.'

'Nevertheless, why did he underline the time and date?'

'You say that this . . . Botulf? I find your Saxon names still difficult to pronounce. You say that Botulf is a good friend of yours?'

Eadulf nodded swiftly. 'We grew up together. He must be in serious trouble, otherwise he would not have written such a message.'

'But he did not explain anything in the message. He must take your friendship for granted if he presumed that you would leave Canterbury and come rushing to him.'

'He would guess that if I was at Canterbury, then I would be travelling to my home at Seaxmund's Ham. He would assume that my path would lie by his door,' replied Eadulf defensively. 'My home is only six miles further on from the abbey.'

'A strange friend, that is all I say,' sighed Fidelma. 'Is he the abbot of this abbey?'

Eadulf shook his head. 'He is the steward. I was told at Canterbury that someone called Cild is the abbot, but I have never heard of him.'

Cynric re-entered, bearing a tray with a hot meat pie on it which he set down at a nearby table.

'If you will be seated at the table, I shall fetch more cider with which to wash your meal down.'

The pie looked and smelled good and soon the howling wind outside was forgotten as they savoured the meal. Eadulf explained something of what Cynric had told him about the conflict between the Christians and pagans. Sister Fidelma looked at her companion with some sympathy.

'It must be difficult for you to hear this. However, it is surely balanced against the pleasure of seeing your home again.'

'It is a long time since I was last at Seaxmund's Ham. I am indeed looking forward to seeing it again.' He glanced anxiously at her. 'I am sorry if I seem selfish, Fidelma.'

Her eyes widened for a moment. She was thinking that *she* was being selfish. She had suddenly realised just how much she was missing her home in Cashel. This land of the South Folk was bleak, cold and inhospitable. When she had agreed to accompany Eadulf to Canterbury and had left the shores of her homeland, it had not occurred to her that he would want to proceed further and journey on to the place of his birth. But that, she realised, had been a silly and egocentric assumption on her part. Of course, after the time in Rome and then nearly a year in her brother's kingdom of Muman, it was obvious that Eadulf would want to spend some time at his birthplace.

She tried to suppress the apprehensive feeling that came over her. She hoped that he would not want to spend any great length of time at that place . . . Seaxmund's Ham. She felt guilty for the selfish thought. Why should she expect him to want to return to her own country? But she did miss her homeland. She had travelled enough. She wanted to settle down.

She realised that Eadulf was smiling at her across the table.

'No regrets?' he asked.

She felt the hot blood in her cheeks.

'Regrets?' she parried, knowing full well what he meant.

'That you came with me to my country?'

'I have no regrets at being in your company,' Fidelma replied, choosing her words carefully.

Eadulf examined her keenly. He was still smiling but she saw the shadow cross his eyes. Before he could say anything more, she suddenly reached forward and grasped his hand.

'Let us live for the moment, Eadulf.' Her voice was earnest. 'We have agreed to follow the ancient custom of my people – to be with one another for a year and a day. I have agreed to be your *ben charrthach* for that time. With that you must be content. Anything more lasting requires much legal consideration.'

Eadulf understood that the people of the five kingdoms of Éireann had a very complicated law system and there were several definitions of what constituted a proper marriage. As Fidelma had explained to him, there were nine distinct types of union in Irish law. The term which Fidelma had used, *ben charrthach*, literally meant the 'loved woman', not yet a legally bound wife but one whose status and rights were recognised under the law of the Cáin Lánamnus. It was, in fact, a trial marriage, lasting a year and a day, after which, if unsuccessful, both sides would go their separate ways without incurring penalties or blame.

The decision had been made by Fidelma not because

they were members of the religious. It would not have entered her mind that this was a bar to marriage. No religious, neither those who followed the way of Colmcille, nor those who followed the Rule of Rome or any of the other Churches of Christ, regarded celibacy as necessary to the religious calling. However, there was a growing minority who had begun to denounce married clergy and proclaim celibacy as the true path of those who were committed to the new faith. Fidelma, in fact, was more concerned that a marriage with Eadulf would be deemed a marriage of unequals . . . if her brother, Colgú, King of Muman, even gave his approval for it. Such a marriage, while recognised in law, meant that Eadulf, as a stranger without land in Muman and not of the same princely family rank as Fidelma, would not have equal property rights with his wife. Knowing Eadulf's character, Fidelma thought it would not be a good prescription for happiness if Eadulf felt less than her equal.

There were other forms of marriage, of course. A man could legally cohabit with a woman at her home with the permission of her family, or she could go away openly with him without the consent of her family and still have rights under the law. The problem was that, having reached the stage of seriously considering marriage to Eadulf, Fidelma was in a quandary about what path to proceed along. Moreover, she had assumed that any future together would be a future in Cashel. The last few weeks with Eadulf in the kingdoms of the Angles and the Saxons had begun to raise doubts in her mind.

She found her thoughts interrupted as Eadulf was speaking again.

'Did I say that I was not satisfied, Fidelma?' Eadulf's smile was a little forced now as he saw the changing expression on her face.

The door opened abruptly with a crash and for a

11

moment it appeared that some strange figure from the netherworld stood framed against the swirling cloud of snow that pushed into the inn. An ice-cold breath of air threatened to blow out the lanterns that lit the main room of the inn. The figure, looking like some gigantic, shaggy bear, turned and had to lean against the door to push it shut against the pressure of the blustery wind. The figure turned again and shook itself, causing cascades of snow to fall from the thick furs which encased the body from head to foot. Then one arm appeared through the furs and began unwrapping part of the head covering. A bearded face emerged from under the wrappings.

'Mead, Cynric! Mead, for the love of the mother of Balder!'

The figure stamped forward into the inn, showering snow about him from his fur wrappings. He dropped his outer garment unceremoniously on the floor. He wore a leather jerkin over a muscular torso and strips of sacking were wrapped around his giant calves and tied with leather thongs.

'Mul!' exclaimed Cynric, the innkeeper, in surprised recognition as he came forward to greet the newcomer. 'What are you doing abroad and in such inclement weather?'

The man addressed as Mul was of middle age, broad-shouldered, with flaxen hair and a skin that seemed tanned by the elements. He had the build of a farmer or a smith. His thick-set shoulders and arms seemed to bulge through his leather jerkin. He had a coarse, ruddy face with a bushy beard. His features made it seem that he had been beaten about the face and never recovered. His lips were constantly parted and showed gaps in his yellowing teeth. He had piercing bright eyes set close to his beak-like nose, which gave him a permanent look of disapproval.

12

'I am on my way home,' the newcomer grunted. 'Where should a man be on this night of all nights?' He suddenly caught sight of Fidelma and Eadulf, seated across the room, and inclined his head in greeting.

'May the spear of Frig and the Desir be ready to smite your enemies!' he thundered in the ancient fashion.

'*Deus vobiscum*,' replied Eadulf solemnly with a hint of reproof in his tone.

The man, whom the innkeeper had called Mul, grabbed the tankard of mead from Cynric's hand and sprawled in a chair near the fire, downing half of it in one great gulp. Then he uttered a loud belch of satisfaction.

Fidelma looked a little shocked but said nothing.

'God look down on us,' muttered Eadulf, his face showing his disapproval of the man's lack of manners.

'Christians, eh?' frowned the newcomer, regarding them with curiosity. 'Well, I am an old dog and cannot be taught new tricks. The gods who protected my father are good enough to protect me. May all and any of the gods protect all travellers this night.'

The innkeeper placed another tankard of mead ready for the newcomer.

'Shall I prepare a bed for you, Mul?'

The big man shook his head almost violently. The gesture reminded them of a big shaggy dog, shaking itself. His hair and beard seemed to merge into one tangled mane.

'Woden's hammer, no!'

'But your farm is six or more miles from here!' exclaimed the innkeeper. 'You'll not make it in this storm.'

'I'll make it,' the burly farmer said with grim confidence. 'I would not let a little blow like this prevent me from going home. Anyway, tonight is the Mothernight and I intend to raise a tankard of mead to Frig and the

Desir at the appointed hour. I shall be back on my farm before midnight, friend Cynric. Apart from anything else, I have animals to see to. If I am not there to tend to them, then they go without. I have been away all day to sell some cheese at the market at Butta's Leah.'

Eadulf saw the perplexity on Fidelma's face and explained in a whisper: 'Tonight is the Winter Solstice, the start of the old pagan feast of Yule which lasts for twelve days. We celebrate with the feast of the goddess Frig and the Desir, the Fore-Mothers of the race. The main feast is dedicated to Woden, the Yule One.'

Fidelma was just as perplexed as before.

'It is a time when we are in darkness and must offer gifts to the gods and goddesses to ensure the rebirth of the sun.'

He did not notice Fidelma's disapproving look, for he had begun to regard the newcomer with some interest.

'Might I ask, my friend, in what direction is your farm? I heard the innkeeper call you Mul. There was a Mul who used to farm Frig's Tun before I left on my travels. Are you he?'

The burly farmer examined Eadulf keenly. A frown crossed his brows.

'Who are you, Christian?' he demanded.

'I am Eadulf of Seaxmund's Ham, where I was *gerefa* before I joined the religious.'

'Eadulf? Eadulf of Seaxmund's Ham? I knew of your family. I had heard one of them had converted to the new faith. You are right. I am Mul of Frig's Tun and, as I told Cynric, I mean to sleep in my own bed this night.'

'Surely the roads are impassable?' intervened Cynric the innkeeper.

The farmer laughed harshly. 'Impassable to people without courage. Another tankard of mead, Cynric, and I will be on my way.'

Fidelma tapped Eadulf on the arm.

'*Virtutis fortuna comes*,' she whispered in Latin. Good luck was, indeed, the companion of courage, but what was meant, and understood by Eadulf, was that one must grasp opportunity when it came one's way.

Eadulf sought to frame the question in a way which might appeal to Mul.

'Your journey must lie in the direction of Aldred's Abbey, must it not?'

Mul paused with his tankard to his lips and regarded Eadulf speculatively.

'And if it does?' he countered.

'My companion and I are anxious to reach the abbey this evening. If there is room on your wagon, then I would make it worth your while to pass the gates of the abbey.'

Cynric, the innkeeper, was disapproving.

'I advise you against journeying on. It is too dangerous. We have not had a blizzard like this in ten years. Why, the dry snow is being driven by this bitter wind and banking up behind walls and hedges and ditches and filling the hollows. You could even miss the path and fall into a lake or frozen stream; break a leg or worse. And there is the marsh to consider.'

Mul drained his mug and wiped the back of his hand across his mouth. He fingered his thick, coarse beard for a moment as if in speculation. Then he sighed and turned to the innkeeper.

'You are an old woman, Cynric. I know the roads like the creases on the palms of my hands.' He glanced at Eadulf. 'My path takes me right by the gates of the abbey. May the gods curse that place of evil. If you can pay, I will take you. But I only have an uncomfortable farm wagon drawn by a team of mules.'

Eadulf exchanged a quick glance with Fidelma.

'I do not approve of your calling a house of the Christian faith a place of evil, friend, nor calling on idolatrous gods to curse it.'

Mul grinned sourly. It made him more ugly than before.

'It is evident that you do not know Aldred's Abbey or what it has become these days. But your opinions are no concern of mine.'

Eadulf hesitated and then said: 'By payment, what had you in mind?'

'If you decide to come with me, then I am sure that you won't begrudge me a penny for my labour.'

Eadulf turned to Fidelma who nodded quickly.

'It is agreed, my pagan friend,' Eadulf exclaimed in satisfaction.

The farmer rose to his feet, grabbing his fur outer garments.

'How soon can you be ready?' he demanded as he began to pull them on.

'We are ready now.'

'Then I will go and see to my rig. Join me outside as soon as you are prepared.'

They were already putting on their woollen cloaks before the burly farmer had disappeared through the door.

Cynric regarded them anxiously. 'Please reconsider. It is a dangerous road. Only an idiot like Mul would attempt the journey. You should know that he is named Mad Mul in these parts. You are much safer waiting to see if the storm breaks tomorrow.'

'And if it does not?' smiled Eadulf as he placed some coins in the hands of the innkeeper to pay for the meal. 'At least we will make the effort this night.'

'It is only your lives that you risk,' shrugged the innkeeper, realising when to accept defeat.

Outside, they found Mul already seated in his wagon, with a team of two patient mules in the shafts, heads slightly bowed against the bitter, moaning wind. The winter night had begun but the farmer had lit two storm lanterns which hung on either side of his wagon and there was light enough by the shadowy reflections on the snow to see by. Great banks of snow were piling up in the gusting winds. Eadulf helped Fidelma climb up onto the wagon, then threw up their travelling bags, before climbing up himself.

'Sit yourselves down there,' cried Mul, above the howling of the wind, pointing down into the shelter of the wagon behind the driver's seat. 'Those woollen cloaks will be scant protection against the cold. There's some furs there. Put them around you and you'll be out of the worst of it.'

Cynric had come to the door of the inn. He raised his hand in farewell.

'I think that you are all crazy,' he called, his voice blurring in the whistling of the blizzard. 'However, as you insist on going, may God be on every road that you travel.'

'God be with you, innkeeper,' replied Eadulf, solemnly, before tucking himself down under the furs beside Fidelma. They heard Mul crack the reins and shout and then, with a jerk, the wagon began to roll forward.

17

Chapter Two

Once they had passed out of the yard of the inn, beyond the surrounding trees, the wind drove at them bringing the snow like icy pellets, dry and hard and painful where they hit the flesh of the face. It was a bitter wind that groaned around them and now and then rose to a shriek like someone in anguish. Eadulf was glad of the furs in the wagon which guarded them from the full rancour of the icy storm.

Heads down, the sturdy little mules strained and tugged as they pulled the wagon through a low snowdrift, the big wooden wheels crunching on the crispy surface while the wagon swayed and tilted as Mul tried to keep it on the hidden track which lay underneath the drifting snow. For a moment it seemed that the wind was receding and then it suddenly came back with a vengeance from another quarter, causing the wagon to shake as if it had been given some life of its own. Then the wheels suddenly went into a skid as they encountered a patch of solid ice.

They heard Mul cursing but whatever he did brought the heavy wagon to a halt. He jumped down and Eadulf, peering over the side, saw him leading his team through a larger snowdrift. The farmer stayed at their heads until they came to the shelter of a stretch of forest through which the roadway was barely coated with white snow. The wind, sweeping through the trees, was like a curious whispering chorus of sighing voices.

Mul climbed back onto the wagon.

'Are you all right, down there?'

His voice was almost obliterated by the sighing wind, but Eadulf heard him.

'We are,' he called in reply. 'Are you sure that it's safe to continue?' Eadulf himself had begun to have second thoughts as they had driven through the unprotected countryside. At least the forest afforded some shelter from the harsh elements. But he knew its protection would not last long.

'Woden's hammer! Of course it's safe. I'm driving, aren't I?' Mul roared with laughter at his own sense of humour.

Eadulf did not reply but turned back to Fidelma. He could not see her face through the slanting snow and gloom.

'How are you?'

'I've been through worse,' came her calm response.

She was about to say something else when the wagon suddenly jolted and came to a halt again. The heavy wheels were slipping, turning on the surface of the icy track without finding a purchase. The animals strained hard to keep the wagon moving forward but to no avail.

'I'll have to get down and find some branch wood to put under the wheels,' shouted Mul.

He was about to do so when from somewhere nearby came the mournful howling of a wolf. Eadulf felt Fidelma stiffen suddenly beside him. Wolves were common and dangerous in her country and Eadulf knew that she had good cause to be apprehensive of them. So had he, if it came to that. He looked over the edge of the wagon again and stared hard in the direction of the sound. Some grey-white shadows were moving among the trees.

Mul noticed the concern of his passengers.

'Don't worry. It's an isolated male and his mate

20

roaming these woods with their cubs. There are no packs here, so far as I know. The wolves are dying out in this country. They won't harm us.'

Fidelma and Eadulf, having had encounters with wolves, were not so sure. Even through the driving snow they could spot the male – a great beast who must have been a full metre high at the shoulder. It had paused on a rock among the trees and was staring at them, its bright sharp eyes glowing red. Fidelma shivered as she observed its massive frame and heavy, slate-grey coat.

Below this majestic form, even in the twilight, they could make out the vixen keeping restless guard over her two leggy, yelping cubs, now and then snapping a reprimand at them with her long, white fangs.

The head of the male wolf went back and a long, mournful wail of hunger echoed through the deep forest. Then the animals turned and seemed to disappear, vanishing among the darkness of the trees. For some moments they could still hear the cry of the wolf as it gradually faded.

To their surprise, they found that Mul had already clambered off the wagon while they had been concentrating on the wolves, and was placing several branches of wood under the wheels to create a purchase for them. A moment later, he was back on his seat and the wagon jolted forward again, but in a skid that swung them into an embankment from which a pile of snow cascaded into the vehicle, almost burying them. They spluttered as they tried to clear it, some of the cold pellets finding their way into the furs and into their noses and mouths and eyes.

The wind dropped a fraction and Mul turned his head and shouted down.

'There are too many snowdrifts along here. I am going to try the marsh road. The wind will be harsher there but there are no hollows for the snow to drift into and hold us up.'

Eadulf raised his hand to show he had understood.

'Are you all right, Fidelma?' he asked again, leaning close to her.

Fidelma grimaced sceptically. 'If you keep asking, I shall suspect that you are worried. Do you know how far off we are from this abbey now?'

'Not far. The marsh road takes us through low-lying country to a river, and the abbey is just the other side.'

'Do we have to try to ford a river in this weather?'

Eadulf shook his head. 'As I recall, there is a bridge, thanks be to God.'

'At least that is comforting news.'

The swinging lanterns illuminated the misty flurries of snow sweeping diagonally this way and that as the wind veered in short staccato bursts. Had it not been so cold, had there been some respite from the raw elements of nature, it would have been a beautiful sight. If anything, the snow-laden gale seemed to be increasing as swirling whorls of icy pellets blinded them.

Abruptly, they felt the wagon slipping again and suddenly it came to yet another halt.

Eadulf saw the figure of the farmer rise on his seat and heard him swear, invoking all the gods of his father. Eadulf pretended not to notice the pagan profanities.

'What is it?' he demanded.

'I'll need to dig her out this time,' Mul responded gloomily.

'I'll give you a hand,' volunteered Eadulf. He turned to Fidelma and added unnecessarily, 'Stay where you are and keep yourself warm.'

'I don't think I shall ever be warm again,' returned Fidelma without humour.

The wagon had slid sideways into a great bank of snow

and almost buried the back wheels above the axles. Mul had seized a spade from the side of the cart, where it had been strapped, and was already digging furiously. Great chunks of snow flew from the blade. He paused, straightened and pointed to where a hedge could be seen on the far side of the track. The driving wind had actually cleared the hedge, heaping the snow on the side where the wagon had become bogged down.

'Try to find some dead wood that we can pile under the wheels.'

Eadulf acknowledged the instruction with a gesture of his hand and set off to fulfil the task.

It was some time before the heavy wagon had been hauled out by the patient animals, with some pushing and yelling from both Mul and Eadulf. Eadulf returned to his perch with his clothing soaked, for he had been up to his waist in the drift and the chill was cutting like a knife through his body.

They had reached the crest of a hill and the force of the wind was almost unbearable as the tiny ice pellets drove against the wagon like diminutive stones beating a rapid tattoo on the wooden boards. Eadulf raised himself and stared over the seat, beyond Mul, along the track ahead. Mul noticed him and indicated with a jerk of his hand.

'Around those trees and we'll turn on the marsh road,' he said encouragingly. 'From that point, were it not for the snowstorm, you would be able to see the River Alde in the distance. The marsh road will take us to the bridge and the abbey is not far beyond.'

'Another mile or so, at most,' confirmed Eadulf with a tone of satisfaction. 'We are quite close and it is well before midnight.'

'Midnight? I'll be in bed at my own farm and asleep before then,' said the farmer.

Eadulf squinted through the slanting snow. As the

23

wagon came around the line of trees he could only just see an indistinct whiteness of landscape, without the shadows of hills or forest, which showed the level marsh. A ribbon of white powdery snow stretched away, free from curves or bends in which drifts could gather.

'Inclement is scarcely a term to describe this weather, my friend,' Eadulf observed, shivering a little. 'Surely, Mul, you will stay at the abbey for the rest of the night rather than journey on to Frig's Tun?'

'Woden's hammer! I would not stay at Aldred's Abbey this night nor any night – even if you paid me treble the penny which you have promised me,' averred the farmer forcefully. 'I call for its destruction!'

Eadulf stared at him through the slanting snow, wondering at the vehemence in his voice.

'What do you fear at the abbey?' he demanded.

'Everyone knows that the devil has come to that place.'

'The devil?' Eadulf's eyes widened a little. 'That is a strong thing to say and a bad thing when you speak of a Christian community.'

Mul shrugged indifferently.

'Have you been away long from this land?' he asked and, for a moment, Eadulf thought he was changing the subject.

'Several years,' he confirmed after a slight hesitation.

'Well, I shall tell you, Eadulf of Seaxmund's Ham, that many things have changed in these parts. Sometimes it is not wise even to confess that you belong to the new faith.'

Eadulf was impatient. He disliked people who did not explain precisely what they meant, and said so.

'I have heard all about the conflict in the kingdom of the East Saxons. But I cannot see what that has to do

24

with Aldred's Abbey and any evil therein. State plainly what you mean, Mul.'

'I can say no more than this; the devil has cast his shadow over Aldred's Abbey. Now, let me drive on before we all freeze to death. Just have a care, Brother; have a care for your companion and yourself. There is a brooding evil at the abbey. I have heard that—'

He halted in mid-sentence, shrugged once more and turned to crack his whip over the mules' heads. The cart jerked forward again, almost sending Eadulf flying back into the wagon.

'Did you hear and understand that?' Eadulf asked, resorting to the language of Éireann as he settled down and leaned close to Fidelma.

Fidelma glanced at him in the twilight.

'I did not understand the nuances but I understood the sense,' she confessed. 'This farmer, Mul, is afraid of the abbey. That I realise. Is it because he is a pagan and fears the new religion?'

'Perhaps,' said Eadulf. 'Maybe it is due to some pagan peasant superstition. Who knows?'

'I presume that your Saxon word *diofol* is the same as our word *díabul*?'

'Aye. Lucifer, Satan . . . the devil.' Eadulf nodded.

Fidelma was thoughtful for a moment.

'A curious thing for a pagan to say about a Christian house. Tell me, this friend of yours . . . the one who sent you the message at Canterbury . . . ?'

'Brother Botulf?'

'Indeed. Brother Botulf. Are you sure that he gave you no explanation, no hint, as to why he wanted to see you so urgently?'

Eadulf looked pained. 'I have kept nothing back from you. You know as much as I do. He merely said that he wanted me to be at the abbey before midnight tonight.'

Fidelma exhaled in frustration. 'But why midnight tonight? Has this day any significance for you?'

'There is no significance to the day that I know.'

'Is he someone given to making a drama out of nothing?'

'Not at all. He was a humorous and happy man. He was converted by Fursa before that blessed man left for Gaul, and he was one of the first to join Aldred in establishing the abbey. Aldred died some years ago and Botulf is now steward of the abbey. It is true that I have not seen him for three years but people do not change their personalities. He is not given to making idle demands. If he wants me to be at the abbey before midnight tonight, then it is for a good reason.'

For a moment or two they sat in silence. Finally, Fidelma spoke again.

'Well, as I have often said, Eadulf, there is no use speculating without knowledge. We will have to wait until we have that knowledge.'

If they had expected the journey to become easier once they reached the marsh road, they were soon disabused of the notion. The wagon continued to advance but in a crazy skidding progress from side to side. Underneath the powdery snow, the surface had become ice. The wind blew great white clouds of snow over the wagon so it was hard to make anything out. Several times, Mul was forced to get down and lead the sturdy little mules, feeling the way along the road before letting them move forward.

Now and then, Eadulf, painfully aware that either of the animals might slip and break a leg, also dismounted to help the farmer. In this fashion it seemed to take an eternity to reach the wooden bridge which spanned the river. Along the river edges were jagged strips of ice. Indeed, the water might well have been frozen over were it not for the torrent pushing down its centre.

At least the bridge was fairly clear, for the wind gusted so strongly across it that it blew the snow from the wooden planking before it had a chance to lie, and there was nowhere for it to bank. Mul led the mules across and brought the wagon to a halt on the other side.

He screwed up his eyes against the blinding ice pellets before pointing with a shout to Eadulf.

'See! There is the light of the abbey. A few hundred paces and we will be at the gates. I will take you up there, but there I shall leave you.'

'You would do well to reconsider that, Mul,' Eadulf replied, examining the continuing drifting snowfall. 'It is going to be a difficult journey to your farm. You will not have me to help you.'

'I have managed thus far, Eadulf of Seaxmund's Ham. I will manage the extra distance.'

The wagon started forward again, and this time it seemed but a short distance up the twisting, tree-sheltered roadway to the dark walls of the abbey. A storm lantern danced in the wind outside the great wooden doors.

'We are here, Fidelma,' cried Eadulf, picking up their bags and tossing them to the ground.

Fidelma had risen from beneath the furs and stood in the wagon, staring in disapproval at the forbidding squat grey stone walls.

'It seems more like a fortress than a house of God.'

Eadulf nodded in the gloom. 'That is probably because it has to act as fortress as well as spiritual centre. We are still a violent society, Fidelma. Often our kingdom here is under attack from the Mercians, or even the West Saxons.'

'I have read the works of Gildas,' she replied solemnly, 'telling how your people invaded this island over two hundred years ago and drove the Britons out or massacred them. It is not a pleasant story. Yet your people continue

27

to live in conflict. When they are not fighting with the Britons then they are fighting with each other.'

'It is not a pleasant world,' rejoined Eadulf defensively. 'It has always been so. All people fight wars. Our gods are gods of war.' Then, realising what he had said, he flushed, glad of the covering of the snow to disguise his embarrassment. 'I mean, this was the attitude before the coming of the word of Christ.'

Fidelma moved to the edge of the wagon.

'The word of Christ has come and still your people fight,' she observed with sarcasm. 'Perhaps they fight with a greater relish, often proclaiming that each side is supported by Christ. My people have a saying: let those who think war is a solution go to war. A war only makes the victor brutal and the vanquished vengeful. Now, help me down, Eadulf.'

Eadulf reached up and helped her climb down.

Mul had been waiting patiently, still seated on the box of the wagon.

'I will be on my way now,' he called.

Eadulf moved forward and reached into the purse at his belt, taking out a coin.

'A penny is what we agreed, Mul.'

He handed up the coin, which the farmer took readily enough.

'May Woden protect you from your enemies,' he called. 'May his hammer smite those who offend you!'

'*Vade in pace*, go in peace!' Eadulf replied as the big wagon began to move off into the whirling snow clouds.

'What was it the innkeeper called him? Mad Mul?' Fidelma asked, as they stood watching the wagon disappear for a moment. 'I would not call him mad. Determined, yes. Nature has a tenacious enemy in a man who can defy her in such a manner.'

Eadulf picked up their bags from the snow-covered ground and turned towards the tall dark gates of the abbey.

'No one seems to be stirring,' Fidelma observed curiously. 'Someone should have noticed our arrival. Do they not keep a watch?'

'There's a bell rope at the side of the door. With this snowstorm, the wind and the darkness, probably no one heard or saw the arrival of Mul's wagon.'

He reached the rope, just by the swinging storm lantern, set down one of the bags and pulled sharply. They could only just hear the distant clang of the bell above the whistling of the wind.

It was some time before there came a rasping sound and a tiny grille in the door was opened. Even peering closely through the aperture, Eadulf could only make out a faint shadow beyond.

'Who are you and what do you seek here?' came a harsh, unfriendly voice.

'I am Brother Eadulf of Seaxmund's Ham, travelling with Sister Fidelma of Cashel. We seek shelter from the storm and a word with the steward of this abbey.'

There was no answer for a moment but then the voice said: 'We have declared ourselves a closed community of brethren in the service of Christ. The abbey is not open to receive women.'

Eadulf flushed with annoyance.

'You will open this door in the name of Theodore of Canterbury whose representative I am,' he replied sternly. 'If we freeze to death on your threshold, the archbishop will demand a grim restitution from this abbey.'

There was a short silence and then the grille door snapped shut. After what seemed an eternity, they heard the scraping of bolts being drawn back. Then one of the two great wooden doors swung inwards a short way.

Eadulf pushed his way forward through the narrow aperture, ensuring Fidelma was close at his back, and the door was immediately shut with a crash behind them.

They were standing in a narrow arched entrance, the grey stones lit by an overhead lantern. The entrance gave way to a large courtyard across which were the main buildings of the abbey and the chapel. They heard the bolts being thrust home with a sound that Fidelma associated more with a prison than with a religious community.

The man who had opened the door now came forward and scrutinised them closely with one dark, sharp eye. He wore a leather patch over the other. In the light of the lantern, Fidelma saw that the doorkeeper was tall, clad in the brown woollen robes of a member of the religious, with a wooden cross on a leather thong around his neck. He was lean, with a prominent, hook nose and thin red lips. His forehead was balding and wisps of grey straggling hair sprouted untidily over his ears and at the back of his head. His single right eye was dark and restless. A livid white scar, the ends of which could be seen even in the lamp-light, crossed diagonally over the left eye socket, under the patch.

'I am Brother Willibrod. I am the *dominus* of the *domus hospitale* of this abbey.' He paused and glanced at Fidelma. 'That is, I am in charge of the guests' quarters . . .'

'Should you wish to speak Latin,' Fidelma interrupted mischievously while speaking in that language, 'I am competent enough in that tongue to follow you.'

The mouth of Brother Willibrod turned down in disapproval. He resorted to Saxon.

'Sister, I have to tell you that this is not a *conhospitae*, a mixed house. We are all brothers of the faith here. There

30

are no women, neither do we provide facilities for female guests.'

Eadulf was almost beyond irritation.

'Are you refusing us hospitality?' he demanded, a threatening tone in his voice.

'Not you, Brother. It is just that we are a closed Order and women are not allowed in this abbey. It is our rule.'

'Where is your duty of hospitality?'

'The hospitality is not open to women,' replied the *dominus* stubbornly again. 'Since the great Council at Whitby, we no longer abide by the rules laid down by the missionaries of Éireann. I am told that Domnoc's Wic is still a mixed house. That is twelve miles from here.'

Eadulf took an aggressive step towards Brother Willibrod. The *dominus* flinched but Eadulf made no further physical threat.

'I presume that you are aware of the condition of the weather and that it is but a few hours to midnight?' he asked coldly.

Brother Willibrod regarded him nervously.

'I can only relay the rule of the abbey,' he replied defensively.

'Dominus, listen to me. I am Eadulf of Seaxmund's Ham, lately come from Canterbury, and—'

The *dominus* nodded rapidly. 'You have said that you are the representative of Archbishop Theodore of Canterbury. That is the reason why I have admitted you. Have you been sent by our new archbishop? Is it true that he is a Greek from the very place where the saintly Paul of Tarsus was born?'

Eadulf's mouth quirked a little in vexation but he thought the air of reverence with which the other spoke of Theodore might be useful.

'I know Theodore well and act as his emissary,' he

31

replied calmly. 'It was my fortune to instruct him in the ways of our country while we were in Rome. In his name, I demand that you—'

'Then you were in Rome itself?' Brother Willibrod's voice was a whisper, filled almost with awe.

'I was. But now, Brother, in Theodore's name, I demand hospitality for myself and my wife!'

Brother Willibrod's jaw dropped a little and he stared from Eadulf to Fidelma.

Fidelma could not restrain her glance of annoyance at her companion and she added pedantically: 'I am only a *ben charrthach*.'

Brother Willibrod was unaware of the fine points of difference in Irish marriage laws and the status of wives. He shook his head sadly.

'I will take your demand for hospitality to the abbot, as it is made in the name of the archbishop sent from Rome and, as you have pointed out, the weather is too inclement for the foreign woman to travel further. But I must give you a word of warning. Abbot Cild is of the party which believes in the celibacy of all the religious. Until the Council of Whitby, this was a mixed house. When the ruling at Whitby went against the Irish, most of the Irish abbots and religious – indeed, many of the Angles and Saxons who decided to continue their teachings – were ordered to quit these kingdoms.

'Cild was appointed abbot here and eventually converted to the Rule of Rome, becoming an advocate for celibacy. The married religious were asked to leave. We became a closed community. It is against my instructions to let any women into these buildings. Only your authority as Archbishop Theodore's representative forces me to present your case to Abbot Cild. He may well refuse you hospitality . . .' he paused and looked uncomfortably at Fidelma, 'especially if he learns that you are of the married religious.'

Fidelma smiled winningly at the *dominus*, deciding that diplomacy might achieve more than trying to exert authority.

'We shall not make a point of stressing our relationship, Brother Willibrod,' she said with a meaningful glance at Eadulf. 'And perhaps you will respect our confidence, if it makes life easier for all concerned?'

The *dominus* hesitated for a moment and then shrugged.

'I will not mention it, if you do not wish it.'

Eadulf was seething with anger, but he did his best to control himself.

'Then instead of standing here in the chill of the evening air, perhaps you will show us to your guests' accommodation so that we may wash and warm ourselves. For I tell you, whatever the views of your abbot, we do not intend to leave the shelter of this house tonight . . . not while this storm howls around our ears.'

Brother Willibrod inclined his head. He seemed to be having an inward tussle with himself. Finally, logic won out.

'I will take you to the guests' chambers across the quadrangle here. Refresh yourselves, by all means. Then I am sure that the abbot will want to see you, Brother Eadulf. He will want to know what messages you bring him from Canterbury.'

'Messages?' Eadulf frowned.

'You are an emissary from Archbishop Theodore of Canterbury. Abbot Cild will want to know why Theodore has sent you here and will have many questions to ask you.'

Eadulf had used Theodore's name merely to gain access to the abbey and now he realised that his bluff had been called.

'Well, first . . .' he began.

'First, I will take you to the guests' quarters,' Brother Willibrod assured him quickly, turning and walking rapidly in the direction of the courtyard. They almost had to run to keep up with him. He moved with quick assurance for a person with one blind eye. Indeed, the pace was such that they did not have breath to spare to say anything further until the tall *dominus* halted outside a door and opened it for them.

'Wait here!' he instructed, and then he disappeared into the darkness of the interior. A few moments later he returned with a shielded candle. 'I will light the way in.'

They were in a long, stone-flagged corridor. Brother Willibrod went to the first door.

'You may wash and refresh yourself in this room, Sister. There is a fire already alight and water ready. We always keep one room in such a condition in case of wayfarers. Your room, Brother, is not yet ready. I will get one of our brethren to lay and light a fire for you, but—'

'We can share this one,' Eadulf said, indicating the warm room where Fidelma was now standing before the sparking logs of the fire.

Brother Willibrod looked shocked. 'I have said that this is not a mixed house, nor are liaisons between religious—'

Fidelma turned and spoke quickly to Eadulf in the language of Éireann.

'For the sake of simplicity, let us obey the rules of this place until it is time to leave.'

Eadulf was reluctant. He had to admit, however, that Fidelma was right. It seemed that they had enough problems without creating more.

'While you refresh yourself from the journey, Fidelma,

I will attend to the reason which brought us here.' He turned back to Brother Willibrod and spoke in Saxon. 'While I am waiting for my room to be prepared, I should like to see Brother Botulf.'

Brother Willibrod's one restless eye widened a little. 'Brother Botulf?'

'He is the steward of this abbey, is he not?'

'So you know already?' Willibrod sounded surprised.

'Know?' Eadulf frowned impatiently. Then he said, 'I would like to see Brother Botulf right away.'

'You want to pay your respects to Brother Botulf right away?' Brother Willibrod echoed, as if he was having difficulty understanding. He hesitated for a moment and then said, 'If you insist, Brother . . . ?'

'I do,' snapped Eadulf, baffled by the other's curious behaviour.

'Follow me, then, Brother Eadulf.'

With a quick puzzled grimace to Fidelma, Eadulf turned and followed Brother Willibrod back across the snow-laden courtyard. The abbey was almost in darkness. A few lights shone here and there but there was no sign of anyone about. It was as if the buildings were deserted.

Brother Willibrod led the way directly through an arched door into what was obviously the antechamber to the abbey's chapel and paused inside to shake the snow from his sandals and allow Eadulf to catch up with him. Eadulf had barely time to clean the snow from his feet before Brother Willibrod swung the inner door open and passed inside.

The perfume of warm, musty incense almost took Eadulf's breath, so sharp a contrast was it to the crisp, cold air outside. The *dominus* genuflected towards the high altar before walking forward.

Mechanically, Eadulf did the same, wondering where

he was being led. Then he halted suddenly. His heart began beating very fast.

Before the high altar, on two trestles, lay a plain wooden box. A large candle in a tall holder stood at the head and foot of the box, the flames whipping in the draught that blew through the chapel, almost extinguishing them but never quite succeeding.

It suddenly seemed that the violence of the wind had died away, its roaring softened to a moaning whisper. There was a dread in his soul as Eadulf allowed Brother Willibrod to conduct him forward to the box. He had already identified it as a coffin.

Brother Willibrod halted and stood aside with his dark restless eye downcast. Eadulf looked at the *dominus*, trying to seek a denial of what he knew must lie in the box. Brother Willibrod's face was graven in respect. It offered him no comfort.

He moved to the side of the coffin and looked down.

As he feared, the body of his friend, Brother Botulf, lay in repose within it, hands folded on his chest, a wooden crucifix clutched in his nerveless grasp. He had already been laid out in grave clothes. Eadulf forced himself to bend down and peer at the discoloured features of his dead childhood friend.

It needed little medical knowledge to realise that Brother Botulf's skull had been smashed in by some heavy, blunt instrument. Eadulf knew that such wounds could only have been inflicted by someone whose strength lay in malice. His friend had been murdered, and the event must have occurred scarcely more than a few hours before.

At that moment, the wind rose again, shrieking like a chorus of souls in torment; howling like a presage of evil.

Chapter Three

'You have arrived just in time, Brother,' intoned Brother Willibrod softly.

'In time?' muttered Eadulf distractedly as he gazed upon the body of his childhood friend. 'How do you mean – *in time*?'

'We shall bury the earthly remains of our dear brother at midnight, as is the custom of the abbey.'

'Midnight!'

Eadulf twisted round and stared aghast at Brother Willibrod. The message that he had received from his friend had urged him to be at the abbey before midnight that day. Could Botulf have known . . . ? Surely not?

'You seem surprised, Brother Eadulf,' Brother Willibrod said calmly as he returned Eadulf's apprehensive stare. 'I am told that it is the fashion in many lands to bury the dear departed at midnight. Why should you appear shocked?'

Eadulf tried to calm his racing thoughts. He turned quickly back to the body, not wishing to betray his emotions further until he could find some answers, and began to examine the wounds with a careful eye.

'Botulf did not commit suicide, did he?' The question came immediately to his mind as an answer to why Botulf had urged him to be at Aldred's Abbey before midnight. He dismissed the idea even as he voiced it, however, for the wounds could never have been self-inflicted.

He was aware that, behind him, Brother Willibrod had quickly crossed himself.

'*Quod avertat Deus!* God forbid, Brother. Why should you think something like that?'

'When did this happen?'

'Sometime this morning, so far as we can tell. His body was found in the small quadrangle at the back of the chapel, just by the entrance to the crypt. Poor Botulf. It was noticed that he was missing at early morning prayers and he was found soon after Matins was sung – at the seventh canonical hour.'

'Just after daybreak, then?'

'Just so, Brother Eadulf.'

'Who found him?'

Brother Willibrod frowned suspiciously at the question.

'Brother Osred. He is the smith of our community and he was crossing the small quadrangle to his forge to start his day's work when he found the body.'

'From the wounds, Botulf was attacked from behind. Has the attacker been discovered?'

'You are asking many questions, Brother,' the *dominus* replied, a distrustful tone now entering his voice. 'When you asked to see Brother Botulf, I presumed that you had come to the abbey having already heard of his death. Yet you seem surprised. Now all these questions. Who are you?'

Eadulf was patient. 'I have told you that I am Eadulf of Seaxmund's Ham, just arrived from Canterbury. Botulf . . .' He hesitated. Perhaps he would do best not to reveal Botulf's message. 'Botulf was a friend of mine. We grew up together. I had not heard the news of his death until you showed me his body.'

Brother Willibrod considered this explanation for a moment and accepted it. He grimaced awkwardly.

'Then I am sorry that I did not prepare you for this sadness. I had assumed . . .' He ended with an embarrassed shrug.

'I asked you if the attacker had been discovered,' Eadulf pressed. The sharpness in his voice caused Brother Willibrod to frown.

'That you knew Brother Botulf does not excuse the tenor of your questions,' he snapped back spiritedly.

'I was also hereditary *gerefa* of Seaxmund's Ham.' Eadulf's voice was cutting. 'I am a magistrate of the laws of Wuffa son of Wehha, first King of the East Anglians, who brought our people to this land from across the sea one hundred years ago.'

He did not mean to sound so proud and arrogant but he knew his words would have an effect on Brother Willibrod. Eadulf neglected to add that his office of *gerefa* was negated under the old laws of his people when he accepted the tonsure of the religious and became a brother of the faith. Brother Willibrod did not question his statement. The *dominus* merely bowed his head.

'Forgive my lack of knowledge and courtesy, Brother *gerefa*.' His tone was more respectful.

Eadulf gave a gesture with his hand as if to dismiss the matter.

'Tell me what you know. Who killed Botulf and why?'

'Abbot Cild has taken the inquiry in hand. It appears that one of our brethren saw a notorious outlaw near the abbey not long after poor Brother Botulf was found. The abbot is certain that this thief broke into the abbey and was accosted by Brother Botulf. The thief slew poor Botulf and made good his escape.'

Eadulf's eyes narrowed. 'And nothing else is known other than that?'

'Abbot Cild is the one to ask about the details.'

Eadulf was silent for a moment or two. Then he looked down at the body of his friend and sighed softly. He reached forward and touched Botulf's cold hand.

'I will discover the truth of this matter, Botulf,' he said under his breath. 'The culprit will be found.' Then aloud he quoted from the Gospel of Luke: '*Nunc dimittis servum tuum, Domine* . . . Lord, now let thy servant depart . . .'

At the door of the chapel, he turned to Brother Willibrod.

'I shall remove the grime of travel, and then Sister Fidelma and I will wish to see Abbot Cild.'

Brother Willibrod looked suddenly nervous. 'I will see if Abbot Cild will receive you, but he will not meet with the woman.'

Eadulf's brows came together threateningly. 'What do you mean?'

'I have told you that the abbot does not believe in mixed houses nor in married religious. I do not know if he will even approve of my admitting her into this abbey.'

A look of disdain crossed Eadulf's features. 'Then you had best ensure that the abbot knows of my authority both as *gerefa* and as an emissary of Archbishop Theodore. And my companion is sister to the King of Muman in the land of Éireann.' He felt a twinge of guilt as he said this, as Fidelma had expressly asked him not to reveal her identity. Hostage taking for ransom was not an unknown practice. It was often better that one's rank was not revealed. He dismissed his disquiet and went on sharply: 'Your abbot would do well to reflect on whose enmity he wishes to earn.'

Brother Willibrod raised his eyebrows with an expression of resignation. 'It shall be as you wish, Brother Eadulf, but the abbot is a man of strict faith and belief and not moved by threats . . . nor by other concerns,' he added quickly to cover up his lack of diplomacy.

Eadulf's lips thinned for a moment and then he said: 'Very well. You may see if he will receive me before the ceremony of burial.'

'I will come by the guests' quarters shortly with the abbot's answer. I will also send one of the brethren to tend to your wants and make up the fire.'

When Eadulf found his way back to the guests' dormitory, Fidelma had washed but was sitting close to the log fire, her robes tightly wrapped around her, and she was shivering a little. She looked up as he entered.

'I think I am developing a sore throat,' she complained. 'This cold has cut me to the bone.'

'Botulf has been murdered,' cut in Eadulf without preamble.

She stared at him for a moment as if not comprehending.

'Do you mean that your friend, the one who sent you the message, is dead?'

'He has been murdered,' repeated Eadulf, 'and the burial ceremony is due at midnight.'

'Midnight?' echoed Fidelma. She frowned. 'He asked you to be here before midnight. Do you think . . . ?'

'He was murdered sometime before dawn today,' Eadulf told her. 'How could he have known there would be any significance about midnight tonight?'

'Perhaps there was another significance?'

'I do not understand.'

'It is not a matter of understanding but of first trying to discover the facts.' Fidelma suddenly sneezed. 'This fire is not even beginning to thaw the chill in my marrow.'

There came a knock at the door and a young religious entered. He was only a boy, scarcely out of childhood, fair of hair and skin, with blue eyes and blood-red lips. He seemed shy and nervous. He carried a tray with a steaming jug on it and two clay beakers. He kept his eyes lowered and did not look at Fidelma.

'I have been asked to bring you some warming broth.' He addressed himself to Eadulf, having glanced nervously at him before dropping his eyes again. 'I am then to light the fire in the next room for you, Brother.'

Eadulf took the tray from the boy's trembling hands and placed it on a nearby table.

'Thank you.' Fidelma smiled at him. 'What is your name?'

'I am Brother Redwald, Sister.' The boy's manner showed that he was clearly apprehensive at being addressed directly by her.

'You have no need to be nervous,' Fidelma assured him.

'The abbot . . .' began the boy. Then he shut his lips firmly.

'We have heard that the abbot does not welcome women into this abbey,' Fidelma replied solemnly. 'Do not worry, you shall not get into trouble for doing your job.'

The boy nodded quickly. 'Then I shall be about that work, Sister.'

The boy was already moving out of the door when Eadulf stayed him with a sharp question.

'Did you know Brother Botulf?'

The boy turned back quickly. There was a look almost of fear on his features and for a moment he stared directly at Eadulf before dropping his gaze once more.

'Everyone knew Brother Botulf. He was the steward of the abbey and had been here when it was founded. He was a companion of the blessed Aldred whose body lies beneath the high altar in the chapel. Our abbey is named after him.'

'Did you know Brother Botulf well?'

'Brother Botulf was kind to me.'

'Isn't everyone kind to you here?' asked Fidelma softly.

Brother Redwald sniffed but did not look at her or respond.

'Do you know what happened to Brother Botulf? I mean, how he was killed?' Eadulf pressed.

The boy shook his head without meeting Eadulf's eyes. 'His body was found this morning. They say someone broke into the abbey to steal from the chapel and was discovered by Brother Botulf. The thief killed him.'

'What was stolen?' inquired Fidelma.

'Nothing was stolen. I heard Brother Willibrod say that Brother Botulf must have prevented the theft and the murderer fled empty-handed.'

'From the fortress-like appearance of this abbey, it would seem a difficult place to break into,' observed Eadulf. 'Have you heard who this thief was?'

The boy grimaced as if to disclaim responsibility. 'They say that it was one of a band of outlaws who dwell in the marshes. They have no love for the religious. I heard that Abbot Cild was blaming the death of Brother Botulf on their leader and said that he would punish him.'

'Who is their leader?' asked Eadulf.

'Aldhere is his name. Now let me be about my work, please, Brother.'

The boy left the room hurriedly. They could hear him stacking the firewood in the next room.

Fidelma sneezed twice.

'Pass me that hot drink, Eadulf,' she asked mildly. 'Perhaps it will give me some warmth.'

'There is something wrong here,' Eadulf said reflectively, handing her the beaker. 'There is a curious atmosphere in this abbey which I do not like. Something very oppressive. Do you not feel it?'

Fidelma smiled thinly. 'I would agree with you in that the death of your friend is oppressive enough.'

'I do not mean that. I grieve for him, but my grief must give way to resolving the manner of his death.'

Fidelma sipped her broth while examining him with some concern. 'What else can it be but a coincidence that he had asked you to be here before midnight?'

'Before midnight,' repeated Eadulf with emphasis, 'and I then find that this is the hour in which his body is to be laid to rest. A coincidence? Why did he want me to be here at that specific hour?'

'A few discreet inquiries might tell us something,' observed Fidelma.

Eadulf did not appear enthusiastic. 'Much depends upon the abbot of this place as to whether I will be allowed to make those inquiries. If Brother Willibrod's word is anything to go by, I do not think that we shall be invited to stay long.'

Fidelma sneezed again.

'I hope that I am not going to suffer a cold from the excesses of our journey,' she muttered. Then she added: 'Abbot Cild seems to have little charity in his heart if Brother Willibrod presents a true picture of the man. Have you planned your further intentions if we are told to leave here?'

Eadulf shook his head. 'We can only go on to Seaxmund's Ham, for there is nowhere nearer to stay.'

'Well, in truth, I shan't be sorry to leave this place, Eadulf. I not only have a chill in my body but I have rarely encountered a place which strikes such a chill in my soul.'

At that moment there was a rap on the door and it opened to allow the one-eyed Brother Willibrod to enter. He looked fidgety and concerned.

'Abbot Cild will see you immediately, Brother Eadulf. Will you come with me?'

Eadulf glanced apologetically to Fidelma. She did not

even look at him but sat hunched by the fire nursing the hot drink in both hands.

Eadulf followed Brother Willibrod through the dark brick-built corridors of the abbey until the *dominus* halted before a heavy oak door and knocked upon it in a discreet manner. A voice barked an order from inside and Brother Willibrod threw open the door, stood aside and motioned Eadulf to enter. When he did so, the door was closed silently behind him with Brother Willibrod waiting outside.

The abbot sat at the far end of a long oak table on which two ornate candlesticks bore tallow candles which fluttered and hissed, sending out a curious light in the darkness of the chamber. He gave the impression of a tall man, seated upright in a carved oak chair, his hands placed palm downwards on the table as he gazed before him with dark eyes.

The abbot's face was long, pale of skin and with sharp, etched features. The forehead was high-domed and surrounded by long, dark hair. It was a face filled with a strength of purpose that Eadulf found unusual in a religious, although such features were often found in warriors. His nose was thin and had a high bridge and strangely arched nostrils. The dark eyes seemed to reflect the light of the flickering candles, causing them to glow with some red aura. The effect was threatening. The thin mouth was fixed and cruel.

'I am told that you are an emissary from Theodore, the new archbishop of Canterbury, that you are also hereditary *gerefa* of Seaxmund's Ham.'

'I am Eadulf of Seaxmund's Ham.'

'This does not allow you to maintain special privileges. At least not in my abbey. You do not appear to have informed Brother Willibrod that your rank of *gerefa* was lost the moment you took your vows as a religieux.'

'Perhaps Brother Willibrod assumed too much. I did use the word "was",' Eadulf replied spiritedly. 'As for special privileges? I do not understand.'

'To bring a woman into this abbey. To persuade my *dominus* to defy my cardinal rule. We are a closed house to womenkind.' The abbot's voice was sharp.

Eadulf coloured hotly. 'My travelling companion is Fidelma of Cashel, sister to the King of Muman and a famed lawyer in her own land.'

'She is not in her own land and this is my abbey where I set the rules.'

'If you glance through the window you will see that the weather makes it impossible for anyone to continue on a journey this night,' Eadulf snapped back.

The abbot was not put out by Eadulf's attitude.

'You should not have attempted any journey in the first place without being assured of a welcome,' he replied with equal firmness.

'Forgive me. I thought that in coming to a Christian house I would find Christian charity,' Eadulf replied sarcastically. 'This is my own country, my own people, and the steward of this abbey was a friend with whom I had grown up. I did not expect to find a Christian house that displays an inflexible, uncompassionate and mean-spirited rule.'

The abbot regarded him without any change of expression. He did not respond to the insult.

'You have been away some time, I am told. You will find many things changed in this land. This abbey, for example, is now under my rule, *mutatis mutandis*.'

'Things having been changed that had to be changed?' Eadulf turned the Latin saying into a question. 'So compassion had to be excluded from this place?'

The abbot ignored the interjection. 'I will show Christ's generosity this night. But tomorrow morning, after Matins, you and the woman will leave this place. In the meantime, she must not move from the chamber in which she has been placed. You, Brother Eadulf, may attend services in our chapel.'

Eadulf swallowed angrily. 'I must protest that—'

'The woman will not be allowed to stay longer and set my rules at naught. Now, I demand to know what business brings you here. Do you have messages from Archbishop Theodore for me?'

Eadulf ground his teeth to control his anger.

'Not for you. No,' he replied with malicious sharpness.

The imperturbable features of the abbot did not flicker. However, his voice rose sharply again.

'Then why did you come here? You gave my *dominus* to believe—'

'I gave him to believe nothing. I merely told him who I was. I came to see my friend, Brother Botulf.'

For the first time the abbot's eyes widened slightly. 'And that is all?'

'Should there be anything else?'

There was a pause. Eadulf noticed a tiny pulse throbbing in the abbot's temple. He wondered at the man's state of nerves.

'Are you saying that you brought a message from Canterbury to my steward? Is that the reason why you have come here?'

'I have nothing further to tell you,' replied Eadulf, feeling irritated by the interrogation.

'I have been told that you have seen the body of Brother Botulf. If that is all, you may leave tomorrow morning with your purpose achieved.'

'My purpose achieved?' For a moment Eadulf found himself speechless. Then he fought to control himself again. Truly, this man was insufferable. Eadulf's voice became tinged with an icy hardness. 'My purpose now is to find out who killed my friend and to ensure that the culprit is brought to justice.'

Abbot Cild's eyelids lowered slowly, paused, and then rose. It reminded Eadulf of a hawk hooding its eyes before a kill. A faint smile now seemed to hover on those thin lips. It was, the thought came to Eadulf, like moonlight glinting on a tombstone. There was no feeling in the abbot's voice other than that tone which implied a sinister threat. Eadulf shivered slightly as the hairs tingled for a moment on the nape of his neck.

'I can tell you that the outlaw Aldhere, a marsh dweller, is to blame. And tomorrow at midday I shall take some of our brethren and go into the marshes and hunt him down like the dog that he is. If we catch him then we shall hang him. Now your purpose is achieved and you will quit this abbey as I have requested. I hope that I have made myself clear, Eadulf of Seaxmund's Ham?' Abbot Cild rose leisurely in one smooth movement, reminding Eadulf of the way he had seen a snake uncoil itself after basking in the sun.

'Is there to be a trial of this man Aldhere?' he ventured, trying to quell the feeling of dread which the abbot seemed to have no trouble in conjuring in him.

'A trial? What need is there for a trial? Aldhere is a murderer. Trials are not for such as him.'

'What was the motive and where is the evidence?' demanded Eadulf, determined not to be put off.

'The motive is theft and the evidence is that Aldhere was seen leaving the abbey shortly after the body of Botulf was discovered.'

'Who saw Aldhere?'

Abbot Cild let out a hiss of annoyance. 'You try my patience too far, Eadulf of Seaxmund's Ham. Now be gone. I have a burial to prepare for.'

He waved his hand in dismissal and Eadulf, in spite of protests, found himself standing outside the abbot's door, so forceful a personality was Cild's.

Brother Willibrod awaited him.

'I presume that you will attend the funeral ceremony?' he asked.

Eadulf nodded moodily.

'Is it clearly understood that the foreign woman will not be allowed to attend services in this abbey?' added the *dominus*. 'I have strict instructions from the abbot.'

Eadulf, still angered by his meeting with Abbot Cild, did not respond to the question.

'What is the evidence against this outlaw, Aldhere?' he demanded. 'He was seen near the abbey but what ties him to the death of Botulf?'

Brother Willibrod took a moment to adjust to the change of subject and then shrugged.

'Do you doubt Abbot Cild's word that he was seen?'

'So far, I have heard nothing to make me accept or reject Abbot Cild's word. I have no doubt that he means to hang this man, Aldhere. However, before a man's life is forfeit it is customary to demand evidence. The abbot tells me that the motive was theft, yet I understand nothing was taken. I am told that someone saw Aldhere leaving the abbey but not who it was. Was it this Brother Osred? The one you told me discovered Botulf's body?'

Brother Willibrod smiled grimly. 'You have been away among strangers too long, Brother. You have forgotten that here we live among animals. Kill or be killed. If a man covets another's land or his wife, and he is strong, then he will take what he wants. The weak will always lose.'

'The faith has reformed our pagan ways,' protested Eadulf.

'Only if we have allowed it to. For some, it is impossible to change. *Naturam expelles furca tamen usque recurret.*'

'You may drive nature out with a pitchfork, but it will still return,' translated Eadulf, showing that he had understood.

'Our faith may alter but not our ways.'

'You are supposed to follow the way of Christ.'

'Only if we live long enough to do so. Those without the law, such as Aldhere, would not have this abbey survive. He is a mad dog.'

'So the dog has a bad name and thus he will be hanged? His guilt or innocence is of no consequence?'

'If he is not guilty of this act then he is guilty of some other. What difference does it make?'

Eadulf was concerned that his friend's killer should be found and punished, but any suspect should be tried under law. Eadulf vowed to himself that if the Abbot did indeed lead a hunting party into the marshes the next day, he would accompany them to see that justice was done. Justice, not blind vengeance.

'And so by such logic we reach paradise?' he protested sharply. 'Come, *dominus*, I would like to see the person who appears to be the only witness in the case of Brother Botulf's murder. This is a matter far too grave to be judged by prejudice. A mistake will reflect ill on this abbey and on anyone who has a hand in any event which may lead to a miscarriage of justice.'

Brother Willibrod still hesitated a moment before finally relenting.

'Brother Wigstan was the person who saw Aldhere. He will be at the funeral service tonight. Will you be able to find your way back to the guests' quarters from here?'

Eadulf nodded and Brother Willibrod turned abruptly and left at his usual rapid pace.

When Eadulf returned to the guests' quarters he went immediately to Fidelma's room and found her in the middle of a coughing fit. He brought her some water. She peered up with reddened eyes.

'Oh, for a good Irish sweat bath,' she muttered. 'A sore throat, sneezing and a cough . . . all because of this awful climate. I have never known weather so cold anywhere.'

'It is because the country is low lying,' offered Eadulf in explanation. 'There is nothing to protect us from the cold northerly winds from the sea. No tall hills nor mountains shield us.'

'So the result is that I have to suffer a cold.'

Eadulf had studied medicine at the great Irish medical school of Tuaim Brecáin and was already searching one of his bags.

'We have a fire and thus a means of heating water, and while we have these things all is not lost.' He smiled confidently. 'I will prepare an infusion of elderflowers and woodbine and stir in a little of the honey that I carry. You will soon be well.'

As he set to preparing his mixture, Eadulf told her of his meeting with Abbot Cild. Fidelma listened attentively, asking one or two questions to clarify points.

'It seems that he is exactly as Brother Willibrod painted him,' she murmured at the end of his recital.

'He brings shame on the faith.'

'He brings shame only on himself,' replied Fidelma. 'A man of such shabby arrogance brings derision only on himself, not on the faith. Let us hope I will be well enough to travel tomorrow morning. But as for tonight, I intend to retire. I am sorry that I shall miss the funeral of your friend, Eadulf.'

Eadulf shrugged. He did not bother to inform her

that she would not have been allowed into the chapel in any case.

'You cannot help Botulf. It is now more important that you recover your health. I have prepared enough of this infusion for you to sip through the night. Do not swallow it in large draughts, only small sips. Remember that.' With a preoccupied smile, he turned for the door.

'I'll remember,' Fidelma called after him. 'And be circumspect with your questions, Eadulf. It seems an easy thing to cause annoyance to the brethren of this place.'

Eadulf left the guests' hostel as a distant bell began to toll the Angelus. He increased his pace along the dark stone-flagged corridor, trying to remember the route to the chapel. It was icy cold and through the arches that gave onto the quadrangle he could see that the snow was still slanting downward from the black night sky. Making his way through a series of covered ways he came to a smaller quadrangle, encompassed by a covered walkway. On the side that Eadulf was proceeding along, a door at the end was illuminated by a storm lantern. He could see a similar lantern lighting another door on the far side. The snow lay thick where the quadrangle was open to the elements. He realised that this was the small area at the back of the chapel where poor Brother Botulf's body had been found. He paused. One of the doors must lead to the crypt.

He was standing by one of the pillars, trying to reason how best to get to the other side of the chapel where the main doors were, when he noticed a movement on the far side of the quadrangle, among the shadows of the covered walkway. A slim figure in a long cloak moved from a darkened recess and strode swiftly, silently, along it. He watched the progress of the figure, frowning. There was something incongruous about it, given the surroundings. The figure paused just by the door with the lantern, hesitated and cast a quick glance around, as if to ensure that it was not being observed. Eadulf's eyes widened a fraction.

The shadowy light revealed the face of a young woman. Even from across the quadrangle, Eadulf had the impression of ethereal beauty, of pale skin – was it too pale? It might have been a trick of the light – and fair hair. The figure was not clad as a religieuse but in some rich, crimson gown and there was evidence of silver jewellery and glittering gemstones.

Then, quickly, silently, the figure vanished through the door.

Eadulf stood for a moment or two wondering who the young woman was and what she was doing in an abbey which he was assured was the preserve only of men pledged to a life of celibacy under the faith. No women were supposed to be allowed within these walls.

When Eadulf reached the chapel, the abbot had already begun the service for the soul of Brother Botulf. He was intoning the blessing and Eadulf was forced to put his questions to one side.

'May the blessing of light be on you, light without and light within . . .'

There were some thirty or more brethren gathered in the chapel. Eadulf took his seat on a bench at the back, not wishing to make himself conspicuous among the assembly.

He glanced around. Most of the congregation were young. They seemed to be sturdy men. Several had features that were harsh and would not be out of place in a battle host, seeming more suited to swords and shields rather than a crucifix and a phial of holy water.

They followed the prayers with a song. Eadulf did not know it and so did not join in.

Abbot Cild then came forward and had just started an

adulatory soliloquy when the two great wooden doors of the chapel opened with a crash.

Eadulf, along with the rest of the congregation of brethren, swung round startled.

A tall man stood framed in the doorway, feet wide apart, a naked sword in one hand, his shield ready on the other arm in a defensive position. That he was a warrior was easy to see but who or what manner of warrior was more difficult to recognise. He wore a burnished helmet on which was fashioned the head and wings of a goose. The goose had its beak open in a warning; its neck was curved and low while its wings were swept back on either side of the helmet. It was a truly frightening image. Eadulf vaguely recalled hearing that in some cultures the goose was an emblem of battle. It seemed so now, for below this helmet was a faceguard and only the bright eyes of the warrior glinted in the candlelight from the chapel, emanating a threatening malignancy.

A long black fur cloak hid the body, although Eadulf saw the glint of a breastplate underneath. The arm that held the menacing sword was muscular. For several long seconds there was absolute silence in the chapel. Then the man spoke, or rather his voice was raised so that it reverberated throughout the building. His Saxon was stilted and accented.

'Know me, Cild, abbot of Aldred's Abbey. Look upon me and know me.'

Chapter Four

There was a moment of utter silence in the chapel.

Abbot Cild must have been a man of iron control for he did not seem perturbed at all by the threatening appearance of the warrior. When he replied it was in a sneering tone.

'I do not recognise men who come armed into Christ's house with their features disguised by war helmets.'

The warrior responded with a fierce smack of his sword across his shield. The sound was like a thunderclap.

'You who pretend not to know the crest I wear on my helmet, you who pretend not to know my voice . . . you know me well. I am Garb son of Gadra. Tell your brethren – do I lie?'

Abbot Cild hesitated.

'If you say so, so you are,' he responded tightly.

'I am Garb of the Plain of the Yew Trees.'

'And if you are,' rejoined the abbot, still not cowed, 'then you commit sacrilege in the manner of your coming. Put down your sword.'

The Irish warrior, for Eadulf had identified the man by his accent as well as the name he had given, gave a sharp laugh.

'I value my life too much to put down my weapon in this place. I will keep my sword.'

'Then tell us what you want and be gone.'

'I will—' The man stopped short and turned quickly

to the side. 'Cild, tell your brethren they are dead men if they come further!'

Two men with drawn bows suddenly appeared at the Irish warrior's sides. Eadulf, too, had noticed that several of the Saxon brethren had been edging along the side aisle of the chapel. To Eadulf's surprise, they carried short swords in their hands. Their obvious intention was to disarm or close with the intruder. Cild rapped out an order. They halted, realising that the arrows were aimed unerringly at them.

Abbot Cild waved them back. 'Return to your places, Brothers. Let us deal with this madman peacefully.'

The Irish warrior turned back to him. 'Madman? That is good, coming from your mouth, Cild. But it is wise that you tell your men to desist for it is not my intention to join poor Botulf there in an early grave.'

Eadulf started at the use of his friend's name on the lips of this warrior who called himself Garb.

'Don't profane his name by uttering it!' cried Abbot Cild, his voice filled with an angry emotion for the first time.

'Botulf was a good friend to my family, Cild, as well you know,' went on the warrior in a calm tone. 'It is in *your* mouth that his name is profaned. It was convenient for you that he was killed on this day of all days. Maybe it is another debt to be added to your account?'

Abbot Cild stared at the man woodenly.

'Brother Botulf was killed by a thief,' he finally said. 'An outlaw breaking into this abbey. He will soon be caught and dealt with.'

'A thief? Perhaps. I still call it convenient.' There was irony in the man's voice. 'By the virtue of my sisters, I still call it convenient!'

'What do you want, Garb?' Abbot Cild's eyes were

suddenly furtive. His change of expression was not lost on Eadulf.

'Ah, you have no difficulty recognising me now, eh?' The voice of the warrior was bantering.

'What do you want?'

'I come from my father, Gadra; from Gadra who was also father to Gélgeis, the wife whom you put from you and killed.'

A gasp of shock rippled through the chapel. Eadulf glanced swiftly from accuser to abbot in astonishment. Abbot Cild's face was white and now etched in sharp lines. The dark eyes were like coals.

'I did not kill your sister, Garb.'

'You would doubtless deny it. You have no shame. Yet shame shall be your portion, Cild. I come as an emissary of my father, chief of the Plain of the Yew and father of your murdered wife. This is not the first time he has accused you of her murder and called upon you to come to arbitration. You have refused to do so. Will you do it now?'

'If I did not do so before, I will not do so now while you threaten me. Go back to your own country, Garb. Go back to your father. You and your people are not welcome in our Anglo-Saxon kingdoms. You cannot cow me with the threat of violence, for you will never leave this abbey alive if I am harmed.'

Garb chuckled softly. 'You are an arrogant fool, Cild! I have merely come to perform the ritual *apad*. I do not threaten you.'

'The what . . . ?' Cild's voice was hesitant.

'I give you notice that my father seeks restitution for the murder of his daughter at your hands. He undertakes the ritual *troscud* to compel you to accept the arbitration of the court. You have nine days, according to our law, to consider your position and then my father will begin the *troscud* . . . he will fast to the death or until you have accepted arbitration.'

Abbot Cild's sharp features moved swiftly to relief and then broke into a sneer.

'And if I do not accept this arbitration and your father merely dies for his mistaken belief in my guilt, what then?'

'If you allow my father to die while fasting for justice, then the shame is yours. Not just in this world but in the next. Every man's hand can be raised against you to strike you down without fear of punishment, for you then lose all rights as a human being.

'I have also to say this. According to our law you are an *airchinnech*, a monastic superior, and so from the time of this *apad* you are prohibited from reciting the *pater* or *credo* or going to the sacrament of the Mass.' The warrior turned his head slightly and whispered something to one of his companions who, relaxing his bow and replacing the arrow in his quiver, hurried forward to the altar of the chapel. From beneath his cloak he took a circlet of twisted willow branches and tossed it to the foot of the altar.

There was a mutter of concern from the brethren as the man trotted back to the side of Garb the warrior and resumed his stance with his readied bow.

'See that withe?' cried Garb. 'That is symbolic of the moral prohibition that is placed on you, not to perform your priestly functions until such time as you concede justice to my father. If you ignore this, then your soul may be damned.'

'This is ridiculous,' mocked Cild. 'Your laws do not apply here. This is not one of the kingdoms of Éireann but the kingdom of the East Angles.'

'You were married to my sister in my father's house on the Plain of the Yew. Your oaths were sworn by the Laws of the Fénechus in front of a Brehon. The same laws now hold you accountable for her death. You have nine days before the *troscud* starts. Now, I have fulfilled my task.'

With that the warrior stepped rapidly back. His companions reached forward and slammed the doors shut. There was a rush to the doors by the brethren nearest them but they found the doors barred on the outside.

Eadulf had not left his seat. Garb had obviously planned this confrontation well and he would have prepared his retreat with equal precision. Eadulf suspected that the warrior and his companions would have made good their escape by the time the infuriated brethren broke out of the chapel. He glanced to where Abbot Cild was still standing at the lectern where he had been interrupted. Brother Willibrod had gone to his side.

'How did they get into the abbey?' Abbot Cild was demanding. 'The doors were shut and secured, weren't they?'

'I will find out,' Brother Willibrod replied, almost rubbing his hands together in his anguish. 'But what should we do?'

'Do?' Abbot Cild had turned and was staring at the withe lying at the foot of the altar. 'First, you may take that and throw it on the fire. Second, you may see to the burial of Brother Botulf. Third, you may ensure that those brothers who will accompany me in the search for Aldhere and his outlaws tomorrow are properly armed. I have a feeling that these Irish bandits will be found with him.'

Eadulf rose and walked across to him. 'Bandits? It did not sound to me as if the warrior, Garb, was a bandit. I have spent some time in his country and what he was saying was a ritual prescribed by law, although I do not understand most of it.'

Abbot Cild glowered at him. 'This is none of your

business, Brother Eadulf. I advise you not to interfere.' Cild glanced to where some of the brethren were still banging on the secured doors of the chapel. 'Stop that nonsense!' he shouted.

They turned, like frightened children, and stood heads hung before the abbot.

Cild turned to Brother Willibrod. 'Take one of the brethren through the underground passage beneath the chapel and open the doors. I should imagine that the wretches are long gone by now. It was merely a means to hold us here while they escaped.'

It seemed a long while before the chapel doors were opened. In fact it was probably no more than ten minutes.

'Where is Brother Willibrod?' demanded the abbot, striding forward. Eadulf noticed that it had stopped snowing and although the wind was still up it was blowing less strongly than before.

'He went to see how they were able to enter the abbey,' said the brother who had opened the doors, backing before the abbot.

At that moment, Brother Willibrod came hurrying up to join them.

'They came over the wall,' he began breathlessly. 'I saw the marks in the snow. Three of them must have climbed up by means of a rope and grappling hook. I went outside and found signs of where half a dozen horses stood, so three others waited outside.'

Abbot Cild rubbed his chin in moody contemplation. 'Did you notice which way the tracks led or came from?'

'The wind was swiftly covering them. The snow is powdery and dry.'

Abbot Cild was clearly annoyed. 'It makes no difference. I am going to my chamber. You may finish the

burial rituals for I have much to do. We will deal with
these villains tomorrow.'

Brother Willibrod gazed unhappily after the retreating
form of the abbot, his one eye blinking rapidly. Then he
saw Eadulf looking at him and shrugged.

'At times,' he confided, 'I wish I had courage enough
to return to Blecci's Hill.'

'Blecci's Hill?' queried Eadulf. 'That's on the banks
of the Ouse, isn't it?'

'You know it?'

'It is just over the border in the kingdom of Mercia.
There was a battle there many years ago.'

Willibrod smiled, pleased that Eadulf knew something
of the history.

'That was before I was even born. It was when the
Northumbrians raided our territory.' He sighed deeply
and then drew his mind back to the present. 'One day
I shall return, God willing, and set myself in a little
hermitage on Blecci's Hill. But now . . .' He turned
round and called several of the brethren to him.

'Resume tolling the funeral bell. We will not insult the
memory of our brother Botulf by allowing this incident
to shatter the solemnity of the occasion. God willing, on
the morrow, we will avenge this insult.'

Eadulf was awake well before dawn. It was still cold,
although in the hearth some ash-covered embers seemed
to have retained a spark of life. There was a curious
grey twilight in the room which was caused by the white
reflection of the snow outside.

He arose from his bed, shivering, and moved swiftly
across to the fire, making sure to put only brittle, dry
twigs on the embers, waiting for them to spark into flame
before stacking more substantial pieces of wood on it. It
took only a few moments to set the blaze going in a more

hearty fashion. Even so, he found himself so affected by the chill room that he had to blow on his hands and stamp his feet to help restore his circulation.

His toilet was perfunctory. He splashed his face and hands in a bowl of cold water, noticing, with a shiver, the tiny particles of ice that had formed around the edge of the bowl. He towelled vigorously, drew on his robes and went softly to the next room.

When he had returned from the chapel, which had been well after midnight, after the burial of Brother Botulf in the small community cemetery which lay alongside the chapel walls, he had gone to report to Fidelma about the curious Irish visitors and their claims about Abbot Cild. But Fidelma had been fast asleep, shivering slightly but sweating profusely as she tossed in an uneasy slumber. He had not disturbed her, realising that she was suffering from a bad ague. Her breathing had been sharp and rasping.

Now, as he moved quietly into the room, he found her still huddled in the bed. Her eyes were shut, although from time to time she uttered a pitiable cough and her nose was red from sneezing. He went straight to the fire and banked it up into a blaze, and then turned to heat some water.

'I feel awful,' came a croaking voice that did not bear any resemblance to Fidelma's usual tones.

Eadulf turned from his task and smiled in sympathy.

'It looks as though you have caught a bad cold from our journey,' he observed unnecessarily.

Fidelma eased herself up slightly against the back of her wooden cot. Sweat still stood on her temples and she coughed spasmodically. Eadulf laid the back of his hand on her moist but burning forehead.

'As soon as I have the water heated, I'll prepare an infusion for you to make you feel better.'

'My throat is dry.'

He handed her a beaker of ice-cold water and told her to sip it gently to ease her throat. The water set off a little coughing fit and he took it from her.

'I will give you an infusion of betony leaf. It will help your headache. It's a favourite herbal remedy of my people. We'll try that mixed with some more elder and woodbine.'

'Eadulf, I don't care what you give me,' she moaned. 'I feel like death.'

'Don't worry,' Eadulf responded brightly. 'You will be back to normal in a day or two. I'll guarantee it.'

Fidelma suddenly sneezed and looked ruefully at Eadulf. Something of her old self shone through as she tried to smile.

'I thought that we didn't have two days?'

Eadulf frowned and then remembered. 'You mean the order of Abbot Cild to quit his abbey? Don't worry about that. I will go to see him and tell him that you cannot be moved. Anyway, there has been a new development here which I must tell you about.'

He turned back to the fire, and while he was preparing the medication for Fidelma he told her about the events of the night before. Fidelma was intrigued, almost forgetting her woe.

'A *troscud*? Are you sure he used that word?'

Eadulf nodded, sitting at the edge of her bed and waiting as she sipped the brew that he had prepared.

'I know that it is some sort of ritual fast,' he offered.

'A very serious one,' she confirmed. 'It does not happen often, for most people are happy to have arbitration in cases of dispute. The law is considered of importance, so both sides will abide by it and one rarely has to force the other to accept it.'

'But Abbot Cild is not subject to your laws here, in his own country.'

'That is true enough,' Fidelma agreed, interrupting herself with another coughing spasm.

Eadulf handed over another beaker of the infusion. She sipped for a moment.

'But you say that this man – Garb was his name? – you say that he claimed that Abbot Cild was at the Plain of the Yews when he married his sister?'

'A girl called Gélgeis,' confirmed Eadulf.

'And he married her according to our Laws of the Fénechus?'

'That is true.'

'Plain of the Yews? Garb was speaking in Saxon and he translated this name into Saxon?'

Eadulf nodded.

'Maigh Eo – Plain of the Yews. It is a place in the kingdom of Connacht. I can see why it would be claimed that Cild should submit to the Law of the Fénechus if he married under it at that place. Is it possible for you to find out any further details about this matter?'

Eadulf grimaced sourly. 'Not from Abbot Cild.'

'Then you must find out where the father of Garb is planning to hold his ritual fast.'

'Does it matter?'

'I think so. In my country, the ritual fast is usually carried out within sight of the door of the person against whom it is directed. It would be sacrilege and a crime for any man to harm the faster while engaged in the *troscud*. But here, in your country . . . I do not know how such a fast could be carried out for, to be brutal, your people would not respect our custom and probably do harm to the person who was fasting.'

'This is a fact,' Eadulf agreed. 'The fast would be a useless gesture among our people.'

Fidelma sank back onto her pillow. She was having

difficulty breathing and her cough was irritating her. She caught Eadulf's hand.

'Try to find out something more. I think Garb's father must have realised this and made some other plan to safeguard himself. But something as serious as a *troscud* could lead to war.'

Eadulf smiled reassuringly at her. 'I will make some discreet inquiries. First, though, I have to tell Abbot Cild that we cannot move from the abbey today. Meanwhile, I will ensure you have enough medication to ease your discomfort.'

After he had prepared more of the infusion from the herbs that he always carried with him, Eadulf left Fidelma fitfully dozing and made his way to Abbot Cild's chamber.

The abbot greeted him sourly. 'I suppose that you have come to bid farewell? You need not have bothered.'

Eadulf controlled the flash of irritation he felt at the abbot's abrupt manner.

'My companion and I cannot leave the abbey this morning—' he began.

He was interrupted by a look of anger which formed on the abbot's features.

'You dare attempt to disobey my orders?'

Eadulf raised a hand, palm outwards, to quell his rage.

'I regret to say that my companion, Sister Fidelma, has been taken ill. She cannot be moved in this weather. She has to stay in bed in the warm with some medications that I have provided for her.'

Abbot Cild regarded him with narrowed eyes. 'I am not accountable for her health. I did not invite you or her into this abbey.'

Eadulf was shocked at the callousness of the man.

'It is your Christian duty to provide visiting religious

65

with hospitality. What manner of holy man are you that you would depart from the rule of the faith in this way?' Eadulf's voice was cold as he sought to control his own temper. 'You refuse hospitality to a member of the faith on the claim that this is a house for males only but you seem to accept women guests who are not members of the religious. By the holy rood, I will ensure Archbishop Theodore learns of it.'

Abbot Cild's face had paled a little as Eadulf swung away.

'Wait!'

Eadulf was forced back by the sharpness of the man's command.

'What do you mean? What are you talking about . . . women guests who are not members of the religious?'

Eadulf smiled maliciously. 'I caught sight of the lady when I was on my way to the chapel last night. Is it some secret that she is here?'

The muscles on Abbot Cild's pale face were suddenly twitching. It seemed, for a moment, that all his aggression had suddenly left him. He sat down and stared up at Eadulf with an almost pathetic expression.

'Tell me exactly what you saw,' he said quietly. The tone was pleading. Eadulf heard a curious catch in his voice.

Tersely, he told the abbot of seeing the young woman in the quadrangle behind the chapel. He suddenly realised that the abbot was trembling slightly.

'Fair, you say, and clad in a red dress with jewels?'

'That is what I said,' confirmed Eadulf, wondering what had produced this astonishing change of attitude.

'You are not lying to me?' The question might have been insulting but the abbot's voice was almost entreating. 'You swear to me that you actually saw this woman?'

Eadulf was about to retort harshly, but the man seemed too pitiful.

'Of course I did,' he replied gruffly. 'I am not in the habit of recounting things I do not see. But enough of this. What I say is that you cannot claim to adopt one set of principles and disguise the fact you do not keep them. I promise that Archbishop Theodore shall hear of your ill treatment of Sister Fidelma. Woe betide you if harm falls on her by your callous indifference to her illness.'

Eadulf turned for the door again and again Abbot Cild halted him. He still seemed nervous, ill at ease, and Eadulf put it down to his threat to inform the archbishop.

'I will send the apothecary of the community to examine this . . . this Sister Fidelma. If he confirms what you say, you may stay here until she is well enough to travel.'

Abbot Cild reached forward and picked up a small bronze handbell. Brother Willibrod appeared almost immediately.

'Send Brother Higbald to see Sister Fidelma and ascertain her condition. Tell him to report directly to me as to the extent of her illness.'

Brother Willibrod looked startled. 'Illness, Father Abbot?' He glanced nervously at Eadulf. 'Is she ill?' he whispered fearfully. 'It is not . . . it is not the Yellow Plague?' He crossed himself quickly.

Abbot Cild gave a snort of displeasure that his order was not being carried out immediately. Gradually, a flush had spread over his features and he seemed to be returning to his old self.

Eadulf shook his head. 'It is only a bad cold for which she needs some warmth, rest, and alleviation of her discomfort. And perhaps some Christian charity,' he added crossly.

Brother Willibrod was immediately apologetic. 'It is just that we still live in fear of outbreaks of the dreadful

Yellow Plague . . . it carried off many of our people, and—'

'The sooner you send Brother Higbald to attend to the woman, the sooner we can confirm what afflicts her, Brother Willibrod,' Abbot Cild snapped.

Brother Willibrod jerked his head in a nervous acknowledgment towards the abbot and turned hastily from the room.

'I should go to explain to the apothecary what I have done for her,' Eadulf suggested but Abbot Cild stayed him.

'I presume that she is capable of communicating with Brother Higbald and will tell him herself?' he sneered. 'It is best if Brother Higbald look for himself without being told what it is that he should see.'

Eadulf's expression tightened. The man was fully back in control, impatient and arrogant. Eadulf did not mean to rise to his antagonism – after all, it was necessary that Fidelma be allowed to recover before travelling on – but he could not help himself.

'Had I been in your position, Abbot Cild, I would have welcomed the happy coincidence that brought such a person as Fidelma of Cashel to your abbey at this time.'

Abbot Cild's eyes narrowed.

'Explain yourself,' he demanded.

'Easy enough. Sister Fidelma is a lawyer of some reputation in her own land. In fact, she was a legal counsel to the Irish deputation at the Synod of Whitby two years ago.'

For a moment Abbot Cild's eyes widened as a memory stirred.

'Sister Fidelma? She stopped the Council from breaking up and the kingdoms plunging into civil war after one of the leading delegates was murdered?'

'That is the same Sister Fidelma. She is a friend of King Oswy of Northumbria and Abbess Hilda.'

Abbot Cild relaxed suddenly, in one of the curious, inexplicable mood swings which Eadulf had observed him to be capable of. He sat back in his chair, gazing closely at Eadulf.

'Why should her presence here be of interest to me? What are you implying?'

'I merely point out that she might be able to advise you on this matter of Gadra's *troscud*.'

Abbot Cild blinked rapidly and then exhaled slowly. 'That is a matter which is of no concern to you or, indeed, to anyone else.'

'Law *is* my concern, Abbot Cild. The rituals of the law take different forms but its morality is not to be denied. If you are a victim then speak out and let Fidelma help find a way to end this ritual fasting against you. If you have to answer before the law, then let someone who knows something of this ritual of *troscud* advise you. If handled wrongly, this matter could escalate into war and much blood will be shed.'

Abbot Cild raised his head to Eadulf, his dark eyes suddenly unfathomable.

'When or if that time comes, I will know how to protect myself,' he said grimly.

'That sounds like a recourse to violence. Surely that is an odd position for one in holy orders to take?' observed Eadulf. 'Why not protect yourself in accordance with law if, as you claim, you are innocent of any wrongdoing?'

Abbot Cild's eyes suddenly flashed brightly and Eadulf noticed his hands gripping the edge of the table.

'I do not have to defend myself to you.'

'Perhaps not,' Eadulf agreed with equanimity. 'Tell me, did you have a wife named Gélgeis?'

There was a colour on the abbot's cheek. He made no reply and Eadulf pressed him further.

'Did you change your mind about the celibacy of the religious before or after you married?'

'I married when I was . . .' began Abbot Cild, off guard for a moment. Then he stopped and stared defiantly at Eadulf. 'I have told you that it is no concern of yours. You are no longer *gerefa* at Seaxmund's Ham.'

'How much of the accusation of Garb was true?' Eadulf asked calmly, ignoring Abbot Cild's outrage.

'Not a word of it!'

'But you have just agreed that you married this girl, Gélgeis. I presume that she was, indeed, Garb's sister, and the daughter of Gadra, and that you married her in the kingdom of Connacht?'

'I do not deny that. But how do you know it was in Connacht? Garb did not mention that.'

'Maigh Eo – the Plain of the Yew – is in Connacht.'

'You are well informed, Eadulf of Seaxmund's Ham,' muttered the abbot.

'You are not the only Saxon who has studied in the universities of Éireann,' replied Eadulf. 'Anyway, the answer to my question is that you did marry your wife according to the Law of the Fénechus?'

'I do not deny that.'

'And she is now dead?'

Abbot Cild's jaw tightened and he rose from his chair.

'She is dead. I know that for a fact. No one can prove otherwise! Do you hear me? I will not tolerate your suggestions to the contrary!'

Eadulf was astonished.

'I have not . . .' he began. Then, observing the look in Abbot Cild's eye, he went on: 'I am merely trying to help. It is a very serious accusation that has been

70

levelled against you. Surely you would wish for advice from someone who knows the law under which you are accused?'

'A foreign law which has no force in this land. If I am attacked, there is a good mediator here.'

For a moment, Eadulf was puzzled. Then he followed the abbot's meaningful glance towards the wall nearby. On it hung a sword and a shield. It had been too dark on the previous night for Eadulf to spot the incongruous items of decoration. A warrior's sword and shield hanging in an abbot's chamber.

Eadulf opened his mouth to speak again but the abbot stayed him with a gesture.

'We will speak no more of this, Brother Eadulf. And you will say nothing about this to anyone. You will not mention the . . . the woman you claim to have seen last night. Do you understand?'

Without waiting for a response, Abbot Cild turned and left the chamber. Eadulf stood for a moment considering the abbot's reaction. The thought came into his mind that he had caught the abbot out in his moral stance. Could the woman he had seen be Cild's mistress, or . . . his eyes widened. He had had an inspiration worthy of one of Fidelma's deductions. Could the woman have been Cild's wife, Gélgeis, and Cild be pretending to the rest of the world that she was dead in order to cover up the fact that he was still living with her while professing to support celibacy? Now that was an idea! Perhaps that was why her family thought that he had done away with her. He wished Fidelma was well enough to discuss the matter but he decided not to bother her. Abbot Cild was undoubtedly a sly fellow.

Chapter Five

Eadulf was leaving the abbot's chamber when a tall, fair-haired brother came striding along the corridor towards him. He was a pleasant-faced man of nearly thirty, his flaxen hair falling in curled ringlets from the *corona spina*, the tonsure of St Peter. He had a fair skin, bright eyes and a friendly smile. He carried himself proudly upright – almost too proudly to be a member of the religious.

'Good morning, Brother,' he said brightly, halting in front of Eadulf. 'I presume that you are Brother Eadulf, the companion of Sister Fidelma?'

Eadulf inclined his head slightly. 'You have the advantage of me, Brother.'

'I am the apothecary of the abbey. My name is Higbald.'

Eadulf relaxed and returned his smile. 'Have you seen Sister Fidelma?'

'I have. A fever brought on by exposure to the harsh elements. You appear to have already prescribed all the necessary remedies. I could do nothing more for her. The sister tells me that you were trained in one of the medical schools of Éireann? They have a good reputation.'

'I studied at Tuaim Brecáin,' confirmed Eadulf. 'But tell me your recommendation, Brother Higbald. Abbot Cild wants us to leave the abbey immediately.'

Brother Higbald laughed pleasantly. 'In this inclement

weather? The snow may have stopped falling, and the sun is high and shining, but the air is without any warmth. It is truly cold enough to freeze a fair-size pond. It is not the weather to go travelling. In her condition, it would not be wise at all. I will tell the abbot so.'

Eadulf gave a little sigh of relief. 'Thank you, Brother Higbald. I am afraid Abbot Cild's hospitality towards Fidelma leaves much to be desired.'

Brother Higbald looked sympathetic and took Eadulf's arm in his in a confiding gesture.

'Let us walk for a moment, Brother Eadulf.'

Eadulf allowed himself to be led along the corridor and out into a covered walkway that opened on one side to the central square, the main quadrangle around which the buildings of the abbey were clustered. It had stopped snowing, as Brother Higbald had said, but the air was chill and the snow lay thick. It was a dry, fine snow which swirled in the sharp gusts of wind.

Brother Higbald spoke in a confidential tone.

'I will ensure, of course, that the abbot realises the situation. However, do not condemn him for his uncompromising attitude. He has been through much. It is merely his means of protecting himself.'

'I understand that all is not well with him,' conceded Eadulf. 'I was here last night in the chapel.'

Brother Higbald grimaced. 'Ah, you mean the somewhat dramatic entrance of the Irish warrior Garb? He appears to be given to dramatic gestures.'

'You know him, then?'

'Know is, perhaps, too strong a word. I have seen him twice, to be exact.'

'And what times were these?'

'The first was when he came to the abbey to speak with Abbot Cild. The second time was last night. On both occasions his appearance was dramatic.'

'Dramatic? When did he first come to the abbey, then?'

'You are inquisitive, Brother Eadulf.' Brother Higbald's look was suspicious but still edged with amusement.

'It is my nature,' explained Eadulf. 'I was hereditary *gerefa* at Seaxmund's Ham before I began to travel for the faith.'

Brother Higbald's smile broadened.

'A *gerefa*, eh? A legal mind as well as a medical one and both in service of the faith. An extraordinary combination, Brother. Well, the warrior Garb came to the abbey about nine days ago. I was with the abbot when he made a similarly dramatic entrance though the door. I was removed from the chamber under guard of one of his warriors. I do not know what passed between them. However, Garb departed in anger. Abbot Cild was upset for some days. Since that day I believe he has become more extreme in his moods.'

Eadulf examined Brother Higbald with some scepticism. 'Are you saying that before Garb came here that first time, the abbot was a different person? How did this metamorphosis manifest itself?'

Brother Higbald chuckled warmly. 'If you mean, was he jovial and good-natured and of a free and easy disposition before that day, then I have to say – absolutely not! Nature did not endow Abbot Cild with such attributes as kindliness and humour. The abbot has always been a man of extreme moods – more or less as you observe him now. I would say that he has become fearful. He has, to my knowledge, always been distrustful and somewhat illogical in his dealings with people.'

'Garb's charge of murder is a very serious one,' pointed out Eadulf.

'Accepting that, how can such a charge be made here under a foreign law?'

'From the viewpoint of our law, it cannot,' agreed Eadulf. 'From the viewpoint of the law of the Brehons it can because Cild was married in Connacht under that law. So, I am told, it is serious.'

'Fate has worked a cruel blow on the abbot.'

'Cruel?' queried Eadulf in surprise. 'In what way?'

'In respect of Brother Botulf's death. Had he been alive, Botulf would have been able to defend Abbot Cild from these accusations.'

'I do not follow you.'

'I only know that Brother Botulf knew the full story about the abbot's wife and was a witness to her death.'

'When did she die?' Eadulf hid his disappointment that his theory that Cild was hiding his wife from the world was so easily demolished.

Brother Higbald shook his head. 'I should not be gossiping about the abbot.'

'I do not ask you to gossip,' Eadulf replied easily. 'I asked for an answer to a question. A date, a time.'

'Gélgeis must have died some months before I joined this community. When I came here, which was the end of the summer, Cild had already established the abbey as a fraternity of religieux in which no women would be allowed to distract our contemplations. But there are still some of the brethren who knew her. Poor Brother Botulf, of course, and Brother Willibrod. Oh, and young Redwald. From what I heard, Gélgeis was not too well liked.'

'Was the abbot's concern about celibacy just a reaction to his wife's death?'

'Who knows what motivates people in their designs?' Brother Higbald observed with a shrug. 'Grief is often a spur in such matters.'

'It is certain that the abbot's wife is dead?' Eadulf asked, struck by a sudden thought.

'Of course. What makes you ask such a question?' The apothecary seemed amused.

'I was wondering about the identity of the lady who is currently a guest in this abbey?'

Brother Higbald's expression was slightly bewildered. 'I presume that you are not referring to your companion . . . ?'

'I am not. I mean the slim, fair-haired and richly dressed woman whom I observed in the cloisters by the chapel last night.'

The apothecary appeared to be serious for the moment. 'Truly, Brother, as far as I know, there is no female in this abbey other than your companion.'

'Yet I have seen her,' Eadulf repeated firmly.

'And you would recognise her again?' asked Brother Higbald quickly.

Eadulf hesitated and then shrugged. 'I am not sure.'

'Well, would we not know if there was a woman here?'

Eadulf decided not to pursue the matter further.

'Does anyone know how Abbot Cild's wife came by her death?' he asked. 'Could it be that Garb's accusation has some truth in it? Abbot Cild acts as though he has something to hide in this matter.'

Brother Higbald shook his head quickly. 'There is no secret about her death. She wandered into a bog and was sucked under. My friend, granted that you were a *gerefa*, my advice to you would be that as soon as your companion is recovered in health, you should move on from here and stop asking questions. It would be unwise to take the side of Garb and seek out a mystery where there is none. If Abbot Cild does not wish to answer Garb, then surely that is his own affair?'

Eadulf returned his level, still humorous gaze for a moment. Yet there was something mysteriously serious about the smiling face of the apothecary.

'There is a mystery here, Brother Higbald.' Eadulf was not deterred. 'Botulf was the friend and companion of my youth. I will not rest until I discover who killed him. I do not like leaving mysteries in my wake. Nor do I react to threats, however diplomatically articulated.'

The apothecary sighed ruefully. 'I did not mean to sound as if I was issuing a threat. The matter is no concern of mine. I simply meant to warn you that Abbot Cild is a man of unstable temperament. He says that Botulf was killed by—'

'I know what Abbot Cild says. Outlaws? Thieves from the marshlands? All because a Brother Wigstan claims that he saw an outlaw called Aldhere in the vicinity of the abbey not long after the body of Botulf was discovered. By the way, as apothecary, I presume you examined Botulf's body when it was found?'

'I did. I was in the chapel when I was sent for. The body was just outside in the courtyard. It was clear that Botulf had been struck several times about the head with a battle-axe.'

'A battle-axe? What makes you say that?'

'I have seen enough wounds in battle to recognise the type of injury inflicted by such a weapon.'

'And what was the conclusion that you reached?'

'That he had been bludgeoned to death.'

'And why would Garb accuse the abbot of having some interest in that act? If Botulf was a witness at Gélgeis's death, is the inference that he was killed because of something he knew?'

Brother Higbald shrugged. 'It is not for me to comment, Brother. I would simply urge you not to delay here unnecessarily. I shall tell the abbot that the sister needs some time to recover from her fever, but after that . . .'

He raised a shoulder and let it drop as if in dismissal.

Eadulf stood gazing thoughtfully after him as the apothecary walked away. Then he turned towards the guests' hostel and went in to see Fidelma.

'I understand we may stay here until I am recovered sufficiently to travel,' she greeted him in between bouts of coughing. 'You seem to have been diplomatic in your plea to the abbot.'

Eadulf smiled broadly. 'Diplomatic? Not exactly. Abbot Cild is of a very peculiar temperament.'

'Did you find out any more about the matter of the *troscud*, the ritual fast against him?' Fidelma hesitated and pointed to the side table. 'Give me some more of that noxious brew of yours, Eadulf. It tastes foul but I am persuaded that it does ease the soreness of my throat and chest.'

Eadulf gave the beaker to her.

'I tried to find out more,' he replied. 'I think there is a bigger mystery here than appeared at first glance.'

He recited in as much detail as possible his conversations with the abbot and Brother Higbald.

'I don't recall you mentioning this strange woman to me before,' frowned Fidelma. 'But if there is a woman here, why are they denying it?'

Eadulf shrugged. 'The matter did not seem important to me before. It was only when Abbot Cild started lecturing me on how women were not permitted in his precious abbey that I brought the matter up.'

'And you say that she was not a religieuse?'

'No. She was well dressed and therefore someone of rank and prosperity but certainly not a member of the community.'

'What made you think that it was the abbot's wife?'

'It was just an idea, that's all. It would have explained his reaction to Garb's accusations.'

'There are some weaknesses in that argument, Eadulf.

If she were still alive, why not simply tell Garb and his father in order to prevent the public accusation against him? And you say that Brother Higbald denied the existence of the woman in the abbey?'

'He did, but one does not necessarily have to believe him.'

'Or, maybe, he and other members of the community simply do not know of her existence. Perhaps she comes and goes in secret.'

'A mistress, perhaps?'

'You do not have enough information to leap to these conclusions, Eadulf,' sighed Fidelma. 'And now, I want to rest a while. Ask more questions and make fewer deductions.' She took another sip of the herbal remedy and then turned on her side.

Eadulf left quietly.

Outside he met Brother Willibrod. He was standing with another member of the community, a broad-shouldered young man. The *dominus* was looking less anxious than before as he greeted Eadulf.

'I understand all is well. It is not the Yellow Plague but an ague. Abbot Cild has told me that you can stay for a few days until Sister Fidelma is recovered. Is there anything that can be done to aid her recovery?'

Eadulf shook his head. 'Rest, warmth and perhaps someone could take her some clear broth at midday?'

'It shall be done. Young Brother Redwald shall be instructed in this. By the way, this is Brother Wigstan. You asked to see him.'

Eadulf looked at the young man. 'I am told that you saw this outlaw – Aldhere?'

Brother Wigstan nodded slowly. 'I was returning to the abbey early yesterday morning. I was hurrying to join the brethren in singing Matins—'

'Where had you been?' interrupted Eadulf.

'I was returning from a visit to the coast, bringing some fish to the abbey. As my cart came along the road nearby, I swear I saw Aldhere riding away.'

Eadulf frowned slightly. 'You do not sound positive?'

'I am positive. It was by the little copse at the side of the abbey that I saw him.'

'And in order to recognise him, you have obviously seen him before?'

'I have been robbed twice by him on journeys to and from the coast,' agreed Brother Wigstan with bitterness. 'I know him.'

'And each time he let you go with your life? He does not sound the depraved villain that I have been led to believe.'

'Is that all, Brother?'

Eadulf nodded absently and when Brother Wigstan had departed, he turned to Brother Willibrod.

'And on such an observation, a man may be killed?' he asked rhetorically. 'It is hardly evidence. I have another favour to ask of you.'

'Which is?' demanded the *dominus* cautiously.

'I have told you that I was a good friend of Brother Botulf. I would like to see his personal possessions.'

'The brethren of Christ have no possessions,' admonished Brother Willibrod gruffly. 'You know the ruling of the *Didache*?'

The *Didache* or *Teaching of the Twelve Apostles* was a book dealing with church order and ecclesiastical life said to have been handed down from the earliest Christian community. But Eadulf had never read it nor consciously followed its rules. He shook his head.

'The *Didache* says,' quoted the *dominus* in sonorous tones: '"Share everything with your brother. Do not say 'it is private property'. If you share what is everlasting,

81

you should be that much more willing to share things which do not last."'

'I have heard the teaching from other church fathers,' admitted Eadulf. 'Do you claim that this is the rule which you practise here?'

'We try to retain the true rules of the faith,' replied Brother Willibrod with some stiffness.

'Even so, I would like a moment in the cell of my good friend.'

'I do not know whether his cell has been cleared.'

'Please?'

Brother Willibrod suddenly shrugged as if to dismiss the matter. 'Very well. A moment of contemplation can be allowed. Come.' He turned and led the way through the abbey, past the main dormitory and refectory buildings. 'Brother Botulf, as the steward of the abbey, had his chamber here,' he said, pointing to a door and standing aside.

Brother Eadulf entered the small chamber.

There was hardly anything within. A robe and a cloak were still hanging on wooden pegs, along with a book satchel. A pair of worn sandals were placed underneath them on the floor. The bed was a single straw mattress on a wooden frame with several neatly folded blankets on it. A candle and a tinder box stood on a small table. There was also a beaker, a jug and a wash basin.

'As you see, Brother Eadulf,' intoned the *dominus* standing in the doorway, 'Brother Botulf had no possessions.'

Eadulf shook his head. 'I find it sad. A life gone by and nothing to show but a few memories of those who knew him. And memory dies, too, and is gone like smoke in the wind.'

'Possessions are an abomination, leading men into temptation,' replied Brother Willibrod in a stony voice.

'Did not St Basil the Great declaim that property is theft? We of the faith must do away with all personal possessions. We are all equal in the faith.'

Eadulf sighed in resignation. 'I think it was Aristotle who said that it was not the possessions but the desires of mankind which required to be equalised.'

He turned to the satchel hanging on the wall. There was a little book of scripture quotations in Latin there. As Eadulf lifted it out he saw a piece of crunched paper beneath it at the bottom of the satchel. He drew it out surreptitiously so that Brother Willibrod did not observe him tucking it in the sleeve of his robe.

'I should remove that book to the *scriptorium*,' Brother Willibrod said, holding his hand out for it.

'Was it not Botulf's book?' queried Eadulf.

'All is common property here,' Brother Willibrod replied.

Eadulf watched the *dominus* return the book to the satchel and take it from the peg. As he did so, Eadulf took the opportunity to secure the piece of paper in the small *sacculus* that he carried on his belt. Brother Willibrod turned back to him.

'Have you seen enough?'

Eadulf bowed his head in confirmation. As they were walking back to the main quadrangle, he asked: 'Tell me, Brother Willibrod, as *dominus* of this abbey you know everyone who comes and goes, don't you?'

Brother Willibrod regarded him curiously. 'What do you mean?'

'I mean that you know all the visitors here, don't you?'

'If you wish to question me about the intrusion last night, I have already explained that the foreign warriors scaled the walls, and—'

'I am not asking about that. I want to know the identity

of the woman who was in the abbey last night. And I don't mean my companion.'

Brother Willibrod regarded him with outrage on his features.

'Are you mad? A woman, here in the abbey? Impossible!'

'Not impossible. I saw her in the quadrangle by the chapel. A slim woman, fair-haired, with a red dress and jewels.'

Brother Willibrod took a physical step backwards. A look of astonishment crossed his face. Then it hardened into a mask.

'There was no such woman in the abbey last night nor any night.' He swung round and walked away so quickly that Eadulf was left staring after him in surprise at his reaction.

As he stood there, the youthful Brother Redwald came round a corner of the building carrying two buckets of water for the guests' chambers.

'Good morning, Brother Eadulf,' he said nervously. 'Is there anything I can do for you and Sister Fidelma?'

'Thank you,' replied Eadulf grimly. 'I think everything that needs to be done is being done.' He was about to move on when he paused and said: 'You could tell me where I might find Brother Osred. I was going to have a word with him last night but didn't get the chance.'

'Brother Osred? The smith?' Brother Redwald pursed his lips thoughtfully. 'I suppose he's gone with the others.'

Eadulf frowned. 'Gone with the others? What do you mean?'

'Abbot Cild led a small group of the brethren out a short time ago. They have gone to the marshes in search of the outlaw, Aldhere.'

'What?' Eadulf recalled his vow to accompany Cild

to ensure some sort of law prevailed if the abbot caught up with the outlaw. A moment later Eadulf was running after Brother Willibrod.

Chapter Six

The lonely bittern with its mournful cry caused Eadulf to draw rein on the mule that he was riding and glance in frustration about him. A short distance away, among the waving reeds, he saw the black and brown streaks of the bird's plumage as it gently climbed the stalks, clutching at them in little clumps with its talons in order to haul itself up to scan the surrounding area. Then its bright eyes spotted Eadulf and it disappeared back into the shelter of the growth.

Only a few months ago, Eadulf knew that these tall reeds would have made a wild and dramatic image against the stormy skies; an image that would have enchanted him by its beauty. Now, however, they were flowerless and bent by the onslaught of the snow; they were humbled by the cold and frosty weather. It was only a passing thought, however, for more important things impinged on his mind.

Eadulf had to admit to himself that he was lost.

He had managed to persuade Brother Willibrod to lend him one of the few remaining mules in the abbey stables in order to ride out after Abbot Cild and the half-dozen armed brethren who had accompanied him. He had allowed the *dominus* to think that Abbot Cild had accepted his offer to go with them, and must have forgotten to wait for him.

'It'll be easy to catch up with them,' Eadulf had

assured Brother Willibrod. 'I can follow their tracks in the snow.'

The *dominus* had agreed to let him go, but with utmost reluctance. The reluctance had been justified, for Eadulf had forgotten that the snow was dry and powdery and that the wind constantly gusted, blowing the snow this way and that. In fact he had only ridden a short way from the abbey when he realised that the wind had covered all tracks of Abbot Cild and his companions.

Eadulf should have turned back but some obstinacy drove him forward, a determination which often helped him overcome adversity. He urged the mule on, but with a less than confident feeling. It was a sturdy animal, strong-limbed and used to the hardship of the cold weather, but it was also renowned for an obstinacy that was the equal of Eadulf's. And Eadulf was the first to admit that he was not entirely comfortable in any saddle. He was not like Fidelma who had ridden almost before she could walk. He was nervous and he found that animals sensed his nervousness, especially this heavy-muscled mule.

In spite of the thick snowy carpet, Eadulf knew he was in the marshlands now and not far from the coast. He had grown up within reach of this countryside but had never really ventured into it. The scenery, the small streams and lagoons, the mixed woodland broken up by stretches of thinly disguised heathland under its covering of snow, were all typical of the low-lying marshes that constituted the coastal strips of the kingdom of the East Angles. But there were no tracks to follow; there was nothing substantial, nothing tangible by way of landmarks to take a bearing from.

From nearby a scolding 'chickabee-bee-bee-bee' sound seemed to sweep close to his head and then fade in the distance. He had a fleeting glimpse of a tiny white and brown shape, with a glossy black crown. The marsh-tit had been disturbed and soon Eadulf saw the reason. A female marsh harrier, identifiable by its large size, dark brown body, and buff shoulders and head, came swooping in search of prey. The raptor fed on the tiny birds as well as mice and other small mammals.

Eadulf found himself hoping that the tiny marsh-tit would elude its hungry pursuer.

He realised that he was very near the sea now. He could smell the salt tang on the air and he saw the snow on the ground thinning slightly as the heath gave way to a stretch of sand dunes and shingle beyond which the sea's long, dim level appeared out of the grey that made sky and water seem momentarily one. Little clusters of sea buckthorn grew here and there among the sand dunes, an ancient little shrub, willow-like, slender, green with a silver underside. Eadulf noticed that it still bore a few of the faintly orange berries which, as a child, he used to gather for his mother to make marmalade. It formed a thicket and was all but indestructible.

Some way ahead he saw a small outcrop of land, a grassy knoll like a tiny headland jutting from a fairly thick-wooded area and rising to a high point from which the land dropped away like miniature cliffs into the sea on all sides except its landward connection. It formed a tiny little peninsula. Eadulf realised that it was a vantage point from which he would probably be able to see a fair distance across the marshlands and he might be able to spot the abbot and his brethren.

He urged the little mule forward towards the wood. He had decided that if he could see no sign of Abbot Cild and his companions from this vantage point then he might as well make his way back to the abbey. He had wanted to be with Abbot Cild if he caught up with Aldhere to find out what the outlaw had to say in answer to the accusation of causing the death of Brother Botulf. He had wanted to make sure that justice was upheld. But he had missed his opportunity, and he was positive that the abbot would not welcome any interference from him.

He made his way through the trees towards the small headland. When he emerged from their cover he saw something which caused him to draw rein sharply so that his small mount grunted in protest as it halted and stamped its forefoot in temper. In the lee of the headland was a Saxon longship. It was close inshore, and there were a score of men milling around it. Its design and pennants showed that it was not from the land of the East Angles but from the East Saxons. The great sail carried the solar symbol associated with the god Thunor, the cross with the broken arms.

Someone among them gave a cry as Eadulf was spotted and several of them, swords unsheathed, came bounding up the rocky incline towards where he sat in momentary surprise. Before he could react, he was aware of a hissing sound in the air. Several arrows sped by him but were not aimed at him. They had been fired from behind him and two found their targets in the oncoming warriors. The men dropped with cries of pain while the others came to a ragged halt.

Eadulf was confused. He suddenly found himself surrounded by several warriors, whose bows rained down deadly missiles on the men from the longship. One of the newcomers grabbed his mule's reins, a thick-set man with a mane of wild yellow hair and a black-toothed grin.

Eadulf was aware of the men below running for their longship, carrying or dragging those who had been hurt, while others were frantically pushing it into the waves. More arrows were unleashed by those around him but they found no human target, although several embedded themselves in the timbers of the boat. The retreating Saxon warriors scrambled into it, hauling themselves over the sides as it began to ride up and down on the waves. Men were swiftly adjusting the lines and ropes, shouting and cursing to each other, causing the big sail to move slightly in order to catch the off-shore winds.

Away it went, dancing swiftly over the water and out of sight round the end of the headland.

A tall warrior who appeared to be the leader of the band who had launched the attack on the Saxons had sheathed his sword and was now examining Eadulf in some amusement. He was more wiry than muscular and carried a great scar across one cheek. His eyes were black and held an inner fire, dark and flashing. His lips were thin and the scar had twisted them into a permanent sneer. There was something about the cast of his features that seemed familiar to Eadulf but he was sure that he had not seen this man before. He was swarthy of skin, a man used to the outdoor life. He was dressed in dark clothes, woollen garments dyed black. Only his leather jacket was studded with polished steel roundels in the manner of body armour. He carried a round burnished shield and his helmet was simple, conical without adornment.

'And who have we here? One of Cild's evil brood, no doubt?'

Eadulf frowned in annoyance.

'What is the meaning of this?' he demanded. 'Do you raise your hand against a religious?'

The warrior chuckled and gestured with a nod at his companions.

'I would have thought that a man of such noble learning as yourself might have deduced that we have just saved your holy life from the East Saxons. You do not appear to be grateful.'

'Why would the East Saxons want to take my life?' Eadulf demanded, trying to match the other's bantering tone but not succeeding. 'And why would you want to save it?'

The tall man's eyes narrowed as he examined Eadulf more closely. The smile did not leave his features.

'What is your name, Brother? I cannot recall seeing you in Cild's festering pile of stones before. Are you a newcomer to this district?'

The man spoke with an easy familiarity which irritated Eadulf.

'I am but recently come from Canterbury and before that I was over a year abroad. However, I am—'

'He's Eadulf of Seaxmund's Ham!'

One of the band interrupted with a shout of recognition as he stepped forward.

The tall man turned to him, as did Eadulf, trying to place the scruffily dressed ruffian.

'Do you recognise this man, Wiglaf?'

The short, sturdy-framed, brown-haired man nodded eagerly.

'He was the *gerefa* of Seaxmund's Ham. I recognise him well. He once ordered that I should have twelve strokes of a birch stick for thieving.'

The tall leader turned back to Eadulf with mock seriousness.

'Is this true? You ordered the punishment of poor Wiglaf here?'

Eadulf's mouth tightened.

'I cannot say one way or another,' he said defensively. 'I do not recognise the man.'

The man called Wiglaf moved closer and stuck his grinning features in front of Eadulf.

'I did not have a beard then, *gerefa*, for I was very young, but the birch stung and marked me for some years.'

'Was the sentence just, Wiglaf?' interrupted the tall leader, with humour still in his voice.

The brown-haired man chuckled. 'That it was. I did thieve a pot of honey from an old widow. The *gerefa* was just.'

Eadulf gave up trying to identify the erstwhile honey thief. He had ordered many such punishments when he had been a *gerefa*.

'Now you know me, but I do not know you,' he ventured defiantly to the tall leader. The man continued to smile.

'I am called Aldhere and these are some of my men.'

Eadulf's eyes widened. The tall warrior saw the expression of surprise and grimaced in amusement.

'I see, by your reaction, that you have heard of me, holy *gerefa*.'

'That I have,' admitted Eadulf. 'From Abbot Cild.'

Aldhere laughed uproariously as if Eadulf had said something really humorous.

'I doubt that you have heard any good of me from that son of a she-devil. Have you become a member of Cild's noxious little brood?'

Eadulf shook his head. 'I am staying at Aldred's Abbey with my . . . with a companion for a few days before travelling on to Seaxmund's Ham. I have been away from these parts for several years.'

The outlaw leader continued to appear relaxed and almost friendly as he digested this news.

'Then, holy *gerefa*, I would advise you to leave that putrefied rats' nest at Aldred's Abbey sooner rather than later.'

'What makes you say that?'

'Because it is an evil place; a place which should be shunned. Abbot Cild is an evil man.'

A frown crossed Eadulf's brow as he suddenly remembered the words of 'Mad' Mul. He, too, had called the abbey a place of evil. It was time that some explanation was given.

'I would have a word alone with you, Aldhere.'

'Then you will ride with us back to our camp and we will talk on the way.'

Eadulf hesitated and then decided that he had to be honest.

'Do you realise that Abbot Cild and several of his brethren are scouring these parts to take and hang you?'

Aldhere raised an eyebrow but the smile did not leave his features.

'I am glad that you have warned us, holy *gerefa*, for it shows me that you are a man of integrity. That is more than I can say of Abbot Cild. However, we watched Cild entering the marshes earlier, and he has returned to the abbey long since. It was no more than a show to impress someone. What could his half-dozen men do against my war band?'

Eadulf suddenly realised that Aldhere had a score of men with him. Cild must have known that he was no match for them. Why would he have put on this show? Whom did he want to impress? Eadulf himself? The community? Garb and his Irish warriors? Or was this just another manifestation of Cild's irrational moods?

They had all mounted horses brought to them by men who had obviously held them in the thickness of the wood while the attack was taking place. Two of Aldhere's men took the lead, riding some little way ahead as scouts, while Eadulf and Aldhere followed. The others brought up the rear.

Aldhere rode in a relaxed position, stretched back in

the saddle. It was clear that he had been raised on horseback.

'Now, what is it that you wish to say that you feel is for my ears alone?' asked the tall outlaw as they began to move forward.

'Abbot Cild believes that you killed Brother Botulf.'

The sardonic snort told Eadulf that Aldhere did not think much of Abbot Cild's belief. But Eadulf's eyes narrowed at the implication.

'So you knew that Brother Botulf has been killed?'

'I knew,' Aldhere replied grimly. 'And if you are looking for a culprit you must speak to Cild.'

'Are you making a counter-claim that Cild was the murderer and not you?'

'Did I not make myself clear?'

'Tell me how you knew that Brother Botulf was dead.'

For the first time, Aldhere's features had become grave.

'What does this matter to you, Eadulf of Seaxmund's Ham? You tell me that you have only just arrived at Aldred's Abbey and, as I have said, if you have sense then you will leave it without delay.'

Eadulf decided to speak plainly.

'It matters a great deal to me, Aldhere. Botulf was a close friend of mine. He was the friend of my childhood and youth. While I was at Canterbury a few weeks ago he sent a message to me asking me to come to the abbey and requesting that I endeavour to get there before midnight last night. I did so, only to find out that he had been killed shortly before I arrived. In support of Cild's accusation of your complicity, one of the brethren insists that he saw you at the abbey about the same time.'

Aldhere was silent for a moment.

'That would have been Wigstan, returning from his

journey to the fishing village with fish for the abbey. I saw him. He was right. I was there.'

Eadulf glanced at him sharply. 'Are you now admitting . . . ?'

'Don't make yourself out to be a fool, holy *gerefa*. Of course I am not. Did Botulf tell you why he wanted you to come to Aldred's Abbey? Or why you had to be there by that particular time?'

Reluctantly, Eadulf shook his head.

'I did not kill Botulf,' Aldhere said abruptly, with a controlled passion. 'He was a friend of mine, too. I had come to the abbey to meet him in secret – also being instructed, like you, to come by an appointed hour at dawn yesterday.'

'And so Brother Wigstan saw you?'

'I have not denied it.'

'But you did not see Botulf?'

Aldhere shook his head firmly. 'While I was waiting for him in the shadow of the copse by the side of the abbey, I heard an outcry. I decide that I would not wait around to discover its meaning.'

'So how did you learn that this outcry was due to the fact that Botulf had been found dead?'

'Through Wiglaf. He had a contact in the abbey and found out that, thanks to Wigstan, Cild was claiming I was responsible.'

'Why does Abbot Cild hate you?'

Aldhere gave a long deep sigh. 'It is a long story. A tale with an even longer preamble.'

'I have plenty of time,' replied Eadulf without humour.

'Then have patience until we reach the camp and then, over a dish of hot soup, I shall tell you that story.'

Eadulf relapsed into silence for a while. He was disconcerted by Aldhere. This was not exactly the image of the marsh outlaw that had been conjured by Cild. In spite of his appearance, which initially fitted Eadulf's concept of a robber, Aldhere was a pleasant-mannered, educated man, with the quiet authority of a thane rather than an outlaw. Eadulf was bursting with questions but he decided to keep his natural impatience in check. As Fidelma was so fond of saying, they succeed who are patient.

They were riding northwards, parallel to the seashore but keeping to the shelter of the woods which grew thick where they were protected from the corrosive sea-salt air. Eadulf began to recognise his surroundings and he felt a slight pang of homesickness as he realised that they were not very far away from his birthplace.

Away to their right lay the shingle seashore and sand dunes marking the extremity of the land but to their left was a landscape of small lagoons, freshwater reedmarsh, and mixed woodland and heath. Then, as they moved through a thick belt of aspen, birch and oak that had seemed impenetrable, Eadulf suddenly found that they had arrived in a clearing with makeshift huts where several people were moving about, men and women and even children.

'Welcome to my camp,' smiled Aldhere, halting his mount and sliding off it.

Eadulf followed his lead and the outlaw conducted him towards one of the huts. Before they reached it, the door was opened and a woman came forward to greet Aldhere. She was slim, and flaxen hair showed beneath a headscarf that covered most of her features. She halted and frowned at the sight of Eadulf.

'Who is he? A prisoner? One of Cild's men?' she demanded in an unfriendly tone. She spoke Saxon with a foreign accent which Eadulf could not place for the moment.

Aldhere shook his head, smiling.

'No, my sweet, this is a guest. This is my woman,

Bertha. This is Brother Eadulf, Bertha. Now bring us mead and hot soup and leave us to talk.'

Bertha sniffed disparagingly but ducked back into the hut, followed by Aldhere and Eadulf. The interior formed a single room with scarcely space for a bed, a table and a few stools. Aldhere motioned Eadulf to be seated, and placed himself on the other side of the table. Bertha set a jug of mead on the board. As she did so Eadulf saw that she had a scar on her right arm, running upwards from the wrist. The soup had already been made and, after a moment, bowls of steaming vegetables and fresh, warm bread were also placed before them. Then Bertha flounced from the hut as if angered by her exclusion.

'Bertha? That is a Frankish name,' commented Eadulf when they were alone.

Aldhere nodded thoughtfully. 'I released her from a Frankish slaver, who was trying to sell her to the East Saxons. The slavers did not treat her well. I saw that you noticed the scar on her arm. She has others and that is why she tends to cover her face in front of strangers. She has preferred to stay with me.'

Eadulf nodded sympathetically. 'A cursed trade is slaving and one that I hope will be outlawed one day. But, tell me, why were the East Saxons trying to kill me? They were never so violent when I was a young man.'

Aldhere took the jug of mead and poured from it.

'It is all to do with King Sigehere who has returned to the worship of the gods of his father. He has declared war on all Christians.'

'I thought that he had his hands full fighting his own people. Why does he send his men to raid our territory?'

'Sigehere is an ambitious man no matter what religion he holds. The kingdom of the East Saxons is too small for him and so he sends warriors to probe his neighbours to test their strengths and weaknesses. There have been several raids against us . . . as you have now witnessed. A Christian holy man would have been a good catch for the warriors of Sigehere. They would have reserved a special entertainment for you.'

Eadulf shivered at the thought and took up the beaker of mead.

'Why would they land at that point? There are no significant settlements in the vicinity apart from Aldred's Abbey.'

Aldhere rubbed his chin, thinking for a moment.

'That is a good point, holy *gerefa*. They usually raid to the north of here, against the lands of the North Folk where King Ealdwulf has his palace and fortresses. Why, indeed, would they land there?'

For a moment or two it seemed that the outlaw was lost in contemplation of the question. Eadulf decided to pull him back to the moment.

'Can nothing be done about Sigehere? I thought his cousin Sebbi was leading a civil war against him. Surely that would curtail his ambitions?'

'Sebbi is no warrior. He is too pious and has to rely on others to fight his battles. At the moment, he is hard pressed to hold his own against his pagan cousin.'

'Is there no Christian neighbour to intervene on Sebbi's behalf?'

'Christian or pagan, kings are only governed by self-interest. What can Sebbi do for them? If it is nothing, then why should they support him?'

'So there is no prospect of stopping Sigehere?'

Aldhere shook his head. 'Short of defeating him in battle, little enough, I suppose. And Sigehere has too many powerful friends who would be willing to take his side. As a matter of politics, he even recognises Wulfhere of Mercia as his overlord, and Wulfhere, for one, would welcome the chance to move into our land of the East Angles if we sent an army against Sigehere.'

Eadulf paused uncertainly for a moment or two and then said: 'You do not speak with the selfish attitude of a robber, Aldhere. You claim that Botulf was your friend. Tell me how this was and all that you know of his death.'

Aldhere set down his tankard of mead and stretched his arms before folding them easily across his stomach. He closed his eyes in thought for a second.

'Botulf was the only one of your faith who did not condemn me when I was declared an outlaw. That was over a year ago now.'

'First tell me how you met Botulf. What were the circumstances of your friendship?'

'You will recall that Wulfhere succeeded his father, Penda, as King of Mercia eight years ago and has been busy ever since trying to re-establish the domination of Mercia over all the kings of the Angles and the Saxons?'

Eadulf nodded. During his childhood the name of Penda, son of Pybba, had been conjured by mothers to frighten their children into obedience. From his kingdom of Mercia he had marched on his neighbours, even killing Oswald of Northumbria, the most powerful of the Anglo-Saxon kings. Eadulf had been a child of six or seven at the time. There had been almost universal joy when Oswy, son of Oswald, who had become Northumbria's King after his father's death, defeated and slew Penda at Winwaed Field. The mighty Mercian empire had collapsed. Penda had been depicted as an ogre because he rejected the Christian faith and adhered to the ancient gods like Woden and Thunor. Yet three years after Penda's death, his son Wulfhere had rallied the kingdom and begun to re-establish its dominance.

Eadulf was frowning.

'What have such matters to do with you?' he asked the outlaw leader.

'I was thane of Bretta's Ham, a warlord of the South Folk.'

Eadulf was startled to realise that his estimation of the man was correct. A thane was one of the lesser nobility; Eadulf knew only that Bretta's Ham was to the south-west of the kingdom. He waited patiently for Aldhere to continue.

'About a year ago, Wulfhere sent his brother Aethelred against the western border of our kingdom. Ealdwulf, our King, sent his Cousin Egric to command the army. It was a short skirmish but a fierce fight, for the Mercians came down on us like the furies of hell. I was given command of the right flank. It was not a good position, for Egric had placed us at the foot of a hill, almost out of sight of the main body. When the attack began, a message from Egric was sent to me to stand fast until we were called. I obeyed. The next thing we heard was that Egric's positions had been overthrown and he was mortally wounded.'

Aldhere was silent for a moment or two and then he sighed deeply. 'Once I learnt this intelligence, I led my men around the hill and came upon the Mercian rear. As I say, it was a fierce but swift fight and the Mercians were suddenly in full retreat.'

Eadulf made no comment as Aldhere paused again.

'When I went to see how Egric fared and to tell him the good news that we had turned the Mercians, I found the life blood ebbing from him but the man still full of bile and recriminations. Instead of taking responsibility for the bad positions and his consequent overthrow – indeed, his own death – he ranted and raged against me even with his dying breath. He claimed that I was

101

a coward. He said I had hidden away until he had been defeated; that I had made no effort to protect his flank. And in his anger, he died.'

There was a silence until Eadulf made the obvious comment.

'But it was his own fault.'

'He was the King's cousin and those in his bodyguard who had survived took his dying words back to Ealdwulf. I was summoned to the King's palace to answer for my cowardice. Those were the very words with which the demand for my attendance was made. I knew, then, that if I went, there would be only one resolution to my situation. My execution.'

'So you decided not to go in answer to the King's summons?'

'That is the reason I am still alive today.' Aldhere gave a wry grimace.

'The King declared you an outlaw?' Eadulf made a sympathetic clicking sound with his tongue. 'Not to answer a king's summons was a wrong course to pursue, I think.'

Aldhere shook his head. 'You believe that I should have gone to argue my case? Those men who were with me decided to go to the King's court, and with them went Botulf.'

Eadulf started. 'Why should Botulf go?'

'Because, at the time, Brother Botulf had come to preach the word of the faith in Bretta's Ham where I was lord. When word came of the Mercian attack, he volunteered to accompany my warband that we be not denied spiritual comfort in our hour of need. He was with my men throughout the fight, standing at my side armed with only the symbol of his faith, a crucifix. He knew the allegations of Egric to be untrue. He went to King Ealdwulf as an emissary on my behalf.'

Eadulf realised that Aldhere must be telling the truth. No one who knew Botulf would doubt such a story. Eadulf knew his friend's courage.

'But he failed?'

'He failed to convince King Ealdwulf, who preferred the word of his dead cousin to those of my men. Those three warriors who went to him, three of my trusted commanders, he enslaved immediately. As for Botulf, he sent him back to Aldred's Abbey, where he had originally come from, with instructions to Cild that Botulf was never to go further from the abbey than one mile in any direction.'

Eadulf was aghast. 'But this is unjust! I did not know this.'

Aldhere smiled sarcastically. 'Tell me about justice, *gerefa*. Only the powerful and rich can afford true justice.'

Eadulf thought of the system that he had witnessed at first hand in the five kingdoms of Éireann and felt a sorrow for his people.

'So this injustice has caused you to become an outlaw?'

'As soon as I heard what had happened to Botulf and my men, I took those remaining loyal to me, and their women and children, and made for the fastness of the marshlands and the woods. Here, through good luck, I made contact with Botulf once again and he was able to tell me where my men had been taken as slaves. We were eventually able to launch a raid to free them and so our band has existed during this last year, sometimes attracting new members who felt that they too had been the victims of malicious injustice.'

'It is a curious tale,' Eadulf commented.

'It is a tale that is common among the South Folk

these days. We give too much power to too few who then dispense it according to their prejudices and not according to what is right and just.'

'Tell me more about Botulf and what you know of the events leading to his death.'

Aldhere nodded. 'I was coming to that. But, as I said, holy *gerefa*, it is a story with a long preamble. Botulf had remained a good friend to me and to my people and hoped to persuade Ealdwulf to rescind his outlawing of our band. But it has been difficult for him, confined as he was to the abbey. A few days ago, I received a message from him that I was to meet him in the copse by the abbey, as I have told you. Dawn yesterday. The rest you already know. But you can be assured that I did not kill him.'

'Have you any idea of why Botulf wanted to meet with you?'

'None at all,' replied Aldhere. 'Though I did presume . . .' He hesitated.

'Presume? What?' prompted Eadulf.

'That it was something to do with his attempts to persuade the King to reconsider his sentence on my people and myself. He had promised that he would make an effort to contact Sigeric, the high steward of the King, and make a new plea on my behalf.'

'Sigeric? Is he still living?'

'Aye, and still an unremitting adherent of the old gods. But he is highly regarded by the King and even the bishops for his knowledge of the law.'

Eadulf reflected for a moment and then returned to the subject in hand. He detested meeting with blank walls.

'I received a message in Canterbury several days ago to come to the abbey. Botulf seems to have learnt that I had returned there. He urged me to be at the abbey before midnight last night. I cannot see how these matters can be connected.'

Aldhere shrugged. 'Nor I. Although last night did mark the start of the twelve-day festival of Yule. That is the only significance I can see in respect of the date and time.'

'I hardly think that it would be significant so far as Botulf was concerned.' Eadulf massaged his forehead with his fingertips for a moment or two. 'One thing still puzzles me. Cild is a very bellicose man for a Christian abbot. He was quick to denounce you and gather a band of his brethren, fully armed, to ride out and hunt you down. I had no doubt that he meant to hang you if he caught you. That was why I rode out to find you – in order to prevent injustice.'

Aldhere chuckled grimly. 'For that, I must thank you, holy *gerefa*. You seem to be a man in the same mould as poor Botolf.'

'One thing I must know,' insisted Eadulf. 'Tell me about your relationship with Abbot Cild. What is the cause of the antipathy between you and him? I doubt that it can merely be because the King has outlawed you.'

Aldhere shook his head with a curious smile. 'Cild was once a warrior as well. He has, at heart, never ceased to be a warlord. He knows enough of warfare to know that during the skirmish of Bretta's Ham, the fault lay not with me.'

'Then how do you explain his intense dislike of you? That he would seize this opportunity to hang you?'

Aldhere's lips thinned a little. 'It is a long story.'

'And you have said that before. A story does not get shorter in the telling if one keeps pointing out how long it is. Let us commence. What is it between Cild and yourself that can cause such dislike?'

Aldhere raised a shoulder in a half shrug.

105

'It has its roots in the fact that Cild and I share the same mother and father.'

For a moment Eadulf was uncertain of what he had just heard. Finally he said: 'Then you are . . . ?'

'Cild and I are brothers,' confirmed Aldhere.

Chapter Seven

In the sudden confusion of thoughts, only one made any sense to Eadulf. Now he knew why he found Aldhere's face so familiar. He was looking at an echo of Abbot Cild's features.

Aldhere was chuckling at his bewilderment. 'You look surprised, holy *gerefa*.'

Eadulf drew his thoughts together. 'I am shocked that Abbot Cild is so violent against his own brother – to the point where he seeks him out to kill him.'

The outlaw grimaced. 'Fratricide is no stranger to our people, my friend, especially among those who seek power.'

'You will have to explain that to me.'

'It is easily explained. Cild and I are both the sons of Bretta. Cild was the elder—'

'But you became thane of Bretta's Ham.' Eadulf frowned quickly.

'Exactly so. Our father, Bretta, did not like my brother. Cild was often given to rages and tantrums as a child. Once, he went so far as to slaughter a black cat which belonged to our mother on the altar of our chapel and declare his allegiance to Woden instead of Christ. Even when he grew up he could be overcome by a terrible temper. He became a warrior who relied on the power of his battle-axe and not his brain to win his victories. He was an individual, not one who could marshal his forces and devise plans. Bretta felt that he had no qualities for the just leadership of our people. He disinherited him and proclaimed that I would succeed him as thane after he died.'

'And Cild disliked you for that?'

'Of course. All through our youth, Cild had assumed that he would become thane. Now I was placed over him – his young brother to whom he would have to bend the knee. He was angry with our father and with me. It was not at first apparent because Cild announced that he was joining the brothers of the faith.'

'Did that come as a surprise?'

'A complete surprise. Cild was not interested in anything but fighting, drinking, womanising and power. My father was right – Cild would have made a bad thane. Anyway, he left Bretta's Ham and the next thing we heard was that he had gone to Connacht in the land of Éireann to enter the service of the faith. Our father died whilst he was away – died in the service of the King fighting his enemies, the forces of Wulfhere of Mercia. Then I became thane. This was three years ago.'

'When did Cild return?'

Aldhere rubbed the bridge of his nose and frowned at the question.

'I suppose it was just before the big council in the kingdom of Northumbria . . .'

'The Synod at Whitby?' asked Eadulf.

'Indeed, the council at the abbey of Hilda.'

'When did you first know that he had returned?'

'When I heard that he was appointed abbot. After his wife died he chased most of the brothers out of Aldred's Abbey and declared it to be a closed community.'

'Your tone tells me that you think this was illegally done,' pointed out Eadulf.

'Not illegally done, holy *gerefa*, for he had the support of Ealdwulf, our King, who followed Oswy of Northumbria in proclaiming that he would follow the Rule of Rome rather than the Rule of Columba.'

Eadulf recalled that the Blessed Colmcille was called Columba by the Angles and Saxons.

'But you suspected . . . what?'

'Suspected . . . ? I do not believe that a fox may turn into a lamb.'

'Nor could your brother change his personality to a man of peace and Christian charity,' muttered Eadulf.

Aldhere grinned broadly but said nothing.

'He must hate you a great deal to wish you dead,' Eadulf observed. 'Have you met him since he returned?'

'I met him once only. When I heard that he had become abbot at Aldred's Abbey, I went to see him.'

'There was no other meeting?'

'He did come to see my disgrace before King Ealdwulf,' grinned Aldhere. 'But I disappointed him by not keeping the appointment.'

'Did you ever meet his wife?'

'He did not deserve her,' Aldhere said quietly. 'She was a gentle young thing. Gélgeis was her name. Yes, I met her. That was when I went to the abbey. Cild had not then claimed the tonsure of Roman and declared for celibacy. Gélgeis was still alive then. They came to Aldred's Abbey together.'

'How did she die? Do you know?'

A curious expression crossed Aldhere's features.

'What makes you interested in Gélgeis, holy *gerefa*?'

Eadulf told him of the events of the previous night in the chapel.

Aldhere sat back with a soft smile.

'If I have understood you well on this business of ritual fasting,' he finally said, 'then these poor fools do not stand any chance of forcing justice upon Cild at all. Who understands this ritual among us? They will simply be killed by my brother's men if given the opportunity.'

Eadulf leaned forward. 'Do you think Gélgeis was murdered by your brother?'

Aldhere hesitated. 'It is possible. I cannot say. She disappeared while crossing the marshes near the abbey one day.'

'Did Botulf ever speak of the matter? I am told that he knew the girl well.'

'Botulf? He never spoke of it to me.'

Eadulf sat back in disappointment. 'What do you know about her death?'

'I know little enough. When I heard that Cild had returned from Connacht, I was prepared to greet him as a long lost brother. As I said, I came to the abbey. Cild's wife showed more friendship and courtesy to me than he did. She was very sweet and charming but frail and gentle. I could not believe that my brother had been able to attract such a creature . . .'

He paused for a minute in his remembrance, then continued. 'As soon as I saw my brother and realised the enmity that he still held for me, I resolved to have no more to do with him. Then came the battle and my downfall. When I was outlawed, my brother went to King Ealdwulf to claim my rank and possessions. Ealdwulf is a wily monarch. He sympathised, approved of my brother's appointment as abbot but said he could not also make him thane of Bretta's Ham nor give him all my possessions. In truth, Ealdwulf wanted them for himself, but he gave Cild one eighth share of my father's treasure. This did not mollify Cild but he could not argue further with the King.'

Aldhere paused and reached for the flagon of mead which stood on the table and poured himself a beaker, draining it with two swift gulps.

'That, holy *gerefa*, is my unhappy story, and indeed the unhappy story of my brother.'

They sat in silence for a moment or two.

'It does raise some further questions,' Eadulf pointed out.

'Which are?'

'Was it Cild or Botulf's presence in the abbey that caused you to set up your base in these marshes?'

Aldhere grinned. 'In truth, it was a mixture of both.'

'How would one set about finding this man, Garb, and his father, Gadra of Maigh Eo? For Garb to come to the abbey in the snowstorm last night and proclaim this ritual would indicate that these Irish warriors must be dwelling in the vicinity. I would like to speak with them and maybe save them from Cild's wrath.'

The outlawed thane pursed his lips in thought.

'A band of Irish warriors would find it hard to conceal themselves in this country. But there are still a few religious houses where the Irish missionaries have refused to abandon them to Roman clerics. That may be your answer.'

Eadulf was suddenly hopeful.

'Do you know where there are such houses?'

Aldhere nodded slowly.

'But I fail to see your interest in this, holy *gerefa*,' he countered. 'You are surely a stranger to all these matters – what are you interested in?'

'I am interested,' returned Eadulf, 'in bringing to justice the murderer or murderers of my friend Botulf. If I have to unravel a ball of twine to reach that end, then so be it. I will do so.'

'You sound a determined man, my friend. Are you such a man? And are you without fear?'

'You may rest assured that I am determined and you may judge whether I am without fear or not.'

'It is not I who will judge that. I think you are up against some strange mysteries, my friend. Strange mysteries and evil people. Be warned.'

'The nearest houses of Irish missionaries – you were about to tell me their whereabouts?'

'I am told there are a few elderly missionaries from Éireann in Domnoc's Wic to the north of here, but that might be too far away . . .' Aldhere paused, then smiled. 'There is the forest of Tunstall, the place of the farmstead, that is much closer, just south of the river. I heard tell that a monk named Laisre and some of his brethren were hiding there.'

Eadulf was eager.

'I know the forest of Tunstall. It is close enough to the abbey to be accessible but it is large and would be impossible to search single-handed. It would be like looking for a needle in a haystack.'

'There is only one place in that forest where Laisre would be, and that is the old farmstead itself. That is easy to find. But there is no guarantee that these Irish warriors are there. However, it is the nearest place where they might receive refuge.'

'It is worth a try,' agreed Eadulf, feeling positive. 'I think that this Garb and his father might know much of the mystery of your brother's wife. And I believe it is linked to the murder of my friend, Botulf.'

'Will you tell my brother that you have seen me?'

'There is an old proverb,' reflected Eadulf. 'Let not your tongue cut your throat.'

Aldhere smiled wanly. 'You are right. And I will give you another old saying of our people that you would do well to remember while you reside at my brother's abbey – be afraid and you'll be safe.'

Eadulf glanced towards the sky beyond the open window. Darkness came early in these winter months and he estimated that it would be less than an hour before it was dusk.

'Speaking of safety, it is time that I returned to the abbey.'

He rose and Aldhere rose with him.

'I'll send Wiglaf to put you on the right path. At least the sky is clear and the snow has stopped falling. Your journey back will be easy.'

'Should I want to get in touch with you again . . . ?' Eadulf left the question unfinished.

Aldhere smiled. 'There is a clump of trees a few hundred yards upriver from the abbey. I will have Wiglaf there who will know how to find me. That was how we used to keep in touch with poor Botulf. The copse was where I was due to meet with Botulf yesterday.'

Eadulf thrust out his hand. He found himself liking and trusting the outlaw.

'God be with you, thane of Bretta's Ham.'

'And luck follow your path, holy *gerefa*.'

The journey back was longer than Eadulf expected and Wiglaf, the former honey thief, was a loquacious travelling companion. He chattered constantly. In desperation, and trying to convert the conversation to something more positive than just idle gossip, Eadulf interrupted to ask him how he had joined up with Aldhere.

The man laughed uproariously and leaned forward towards Eadulf, pulling down his collar. There were faint red marks around his neck.

'See that? Marks of a slave collar, *gerefa*. That was the price of the path I started on in my youth. I'm afraid your birching did not persuade me to alter my ways. I progressed, was caught and became a slave. It so happened that when Aldhere raided the King's fortress at the mouth of the Yar, in search of his men, I was there and chained to one of them. That is why

I am now here. He couldn't take his man without taking me.'

Eadulf looked at him suspiciously. 'And you have not repented of your ways? Are you still a thief?'

The man smiled broadly. 'And still a good one. Aldhere does not need the religious, he needs thieves to help him stay alive in this marshland. It is all very well taking a stand against injustice, but when one is still declared outlaw, then one must live without the law.'

He roared with laughter at his own joke.

'Do you have any principles, Wiglaf?' Eadulf demanded in disapproval.

'Why, yes, *gerefa*. To stay alive and not be caught again,' replied the thief, unabashed.

'Aldhere, for all his outlawry, appears to me to be a moral man. I wonder that he has any dealings with you.'

Wiglaf turned towards him. The gloom of descending dusk obscured everything but Eadulf was sure that the man winked at him.

'Appearances? Remember that they are not all saints who use holy water, *gerefa*.'

Eadulf shook his head sadly. 'I wish that you had learnt the lesson which I tried to give you when I was *gerefa*, Wiglaf.'

'I have no illusions as to what I am nor what my fate will be,' replied the thief.

'Do you not? I wonder. Surely, you must know that the path to crime leads to one destination? You cannot have sunshine without shadows.'

'Spoken well, *gerefa*,' agreed Wiglaf with humour. 'But there is a saying that a man born to be hanged will not drown. I don't doubt I will probably hang but I will not drown first.'

'So be it. Tell me, you were rescued by Aldhere and

his men simply because you were chained to one of the men he wanted to rescue. Is that right?'

'You have the truth of it, *gerefa*.'

'How did you manage to persuade him to accept you in his band? I would have thought that he would have left you to your fate, he being a moral man and fighting to clear his name and those of his men from any hint of wrongdoing.'

Wiglaf chuckled. His sense of dark humour was constant.

'You have a good mind, *gerefa*. That was the very thing he proposed to do.'

'Then how . . . ?'

'Good luck was on my side. He was persuaded.'

'And how was that?'

'My cousin persuaded him, knowing that he would need someone who knew these marshes well and could move about them with speed; someone with my special talents.'

'I see. So your cousin was known to Aldhere?'

'And to you also, *gerefa*. Have you forgotten that I come from Seaxmund's Ham also?'

Eadulf was not following his logic and said so.

'Why, my cousin is . . . was,' Wiglaf corrected with a droop of his mouth, 'Botulf.'

Eadulf sat up in surprise, jerking slightly at the reins of his mule which snorted in protest.

'Botulf was your cousin?' he asked incredulously.

'Did I not say so?' replied the thief with humour.

Eadulf was furiously trying to remember back to his youthful days in Seaxmund's Ham. Vague memories did come back then, of course. Botulf had spoken of his cousin who had been disowned by the family. Wiglaf had been brought up on a farmstead outside the tiny village and did not enter it much.

'You know that I was Botulf's close friend, don't you?' Eadulf said after a while.

'He spoke often of you, *gerefa*, and wished that you had not left the land of the South Folk in your journeying.'

'Did you know it was because of him that I have returned?'

'I do. It was I who took his message on the first stage of its journey to you at Canterbury. Botulf was pleased when he heard that you were there. I took the message to the port at Domnoc's Wic and entrusted it to a sea captain I knew.'

'So you knew that it was urgent? You were told that Botulf's need to see me was imperative?'

'That's a long word that I have no understanding of, *gerefa*. But I knew that he wanted to see you urgently, if that is the meaning of it. I knew that he also wanted to see Aldhere. I brought the message to Aldhere from him. Botulf did not confide everything to me. Of that which he told me, I remember little.'

'But why did he want to see Aldhere? Why did he want to see me?' cried Eadulf in frustration.

'If I knew that, there would be no mystery. He did say this, and you must interpret it as you like – he said that there was great danger to the kingdom lurking in the abbey. He said that it was an evil which had to be confronted before we all perished.'

Eadulf frowned. 'An evil?' It was that word 'evil' again that caused a shiver of apprehension to go through him. 'And danger to the kingdom – to Ealdwulf's kingdom? From whom?' He sighed in his frustration. 'This is more baffling than ever.'

They rode on in silence for a while as darkness began to descend across the marshes.

'Not far now, *gerefa*. Soon you will see the river and to the right the dark shadows of Aldred's Abbey.'

It was as they were rounding a bend in the road that they came upon a figure hurrying in their direction. It suddenly appeared out of the gloom before them, startling their mounts, and by the time Eadulf had brought his mule under control the figure had scrambled from the roadside. It was lost among the dark trees to their left, away from the low, flat marshlands. Eadulf could hear the panting scramble and breaking of twigs as it progressed through the growth.

'In the name of . . . !' he exclaimed.

He retained an image of a slim figure, a woman, long hair and no more.

Wiglaf was chuckling to himself.

'What do you find amusing?' demanded Eadulf. 'Who was that?'

'That was Lioba. She's a . . . a friend of Aldhere and others, if you know what I mean.' He chuckled lewdly. 'A local girl.' He paused for a moment and then continued. 'As I was saying, we are not far from the abbey now.'

Eadulf nodded absently. His mind immediately returned to their conversation. He wanted to pursue it further before he bade farewell to Wiglaf.

'When did you last see Botulf?' he asked as they set off again.

'A few days ago. I was Aldhere's intermediary and would take messages to and from the abbey. But my cousin was no fool. He kept his own counsel in these matters. I was just a messenger. As I have told you, all I know is that he felt there was danger in the abbey.'

'But you must have had some idea of what was happening at the abbey?' Eadulf pressed. 'Your cousin is dead, Wiglaf, and I desire to bring his killers to justice.'

'I understand that. I do not think that you have to come out of the gates of the abbey to find his killer.'

117

'Do you mean that you think it was the abbot who killed your cousin?'

'Abbot Cild is a ruthless man, and if he suspected Botulf of being in league against him . . .' He ended with a shrug.

'But he must have known that Botulf was in touch with Aldhere? That much is obvious.'

Wiglaf did not reply. It was now too gloomy to see each other's faces clearly. It was going to be a dark night, cloudy, with no stars nor moon to reflect off the white carpet of snow and provide some illumination.

'It will snow before daybreak,' remarked Wiglaf absently. Then he added: 'I don't think Cild knew that Botulf was in contact with Aldhere. That was not the reason for their enmity. There was something else. What it was I am not certain.'

'Last night, at the funeral, Cild was claiming to have been a close friend of Botulf and lamenting his passing. Do I understand that you are saying his statement was far from the truth?'

Wiglaf gave a sardonic bark of laughter which answered Eadulf's question.

'Are you sure there is nothing you can suggest that might shed a light on these matters?' Ealdulf asked desperately.

'A word of advice, *gerefa*. There is a saying that a habit does not make the religious—'

Wiglaf stopped short and Eadulf, seeing the tension that suddenly filled his body as he stared out across the flat marshlands, also halted and glanced in the same direction.

Several hundred yards away across the gloomy white-carpeted marshland he could see a strange fluorescent glow. At its centre was a blue light which dispersed across an area of ground, flickering now faintly now brightly.

Eadulf felt a chill run through him and quickly crossed himself.

Wiglaf caught sight of his action and guffawed.

'No need to seek the protection of the Almighty, *gerefa*,' he said. 'That is only—'

'I know what it is,' snapped Eadulf in annoyance. '*Ignis fatuus* . . .'

'Aye, fool's fire. We call it firedrake.'

'I said, I know what it is. But can you explain *why* it is?'

'The marsh dwellers have many tales to tell about firedrake.' Wiglaf smiled. 'I believe none of them. If I did, I would never venture into the marshlands at all, far less ride them in dead of night. Look, it has already vanished.'

Eadulf shivered and nearly crossed himself again but he did not want to give his companion the opportunity to mock him. In his youth the *ignis fatuus* was called corpse fire for it was said that the spirit of the troubled dead rose in the form of a blue flame to appear to those from whom it wished to seek justice. Indeed, at this very time, the beginning of the feast of Yule, the gods and goddesses allowed wronged spirits to visit their vengeance on the living.

'Anyway,' Wiglaf was saying, 'from those trees ahead you will see the lantern outside the gate of the abbey. A short ride, that is all. Have courage, *gerefa*!'

Eadulf opened his mouth to chide the insolence of the thief, but Wiglaf turned his horse and went trotting back along the track into the darkness.

Eadulf glanced again across the marshes but saw no sign of the blue fluorescent light. He felt another shiver course down his back as he urged the mule forward. It seemed to sense that it was nearing home for it trotted at a speed which amazed him, coming up to the trees from which he caught sight of the river before spotting, a little way ahead, the dark walls of the abbey. There was the lantern flickering by the gates. He felt a wave of relief come over him. It was still only very early evening. If he estimated the hours correctly, it was not even time for the evening Angelus bell to sound, and yet he felt it was so cold and dark that it could be midnight.

It was the *dominus*, Brother Willibrod, who swung open the abbey gates for Eadulf to enter after he had tugged at the bellrope. Thankfully, Eadulf slid from his mule and stretched his aching limbs.

'God be praised that you have returned safely, Brother Eadulf,' the *dominus* began immediately, his single dark eye blinking rapidly. 'It was early morning when you left and now the hour grows late. We had presumed that you had met with an accident or something worse . . .'

'Something worse?' mused Eadulf.

'Aldhere's outlaws wander the marshlands, as well you know. The abbot returned after the noon Angelus having given up his attempt to track them down. He said that you had not overtaken him and was angry with me for letting you go after him.'

Eadulf tried to keep his features impassive.

'As you see, Brother Willibrod, I have returned safely.'

Brother Willibrod gestured to a passing member of the brethren to take Eadulf's mule and instructed him to unsaddle and feed and water the animal. Eadulf started to walk across the main quadrangle. To his surprise, the *dominus* hurried after him. Eadulf began to get the impression that he was concerned about something other than Eadulf's late arrival. He felt that the *dominus* was trying to find the right words to approach the subject. Eadulf was initially determined that he would not help the man. However, he could not help feeling some sympathy for him as he saw the anxious expression on his features. Finally, as they reached the far side of the quadrangle, Eadulf asked: 'Is there something on your mind, Brother?'

'Something strange has happened, Brother Eadulf.'

'Strange?'

The concern in the voice of the *dominus* was apparent. Then a sudden thought hit Eadulf.

'Sister Fidelma . . . her illness has not worsened?'

To his relief, Brother Willibrod shook his head immediately.

'No, her illness has not worsened. It is young Brother Redwald who . . .'

Eadulf was frowning. 'Who is Brother Redwald?'

'The young man who attends to the chores of the guests' hostel.'

'Yes, I remember the boy. What is the matter with him?'

'He has had to be locked in his cell and given strong liquor to calm him.'

Eadulf waited a moment and then gave an exasperated sigh.

'For goodness' sake! Am I to extract this story sentence by sentence? You are clearly upset at something which concerns Brother Redwald, though how it concerns me I do not know, nor probably care unless you can explain to me why I should.'

'Be seated a moment, Brother,' said the *dominus*, pointing to a nearby stone bench, 'and I will tell you.'

Compressing his lips to hide his irritation, Eadulf allowed himself to be guided to a bench and be seated. Brother Willibrod sat down beside him. His features were lit by a flickering storm lantern above them. It produced an eerie effect.

'It happened just after dusk had fallen,' began the

dominus. When Eadulf groaned, Brother Willibrod reached out a hand. 'Patience, Brother. Redwald is ill and now confined for his own protection. His mind is quite frantic.'

Eadulf controlled himself. The *dominus* continued.

'Redwald went into the chamber of Sister Fidelma to see if she needed anything. By the bed of your companion Brother Redwald saw a woman standing. Brother Redwald recognised her.'

Brother Willibrod paused dramatically.

'And who was the person whom Brother Redwald recognised?' Eadulf asked wearily.

'Redwald came to our community when Abbot Cild's wife, Gélgeis, was still alive. Redwald recognised this woman . . . it was Gélgeis or the shade of Gélgeis. He went out of his mind with fear because he knew that she was dead. But there she stood, pale but almost as if she were in life. She stretched out a hand to him and he went screaming from the chamber. We have barely made sense from his story . . .'

Eadulf felt a coldness creeping up his back. He remembered the figure of the woman he had seen the previous night near the chapel and everyone's reaction to it.

'This . . . this apparition was in Fidelma's room?'

'It was.'

'But you said that she was all right?' Eadulf began to rise hastily.

'She was in a feverish sleep; we could not rouse her when we went to investigate. There was no sign of the woman.'

Eadulf was keen to be gone. 'I am sure you are eager to attend to Brother Redwald, but now I am equally anxious to ensure that Sister Fidelma has come to no harm through this incident . . . whatever the reason for the incident may be.'

'Wait, Brother,' cried the *dominus*, rising to restrain him. 'Wait, I have not told you all.'

Eadulf whirled round, his eyes narrowed in sudden apprehension.

'What have you not told me?'

'Abbot Cild came to investigate. He told me that you had also seen what you claimed to be a woman near the chapel and that you had described Gélgeis to him. You told me that you had seen such a woman by the chapel. Now Brother Redwald has seen her. And the abbot is almost beside himself with fear, though I should not tell you that. Cild claimed several times that this wraith had been seen by him. Now it is appearing to others. It is clearly black witchcraft.'

Eadulf snorted sardonically. Inwardly, he felt a fear born of the age-old beliefs of his people.

'That is Abbot Cild's problem,' he said in irritation, turning again.

'Abbot Cild believes that it is the ghost of his dead wife,' cried the *dominus*. 'Further, he believes that this witchcraft came into the abbey when you and your companion arrived in this kingdom. There can only be one explanation.'

Eadulf had whirled back towards Brother Willibrod, his heart beating fast.

'One explanation? What do you mean?'

'The abbot believes that your companion has conjured the spirit of his dead wife by foul rites. We have locked Sister Fidelma in her chamber to await her punishment for witchcraft.'

Chapter Eight

Eadulf halted abruptly outside the door of the guest chambers. Further progress was impeded by a thick-set, muscular brother who stood, arms folded and immovable, in front of it. For a moment it seemed that Eadulf would fling himself physically on the man but Brother Willibrod came up behind him.

'Let him through,' the *dominus* instructed.

The brother stood aside immediately and Eadulf moved into the room at once.

Fidelma lay in the bed, her breath coming in deep rasping tones.

Eadulf halted inside the door for a moment and brought himself under control. He then walked slowly forward. Fidelma appeared to be asleep, but not exactly in a natural sleep. The perspiration stood out on her forehead and she lay in a profusion of sweat. It was clear that her ague had reached a point where she was in a serious fever; a fever which must break that night or become dangerous. Eadulf had seen such fevers before.

He turned as he heard the soft tread behind him.

Brother Willibrod had entered and stood at his side.

'I told you that your companion was not harmed,' he said softly. 'No one has been near here, only Brother Redwald and whatever it was that he saw.'

Eadulf glanced down at the medication that he had left on her side table.

'And no one has given her anything except what I have prescribed for her?'

'Brother Redwald only gave her some water this morning and then, at lunchtime, he came in and found her in this sleep. So he left her alone. Brother Higbald looked in on her a short time ago. She has not been neglected.'

'And when was Brother Redwald supposed to have seen this apparition?'

Brother Willibrod looked uncomfortable.

'Brother Redwald came here just after dusk to light candles and see if she needed anything else.'

'And when did the pious brethren try and condemn her for witchcraft?' Eadulf could not keep the bitterness out of his voice.

Brother Willibrod shuffled his feet awkwardly.

'No one has tried her . . . you must see Abbot Cild for it is on his order that she is confined. He asked that you be escorted to his presence as soon as you arrived back.'

Eadulf's lips thinned in irritation.

'Abbot Cild can wait. I need to attend to Sister Fidelma first. She is at a crucial stage of this ague she has contracted.'

Brother Willibrod's one eye widened in dismay.

'But the Father Abbot will be angry . . .'

Eadulf wheeled round, thrusting his face directly to an inch before that of the startled *dominus*. The man flinched before his gaze.

'I am angry now. Angry that a man who calls himself abbot of a holy community can talk of witchcraft, of ghosts and demons, and . . .'

Eadulf pretended he was too worked up to continue, but what made him pause was a remembrance of his own emotions a short while before when he had seen the *ignis fatuus* dancing on the marshes. He turned back to Fidelma to hide his confusion.

There was no doubting that he had also seen a woman, a woman whose description had clearly had an effect on the abbot. What was the mystery here? Did the abbot really think he was being haunted by the ghost of his dead wife? The woman Eadulf had seen had corporeal existence. She was no shade, he was sure.

'Is there any hot water ready?' he demanded.

The *dominus* indicated the fireplace without speaking.

Eadulf moved to the simmering pot and took a beaker to scoop out a little of the liquid. He began to busy himself mixing an infusion of fresh herbs which he chose carefully from his bag. The *dominus* watched him with growing impatience. Finally, he said: 'I will go to the abbot to tell him that you have returned and will see him as soon as you have finished your administrations.'

Eadulf did not bother to respond and was barely conscious of Brother Willbrod's exit. He bent to the task of mixing the concoction before moving back to Fidelma's side.

'Fidelma,' he whispered.

She moved and moaned in her fever.

Gently, he put a hand behind her head and raised it and then, taking the beaker of his medicinal infusion, he placed it against her lips.

'Drink this. It will do you good. A few sips only.'

He let the liquid dribble against her lips. As some of it reached her mouth she swallowed automatically without waking or opening her eyes.

Eventually he let her head down slowly to the pillow and placed the beaker back on the table.

He felt her forehead. It was still hot and damp.

It was going to be a long night. The fever had to break. Meantime, he had Abbot Cild to deal with.

He turned to the door. The burly brother was still standing outside. He stood aside to let Eadulf out but he did not speak. His eyes merely observed Eadulf, watchful but not unfriendly.

'Where will I find Brother Redwald's cell?' Eadulf demanded. He was not going to confront the abbot until he knew precisely what young Redwald had seen.

The big guard merely pointed to his mouth and shook his head. It became obvious to Eadulf that the man could not speak. Before he could do anything further, the brother had taken his arm and pointed with one hand along the cloisters. Then he held up four fingers.

'The fourth door along that passage?' asked Eadulf.

The man nodded without a change of expression.

Eadulf walked swiftly in that direction and counted the doors along the shadowy passageway. Outside the fourth door he saw some of the brethren were gathered. They were talking softly. For some reason Eadulf found himself drawing back into the shadows.

'Come, Brother Wigstan,' one of the religieux was calling. 'It is time to sound the bell for supper. Leave him. He will come to his senses soon enough.'

Eadulf saw Brother Wigstan come out of the doorway and join the others. They moved off together, their leather-soled sandals slapping the granite flagstones and dying away in the distance.

Eadulf waited a moment or two and then entered through the door. To his surprise, it was not locked but latched from the outside. On opening it he found himself in a small cell-like room. Young Brother Redwald was sitting on the bed, his arms crossed over his chest. The boy glanced up in terror.

'It's all right,' whispered Eadulf, holding up a hand. 'I mean you no harm. I must speak to you about what you saw.'

The boy shook his head. His lips were trembling.

'It was a demon, I tell you. It was . . .' He glanced at

Eadulf with another terrified look. 'The abbot says that the Irish woman has conjured the demon up . . . and she is your companion!'

He began to back across the bed away from Eadulf.

Eadulf shook his head. 'I mean you no harm, Redwald. Neither does Fidelma. She is ill and would be no more capable of conjuring spirits than you are. Put this idea out of your mind. Tell me what you saw. Describe it to me.'

The boy appeared to calm himself a little.

'It would be a great wrong if Sister Fidelma was blamed for something that she is not responsible for,' insisted Eadulf in a gentle tone. 'Only you can tell the true story. So tell me and I swear that you will come to no harm.'

The boy began to look less terrified but scarcely reassured. However, with a little more coaxing, Eadulf managed to get the story from the boy. It was substantially as Brother Willibrod had told him.

'I went to the guests' chamber to see if there was anything I could do for the Irish sister,' the boy confided. 'I suffered an ague like that once . . .'

'And you went into the chamber. What then?' coaxed Eadulf as the boy hesitated.

Redwald raised a horror-stricken face to his.

'That was when I saw . . . her!'

'Go on. Who was this woman who has terrified you?'

'It is the lady Gélgeis. I swear it. I came to the abbey when she was still alive. I know what she looked like. It was she who nursed me when I had the ague. That was why I knew that I should try to help the Irish sister.'

'I see.' Eadulf waited patiently as the boy gathered his thoughts. 'And you thought that the lady Gélgeis was in the room with Sister Fidelma?'

The boy was adamant. 'I did not think. I saw her. As I entered she was bending over Sister Fidelma and bathing her forehead . . . exactly as she used to do with me.'

129

'Describe her.'

'She is young and pretty.'

'Yes? Go on? Describe her hair.'

'She had red hair, more gold than red, and her skin was pale, very pale even by the candlelight. She was clad in a rich, crimson gown with jewels – glittering jewels. I stood there and . . . and she raised her head and looked at me. Holy Mother of God! Her face was exactly as I remembered it – but she is dead, Brother! She is dead! Everyone says she is dead. It must be so.'

'Calm yourself, Redwald,' Eadulf said, patting the boy's shoulder. 'Just tell me what happened then. She looked at you. Did she say anything?'

'Forgive me, Brother, but I raised a cry and fled the chamber. I spared no thought for the Irish sister lying on the bed. I ran. I ran straight to Brother Willibrod who insisted that I go with him back to the room. We went back . . .'

'What did you find?'

'The room was deserted except for the Irish sister. There was no sign of Gélgeis.'

'What then?'

'I told Brother Willibrod the details of what I had seen. He insisted I tell the abbot. I believe that Abbot Cild was very displeased. My nerves were all to pieces and Willibrod gave me strong liquor to calm them and brought me here to rest. That is all I know.'

Eadulf leant against the wall and rubbed the side of his nose with a forefinger.

'When you returned, there was no trace of this woman you saw?' he asked finally.

'How could there be? It was an apparition, a ghost.'

'You are convinced that it was the lady Gélgeis?'

'It was no one else but the lady Gélgeis as I knew her. She has been dead this long year or more.'

'I see. But tell me this, Brother Redwald: did you ever see the lady Gélgeis dead?'

The boy frowned. 'It is well known that her body was never recovered from the marsh. It rests in a quagmire not far from here. Some of the brethren said that she missed the path coming back alone to the abbey one evening and wandered into it. It is an evil place that has claimed several animals who have been caught in its muddy maw. They call it Hob's Mire.'

Eadulf was frowning. 'Not far from here, you say?'

'Aye, there is a track to a little copse and then beyond it stretches the marshes and that's where Hob's Mire is.'

Eadulf suppressed a shiver, suddenly remembering the blue fluorescent light that he had seen about the very place the boy was describing. He found his hand shaking and tried to stop it by a surge of anger. Fidelma would not approve of the thoughts that were streaming through his mind at that moment. He had been brought up in this land worshipping the old gods, the old ways, and was not converted to the new faith until he was well into his maturity. But the blessed water with which the Irish hermit who had converted him to the faith of Christ had baptised him had not been powerful enough to wash away all his pagan beliefs.

The wraith of Gélgeis – which he, too, had seen that first night near the chapel; the blue flame – whether it be the firedrake or not – and now the story Brother Redwald was telling him drew him back to the ancient beliefs of his people like tentacles reaching out and drawing him back into the tenebrous ways of the shadowy religion from which he had fled.

He set his jaw firmly. In his mind he could hear Fidelma's chiding tones.

'What is the supernatural but nature that has not yet been explained?'

As soon as he said it, Eadulf realised that he was merely repeating something Fidelma had said. She would doubtless argue that if people of sound reason had seen the woman and she had been clearly recognised as a woman thought to have been dead, then there were two possibilities. Either the woman was alive or someone was impersonating her. Wraiths and spirits of the dead would not enter into her reasoning. It was as simple as that. Yet this was not her country nor her culture. Eadulf even felt a momentary resentment. How would Fidelma be able to understand the brooding evil that shrouded the dark Saxon winters? Then he felt disloyal for the thought.

The boy did not seem convinced by his argument.

'It is Yuletide, Brother. You remember what that means?'

He knew well enough. During the twelve days of the feast of Yule the pagan deities of the Saxons came closest to Midgard, the middle world in which humankind dwelt. This was when the dead were free to seek out those who had wronged them in life, when trolls and elfin people were sent to punish the wrongdoers. Eadulf felt guilty at even thinking it, but a culture one has grown up with is hard to discard.

He leaned forward to the boy and patted him on the shoulder again.

'There is nothing supernatural here, son,' he assured him confidently, although he felt he was an outrageous liar and that it must show. 'It is just some mystery that we will get to the bottom of. Believe in your faith and be firm in the protection of the Christ.'

He left the boy in the small cell and made his way back to the main quadrangle. From there he followed the route which he knew would lead him to the abbot's chambers. Abbot Cild was waiting for him, seated at his table, his hands spread palm downwards and an angry scowl distorting his features.

'Did you not understand that I had sent for you to

come to me immediately you returned to the abbey?' he demanded belligerently.

'I had more pressing matters to attend to,' Eadulf replied coldly, his demeanour showing that he was not browbeaten by the abbot.

Abbot Cild's scowl deepened.

'Your lack of respect to me has been noted before, Brother Eadulf. Your duty is obedience to me as abbot.'

'I have other duties,' Eadulf responded. 'My duty is to Archbishop Theodore, your superior in the faith. I have been appointed his emissary and may speak on his behalf. That is my sole area of obedience.'

As he spoke, Eadulf crossed his fingers superstitiously. What he had said was true in that this had been his role when Theodore had appointed him as emissary to King Colgú at Cashel, but it was his role no longer. Eadulf, however, suspected that Abbot Cild was not going to challenge him outright and send to Canterbury to ask Archbishop Theodore for verification. By all accounts, Cild himself was not one to stick to the truth. Within a few days, Eadulf hoped that he would have resolved the matter and he eased his conscience by remembering an old saying of his people – falsehood often goes further than truth when dealing with a liar, and such a lie will eventually pass away while only the truth remains.

Abbot Cild regarded him with mixed emotions. A tiny muscle twitched at his temple; his lips thinned.

'Are you claiming to have superior authority to me?' he demanded threateningly.

'I am simply pointing out that you have no power over me, Cild,' snapped Eadulf. 'Now, Sister Fidelma is ill. The crisis is close; her fever either breaks or she worsens. I shall be her nurse this night. So remove your guard on her chamber door.'

Abbot Cild appeared stunned by Eadulf's assertive

manner. He was obviously totally unused to anyone challenging his power.

Eadulf continued, unperturbed: 'Next, remove this stigma of black magic and evil doings from her name. That a man intelligent enough to claim the position of abbot of this house should give credence to such tales of witchcraft is beyond belief.'

Abbot Cild rose rapidly from his chair.

'I shall not! I am abbot here, not you, and let Archbishop Theodore come here in person if he would challenge me.'

Eadulf had not really expected his demand to be accepted immediately and without trouble.

'That he might well do, for many things have come to his attention about this house.' Eadulf realised that he was going out on a limb here by departing from the facts.

Abbot Cild's eyes narrowed.

'Explain your meaning,' he demanded.

'I intend to. But questions first. Why are you so afraid of this reported apparition?'

The question was unexpected and Cild blinked and sat down again with abruptness.

'What . . . what makes you think that I am afraid?'

Eadulf merely smiled. 'I saw a lady near the chapel last night. You were afraid when I described her. Tonight, Brother Redwald saw the same woman in Sister Fidelma's room. This time, Brother Redwald claimed it was your wife who, it is reported, is dead. Is she dead?'

Abbot Cild's expression became angry. 'Dare you call me liar?'

'I am asking a question.'

'She is dead. And only a person who practises the black arts could conjure up her image. Nothing happened until you arrived here with the foreign woman.'

'But I am told that this wraith was seen before we came to the abbey,' protested Eadulf.

'The spirit appeared as soon as you entered this kingdom. The foreign woman's witchcraft must be powerful to conjure the spirit at a distance,' replied Cild, unabashed. 'You forced your way in here and demanded hospitality. I should have expelled you both at that very moment. I relented and let you stay. Immediately, the wraith appears. And I have not forgotten that your coming heralded the arrival of Garb and his men who make such vile claims against me. I have not overlooked the fact that Garb and your companion are from the same country. Perhaps they are kin and in conspiracy? I am a logical man. It was your coming that brought this evil into Aldred's Abbey. Nothing evil had happened until last night, when you both demanded the hospitality of this abbey.'

Eadulf heard him out quietly and then smiled sadly.

'But it did, Cild. Yesterday morning my good friend Botulf was murdered. And it was by his wish that we came here – too late!'

Eadulf saw no reason to withhold this information any longer. He judged that now was the moment to use it, and he was right, for Cild was quiet for some time, trying unsuccessfully to make his face an expressionless mask.

'Why did Botulf ask you to come here?'

Eadulf smiled knowingly. He would play mind games with the abbot now.

'Did someone in the abbey know that he had sent to Canterbury to request my presence at this place?' Eadulf made his voice reflective.

'I certainly did not know.' Abbot Cild's voice was tight with suppressed anger.

'I realise that Botulf and you were not the close associates that you would have had people believe at the funeral service. What enmity lay between you?'

'Did Botulf tell you that there was enmity between us?' demanded the abbot.

'Do you deny it?' countered Eadulf.

'I do not. I point out that your friend Botulf was forced upon me by the wish of King Ealdwulf. If you must know the truth, Botulf tried to defend a traitor and coward and was ordered by the King to remain in this community, moving no more than a mile from it, until he had expiated his crime. I did not like the arrangement but accepted the order of the King.'

Eadulf nodded slightly. This agreed with the version which Aldhere had told him.

'Yet you must have found Botulf a useful member of the community to allow him to remain as steward of the abbey?'

'He had his uses,' Cild reluctantly agreed.

'So my friend, Botulf, who helped Aldred found this abbey some years ago, was returned here to serve you as the new abbot?'

Abbot Cild pursed lips thoughtfully. 'Botulf was one of Aldred's first community here. But then he was sent to a western part of the kingdom to preach and it was there he fell in with the man who was to be a coward and traitor to the King . . .'

'Aldhere?' The question was swift and caused Cild's eyes to widen a fraction.

'How did you know that? From Botulf?'

'No. I happened to fall in with your brother earlier today.'

There was a silence while Abbot Cild digested this information.

'You are trying to play games with me, Brother Eadulf,' he said quietly. 'And what lies has my young brother been telling you?'

'Should he be telling any lies?'

'He doubtless justified to you why he lives outside the law.'

'He claimed to be innocent of the murder of Botulf for which, as I remember, you were insistent upon hanging him had you caught him earlier today. I seem to recall that Aristotle wrote that the strife between brothers is bitter and cruel. Would Aldhere have done the same to you, I wonder?'

Cild glowered in annoyance. 'He has done worse to me by using guile to rob me of my inheritance.'

'Was that not your father's decision?'

'My father was in his dotage and was influenced by Aldhere.'

'But you went into the Church. Surely that is an end of the matter?'

'I did not make Aldhere a traitor and coward. Shortly after I returned here, Aldhere came under sentence of outlawry from the King. I merely attempted to regain what was mine by right.'

'And King Ealdwulf did not agree with you?'

'He agreed on the principle but not on the practicality, for he decided that there should be no future thane of Bretta's Ham.'

'Do you hate your brother to the point where you would personally encompass his death? That is hardly in keeping with the cloth you wear.'

'Where is it written that I should forbear from vengeance?

"Sing psalms to the Lord, who dwells in Zion
proclaim his deeds among the nations
for the avenger of blood had remembered—"'

Eadulf interrupted the abbot's quotation with a sharp gesture.

'I would have thought that you might have considered the story of Cain from the text of Genesis. Cain murdered his brother, and when God came to pass judgment on Cain, Cain fully expected that his life would be forfeit as vengeance. But God told him "No; if anyone kills Cain, Cain shall be avenged sevenfold." God merely set a mark on Cain so that anyone meeting him should not kill him. For vengeance begets vengeance.'

Cild smiled thinly. 'Brother Eadulf, I should advise you to read Exodus as well as Genesis – "then shall thou give life for life, eye for eye, tooth for tooth, hand for hand, foot for foot, burning for burning . . ."'

'I know the lines, Abbot, but blood cannot wash out blood. Vengeance will prove its own destroyer.'

'Then, Brother Eadulf, am I to understand that you will disobey the words of the Scriptures?'

'Are they there to be obeyed without question?' demanded Eadulf.

'They are the words of the holy men inspired of God.'

'They are the words of men who set them forth for the obedience of fools and the guidance of the wise.'

'Now I see why you travel with a witch. You have no religion!' snapped the abbot.

Eadulf was forced into silence by the cold illogic of the man. Finally, he found his voice, but he realised that Abbot Cild was a man of narrow mind and total self-absorption. And it brought him back to the main purpose of his argument with the abbot.

'How can you believe that Sister Fidelma is capable of that which you accuse her of?' he asked softly, realising, as he asked the question, that it was a weak argument.

'I have given my reasons. They are plain enough. And it seems that your irreligion makes you blind to her guilt. These mysterious happenings only occurred after you both arrived in this kingdom. That is the reason I accuse her. I believe that she is one who works for the devil, or by some devilish and curious art has conjured images which the devil

138

has devised to entangle and ensnare the souls of the pious brethren in this community. It is my responsibility to save them from damnation!'

'Without the trial of her whom you accuse? While she lies ill and in no position to defend herself?' Eadulf was seething with anger. 'I tell you, Cild, you exceed your authority. You believe in an eye for an eye. So be it. Should harm befall Sister Fidelma, you will truly know what vengeance is. I swear it.'

Abbot Cild sat back and examined Eadulf's angry features. His mouth turned down.

'One thing you do not lack, Eadulf of Seaxmund's Ham, and that is courage. You threaten me in the sanctuary of my own abbey? I could have you taken out and flogged, aye, and even burnt as a pagan heretic for daring to ignore the holy words of the Scriptures. I have armed brethren within call. What do you think I should do in the face of your threats, Brother Eadulf?'

Eadulf stared back defiantly.

'I do not know what you will do, Cild. I cannot predict what you will do, for you do not seem to be answerable to anyone for your actions. I will tell you this, though. If anything happens to Sister Fidelma or to me, then the retribution that you will bring down on yourself might be more than you bargain for.

'Sister Fidelma is blood sister to the King of Cashel. She is highly respected in the faith having been a delegate at Whitby. She attended the Lateran Palace at Rome, and is a lawyer of her people. Do you think that you can act against her with impunity? I, an emissary of Archbishop Theodore, am as of no consequence compared with her. However, of little worth as I am, Archbishop Theodore will want an accounting of King Ealdwulf if harm befalls me, and Ealdwulf will want to know why his tranquillity is disturbed by Canterbury.'

There was a lengthy silence after Eadulf stopped speaking.

Then Abbot Cild actually smiled. It was not a pleasant smile.

'You have put your case very well. I shall now tell you what I shall do. I shall wait until Sister Fidelma is recovered from her illness and then we shall have a formal hearing about the matter. If it is proved that she has had no hand in conjuring spirits in this abbey, then you may continue on your journey. Whatever whispers of the dead brought you hither can be consigned back to the dead. Do you understand me?'

'How can one defend oneself against such an intangible accusation as conjuring images of the dead?' demanded Eadulf.

Abbot Cild spread his hands. 'That is not my concern. If she is innocent then let her prove it.'

'And who will decide her innocence or guilt?'

'I will,' returned the abbot blandly.

'And if you decide that she is guilty?'

'The punishment is prescribed by the laws of the Wuffingas, the laws of our people handed down to us by Wuffa son of Wehha.'

A coldness went through Eadulf. As a *gerefa* he knew the laws well, but what was more terrifying was the fact that it was obvious that Abbot Cild was demented, and in his state of mind the man was without mercy.

'As amended by the ministration of the new faith?' he asked hopefully.

Abbot Cild shook his head. 'I see no reason why the laws of the Wuffingas should be amended. The penalty for conjuring demons and ghosts is clear . . . the guilty woman is placed face downwards in a grave and buried – alive!'

140

Chapter Nine

As Eadulf was leaving the abbot's chambers he encountered the flaxen-haired Brother Higbald, the abbey's apothecary. Higbald greeted him in a concerned but friendly fashion, still wearing the bright and humorous appearance he had that morning. Humour seemed a natural attitude to him. He had that ease of manner which reminded Eadulf of Aldhere's jocular attitude to the world.

'So, Brother Eadulf, you have heard that mass hysteria has taken over our poor community?'

Eadulf halted, frowning. It took him a moment to realise what the apothecary was referring to. His eyes lighted.

'Then you do not believe in this ghostly apparition?'

Brother Higbald shook his head. If anything it seemed his smile broadened.

'I cannot believe we have a wraith or phantom wafting through these dismal corridors. I believe that young Redwald was imagining things. Yet I have to point out that it was you who first raised the image of a woman who, by poor Brother Willibrod's account, bore a striking resemblance to the dead wife of the abbot. Perhaps young Redwald overheard you talking about the matter and then, with an overfull imagination, he embroidered something he saw in the shadows. That's all.'

Eadulf put his head to one side reflectively.

'That is a possibility, though I have spoken to young Redwald and his fear is genuine enough.'

'It might well be. It is possible to convince yourself that you have seen something when you have not. Youth is impressionable.'

Eadulf smiled grimly. 'Granted that is so. Can the same explanation be ascribed to my sighting of the lady?'

Brother Higbald chuckled. 'I do not know you, Brother, and therefore I cannot say. All I know is – as I told you this morning – we are a small community and I would know if there was a woman in this place.'

'But would you know if it were a shadow, an image from the Otherworld?' demanded Eadulf.

Brother Higbald shook his head firmly. 'You do not believe in such things, my friend. Neither do I.'

'Unfortunately, your abbot and many of the brethren here do.'

'That is a difficulty, I know. In fact, I was just on my way to see how Sister Fidelma is faring. I'll accompany you, if I may?'

'She has fallen into a fever,' Eadulf said as they walked together along the corridor.

Brother Higbald did not appear perturbed.

'It is usually the way with such agues. The fever comes and must break naturally, although we can help with some medication. Usually, the fever breaks in the early hours of the morning. There is nothing we can do but wait.' Higbald paused and glanced at him. 'Where did you disappear to this morning?'

'I rode out after Abbot Cild and his party,' Eadulf replied. 'I did not catch up with them, but I caught up with the abbot's brother.'

Brother Higbald halted almost in mid-stride and stared at Eadulf.

'You met and spoke to Aldhere?'

Eadulf nodded. 'An interesting man. Not quite as the abbot would describe him. There seem some interesting undercurrents here. If I had my way, I would turn the matter over to the King's high steward to investigate.'

Brother Higbald resumed the walk and Eadulf fell in with him.

'I try to avoid fraternal strife. But you are aware of where Abbot Cild's accusation against Sister Fidelma may lead?'

Eadulf nodded grimly.

'Would you accept some advice?' Brother Higbald asked.

Eadulf gave him a curious glance. 'Advice?'

'As soon as your companion's fever has broken, I would leave this place.'

Eadulf sighed with resignation. 'I think that is exactly what you counselled me this morning.'

'It is the best advice I can give,' replied Brother Higbald. 'I will show you a means through which you may pass out of the abbey unnoticed; one which is not generally known to the brethren. With luck, you could escape Cild's wrath with ease. I, for one, do not want innocent blood on my hands.'

Eadulf glanced at him in surprise.

'If you are so sceptical of your abbot, why do you stay here, Brother Higbald?'

The apothecary chuckled dryly.

'We all have reasons for being where we are in life. I choose here. My reasons are of no consequence to this matter.'

A thought suddenly struck Eadulf.

'Didn't you tell me this morning that Brother Botulf had been a witness to the lady Gélgeis's death? I have heard that she was returning alone to the abbey one night and wandered into a quagmire, Hob's Mire, and disappeared. No one saw the body afterwards. So who told you that Botulf was a witness to her death?'

Brother Higbald paused again and turned to Eadulf. There was a frown on his face.

'I never heard that she was alone when she met her death,' he said with some hesitation. 'Indeed, I think that it was Brother Botulf himself who told me the story.'

'Tell me what Botulf actually said. Can you remember?'

Brother Higbald thought for a moment.

'It was several months ago. The subject of the abbot's wife came up, I can't recall why. Brother Botulf said . . . oh, something about failing the lady. That it was his fault that she was killed. Something like that. That . . . ah, I recall now! Botulf said that he had failed to protect Gélgeis from the evil she had found here. That her face, in death, haunted him. Then . . . that was all. He ended the conversation abruptly.'

Eadulf was silent for a moment or so, reflecting on the words. He could find nothing substantial in them but much to give him food for conjecture. He sighed softly.

They had reached the guests' chamber but the burly silent brother still stood guard outside. Eadulf had realised by this time that the man was a mute.

Brother Higbald greeted him with mockery in his voice.

'How is your prisoner, Brother Beornwulf? Has she tried to escape and overpower you with the forces of the Evil One?'

Brother Beornwulf shifted his weight from one foot to the other and scowled at the jocular apothecary.

'I know, I know,' Brother Higbald said pacifically, patting him on the arm. 'You do what you are told. The abbot told you to remain here and so you remain here until he tells you not to.' He shook his head at Eadulf.

'It is good to know one's place and duty,' he said, still smiling. Then he opened the door to the guests' chamber and went inside, motioning Eadulf to follow him. As he closed the door he turned and grimaced at Eadulf. 'A good strong arm is Brother Beornwulf. But what he possesses in strength, he lacks in mental agility. He does what he is told. No more, no less.'

Fidelma still lay in the cot, huddled under blankets, and still in the grip of the fever.

Brother Higbald felt her moist forehead with the back of his hand. She moaned softly but did not open her eyes.

'Ah, *febricula incipit* – still feverish. There is no change as yet, Brother Eadulf,' he said. 'That is to be expected. You understand these things, don't you?'

Eadulf nodded. 'I would prescribe something to help her fight the fever and reduce it, though.'

'I agree. What would you suggest?'

'An infusion of wormwood, catnip . . . ?'

'*I* would suggest devil's bit,' replied Brother Higbald firmly.

'Equally good,' agreed Eadulf.

Brother Higbald took the small sack-like bag he carried over his shoulder. 'It so happens that I have already made up a potion of it.'

Eadulf took the miniature amphora that the apothecary gave him, unplugged the cork and smelt the contents. Then he nodded.

'Shall I administer it?' he asked.

Brother Higbald indicated his assent.

Eadulf carefully placed his hand behind Fidelma's hot, perspiration-soaked head and lifted her up. She groaned in protest but Eadulf placed the small amphora at her lips, gently forcing them open and making the liquid trickle into her mouth.

'A good swallow or two,' instructed Brother Higbald. Eadulf painstakingly administrated the dosage.

'You may give her another dose later if the fever is not abating. But she is a strong, healthy woman. I think that is something we should be thankful for.'

Eadulf put the amphora on a side table.

'Now we must wait,' Brother Higbald said approvingly. 'I will leave you to your watch, my friend, but I earnestly believe that you should take my advice and leave this place at the first opportunity.'

He crossed the room rapidly to a wall where a large tapestry denoting some religious scene was hanging. He turned and looked about him with a conspiratorial air.

'Behind here you will find a small passageway which will lead you outside the walls of the abbey. Remember it.'

He pulled the drape aside. To Eadulf's surprise, there was a small doorway behind it. It opened inwards and was not locked. Brother Higbald opened it and pointed through into the darkness.

'Following the passage, take the first two left turnings and then the first right. Remember that. Two left turns and one right. The abbey has several such tunnels, for it was built on an old Welisc fortress that was overthrown by Tytila, son of Wuffa, when our people conquered this area.'

'I'll remember that, Brother Higbald, and your advice, for which I am most truly grateful.'

The apothecary said nothing but shut the door and returned the tapestry to its original position. Then he smiled briefly and raised a hand in a gesture of farewell before leaving the chamber. Eadulf heard him speaking to Brother Beornwulf outside. He hesitated for a moment and went to look down at Fidelma. Then he crossed to sit in the chair near the hearth.

146

He suddenly realised how tired he was. It had been a long day. He had ridden far on muleback and ached all over. He sat back, hands resting his lap, and closed his eyes.

The events of the day revolved slowly in his mind and he tried desperately to connect them.

Above all, the danger to Fidelma kept nagging at his thoughts. She lay on the bed before him oblivious of that danger, fighting the more immediate threat of her fever. His first duty was to protect her. Brother Higbald had, at least, shown him an alternative to waiting for Abbot Cild's inquisition. But flight from Aldred's Abbey was surely the last resort?

What had he learnt of this mystery? He had been summoned by his good friend to the abbey. That friend had been murdered hours before he arrived. He found the abbot and his blood brother locked in a deadly quarrel and the abbot blaming that brother, Aldhere, for Botulf's murder. In return, Aldhere accused his brother, the abbot, of the murder. In addition, Garb, from Maigh Eo in the kingdom of Connacht, had appeared to accuse the abbot of the murder of his wife, Gélgeis, who had been Garb's sister. A ritual fast against the abbot had been announced. The facts of Gélgeis's death seemed unclear. A woman had been seen in the abbey, by both Eadulf and young Redwald. Brother Redwald claimed the woman was the dead Gélgeis. And now the most ominous fact of all – Fidelma was accused of conjuring the spirits of the dead.

Eadulf could have dismissed Brother Redwald's tale of seeing the ghost of Gélgeis as some hysterical reaction of youth. However, he was unable to reconcile the fact that he, too, had seen a woman outside the chapel on the previous night. Both Abbot Cild and Brother Willibrod had appeared to recognise his description. It was evident that both men thought that Eadulf was describing Gélgeis, the dead wife of the abbot.

Eadulf groaned slightly and shook his head.

Nothing seemed to have a logic to it; nothing made sense. It was at that moment that he suddenly remembered the piece of paper he had taken from the book satchel in Brother Botulf's chamber. He fumbled with the *sacculus* hanging on his belt and took the paper out, spreading it on his knee. It consisted of a few notes in Latin and Eadulf recognised the firm hand of his friend Botulf.

The first sentence Eadulf saw was from the Book of Samuel. 'The Lord sees not as a man sees; for man looks on the outward appearance, but the Lord looks on the heart.'

Eadulf frowned. There seemed something familiar about this admonition and he could not recall why.

The next line he did not recognise but Botulf had written the name Lucretius beside it: 'Whenever a thing changes and quits its proper limits, this change is at once the death of that which was before.' Then added and underscored: 'The change is definite – how long before the death?'

Then there followed a passage almost revealing but totally perplexing. 'God willing, my friend will be here soon. Is it not written that mercy is the support of justice? Not so in the man of Merce. We will be destroyed by the people of the . . .' Eadulf paused, trying to make out the word, which was distorted by an ink blot. It looked like 'marshes'. He thought of Aldhere and his marshland outlaws and shivered slightly. 'God willing, my friend will be here soon.' It could only be a reference to Botulf's wait for Eadulf's arrival, and he had arrived too late to help his friend.

The final note was also curious and again Brother Botulf had noted its provenance. 'Can a man carry fire in his bosom, and his clothes not be burned? Or can one walk upon hot coals, and his feet not be scorched? Proverbs.' Added was the line: 'Thus is it with Bretta's son.'

Eadulf sat back frowning and trying to make sense of these notes by his dead friend. What was going on in Botulf's mind? The only thing that made some sense was the comment about Bretta's son. As he had learnt, Aldhere and Cild were Bretta's sons and both certainly had 'fire in his bosom', but nothing else made sense. He put the paper back in his *sacculus*.

He stood up thoughtfully and walked to the bed to have another look at Fidelma. There was no change. Perhaps Higbald was right. His wisest course was to leave the abbey with Fidelma as soon as she was able.

He returned to his seat and tried to relax.

What choice would Fidelma make in the circumstances? He knew that she would want to get to the bottom of the mystery which permeated this dark, brooding abbey. He also knew that safety must come first. It was evident that Abbot Cild had no compunction about fulfilling his threat. Rank or station did not cause him a second thought.

Eadulf had come back to the abbey intent on going to find Garb and his men. He had learnt that the most likely place would be among a community in the forest of Tunstall which lay south of the abbey. That had been his intended goal. Perhaps that ought to be where he should take Fidelma when she was sufficiently recovered? At least, she would be with her own kind who would protect her because of her rank and office.

Eadulf's thoughts seemed to be becoming slower and slower in registering, drifting, diverging; and then he was sleeping an uncomfortable slumber full of apprehensive visions, jumbled images which made no sense at all.

He was aware of someone shouting at him; angry, demanding.

He awoke with a start. He was slumped uncomfortably in his chair. A foot or so from his face were the scowling features of Abbot Cild. Eadulf started up.

'What is it?' he demanded, trying to gather his wits.

'Do you claim that you have been asleep here?'

Eadulf was still trying to shake the fuzziness from his head. He saw an anxious-looking Brother Willibrod hovering behind the abbot, wringing his hands in his anxiety. To one side stood the implacable Brother Beornwulf.

'It is as I said, Father Abbot,' Brother Willibrod intoned, 'neither the woman nor the man has left this chamber. Brother Beornwulf has been outside the door all night.'

Eadulf was now wide awake and he rose, causing the abbot to step backwards, for he had been leaning right over the chair.

'What is the meaning of this?' demanded Eadulf, his voice strong but hushed. He glanced towards Fidelma and then, frowning, he went to her side and felt her forehead. A surge of relief rushed through him.

'Good! The fever has broken. She is on the mend.' Eadulf swung round to the surly abbot. 'Let us leave her to a natural sleep.'

By force of personality, he was able to push the abbot, the *dominus* and the bodyguard out of the chamber into the corridor outside. After he closed the door he turned his scowling features on them. His voice rose sharply.

'I hope you have some good explanation for bursting into a sickroom in the middle of the night?'

Abbot Cild was not abashed.

'Have you and your companion been in that room since the time you left me last night?'

Eadulf was aware of a soft light permeating the windows. He suddenly realised that it was not far from dawn. There came the distant sound of waking birds. He must have been asleep for several hours.

'Where else would I be?' he countered brusquely. 'And certainly Sister Fidelma is incapable of leaving her bed.'

'It is as I have said, Father Abbot,' repeated Brother Willibrod sulkily. 'Brother Beornwulf has been outside the door all night.'

'What are we supposed to have done now?' challenged Eadulf. 'Have you invented some new claim against us?'

Abbot Cild looked ready to explode with anger but Brother Willibrod reached forward and laid a restraining hand on his arm.

'Come with me, Eadulf of Seaxmund's Ham,' Abbot Cild finally said, turning and leading the way at a swift pace along the corridor and through the quadrangle towards the chapel of the abbey. There were a few of the brethren about who passed with lowered heads and hands folded before them. Eadulf was conscious of their eyes watching as he followed the abbot. Behind him came Brother Willibrod. Brother Beornwulf had been ordered to remain behind at his post outside the guests' chamber.

Abbot Cild made his way directly to the chapel and entered. Inside, he did not pause but marched straight towards the high altar. Then he halted. He threw out one hand in a gesture towards it.

He did not speak. He did not have to, for what he had brought Eadulf to see was plain and its implications were obvious.

On the centre of the high altar was a dead cat. Skewering the animal to the altar was a bone-handled knife. Eadulf had seen such knives before. In the old days, before the new faith had reached the people of Wuffa, in the land of the East Angles, the priests of Woden and Thunor had carried such implements, with the elaborately carved sacred symbols on their bone handles. They were sacrificial knives.

'It is the sign of the pagan worship,' whispered Brother Willibrod, genuflecting. 'We all know this is the feast of Yule.'

In spite of himself, Eadulf could not prevent a shudder catching him. He tried hard to recall where he had recently heard about a black cat being sacrificed on an altar.

'The conjuring of a spirit and now . . . this!' muttered Abbot Cild.

Eadulf glanced quickly at him.

'You appear to link the two things together?'

'They both smell of the evil arts!' cried the abbot.

'They smell of an evil mind,' retorted Eadulf. 'The question is . . . whose mind?'

'My answer is not altered. Nothing like this happened at Aldred's Abbey until you and the foreign woman came here.'

'And I have said, that is no answer at all. What would an Irish religieuse know of pagan Saxon gods and practices? We are not responsible for this' – he gestured towards the high altar – 'this desecration any more than we are responsible for any of the evil acts that have take place in this abbey.'

'That you will have to prove,' snapped the abbot. 'Brother Willibrod, you will see to it that this is cleared away. I shall have to bless and reconsecrate the altar.'

'It shall be done, Father Abbot,' muttered the *dominus*, casting an almost apologetic glance at Eadulf. He moved off to do the abbot's bidding.

The abbot regarded Eadulf with a look in which dislike was tinged with something else. Eadulf suddenly realised that the man's eyes held fear. Abbot Cild was actually afraid of him.

'You will return to the guests' chambers and remain there until I send for you. That I shall do when I am ready to hear the charges formally and give judgment.'

Eadulf was astounded. 'What of my right to present a defence for Sister Fidelma and myself?'

'You will have that right at the proper time.'

'But have I not the right to my freedom in order to investigate and prepare a defence?' he demanded.

Abbot Cild's eyes narrowed. 'You have no right to freedom now. After this desecration you have no right to freedom at all. Were I a less benign man, I would have you both taken and burnt to death immediately for the evil you have visited on this abbey.'

Eadulf snapped his mouth shut. He realised that there would be no moving this man's locked mind. At that moment he knew that Brother Higbald was probably right. He would have to take Fidelma to safety as soon as possible. Yet, coming out of such a fever, it would be reckless in the extreme to attempt to move her into the cold, snowbound world outside without a few days to recuperate.

'Very well, Abbot Cild,' he replied slowly. 'I see that you are intent on pursuing your course against us, blind and malicious as that course is. I shall not come out of the door of the guests' chambers until I am summoned to come through it. You accuse us of evil, yet it is a perverse course upon which you have embarked. In appealing to whatever humanity is left in you, I ask only this – it will take a few days for Fidelma of Cashel to recover from the infirmity she has suffered. In the name of the God that you claim to represent, allow us that time for her to recover before you drag her forth to enact your blind cruelty.'

Eadulf spoke evenly but his voice was filled with a vehemence which made Abbot Cild blink.

'I am not an inhumane man,' the abbot replied defensively. Eadulf noticed that the fear had not left his eyes. 'But I cannot allow further evil to be visited on this place. The woman will have two days to recover – no more. Then you can prepare to defend yourselves.'

He turned, finding the *dominus*, Brother Willibrod, returning with several of the brethren with pails and brushes ready to clean up the mess on the high altar.

'Brother Willibrod, you may escort Brother Eadulf back to the guests' chambers. He is to remain there until further orders from me.'

The *dominus* bowed his head and then gestured to his companions to continue with their work while the abbot left the chapel. Brother Willibrod then glanced apologetically at Eadulf and fell in step beside him.

'I do not know what to say, Brother,' he muttered. 'These happenings are strangely disconcerting.'

'You surely don't believe that the shade of Gélgeis is haunting these walls, do you?' Eadulf demanded. 'There is a human agency at work here.'

Brother Willibrod shrugged. 'Yesterday, I recognised your description of the woman you said you had seen outside the chapel.'

'I saw you were disturbed by it,' agreed Eadulf.

Brother Willibrod pursed his lips for a moment.

'In truth, it did sound like the Lady Gélgeis. And what young Redwald saw seems to confirm that opinion.'

'So you do believe that the shade of Gélgeis is haunting the abbot? Why?'

Brother Willibrod pulled a face, but Eadulf was not sure what it was meant to express.

'I would say that it is precisely the sort of action Gélgeis would take if she had the power to do so.'

'I don't understand.'

Brother Willibrod halted and suddenly looked around with a quick, conspiratorial glance.

'I will tell you the truth. The lady Gélgeis was not the most malleable of women. She was hard, dominant, and ruthless. I might even say that I could understand if Cild was pushed so far from propriety as to rid himself of her.' He hesitated and a flush came over his face. 'I am not saying that he did,' he added quickly. 'In fact, I do not believe that he did. But the lady Gélgeis was spiteful and immoral.'

Eadulf stared at him in surprise.

'Did you know her well?'

'As well as my role of *dominus* here would allow.'

'How long have you been *dominus* here?'

'I was in the abbey when Cild and Gélgeis came here.'

'Did anyone else share your views about her character?'

Willibrod sniffed with disdain.

'You will have to ask them, although most here did not know her as long and as well as I did. I have my opinion. It is not an opinion that I share with Abbot Cild, so I wish you not to reveal that I held his wife in such low esteem.' He paused and indicated along the passage with a jerk of his head to where Brother Beornwulf was seated on a three-legged wooden stool, his massive arms folded across his chest. 'You will remain in your rooms in accordance with the abbot's orders. I am sorry that things have come to this, Brother Eadulf.'

He turned and walked swiftly away.

Eadulf returned to Fidelma's chamber and found himself feeling cold apprehension. Spirits walking abroad, desecration of a high altar, and people who had known the abbot's wife in life swearing that it was her form returned

155

to haunt him. In spite of his dread he went to check on Fidelma and found her deep in a natural sleep.

He sat down in his chair and tried to pick up his scattered thoughts.

There was no decision to be made now. They had to accept Brother Higbald's suggestion. Safety came before the solution of this mystery. His mind full once more of conflicting thoughts, he fell into another troubled slumber.

When he awoke again, a brilliant morning light illuminated the room. He realised that he had been disturbed by young Brother Redwald who had entered bearing a tray with two steaming bowls, some bread and apples on it. He started up.

The young boy smiled apologetically. He seemed embarrassed.

'I have brought you and the Sister breakfast, Brother.'

Eadulf examined him cautiously.

'How do you feel now?' he asked.

The boy set down the tray.

'I apologise for my condition of last night. I was truly alarmed. I have calmed down this morning and am able to fulfil my duties.' He bobbed nervously and moved to the door. 'If there is anything else you need, Brother Beornwulf will be outside the door.'

He hesitated still, as if trying to make up his mind. Then he smiled quickly at Eadulf.

'You have shown consideration to me, Brother. I am sorry to see you in this predicament. I hope no action of mine has brought it on you. But I did see the lady Gélgeis, I swear it. If she be spirit, then she seemed to mean me no harm, so I regret if harm will follow.'

Eadulf responded reassuringly.

'Do not worry, Redwald. You cannot be held responsible for the actions of others.'

156

When the boy made to leave, Eadulf stayed him.

'Did you like the lady Gélgeis?' he asked.

The boy looked bemused for a moment and then nodded.

'She was kind to me. I have told you that she nursed me when I was ill.'

'I remember. You were a boy newly come to the abbey. So you liked her?'

'I think I did.'

'Aren't you sure?'

'I thought she was an angel, when I was ill. But later on, when I was well and growing, I found that she was distant, as if she cared little about me.'

'Are you scared of seeing her image now?'

The boy considered the question and then shook his head.

'The abbot told me that I have the faith to use as my shield. If I am steadfast in the faith, I need not fear.'

The boy left abruptly and Eadulf turned back to the tray and the bowls of steaming broth. He realised that he had not eaten for some time.

'Water,' came a croaking voice from the bed. 'I need a drink.'

'Fidelma!' Eadulf turned and found a pale but more normal-looking Fidelma easing herself up against a pillow.

'I feel like death,' she added.

'You should feel like life, having come through a dangerous fever,' smiled Eadulf, sitting at the side of the bed and taking her cold hand in one of his while he held out a beaker of water with the other.

She sipped cautiously.

'How long have I been in the grip of the fever?'

'Only twenty-four hours.'

'It seems longer. I had the most bizarre dreams, if

157

dreams they were. People rushing in and out and shouting and anger, lots of anger. Are we still at the abbey of . . .' She frowned.

'Aldred's Abbey,' Eadulf supplied. 'We arrived two nights ago. Do you remember anything?'

Fidelma tried to recollect.

'The last thing I remember was a visit from the apothecary, and something about a woman being seen in the abbey. After that things have become extremely hazy. I must have gone into the fever then.'

Eadulf turned and picked up the bowl of broth and some bread.

'After a fever is passed, it is necessary to get some sustenance into you. Have that and afterwards I shall tell you what has been going on here.'

It became obvious during the meal that Fidelma was still weak and unstable. Her hands trembled as she tackled the soup. Eadulf had to help her. She seemed exhausted. Eadulf realised that there was no way they would be able to move her that day.

She finished half of the bowl of broth and nibbled at a piece of bread, before pushing the rest away from her. Eadulf took it and she lay back down on the pillow and closed her eyes.

'You were going to . . . to tell me something,' she yawned.

Eadulf shook his head. 'Not at the moment. You need to sleep awhile.'

'I feel so . . . tired . . .'

A moment later, Eadulf realised that she had passed again into a natural sleep.

He finished his own meal and then sat back to reconsider matters.

Over the next hour or so he did not progress far with his thoughts. The door opened softly and Brother Higbald entered. He nodded to Eadulf and glanced at Fidelma's recumbent form.

'The fever's broken,' Eadulf replied in answer to his raised eyebrow. 'She's having a natural sleep now.'

Brother Higbald pointed to a corner of the room, indicating that he wished to talk without disturbing Fidelma.

'I heard what happened last night,' he whispered. 'Someone profaned the high altar.'

'And we are blamed for it,' Eadulf cut in sharply, in irritation. 'I know. I am now determined to follow your advice. It is foolish to remain here in harm's way any longer.'

Brother Higbald was approving.

'A wise choice of action. But when will Sister Fidelma be able to travel?'

'Not before tomorrow at the earliest, I think.'

'Does she know of what she is accused?'

'I have not told her yet. When I do, I doubt if she will have any understanding of it. Such things do not happen in her country.'

'Well, the sooner you are gone from here the better.'

'Have you heard anything more about what is happening?'

Brother Higbald shook his head. 'I believe Abbot Cild is scared of something. However, he blames you both as being the cause of it.'

'There is some mystery going on that I do not understand, Brother Higbald. You seem to be the only person here that I can get sense from. What is this darkness that enshrouds this abbey? Do you have any idea?'

Brother Higbald shrugged. 'I have never seen it as a darkness. Abbot Cild is a man of uncertain temperament, as are we all – each to his own. There are undercurrents of emotion between us all. Jealousies, suspicions, rivalries. But that is surely normal? Not until the death of Botulf and the subsequent events of the other night was there any hint that there was a real problem.'

'Nothing at all?' demanded Eadulf in frustration. 'No hint that Botulf was in danger? No hint of suspicion about the death of the lady Gélgeis?'

'Well, there were Cild's changes of mood after Garb's first visit and there was always gossip among the brethren. I think we were all shocked when Botulf's body was found. But Brother Wigstan said he had seen the notorious outlaw Aldhere nearby at the same time. There was no cause to question Abbot Cild when he pointed the finger at Aldhere.'

'Even though Aldhere is Cild's own brother?'

'Wasn't Cain the brother of Abel? Being brothers does not make men of the same mind.'

'You never questioned Cild's antipathy to his brother?'

'The King himself, King Ealdwulf, had outlawed Aldhere. That was all one needed to know.'

'So when Garb, the Irishman, arrived here the other night, identified himself as the brother of the lady Gélgeis, and accused Cild of her murder, what then?'

'Most of the brethren were shocked. I had seen him before, you remember.'

'Then one further question; given all these things, why are you so willing to go against Abbot Cild and help Sister Fidelma and myself?'

Brother Higbald looked a little surprised at the question and reflected on it for a moment.

'Perhaps it is because I do not believe in spectres or witchcraft. In this matter, I believe that Abbot Cild acts unjustly. But I say that he acts from fear and not from any maliciousness.'

'But what does he fear? If he acts in the certainty of right, what should he fear?'

'If, my friend, you are able to find an answer to

that, maybe you would find the key to unlocking all these mysteries.' Brother Higbald smiled. 'Now, what time shall you leave? Do you remember the way that I showed you?'

'Two turns left, one right. I know. I have no idea when – it depends on Fidelma and how she feels.'

'Let me know when you intend to leave and I will do my best to help you.'

'Thank you, Brother Higbald. I am grateful for all that you have done.'

After Brother Higbald left, Eadulf sat himself down to consider matters again but he had scarcely begun when he realised that Fidelma's adage that you cannot speculate without information applied to this case. He had no information at all to speculate with.

It was after midday when Fidelma emerged from her natural sleep.

'Eadulf?' She raised herself uncertainly and then fell back.

Eadulf went forward with a beaker of cold water and she sipped it gratefully.

'How are you feeling now?' he asked.

'Terrible. How ill was I?'

'Ill enough.' He placed a hand against her forehead. 'At least the temperature has completely gone now.'

'I have a terribly sore throat.'

'You had a bad fever. However, you have pulled through it, *Deo gratias*.'

'Are we at the abbey?'

Her eyes were bright and alert to her surroundings now.

'We are.'

'How long have I been out of the world?'

'Do you remember coming out of the fever this morning and asking me the same question?'

Fidelma considered and then smiled.

'I do. We have still been here only two days?'

'It is just after midday on the day your fever broke. You must now rest, relax and get stronger.'

Fidelma nodded slowly. 'And you have nursed me during this time?'

'I did. I was helped by the abbey's apothecary, Brother Higbald.'

Fidelma frowned thoughtfully.

'I thought that I asked a question earlier . . . about something which was troubling me.' She paused. 'Ah, yes. I felt some antagonism while I lay ill. Of people . . .'

Eadulf interrupted. 'Patience. If you feel up to it, I will run through the events since we arrived here. They are not pleasant.'

Fidelma regarded him with a faint smile.

'I am well enough now,' she replied quietly. 'Tell me what is troubling you.'

Eadulf began, slowly at first and then having to fight hard to keep his voice from cracking with emotion as he recounted the narrow attitude of Abbot Cild.

Fidelma lay quietly, listening to the story. She did not interrupt for Eadulf was excellent when it came to recounting events without missing any detail.

Her face was grim as he ended his narrative.

'So I am to be sacrificed to the fears of this strange abbot? Cild is his name?'

'It won't come to that. I have a plan to get you away from here as soon as you feel up to it.'

Fidelma grimaced with a cynical humour.

'I think the idea of being ceremonially buried alive, face downward, has improved my health and motivation very rapidly.'

Eadulf looked sympathetic. 'The drawback is that while the snow no longer falls, the skies are clear which means the temperature is freezing outside. It will be a long walk whichever direction we go.'

Fidelma's mind was clearly elsewhere for she said: 'You are absolutely certain that you saw this woman, the one identified as Gélgeis?'

'Absolutely certain,' Eadulf said. 'She was as tangible and as real as you or me.'

'Then the obvious must be true. There is a real woman in this abbey. Has any search been conducted?'

Eadulf smiled indulgently as he shook his head.

'There is some hysteria here about ghosts. Only Brother Higbald, the apothecary, seems sane and treats the matter with any degree of rationality.'

'There is no chance of doing some investigation into this matter?' pressed Fidelma.

'None at all. Abbot Cild is not the best person to deal with. His authority seems absolute. He has already made up his mind on the matter.'

'I am not going to suffer for his fear and ignorance. But from what you say, there is a great mystery here, Eadulf. It is obvious that your friend Botulf had discovered some answer to the mystery, which was why he was killed.'

'Before this matter of the haunting came up, I was going to seek out Garb at Tunstall, where I think he will be hiding. He, or his father, may be able to provide some answers.'

Fidelma nodded approval. 'A good method of proceeding, Eadulf. I agree. I should soon be able to start to make inquiries myself.'

Eadulf looked embarrassed. He coughed nervously.

'What is it, Eadulf? Do you have something else on your mind?'

'I just want to say that you must remember that, apart from any other consideration, you are in the land of the Anglo-Saxons and, apart from the courtesy shown you at the Council of Whitby, the law does not recognise your authority.'

'I understand that.'

'I mean that women are not accorded the same place here as in your country, Fidelma. Be circumspect if you seek to question the people here. It is thought wrong for women to exert authority.'

Fidelma grimaced. 'I cannot pretend to be what I am not.'

'All I say is that you should be prudent.'

'If I am not, then I am sure that you will caution me.' She smiled brightly.

'Well, wisdom dictates that our first priority is to remove ourselves from the reach of Abbot Cild.'

'But you wish to resolve the mystery of the death of your friend?'

'I do,' asserted Eadulf with quiet vehemence.

'Then we shall do so. Now, if you can mix me some of your noxious brews to cure a sore throat and a headache, perhaps I will soon feel well enough to join you in this trip to Tunstall.'

Chapter Ten

The day passed in an agony of slowness for Eadulf. Fidelma rested and slept through most of it. From time to time, Eadulf paced the room in an attempt to relieve the tension he felt. Only the fact that Brother Higbald had shown him an escape route kept his frustration from boiling into uncontrollable rage. Brother Higbald and Brother Redwald were their only visitors during the course of the day. On these occasions Fidelma was awake but decided to feign sleep when they entered the room in order that her improved condition would not be reported to Abbot Cild.

Brother Redwald, who brought their meals, stayed only long enough to leave the steaming bowls of broth and plates of cold meats, cheeses and bread or to pick up the empty trays. Brother Higbald on his visit was more relaxed and forthcoming about what was happening in the abbey. He informed Eadulf that Abbot Cild was making preparations for the tribunal at which the charge of conjuring spirits was to be made against Fidelma. The abbot was going to be both prosecutor and judge. He had informed Brother Willibrod that he would give Fidelma only one more day to recover from her illness. After that, whatever her condition, she would be brought before him and the charges made. Brother Higbald was emphatic in his advice that they should leave as soon as possible.

Eadulf listened attentively, nodding agreement without

committing himself. Fidelma had advised Eadulf to keep his own counsel, trusting no one in the abbey, not even Brother Higbald. When Eadulf pointed out that he trusted Brother Higbald implicitly, Fidelma had reproved him.

'In such circumstances, you should trust no one. How do you know that he has not been sent by the abbot to provoke us into action?'

Eadulf accepted her advice, and when the apothecary pressed them as to what time Eadulf thought that they would depart, Eadulf was vague and pointed out that it would depend on when Fidelma had recovered.

For Eadulf, the night passed uncomfortably. He decided to stay once more in Fidelma's room, sleeping in the chair by the fire. He dozed in short restless periods but each time he awoke he saw that Fidelma was sleeping a comfortable sleep and her temperature was normal.

He finally awoke with a grey light seeping into the room. Dawn was late coming in winter and, by the sounds about him, the members of the abbey had already been at their devotions and work for some time. In fact, he heard the sounds of an unusual bustle and preparation. Then he realised what the day was. It was the Eve of Christ's Mass, the eve of the birth of the Saviour. He felt a sudden guilt that he had not given the date any thought before.

He rose anxiously and, to his surprise, he found Fidelma already washed and dressed.

'You must be careful,' he said without preamble. 'If Abbot Cild saw you now he would observe that you are fully recovered.'

'*Deo favente*, I am well,' smiled Fidelma. 'Do not worry. I think I am well enough to travel and so it is now time to test your escape route.'

Eadulf was about to go to the tapestry to show her the route when there was a deferential tap on the door and a moment later Brother Redwald entered. As usual he came bearing a tray of food.

His eyes widened a little in surprise when he saw Fidelma standing up and dressed.

'It is good to see you well, Sister,' he muttered awkwardly as he put down the tray.

'Brother Redwald, is it not?' Fidelma smiled gently at the youth. 'I am afraid that I have not been cognisant of things the last day or two but I remember your kindness when I arrived at this abbey.'

The boy coloured hotly.

'Sister, I confess that I have done you a disservice.'

'Brother Eadulf has told me that you merely reported what you saw in this room when you entered it the other day,' replied Fidelma. 'It is others who have misconstrued it, so there is no blame to you. Can you describe what it was that you actually saw?'

The boy shifted his weight and glanced towards Brother Eadulf.

'I told him—'

Fidelma interrupted with a slight gesture of her hand but she continued to smile.

'It is not the same as telling me. Describe what it was that you saw.'

'There is not much to add. I came into the room to see if there was anything I could bring you. You were lying asleep or in a fever. By the side of the bed, bending over you was a figure. It was that of a woman. As I entered, she straightened and turned towards me. She looked directly at me. I recognised her, for when I came to this abbey Abbot Cild's wife was alive. It was she. The lady Gélgeis who they said perished in the mire not far from here.'

Fidelma regarded him thoughtfully.

'How did she appear? I mean, was she as substantial as I am? You see, if she were truly a ghost, as everyone apparently believes, then surely she would have been a figure of ethereal quality. There would have to be something about her that was not of a temporal nature.'

The boy was quiet, reflecting.

'She was substantial, truly. But she was a ghost. What else could she be when she was dead? Anyway, it was clear that she was a ghost in spite of the substantialness.'

'How do you know that?'

'Because her face was ghastly white. Even in the flickering candlelight, her face was pale, white . . . Truly, she was not of this world.'

Fidelma pressed her lips together in thought. She realised that Brother Redwald was trembling slightly and she felt that it would not be wise to press him for further information. She was about to dismiss him when the sounds of hurrying footsteps halted outside the door. Brother Higbald opened the door and entered without knocking. He looked agitated. His eyes fell first on Sister Fidelma. He smiled and was about to say something when he noticed Brother Redwald.

'Go to your cell and I will meet you there in a moment. Hurry, do not delay.' His tone was curt.

Eadulf and Fidelma exchanged a glance of surprise.

'What is the matter?' demanded Eadulf, as the young boy hurried obediently away.

Brother Higbald paused, glancing after Brother Redwald, as if to make sure that he was out of earshot. Then he spoke softly and urgently, speaking directly to Fidelma first and then to Eadulf.

'Look to your safety, Sister Fidelma; look to your safety, Brother Eadulf.' His voice was filled with foreboding. 'Terrible news . . .'

'News? What news?' inquired Eadulf.

'Warriors of the East Saxons have landed on the shore,

not far away from here. Word has come that they are marching in this direction.'

Eadulf was dismissive. 'It is probably the men I encountered from the longship two days ago. There were but a few men. They can surely do you no harm?'

Brother Higbald was still worried.

'The news is that there are many longships and it may well be that they are Sigehere's men come to destroy all the Christian houses that give succour to his Cousin Sebbi. The word is that they are marching this way. Take my advice and look to your own safety now! You know what to do, Brother. I must go to prepare our own defence.'

He gave them one last pleading glance before leaving hurriedly.

Eadulf turned back to Fidelma. His face was anxious.

'This is bad news. But it might be to our advantage. I think we must do as he asks. Are you well enough to travel now?'

Fidelma hesitated and then nodded in silent agreement.

'I suggest that we leave immediately, before Abbot Cild claims that you have conjured an army of the East Saxons to fall on his abbey,' Eadulf said.

'Perhaps you are right.' Fidelma smiled softly. 'This does seem an appropriate time to make our departure.'

Eadulf grabbed the bread and cold meats which Brother Redwald had just brought them and thrust them into his bag. He uttered a small prayer of thanks for his wisdom in transferring his belongings to Fidelma's room while he was nursing her. He helped her put on her cloak and slung his own around his shoulders.

Her steps were unsteady in her weakness but Eadulf held out a hand to balance her. She steadied herself and looked questioningly at him.

'Now, where is this escape route? We would be spotted trying to leave the abbey any other way now that there is such an alarm.'

Eadulf went directly to the wall behind her bed and drew aside the tapestry.

Fidelma's eyes widened a little at the door which Eadulf pushed. It swung inwards.

'A secret tunnel?' she asked.

'It is supposed to lead to the outside.'

'And if our ghost is tangible, this is doubtless the way she came into this chamber and departed without being seen by anyone other than young Redwald.'

Eadulf had not given the matter a thought but realised that it was a logical deduction. But now they had no time for such contemplation.

They entered the tunnel. Just inside was a wooden shelf on which there was a tallow candle. Eadulf returned to the room to secure a light from the glowing embers of the fire and then rejoined her, drawing the tapestry down behind him and swinging the door shut. The dark stone tunnel was damp and musty and, as they moved cautiously along it, they heard the alarmed squeaking as mice scampered before them.

Eadulf realised that the tunnel was not a single one but part of a network which must cover the entire abbey. He was trying to concentrate on remembering the directions that Brother Higbald had given him. Had it been two turns to the right and one to the left or the reverse? He uttered a silent curse as he realised that he had forgotten. The only thing to do now was trust in luck. He dared not tell Fidelma that he had forgotten such simple instructions.

They came to an intersection, one way going right and one going left. Eadulf hesitated for a moment and turned right. The tunnel narrowed slightly. There was another intersection and he turned right again. It was damp now, the walls fairly dripping with moisture. Behind him he heard Fidelma coughing. This atmosphere was not going to be good for her after her bout of illness. He moved on as rapidly as he could.

'There's some light ahead,' came Fidelma's whisper from behind him. Eadulf had already seen a flickering glow. It was obviously torchlight which seemed to emanate from a side chamber. He turned quickly.

'We should proceed quietly,' he whispered. It was an unnecessary instruction.

They moved silently towards the chamber from which the light was coming and Eadulf halted before the open entrance. Stealthily he peered round. A torch lit a chamber beyond the archway. Thankfully, it was empty – empty of people, that is. There were benches and wooden pegs along one side of the wall from which hung an amazing array of shields, swords and lances. Eadulf took a step forward and regarded the warriors' accoutrements with bewilderment. They were all brightly polished and well kept.

'Curious,' he whispered.

Fidelma peered over his shoulder.

'Didn't someone say that this had been an old fortress before it became an abbey?' She spoke irritably, distracted by another bout of coughing.

'Torches do not burn for a hundred years, nor do weapons and shields keep their sheen,' Eadulf said reprovingly.

Fidelma was too concerned to get out of the damp atmosphere to be inclined to linger.

'Well, you told me that Abbot Cild was once a warrior. Perhaps he finds the habit hard to break. Let's move on. I am cold.'

'But the shields bear Iclingas images, and—' Eadulf's jaw clenched shut and he moved forwards into the chamber. He had caught sight of an object on the floor beneath a row of shields. It was a small dark leather purse of rectangular shape with a pattern branded on it which struck a distant chord in his memory. He reached forward and picked it up, noting that it had obviously been wrenched off someone's belt with a degree of violence for the leather thongs were stretched and torn.

'Merciful God!' he breathed as he examined it.

Fidelma stood impatiently at the door. 'What is it?'

He turned and held it out so that she could see it in the light. Burned onto the leather below the patterned symbol, probably by means of a red-hot needle or similarly pointed object, was a name. The name was 'Botulf'.

'It is empty,' she observed, quickly peering inside. 'What is your friend's purse doing here?'

Eadulf had been looking closely around the spot where he had found it. There were dark stains there. He followed a splattering of them to where some steps led upwards to be blocked by an old, wooden door, bolted on the inside.

Fidelma had recognised the stains.

'Blood. I think your friend Botulf might have met his death here?' she observed softly.

Eadulf shivered and not with cold. He was aware that she was coughing again.

'I'll wager that door leads through the crypt to the small courtyard by the chapel. Poor Botulf's body was found there. I'll keep this,' he said, putting the purse in his *sacculus*. 'We'd best move on. We can consider this matter later.'

The passage seemed to continue for ever and he was coming to the awful conclusion that he had mistaken the directions. Perhaps it had been two left turns after all, instead of two right? He was about to suggest that they turn back when he saw some light up ahead.

It was the end of the tunnel. The exit was covered with creepers. Trailing growths hung over it like a curtain. Eadulf had a little difficulty in pushing them aside, halting to draw back the foliage for Fidelma to squeeze though. Clearly no one had been through this way in some time.

Cautiously he moved forward. The dankness and cold of the passage had prepared them for the chill of the day outside. Although the sky was clear and blue, the snow lay like a crisp covering over every exposed place.

They had actually emerged twenty or so paces from the abbey walls, in the shelter of a hillock where trees provided a thin screen from watching eyes.

Eadulf peered cautiously round.

'Down!' he suddenly hissed.

Fidelma obeyed him without question.

Close by the south wall of the abbey were gathered half a dozen men. With them, seated on horseback, was a slim figure with long red hair. It appeared to be a girl. One of the men was talking to her. Then she raised her hand in acknowledgment and urged her horse forward, straight towards their hiding place. The track brought her very close to where they were concealed, but the black mare she was riding raced by without their being spotted. Eadulf was frowning as he gazed after her vanished form.

'What is it?' asked Fidelma, noticing his curious expression.

'I could swear that was the same woman I saw the other night – the one everybody is making such a fuss about.' He looked back towards the men by the abbey walls. 'I wonder what they are doing?'

Fidelma followed his gaze.

'Men from the abbey preparing for this Saxon attack?'

Eadulf shook his head.

'A strange place to set up a defensive position,' he said. 'Any attack from the sea is going to come from the east.' He paused and listened. There was no sound of any approaching warband, nor of any personal pursuit. He looked around cautiously. 'I am afraid that it is going to be a fair walk to Tunstall. I wish we could have procured some horses.'

Fidelma, feeling much better since leaving the dark, damp confines of the tunnels, was mischievous.

'I thought that you did not enjoy riding?'

Eadulf smiled briefly. Her humour was a sign that she was returning to her old self.

'I am worried for you. It is a long way to trudge through the cold snow in your condition.'

'Don't worry, Eadulf. It is true that I would prefer to be seated before a good fire with a hot drink but beggars cannot choose. The sooner we start, the sooner we will arrive.'

Eadulf nodded but he insisted on carrying both their travelling bags so that Fidelma would not be burdened with hers. They moved deeper into the woods and Eadulf tried to find tracks that were clear of snow and so would not leave a trail that could easily be seen by those wishing to pursue them. He kept a slow but steady pace but, even so, Fidelma had to rest now and then for her breathing was fast and shallow. It was obvious that she was not entirely recovered from the illness.

Picking his way carefully, Eadulf led the way through the forest and undergrowth. After some time he glimpsed what appeared to be a woodsman's cottage through the trees. It was a short distance above them on the slopes of the hill. A thin blue wisp of smoke was curling from the chimney. Although they had not come very far from the abbey, Eadulf felt it might be a suitable place for Fidelma to rest in comfort for a while.

He turned to Fidelma who was only just catching up with him.

'I am going to see if we can claim hospitality at that woodsman's hut,' he told her. 'Why don't you sit down on that log for a moment while I go up there?'

Fidelma sank down thankfully onto the log to recover her breath. She glanced up towards the hut.

'Aren't we too close to the abbey to rest for a while? If the abbey is attacked then the attackers may well march in this direction.'

Eadulf shook his head. 'I think we will be safe for a while yet.'

'I would prefer to put as much distance as possible between ourselves and the abbey, but . . .' She shrugged. She was too weak to argue with him.

Eadulf left her and made his way towards the woodsman's hut. From the outside it appeared deserted as there were no dogs or other animals about. But the wisp of smoke indicated there was a fire lit inside and where there was a fire there must be someone to stoke it. He walked confidently to the door. Then he saw a horse, still saddled, with its reins hitched to a nearby post. It was blowing a little as if it had just had a hard ride. It was a black mare.

He drew near and was about to raise his fist to the door to announce his presence when a scream stopped him. It was a female scream which ended in a peal of laughter. Then a voice, a woman's voice, began to speak. The words were punctuated with squeals and groans.

'Come, lover . . . oh, it is good . . . good . . . oh . . .'

It was obvious what was taking place inside and Eadulf dropped his arm. He felt a surge of embarrassment. Then he suddenly realised, with some shock, that the voice was speaking in the language of Éireann.

He hesitated, wondering what to do. Half of him

wanted to turn away and the other half of him was curious to know who was speaking in such a fashion.

He suppressed his embarrassment and moved cautiously along the wall to where he had seen a window. There was no glass in it and the piece of sacking was torn. He edged near and took a quick glance into the hut. Then, ascertaining that he was not being observed by those inside, he took a longer look, feeling like some heteroclite; like some perverted peeper.

He saw what he had expected to see: a man and woman making love. It seemed that the woman was more active than the man, talking and moaning all the time. She was young and slim, with a shock of reddish-blonde hair. Above her naked body was a thick-set man of middle age. The first thing that Eadulf noticed about him was that he wore the tonsure of St Peter. Then the man raised his face but, fortunately for Eadulf, his good eye was tight shut in his ecstasy. The other was still covered by its leather patch.

It was Brother Willibrod, the *dominus* of Aldred's Abbey.

Eadulf turned swiftly away, swallowing hard. He paused for a moment, gathering his breath, and then went back down the hill and through the woods to where Fidelma was patiently waiting.

'We will get no hospitality there,' he said shortly, responding to her questioning look. 'We should move on immediately.'

Fidelma saw his anxiety and did not press him with questions. Eadulf would tell her what disturbed him in his own good time.

They moved as fast as her ability allowed and it was not long before they found that their road, if they intended to proceed south to Tunstall, had to cross the River Alde. Fast flowing and icy cold, it was too deep to wade across. Eadulf had forgotten that, being denied the use of the bridge by the abbey, they would have to continue along the river bank until they came to a suitable ford, which might take them miles out of their way.

They had managed to walk a distance of what he judged to be a further two miles or so when Fidelma said: 'I am sorry, Eadulf, I must rest for a little while again.'

Eadulf could see that she was exhausted. He realised that they ought to find some shelter and soon. He stopped, and then was glad that he had halted, otherwise he might not have heard the sound. It was a creaking of wood, overlaid by a squeal of protest. Then a heavy snort.

'A heavy wagon,' commented Fidelma, whose hearing was acute.

'Wait here,' muttered Eadulf and moved hurriedly forward towards the track from which the sound was emanating. The track proved to be close by and led down to the river. A heavy-looking, four-wheeled wagon pulled by two mules came swaying along it, driven by a man in a leather jerkin. He had a ruddy face and heavy jowls. Seated by him was a second man with a swarthy complexion. The driver was easing the wagon down the incline towards the river with the obvious intention of crossing.

Eadulf seized the opportunity without thinking further. He stepped through the bushes almost into the path of the wagon.

'Good day, brothers!'

Startled, the driver heaved on the reins, bringing the vehicle to a halt. His companion's hand went to the knife in his belt. When they saw that they were being accosted by a religious, they both relaxed a little.

'Good day, Brother,' the driver said in a strangely accented voice.

Eadulf raised his voice so that Fidelma could hear him and would come to join him.

'Forgive me, brothers, but are you travelling southwards?'

'As you can see,' replied the driver. 'We are bound for the port of Gipeswic.'

'Ah,' smiled Eadulf. 'My companion is exhausted and our destination lies a few miles along your road. Is it possible that you might have room on your wagon? It would facilitate our crossing the river.'

The driver was frowning, a refusal forming on his lips. Eadulf heard Fidelma come up behind him. The driver suddenly relaxed and glanced at his companion who nodded briefly.

'There is room, indeed, Brother. We are merchants from Frankia. Forgive our wariness but it is said that outlaws throng these woods. Your companion seems to be from the land of Éireann.'

'How did you know?' Fidelma smiled weakly.

'By the cut of your robes, Sister. We come from Péronne where there is a community of Irish religious under their abbot named Ultan.'

Eadulf looked surprised. 'Ultan? Surely he is bishop at Ard Macha?'

Fidelma was indulgent in her explanation: 'It is a name given to any man from the kingdom of Ulaidh. But I know the Ultan you mean,' she said, turning to the Frankish merchants. 'He is brother to Fursa who once led a mission to this land of the East Angles.'

Eadulf's eyes widened a little. 'That Ultan still lives and is abbot in Frankia?'

The driver grinned. 'He was when we left six months ago to bring some trade to this land.' He turned to his companion. 'Get down, Dado, and help the good sister into the wagon. Have you travelled far, Brother?' This to Eadulf. 'Your companion looks tired and weak.'

'We have travelled some distance,' Eadulf replied ingenuously. 'We are most grateful for your charity.'

They climbed onto the wagon and seated themselves behind the driver, a man called Dagobert, and his companion Dado. Eadulf noticed the wagon was full of trade goods. Many were local items which he realised must have been swapped for the goods brought from Frankia.

'Have you had a successful journey, brothers?' inquired Eadulf as the wagon lurched forward, continuing down towards the river.

'There is little trade in this poor land, Brother,' the driver replied, as he cracked his whip over the heads of the mules.

'There seems a scarcity of gold and jewellery in your land,' added his companion, Dado. 'We brought some plate garnet and amethyst. Your smiths seemed to want our Frankish coin only to melt it down to use the gold.' Dado pursed his lips and made a spitting sound without actually spitting. 'The smiths here seem a poor lot. And the pottery production!' He raised his eyes heavenward. 'Many still seem to construct their vessels without a potter's wheel and bake it with an uneven firing by building nothing more elaborate than a bonfire over a stack of sun-dried pots. What do these people have to trade? We shall not be coming this way again.'

Eadulf felt a little uncomfortable at these merchants' assessment of his homeland.

'Surely there is trade to be gained in the manufacture of wool or weaving of cloth?' he demanded irritably.

'Better quality is to be had elsewhere. The people here are more a warrior people, living on subsistence farms,' replied the man. 'Even for the grinding of the corn they have to send for quernstones from Frankia. That is what we have brought across, lava quernstone and millstones to grind the grain of the Saxons. What is offered in return? Slaves? There are too many Anglo-Saxon slaves on the market. It was the discovery of such slaves in the markets in Rome which caused the blessed Bishop of Rome, Gregory, to send Augustine to the kingdom of Kent. There are still many parts of this land that are pagan, but Christian or pagan, the only export seems to be slaves.'

Eadulf compressed his lips sourly.

Fidelma, however, seized the opportunity to gain more knowledge from the gossip.

'I have heard that the East Saxons have gone back to their old gods,' she said.

Dado, who appeared to be the more talkative of the two once he had started, nodded immediately.

'We heard many stories when we first arrived at the port of Gipeswic. They say that King Sigehere was burning down all the Christian centres and rounding up the religious as slaves . . . those he does not kill, of course.'

'I was wondering if you had heard any news of a warband landing downriver?'

Dado whistled and glanced at Dagobert with a shake of his head.

'We have heard nothing. When was this?'

'This morning.'

'That is curious,' said Dado, frowning.

'Curious?' Fidelma pressed.

'An hour or so ago we had paused to take some refreshment when we met another traveller – a rider on horseback. He had come directly from the coast this morning and made no mention of any raid. But it is probably best that we are returning to our homeland. I suggest you do the same. This has proved an inhospitable land. Poverty, slaves and warfare. God speed our return to Frankia.'

'Amen to that, Dado,' muttered the driver.

Eadulf sat silently, a red flush on his cheeks. Something angered him about these strangers speaking of his country in such a manner. The trouble was that he could not think of any counter argument. His people were a warrior people who had swept through Europe guided by what they could seize at the point of the sword. Before the faith came, the greatest end that any one of them could meet was a death in battle, sword in hand, and the name of the god Woden on his lips.

It was less than one hundred years ago that Wuffa, son of Wehha, had led his people to this land and made himself the first King of East Anglia, driving the Britons westward. Ten kings had succeeded Wuffa, who was descended from Woden himself, from Casere the fourth son of the great god. Eadulf as *gerefa* could recite the eight generations between Woden and Wuffa. More, he could recite the ten generations that separated Wuffa from King Ealdwulf.

Wuffa's son Tytila who was killed in battle against Ceolwulf of Wessex; Redwald who became *bretwalda* or overlord of the Saxon kingdoms; Eorpwald who was murdered by his brother because he converted to Christianity; Ricbert the Pagan who met with an end that was uncertain; then Sigebert, Egric, Anna, and Athelhere who all died in battle, sword in hand. Then Athelwold who ruled for nearly eight years before Ealdwulf came to power. Normally, Eadulf would have been proud at the recitation of the kings of the East Angles. But he had travelled extensively and seen much and now he began to wonder if there was anything to be proud of in coming from a warrior nation that could offer no trade to others except a trade in slaves.

He shivered and drew his robe closer around him. Surely he had been too long in the five kingdoms of Éireann that he was now questioning the values of his own people? It was not so long ago that he, as a young man, would have been proud to grasp his sword and run into battle crying for the blessing of Woden, Thunor or Frig! But there are no footsteps that lead backwards. He had moved on and it was not merely his time outside his own land that made him question its values but the new faith itself. That was calling into question all the old ways; all the old values.

'You are quiet, Eadulf. Is anything wrong?'

He turned at Fidelma's soft whisper and forced an answering smile.

'Just thinking, that is all.'

The cart was moving slowly along the track; the mules were sure-footed and hardy beasts and had seemed to make light of pulling the heavy vehicle across the river.

'You were saying that you heard there were outlaws in the woods, my friend.' Eadulf suddenly addressed the driver, Dagobert. 'Have you heard stories of an outlaw called Aldhere?'

Dagobert inclined his head but it was his companion Dado who answered.

'We met with many who talked of this bandit, Aldhere,' he said. 'Thanks be to the Almighty that we did not encounter him, otherwise we would be returning home even poorer than we are at the moment – that is, if we had been in a condition to return home.'

'A fierce outlaw, then?' Eadulf pressed.

'Not so,' interrupted Dagobert before his companion could speak. 'My friend Dado neglects to tell you that we heard much talk but little bad said of him.'

'Little bad?' queried Eadulf. 'That is unusual, isn't it? Outlaws tend to be cursed by the local population.'

'Not this man,' said Dagobert.

'It seems that most people think he is a man unjustly outlawed,' Dado explained. 'The story goes that he was a brave warrior unjustly accused of cowardice who had to take to the marshes nearby to save his own life.'

'Was anything said about a brother of this outlaw?' Eadulf asked innocently.

'A brother?' Dado looked at his companion and shrugged.

'No brother was ever mentioned. Do you know some more of the story then, my friend?' inquired Dagobert.

Eadulf shook his head. 'I heard the same story as you have recounted but I thought I heard mention of a brother who played a role in ensuring that Aldhere fell under the King's displeasure.'

Dado sniffed. 'We did not hear that. In truth, we were only concerned that we did not fall foul of the outlaw and his band. There are many stories to pick up along the road. I suppose this is one of the pleasures of travelling. Every traveller has a fascinating tale to tell.' Dado suddenly looked at them with a sly smile. 'Take yourselves. A Saxon religieux and a woman from the land of Éireann travelling in this wild place on foot. Now you must have a story to tell, surely?'

Eadulf immediately shook his head but Fidelma gave a low laugh and entered into the spirit of the moment.

'There is a story, indeed, Dado of Frankia,' she said. 'But our journey needs must be a long one in order to accomplish the telling of it.'

The man's face was full of disappointment.

'Surely you can give us some idea of the nature of this tale?'

Fidelma dropped her voice to a confidential tone.

'It is a story of a king's sister and her lover who run away to seek happiness in a strange and frightening land . . .'

The man's eyes widened, and his mouth opened a little.

'Go on, go on,' he whispered. 'It sounds a good tale and great in the telling of it.'

'Indeed, for they are pursued in this strange land by both men and phantoms, and they travel quickly under constant threat . . .'

'A tale, indeed,' rejoiced Dado, who was clearly a romantic as well as a gossip. 'Tell us more . . .'

'Well . . .'

'Well,' intervened Eadulf in harsh disapproval, 'it must be left to your imaginings for this is where we must alight. God's blessing on your charity, my friends; our thanks for giving us the comfort of your wagon for part of our journey. It would have taken some hours to reach this spot on foot in these treacherous snowbound conditions.'

Dagobert halted the wagon and looked around with surprise.

'There is nothing but thick forest in all directions here, Brother. Are you sure that this is where you want to be left? You have but an hour of daylight left and we mean to halt and make camp for the night soon.'

'Aye, stay and continue your story,' urged Dado.

Eadulf shook his head firmly. 'Our destination is not far from here and we must reach it before darkness falls.'

Dado looked disappointed. 'If you are sure . . . ?'

Eadulf was already out of the wagon, having thrown down the travelling bags, and turned to help Fidelma alight from the vehicle.

After thanking their Frankish hosts, they stood by the side of the track watching the wagon swaying through the tree-lined path, disappearing out of sight between the wintry evergreens.

Fidelma looked around at the darkening woods and shivered slightly.

'I hope that you are right, Eadulf, when you say we

have not far to go. Are you sure that this is where you want to be?' she asked. 'You were not making an excuse to leave our inquisitive friends? I could have spun a story to keep them amused.'

Eadulf looked hurt. 'I do not doubt that you could have told them some story. However, this is Tunstall Wood and this is where Aldhere says that there is a community of religious from the five kingdoms of Éireann, still hiding out after the edict from Whitby. If anyone knows where Garb and his family are hidden, I am sure we will find them here.'

'Let us hope so, for as our friend Dado said, it will soon be dark and darkness brings a weakness upon me. I probably should have rested for another full day to complete my recovery.'

Eadulf was painfully aware of the fact and was trying his best not to show his concern for Fidelma because he realised that she would disapprove of it.

'If I remember the old place, it is less than a mile in that direction,' he said, pointing along the track.

The woods were so thick that little snow had lain on the paths that crisscrossed them. Some memory, some instinct, drew Eadulf along the track, crossing paths that might have tempted them in other directions and maintaining a south-easterly course through the woods.

They stopped now and then, for Fidelma was growing increasingly uncomfortable in the night chill. The journey through the woods was not easy. They could hear animals scuttling around them and now and again came the staccato bark of foxes. The path came upon a stream and led along its bank, around a large hillock on which stood the overgrown earthworks of some ancient fort. It was almost concealed, with brush and trees growing over it.

Abruptly they came to the edge of a clearing. In the

clearing were several wooden buildings and smoke was rising from a number of them.

Eadulf turned to Fidelma with triumph, although a closer observer might have noticed a predominance of relief in his eyes.

'Tunstall. This is Tunstall. We have reached safety.'

Fidelma, her breath almost gone in the icy cold dusk of early evening, simply nodded.

There came a warning shout across the clearing. They had been spotted. Several men emerged from the buildings, most clad in the robes of religious and most wearing the tonsure of the Blessed John.

As Eadulf and Fidelma began to walk across the clearing towards what Eadulf presumed was the main building of the settlement, Eadulf noticed a small group of warriors. They were clearly not Saxons and Eadulf felt a surge of relief as he realised that he had been right. He did not doubt that these were Garb's men. He felt a quickening of his pulse as he thought that soon the mystery of the death of his friend Botulf might be explained.

He halted, for one of the warriors had given a cry and was running towards him with an upraised sword.

A religious was also running forward as if to intercept the warrior, who skidded to a halt a sword's length away. To his surprise, Eadulf saw that his antagonist was Garb himself.

'Stand back, Brother,' Garb cried in Irish to the religieux, who had come to a halt next to him and was looking bewildered. 'This man is one of Cild's evil brood. I recognise him. He was in Cild's abbey when I delivered the ultimatum. It means that murdering abbot has tracked us down. Stand back while I kill them, and then we must be prepared to abandon this place.'

Chapter Eleven

'Put up your sword, Garb of Maigh Eo! We are not members of Abbot Cild's fraternity,' snapped Eadulf.

Garb sneered in disbelief. 'I saw you among the brethren, Saxon. You are a liar!'

'He does not lie!' Eadulf suddenly found Fidelma had stepped between him and the Connacht warrior, her hand raised, palm outward. 'I am Fidelma of Cashel. Put up your sword, Garb. You would not wish to kill innocent people!'

Garb had actually started to swing his sword back and now he hesitated, momentarily confused.

'I said, put up your sword,' ordered Fidelma once again, 'unless you wish to kill an advocate of the Laws of the Fénechus and a king's daughter.'

The warrior examined her closely with narrowed eyes. Then he slowly began to lower his sword.

'You say that you are Fidelma of Cashel?' It was the religieux at his side who spoke. 'Are you Fidelma the *dálaigh*, the advocate who solved the mysterious theft of the High King's sword?'

'I am Fidelma the *dálaigh*,' she confirmed without embellishment.

The religieux now regarded her with an expression of surprise mingled with awe. He was a man of middle years, his grey hair shaven in the style of the Irish tonsure. His face was still handsome, commanding, with dark eyes and a firm mouth.

'Are you Fidelma, sister to King Colgú?'

'I am.'

'What are you doing here, in this place, and with this Saxon?' demanded Garb gruffly. His sword was lowered but still held in his hand. 'I saw him in the abbey run by Cild only two nights ago. How is it that he claims not to be one of Cild's men?'

'I was also in that abbey, Garb,' she said to him. 'Brother Eadulf is my companion and emissary of Archbishop Theodore of Canterbury. We were guests there, having just arrived that night. I was ill and Brother Eadulf here was attending the funeral rites of his friend, Brother Botulf, when you made your unorthodox entrance.'

Garb frowned suddenly. 'Was Botulf your friend?'

'He was a friend of Brother Eadulf,' confirmed Fidelma. 'So perhaps you should think with your head instead of with your sword hand.'

Garb was still suspicious.

'What are you doing here? Did Cild send you?'

Fidelma gave an impatient gesture with her hand.

'He did not. We became prisoners in the abbey. Cild planned my execution and we thought it wise not to wait for it. Because of the remarks about Botulf which you made to Cild in the abbey chapel, Brother Eadulf and I came in search of you. You are not hard to find.'

The religieux came forward with hands outstretched, ignoring the petulant warrior.

'I am Brother Laisre. I am leader of this small religious group here and I would bid you welcome, Fidelma of Cashel. Welcome to Tunstall. I welcome your companion also. Let us go in by the fire so that we may hear your story and why your footsteps have been guided here.'

They followed Brother Laisre to one of the wooden buildings, with Garb following, his sword now sheathed, although he still regarded Eadulf menacingly. The warmth in the building was a welcome contrast to the chill of the dusk outside. It was clear that the early evening meal was being prepared for several religieux were busy about various tasks and there was an aromatic smell emanating from a steaming cauldron of stew which simmered over the fire.

'You will be our guests here for as long as you like, Fidelma of Cashel,' said Brother Laisre, smiling. He turned to Eadulf and began to translate what he had said into Saxon but Eadulf sniffed impatiently.

'I have studied in the island of the five kingdoms,' he said brusquely. 'I speak your language fluently.'

Brother Laisre looked relieved.

'It is good to have a language in common,' he observed, indicating that they should be seated.

Fidelma was glancing round, noting the small *scriptorum* at the far end of the room. In fact, the building seemed to act as a general refectory and library for the entire community.

'I am surprised to find that there is still a community in this land which cleaves to the rituals of our Church, Brother Laisre,' she commented. 'I thought that after the decision of Whitby whereby the Angles and the Saxons opted to follow the Rule of Rome, all our clergy had departed from these lands.'

Brother Laisre grimaced humorously. 'Some of us made the decision not to give in without trying to save some of our principles. Oh, I know after Whitby, Abbot Colman led many of the Irish missionaries and those Angles and Saxons who were of like mind to the island of the white cow – Inis Bó Fin – off the coast of Connacht. Some of them – mostly the Angles and Saxons – set up another centre on the mainland which is called "Maigh Eo of the Saxons". But we refused to follow Colman and retreat from this land and accept the defeat of our cause. So here we remain – missionaries from the five kingdoms – trying to spread the great truth.'

He turned and regarded Brother Eadulf's tonsure, the tonsure of Peter, which indicated his acceptance of the Roman Rule.

'I see that you, Brother, do not follow our path?'

Eadulf shrugged. 'Not in all specifics. But there is more to unite us than the little which divides us. Like Sister Fidelma, I was in attendance at the great council at Whitby. If we believe in the one God, then there is room for all our ways of worship.'

Brother Laisre frowned briefly. 'I would not agree with that. Had I thought that the revisions of the faith made by the bishops of Rome were right then I would no longer dwell in this inhospitable land but take me back to my own green valleys by the great river An tSiona.'

Fidelma cleared her throat. She did not want to get sidetracked into arguments of theology and liturgy.

'I presume that this is where Gadra, the chieftain of Maigh Eo, will be carrying out the *troscud*?'

Garb started forward. 'How . . . ?' His eye fell on Eadulf and he relaxed then. 'I see. You are clever, Fidelma.'

Fidelma shook her head.

'It was Brother Eadulf who made the deduction. The point is, does your father Gadra realise that Cild does not even respect the laws of his own people and is far less likely to respect the laws of our people? He would be throwing his life away unnecessarily.'

Garb pushed out his lower lip and half nodded.

'My father is a stubborn man who cannot conceive of such a thing.'

'I would speak with him.'

'You may, but he is resting now. First, I would want

to know what brought you into this affair. You say it was something to do with Brother Botulf?'

'That is so,' agreed Fidelma. 'But the story is Eadulf's and I am sure that he will have no objection to the telling of it.'

Eadulf agreed. 'I have none, providing that we can exchange some information. Do we agree that there is some evil mystery at the abbey of Aldred?'

'There is one evil there,' said Garb curtly. 'That is the Abbot Cild.'

'The abbot seems to be a man of extreme opinions and actions,' Fidelma intervened, 'but whether this constitutes evil is a point which we may later consider.'

Brother Laisre snorted. 'I think there is no question about his evil. Cild has been responsible for hanging two of my brethren whom he took captive. He had them executed as heretics to the faith – or rather to his particular interpretation of the faith.'

Fidelma's eyes widened a little.

'We agree,' broke in Eadulf, 'that Cild is a harsh man. You have only to ask the brother of his own blood what his opinion is. But we need information, as I have said before. I came to the monastery because I received a message from the friend of my youth, Brother Botulf, but when I arrived I found that he had been murdered. In the chapel, the other night, you seemed to imply that Abbot Cild had murdered Botulf. Why?'

Garb glanced at Brother Laisre and then he sighed.

'You say that you are Brother Botulf's friend? I would hear what you have to impart and then I will tell you what we know.'

Eadulf exchanged a look with Fidelma, who gestured her approval.

'We must begin somewhere,' she said. 'Information for information.'

Briefly, though not sparing the important details, Eadulf recounted why they had made the journey to Aldred's Abbey and what had befallen them there, including his dealings with the outlaw brother of the abbot.

When Eadulf ended his narration, Brother Laisre suggested that they continue over bowls of hot stew. When they were seated round the table, it was Garb who now commenced his story.

'Three summers have passed since my family came to know Cild. He was one of a number of Saxon brothers who came to study at the religious house of Maigh Eo, the Plain of the Yew, where my father Gadra is chieftain. He was not like the other religious that I have known. He was more like a warrior, angry, aggressive and demanding.'

Garb paused as if gathering his thoughts into some order.

'We were not too interested in him until he began to impress my younger sister, Gélgeis. She became besotted by him.'

Fidelma leaned forward. 'You do not say that she fell in love with him. How old was Gélgeis?'

Garb glanced at her. 'Oh, she was over the age of choice, if that is what you are asking. She was also determined. She was as stubborn as my father is stubborn. My father and I tried to dissuade her from marrying Cild. Even my sister, Mella, tried to discourage her. But Gélgeis was totally intoxicated by Cild. No, I do not say that she loved the man. I believe she was mesmerised by him. Before we could do anything further, she and Cild had left to come to this country.'

'Do I then presume that you also believed that Cild was not in love with your sister?'

'Cild is capable of many emotions,' replied Garb. 'I do not think love can be numbered among them. He wanted my sister for the material benefits which he thought he would gain. He did not fully appreciate our laws. He thought that once he was married, my father would set him up with wealth and position.'

'But Cild came here and achieved a position as abbot.'

'A poor abbot at that. However, my father saw the finality of my sister's situation and so sent word to Gélgeis that he had forgiven her for breaking his heart by running off with the Saxon. But there would be no dowry and Cild would not be welcome in Maigh Eo. Thereafter only two messages came from Gélgeis over the next year.'

Eadulf was interested. 'Messages? By whom were they sent?'

'By a religieux named Brother Pol. As Brother Laisre mentioned earlier, the community of Maigh Eo is called "Maigh Eo of the Saxons". There is much contact between Maigh Eo and some of the Saxon religious. Gélgeis knew how to cut the Ogham and send her message on hazel wands so that few outside our circle would know what she had to say.'

'And what did she have to say?' Fidelma pressed.

'The first message told us that Cild had been elevated to become abbot of Aldred's Abbey and that she and he were living there. She said that she was happy but very homesick.'

He paused for a moment.

'It was the way she worded the message that made us think that she was not being entirely honest and that she was unhappy with her life. The second message confirmed our anxieties. She was unhappy but she did not explain why. But Brother Pol told us that he thought Cild was treating her badly for he had noticed the searing wound of a whip on her arm. We asked Brother Pol to contact Gélgeis and bring further messages on his next trip.'

Fidelma's eyes widened a little. 'You did not think the news of her unhappiness was enough to bring one of your family to escort Gélgeis back home?'

Garb looked uncomfortable. 'My father felt that brother Pol's intermediacy was sufficient. But we did not hear from him again and after many months we decided to ask Brother Laisre here to make contact with her . . .'

'Just a minute,' Fidelma interrupted. 'How did you know Brother Laisre?'

It was the Irish religieux who answered.

'Brother Pol, the intermediary who took Gélgeis's messages to Maigh Eo, had told Gadra about our little group here in Tunstall. So Gadra communicated with me to see if I could make contact with Gélgeis and ascertain what was happening. At the same time he was anxious to learn the reason why he had not heard from Brother Pol.'

'And did you contact Gélgeis?'

'I tried, and that was when I discovered that Gélgeis was dead.'

'One thing I would like to ask,' intervened Eadulf. 'You must know all the Irish in this area. Who is the young woman of Éireann with the red-gold hair who dwells close by the abbey?'

Brother Laisre looked blank. 'A young woman with red-gold hair? I know of no such woman of our people in the land of the South Folk.'

Eadulf was surprised. He had told Fidelma on the journey what he had seen at the woodsman's hut.

'Perhaps she is a newcomer?' suggested Fidelma.

Brother Laisre shook his head. 'I would know of such a newcomer from our land and, if the truth be told, Sister, she would not long escape attention.'

Fidelma sighed. 'Very well. I think, however, that you need to provide us with more details about your contact with Gélgeis. How did you set about getting in touch with her?'

'She was dead by the time I tried to do so,' explained Brother Laisre. 'I went to the abbey disguised as a merchant and, by chance, it was Brother Botulf who spoke with me. I knew him before this nonsense decided at Whitby which has caused the split between us. He was a sympathetic man. It was from him that I learned that Gélgeis had, as her father and brother believed, grown unhappy. Cild was a vain and cruel man. He was unfit to be an abbot. Botulf said the girl had wandered into the marsh.'

'Did Brother Botulf give any details of her death?' Fidelma pressed.

'No. He gave no details. Just that she had wandered into the marsh and that Cild was responsible. Those were his very words. Cild was responsible. There can be no interpretation to be placed on it other than murder. He told me that the body was lost in Hob's Mire, an evil swamp of a place not far from the abbey. He said there was no use searching the quagmire for her body. He asked me to send word to her family that they should assume their daughter was dead to them.'

'And Brother Pol had not returned with messages to Maigh Eo because he was one of the brothers Abbot Cild had hanged for not submitting to the Rule of Rome?' Eadulf was incredulous.

Brother Laisre simply nodded.

'Not long after my meeting with Botulf,' he continued, 'Cild declared the abbey a closed house for the brethren believing in his rules. He drove several of the brethren out of the abbey. Some of them came here and joined me.'

Eadulf was eager. 'Did you speak to Botulf again?'

'Indeed, these events took place a few months ago. The messenger that I had sent to Maigh Eo had taken a long time reaching the sanctuary of Gadra's fortress. His ship had been wrecked on the island of Mannanán Mac Lir, which lies between here and the land of Éireann. He was some time in finding a vessel to continue his journey. Gadra finally sent word back that he was coming here to seek reparation . . .'

Here Garb intervened.

'My father is from the line of the kings of the Uí Briúin, kings of Connacht. He is a chieftain in whom the blood of the High King Niall of the Nine Hostages runs. He is proud and stubborn. Gélgeis is of his blood. He therefore determined to come to this strange land and seek reparation from Cild.'

Fidelma pulled a sceptical face. 'The *troscud*.'

'Aye, lady, the *troscud*,' Garb replied firmly.

'Truly,' Eadulf put in, 'your father must have loved his daughter with great emotion to embark on this course.'

'He loved her as only a father loves,' agreed Garb. 'But we are also bound by honour as well as love and the *troscud* is our court of last resort. By the ritual fast we seek justice when our enemies are too powerful and arrogant to give it of their own volition.'

'One thing that intrigues me, and forgive me for asking, but, as you perceive, I am a foreigner in these matters. What manner of person was your sister?'

Garb regarded Eadulf with some perplexity.

'I do not know if I have understood your question, Saxon.'

'I mean her temperament. Was her nature so unusual that her father, and perhaps yourself and your warriors, might give their lives willingly in her memory?'

Fidelma was slightly puzzled. She thought that Eadulf had understood the essence of the *troscud* and was wondering why he asked this question. Something made her realise that it was for a purpose.

Garb was not annoyed at the question. He smiled indulgently.

'Gélgeis was my favourite sister. She brought tranquillity to any situation. She made a grey day fair, made the storm peaceful, made the troubled blithe of spirit. She was possessed of such a nature that she brought happiness to all who knew her.'

Eadulf blinked, thinking of Brother Willibrod's words. Garb's words sounded almost glib. While he hesitated, Fidelma took up the questions again.

'Is there no dissuading your father from the course on which he has embarked? You must see that it will mean nothing to a man of Cild's culture and, especially, to a man like Cild. Your father will simply be allowed to die. Cild – indeed, any Saxon not used to our ways – might simply regard the *troscud* as a joke.'

'My father believes in the old ways and is determined.'

'I will speak to him, for he must be dissuaded,' replied Fidelma.

'You will speak to him in vain.'

Eadulf was sitting staring ahead of him, his eyes unfocused as he turned over the facts and the differing pictures of Gélgeis that had been presented to him.

'Brother Laisre, have you spoken to Botulf again? More recently?' asked Fidelma.

'A few weeks ago. That was when Gadra, together with Garb and his men, arrived here. I contacted Botulf and explained matters to him.'

'How did Botulf react to your news?'

Brother Laisre glanced uncomfortably at Garb.

'To be truthful, Brother, he shared your feelings that it was a waste of time. I explained the meaning of the *troscud* to him and he felt that no Saxon would truly understand its intent. I explained how Garb would have to come to the abbey to announce the start of the ritual and he promised to help.'

'Did he?'

'Oh yes. He managed to get Garb in to see the abbot on his own. That was a preliminary contact to ensure the abbot knew what was to take place. Cild laughed at Garb.'

'Did Botulf warn you that this would be Cild's reaction?'

'Botulf said he was fearful . . . fearful for the relatives of Gélgeis. He said that there was an old saying of the Saxons – woe to him who is in a country where there is none to take his part.'

'So he advised against the *troscud*?'

'His advocacy was strong but I could only act as an intermediary. I told him the time and day that Garb would present himself at the abbey for the official announcement. We agreed that it would be on the tolling of the midnight Angelus bell when the brethren had been summoned to prayers in the abbey chapel. The announcement had to be made before the community.'

'And it turned out to be the hour of Botulf's funeral,' muttered Eadulf.

Fidelma was thoughtful. 'So Botulf knew that this would happen at the precise hour that it did?'

'Indeed he did.'

'No other words were exchanged?'

'He mentioned that he knew that a friend of his was at Canterbury who knew something of the laws of both our peoples. He was going to send for that friend to come to the abbey.'

Eadulf's shoulders slumped. 'That was myself. I received the message from him asking me to be at the abbey before that time and on that day. Sister Fidelma and I arrived – but Botulf had already been slain.'

'Did Botulf provide you with any other facts concerning Gélgeis's death?' Fidelma asked.

Brother Laisre shook his head.

'What worries me,' Eadulf intervened reflectively, 'and I say this with all sincerity, is the lack of basis in law for any accusation to be made against Cild. Suspicion does not make for fact.'

Garb turned angrily on Eadulf.

'Do you seek to defend Cild?'

'Remember, I was the friend for whom Botulf sent. I seek what we should all be seeking. That is the truth. So far as I can see, we have only suspicion. We suspect that the lady Gélgeis met her death by foul means. We suspect that it was her husband, Cild, who encompassed that death. But so far, I have not been offered proof, only hearsay. The *gerefa* in me cries out for evidence.'

Brother Laisre stared at Eadulf aghast.

'Cild's reputation goes before him. He is evil. He is responsible for many deaths . . .'

'A reputation does not make a man guilty. Nor does the fact that he is known to have killed others in the name of his religion make him guilty of the murder of Gélgeis.'

Fidelma, seeing the anger on their faces, intervened quickly.

'Hurtful as it may sound to you, who believe that Cild is guilty, my comrade has a point. A belief is not evidence in law.'

'Cild's reputation is black. Doesn't the old saying go that every colour will take black but black will take no colour?'

'In other words, the cow with the longest horns will always be accused of butting,' pointed out Eadulf with cynicism.

'Truly,' Fidelma sighed, 'you are embarked on a bitter course of vengeance.'

'Sometimes, *dálaigh*,' replied Garb, 'there is little between justice and injustice but much between justice and law.'

'Is it not better to get more facts about what happened to your sister before this course is undertaken?' demanded Fidelma. 'Just as we must also find out what happened to Botulf?'

'We know the hand that struck down both Gélgeis and Botulf,' Garb said firmly.

Fidelma glanced at Eadulf and shook her head warningly. It was useless to pursue the matter of evidence among people intent on vengeance.

'Brother Botulf was a kindly and generous man,' Brother Laisre was saying. 'We would have had a good ally in him. I had already gathered that Botulf was at the abbey because of a punishment decreed by King Ealdwulf and that there was little love lost between him and Cild. I trusted Botulf. I fear his involvement with us was the cause of his death.'

'The abbot must have found him out and slaughtered him as he had slaughtered others,' Garb added. 'Evil walks with him and in him and he must pay for it.'

'Well spoken, my son,' came a new voice, quiet and firm. 'But it shall be done within the law.'

They turned towards the door.

An elderly man stood there. His features showed a resemblance to the younger man, Garb. He was tall, firm-jawed in spite of his advancing years. On his shock of white hair sat a silver circlet showing his rank. His eyes were deep blue, almost violet. His mouth was thin but firm. The graven lines on his face spoke of grief and suffering. He was dressed with the finery that bespoke his chieftainship.

There was little need to have him identified as Gadra, chief of Maigh Eo.

They stood respectfully as the man walked forward and sat down at the table.

'There are strangers among us, Brother Laisre. Perhaps you will be good enough to introduce your guests to me?'

Brother Laisre inclined his head.

'This is Brother Eadulf, emissary of the Archbishop Theodore of Canterbury, who travels with Fidelma of Cashel.'

The old chieftain's eyes showed that he recognised the name.

'Fidelma, sister of King Colgú of Cashel? Your fame as a *dálaigh* and dispenser of justice precedes you, Fidelma. My heart rejoices to see you here, for you may guide me in matters of law. I am about to undertake a course that may lead to serious consequences.'

'Father,' Garb cleared his throat nervously. 'Sister Fidelma has already been acquainted with the facts of the action you are about to undertake.'

The old man inclined his head.

'That is good. I do not wish to die in a foreign land with my name unrecorded and my fate unknown, and yet I fear it may be so. Yes, I do fear it.'

Eadulf shook his head slowly. He thought that most of the time he knew and understood these people. But it was at times like these that he came face to face with the fact that they were of an entirely different culture. This matter of the *troscud*, of ritual fasting to death to obtain one's rights, to obtain justice, was alien to him. In his culture, if a person wanted to obtain rights they did not harm themselves; they took their sword and forced their antagonist to give them what they wanted. To ritually starve to death just to shame their enemy was a bizarre concept. He would never understand it.

'Are you truly set upon this path, Gadra?' Fidelma

asked softly. 'Is there no other way of seeking the truth than by the *troscud*?'

Gadra smiled with humour. 'The ritual began when my intention was announced. The words have left my son's mouth and cannot be returned to it.'

Garb nodded slowly. 'If my father dies during the *troscud* and Abbot Cild has not come to arbitration and confessed his guilt, then the shame is his and he is cursed in this life and the next. Any man may slay him with impunity. I shall be that man, and if I am not, then my clansmen will see that retribution is taken.'

'The people of this country will not see the justice in that,' Eadulf pointed out.

'But the people in my country will,' replied Garb with equanimity.

'I would still want to find the truth by some other means than this,' Eadulf said stubbornly.

The old chieftain turned to him, his eyes sparkling.

'There is nothing stopping you. You may proceed in your way but do not seek to prevent me proceeding in mine.'

Fidelma nodded solemnly. 'No one will do that, Gadra.' She glanced warningly at Eadulf and continued. 'But as for seeking the truth by any other means, the problem is that all the witnesses as to what exactly happened to Gélgeis are dead.'

'Save for the very man who killed her. May her shade haunt him to his grave,' snapped Garb.

Eadulf jerked his head up. His eyes widened.

'Haunt?' he exclaimed. 'What makes you say that?'

Garb laughed outright.

'Do not tell me that your people are afraid of spirits from the Otherworld? If so, may the abbot share that fear for then I will rejoice if the shadows cause him to look twice to each corner of the room, or down each dark corridor that he traverses.'

Eadulf saw Fidelma shake her head so slightly that no one else noticed the gesture. She stood up and stretched uncomfortably.

'I am afraid that I must beg your forgiveness.' She smiled around the assembled company. 'I would like to find a bed to rest for this night. It is not that the hour grows late but I am still weak from the days of illness that caused my confinement in the abbey.'

Brother Laisre moved forward with concern on his features.

'Of course, Sister. But have you forgotten what night this is? At midnight we celebrate the birth of the Christ child.'

Fidelma looked embarrassed. She had forgotten that it was the eve of Christ's Mass.

'If I may lie down until it is time to celebrate . . . ?'

'Even in our poor circumstances, dwelling in these woods, we have made a little guests' hostel,' Brother Laisre replied with dignity. 'Allow me to instruct one of the brethren to take you there and see that the fire has been adequately prepared.'

Fidelma glanced at Gadra.

'You will excuse me, Gadra of Maigh Eo?'

'Rest well,' the elderly man replied gravely. 'We will talk further in the morning.'

She was moving to the door when a thought struck her and she turned back.

'There is one thing that occurs to me before I retire, Brother Laisre. I presume that you will be in touch with the abbey to let the abbot know of the progress of the *troscud*. It seems to me that unless he knows and is informed of the progress of the ritual it would have little effect. Who replaces Brother Botulf as your contact within the abbey?'

It was Gadra who answered.

'You have a sharp mind, Fidelma, as befits a *dálaigh* of your standing. A means of communication was opened up through the apothecary of the abbey. He has agreed to keep the abbot informed.'

'The apothecary? Brother Higbald?' Eadulf was surprised. 'And how is he told?'

'We have a number of brothers who take it in turn to watch the abbey and leave messages at a prearranged spot where this apothecary can pick them up or, indeed, leave messages for us if he feels it necessary.'

Fidelma was thoughtful.

'How did Brother Higbald come to agree to act as your new intermediary?' she asked.

'Two days ago, the abbot led a party out into the marshes,' Garb said. Then he smiled. 'Not long afterwards one of the abbey brethren set out alone on a mule in the direction they had taken. We were going to waylay him . . .'

Eadulf looked astonished and was about to identify himself as the lone rider when Garb continued.

'Then we saw another member of the brethren following. It turned out to be Brother Higbald. He turned in the same direction. My men and I waylaid him instead. We did so as soon as he was in the shelter of the woods . . . I hasten to say that we stopped him at swordpoint otherwise I doubt whether our conversation would have been very fruitful.'

'He had no prior knowledge of the task you wanted him to fulfil for you?' asked Eadulf with interest, wondering why Higbald was following him from the abbey.

'None. In fact, we argued for a little while as to whether he would do it. He finally agreed when he saw that it was better to have some information than no information at all.'

'What was agreed?'

'That in a hollow tree, in a certain spot by the abbey walls, a message would be left recording the day the *troscud* started and counting each day of the ritual until Cild came to arbitration or . . .'

Garb shrugged and looked at his father under lowered brows.

'Until I die!' snapped the old chieftain angrily. 'Do not be ashamed to say it.'

'Does Cild know of the role that Higbald plays?'

'Higbald only agreed to this provided Cild remained unaware of his contact with us. It was up to him to explain how he obtained the information.'

'And what if Higbald betrays this hollow tree where the messages are left to Cild? What if Cild has armed followers waiting to catch the man who leaves the messages?' demanded Eadulf.

Garb grimaced wryly. 'It is possible, I suppose. But again, such a course of action would bring shame on Cild and on Higbald. In our culture, it would be unheard of . . . however, my friend, we are not fools entirely.'

Eadulf looked puzzled and Garb explained: 'Our man will be watching the abbey carefully and ensure that he goes to the tree to leave his message when there is no threatening danger.'

Fidelma was looking suddenly alert.

'Tell me, is someone watching the abbey now?'

Garb nodded. 'We have had the abbey under surveillance since the pronouncement of the ritual.'

'When does your man get replaced?'

'They stay there from sunrise to sunset and then a second man stays from sunset to sunrise. It is quite simple.'

'The person who has been watching the abbey all today, when does he come back to Tunstall?'

Brother Laisre was bewildered at her eagerness.

'He has been back half an hour. Why?'

'And what has he to report?' Fidelma was almost waspish with impatience.

'Nothing. What should he report?'

'Nothing?' Fidelma was incredulous.

Eadulf was nervous at her change of tone and could not understand what was irritating her.

'Well,' he offered in placation, 'there would not be anything to report until the ritual started, would there?'

He realised that Fidelma was looking pityingly at him. Everyone else was bewildered.

'Think, Eadulf, think! What made us follow the escape route that Brother Higbald showed you and flee from the abbey this morning?'

'To avoid Abbot Cild's trumped-up trial of you for sorcery,' began Eadulf.

Fidelma's impatience was undisguised.

'No, the abbey was supposed to be in a panic. We were brought the news that a Saxon warband had landed on the coast not far away and were marching on the abbey. Now that would surely be something for your man to report, wouldn't it, Brother Laisre?'

Garb was at the door calling for someone by name. A tired-looking brother entered and glanced round in bewilderment.

'You were watching Aldred's Abbey from sunrise today?' demanded Garb.

The man nodded. 'Until I was relieved at sunset by Brother Tola. Then I returned—'

'Did anything untoward happen today?'

The religieux was bewildered.

'Not a thing. Well, soon after dawn some brethren came out of the monastery and they seemed armed. They walked around the walls to a point where they halted and took up positions as if waiting for some-thing.'

'Ah, were they watching the roads from the east?' inquired Eadulf.

The religieux shook his head.

'They seemed more concerned about watching the abbey wall. I think they were covering some hole there. I am not sure. Then, after some time, someone called to them and they returned into the abbey. I did not think that was worth reporting,' he added defensively.

'You saw and heard nothing of any Saxon warband marching from the east?'

The man looked startled. 'A warband? There was no warband.'

'No raiding party?'

'Whoever told you such a thing had happened?'

Garb glanced towards Fidelma who nodded and he dismissed the man.

Eadulf was confused. 'I do not understand this.'

'There are two possibilities,' Fidelma said, pursing her lips in thought. 'One possibility is that it was a ruse to send us deliberately down the tunnels into the hands of the waiting armed brethren so that we might meet our end. I cannot understand why, seeing that Abbot Cild was determined to kill us anyway.'

Eadulf gave a soundless whistle.

'But we did not emerge from the tunnel at . . . oh!'

He suddenly remembered that he had not been sure of the directions Higbald had given him. Perhaps some good fortune had caused him to take another route which had led them safely out of the abbey and away from the ambush.

Gadra the old chieftain was still seated impassively.

'You said that there was a second possibility, Fidelma of Cashel. What is that?'

She glanced at him with a serious expression.

'The second possibility is that it was still a ruse to send us deliberately down the tunnels but this time in the hope that we would do exactly what we have done; to come to find you and by so doing . . . lead Abbot Cild and his men here.'

Chapter Twelve

Fidelma's fear of the second possibility proved without foundation for the night at Tunstall passed moderately peacefully. She had dozed until being roused for the midnight celebration to mark the birth of Christ. As was usual in the Church which followed the Rule of Colmcille, the service was in Greek as the tongue of the Gospels. Brother Laisre had conducted the Offering, as it was called, while the Roman clerics called it the Mass, from the *missa* or dismissal.

Brother Laisre stood facing the altar, not behind it, while preparing the Eucharist, the bread and wine. Prayers were said and the community joined in the psalms and the hymns, making their responses with eagerness. The blessing was given before the communion with Brother Laisre holding up his first, third and fourth fingers to symbolise the Holy Trinity, unlike the Roman fashion in which the priest would hold up the thumb, first and second fingers.

Eadulf thought it was significant that the main song of the service, chosen by Brother Laisre, was a traditional invocation for justice.

I will wash my face
In the nine rays of the sun
Just as Mary washed the Holy Child
  in rich fermented milk.

Love be in my countenance
Benevolence in my mind
Dew of honey on my tongue
    my breath as calming incense.

Black may be yonder fortress
Black may be those within
Yet I am as a white swan
    raising myself above them.

I will travel there in the name of God
In the likeness of a deer, in the likeness of a horse
In the likeness of the birds, with the bearing of a
    king
Stronger shall I be than the evil I will encounter.

At the end of the Offering, Fidelma returned directly to her bed. Eadulf was not long in retiring also for he, too, had not enjoyed one full night's sleep in days. He had expected to pass another uneasy night but, so exhausted was he, it seemed as if as soon as he lay down he was being roused by the weak winter sun shining in on them. To his surprise he found that Fidelma was already up. She was outside with Brother Laisre.

'The blessings of Christ Saviour be with you on this day's joyous morning and every day hereafter, Brother Eadulf,' the leader of the community greeted him.

When Eadulf had responded, Brother Laisre turned back to Fidelma. He had obviously been answering a question.

'Indeed, Sister, we had lookouts posted throughout the night on all the approach roads. There was no sign of any movement at all. No one appears to have followed you to this place.'

Fidelma seemed relieved. 'So it seems that my second interpretation was incorrect. Did Brother Higbald use

210

false news about the Saxon warband to force us to flee the abbey? Did he mean to drive us out into some ambush?'

Eadulf shook his head. 'I cannot see the purpose of that. Why go to those lengths simply to kill us? As you said, the abbot was hell bent on doing that anyway and sooner rather than later. Why would Higbald want to waste his energies when the job would have been done for him? Perhaps the simple answer is that Higbald was given false information knowing that he would pass it on to us.'

Fidelma regarded him in surprise. 'Sometimes one cannot see the wood for the trees. Well done, Eadulf. It is a possibility that escaped me.' She turned back to Brother Laisre. 'There is no further word about any warband marauding along the coast?'

'None at all,' confirmed the leader of the community. 'Before sunrise, I sent one of my brethren to the nearest of the coastal villages to make inquiries. There have been no raids anywhere along the coast in the last forty-eight hours. And, if you would take some advice . . . forget this matter for the moment and let your day begin with breaking your fast. Solemn thoughts often make more sense on a nourished stomach than in the clawing pangs of hunger.'

Fidelma smiled. 'You are wise, Brother Laisre. It is advice that I will gladly accept. However, had you forgotten that this is the day of Aoine – the day the Saxons call Frig's Day, which is meant as a day of fasting and abstinence before tomorrow's Sabbath?'

'Yet it is also Christ's birthday and we are allowed to celebrate as well.'

Brother Laisre led the way to the small refectory building.

As they fell to eating, the leader of the Irish community of Tunstall asked: 'What is your plan now that you have escaped from Aldred's Abbey? Do you intend to travel back to Canterbury?'

Fidelma shook her head quickly. 'I should have made my intentions clearer last night. A *dálaigh* cannot walk away from a situation where a chieftain has embarked on the ritual of the *troscud* leaving no other legal witness present.'

Eadulf noticed with relief and satisfaction that she now appeared to have recovered all her former strength and determination. She was her old assertive self.

'Does that mean that you will stay here?' asked Brother Laisre.

'I have tried to dissuade Gadra of Maigh Eo from the course on which he has embarked. He is determined. So I must remain and see that the ritual is carried out in legal fashion. My honour as a *dálaigh* is at stake.'

Eadulf regarded her in some surprise but it was Brother Laisre who articulated his thoughts.

'But what of Cild? He will not be happy with you since you absconded from the abbey. He will be determined to destroy you.'

Fidelma's chin raised a fraction.

'Better men and women than Cild have tried,' she said almost under her breath. Then she spoke normally. 'It is true that we must be careful of Cild. However, there is a mystery at that abbey which involves not only the fate of Gadra and this *troscud* but also the death of Eadulf's friend, Botulf. We cannot walk away from it without attempting to bring the truth to light. So we must stay and attempt to find that truth.'

Brother Lasire shook his head in bewilderment.

'But the truth lies in the abbey. You cannot return to it in order to question those who might lead you to it. So how can you find what is the truth?'

Fidelma smiled quickly. 'You have an astute mind, Brother Laisre.'

Brother Laisre waited for a moment and when she made no further comment he rose, frowning.

'Well,' he said irritably, 'you do not have to tell me your plans.'

Fidelma nodded as if in agreement. 'The less people know of them, perhaps, the better.'

Brother Laisre clearly felt that he should be included in her designs but now he left them showing his wounded pride.

Eadulf grimaced at Fidelma. 'He feels upset.'

'But I am right. The less people know, the less they can tell.'

'But you must have a plan. I know you.'

Fidelma glanced at him. 'Laisre was pointing to the obvious when he said that I could not go back to the abbey to find the truth which is buried there.'

'That is basic logic,' agreed Eadulf.

'So basic that everyone would think it. That is why I am going back to the abbey. After all, we know a secret way inside through those curious tunnels.'

Eadulf stared at her, horrified.

'Go back into the abbey?' he stuttered. 'I don't believe you can be serious.'

'On the contrary, I am perfectly serious. I do not like having my life threatened and I do not like leaving behind unsolved crimes and mysteries. I am determined to resolve this.'

'But how . . . ?' Eadulf raised his arms in an almost hopeless gesture.

'If one woman can traverse the corridors and chambers of the abbey undetected then so can I.'

'But . . .' Eadulf began to protest.

Fidelma looked at him with disdain. 'Come now,

Eadulf, you do not believe in apparitions and phantasms?'

Eadulf flushed, for deep within him he had to admit that he did believe in such things.

'I say that to return is to court an unnecessary danger,' he said stubbornly.

'Yet to do nothing is to let matters take an inevitable and tragic course. You do not have to come back with me,' she added mischievously, knowing full well that her words would goad him.

Eadulf rose to the bait.

'If you go, of course I will come.'

'Then it is decided,' smiled Fidelma sweetly. 'But first we have some other matters to deal with.'

Eadulf looked nervous. 'Other matters? What matters?'

'Do you think that Brother Laisre and his community might provide us with horses?'

Eadulf's nervousness increased.

'Why would we need horses?' he ventured. 'If you mean to return to the abbey, then it is best to come upon it on foot so that we are not observed.'

'We have a journey or two to make before that event and it is best if we can do it with relative comfort and more quickly than merely walking in this inhospitable weather.'

'Journeys to where?'

'I want to meet Cild's brother, Aldhere. You have given me an excellent report of matters, but I would like to make some personal assessment of him before I reach any conclusions.'

Eadulf exhaled deeply in resignation.

'That presupposes I can find my way back to his hideout and that he has not moved from it since.'

'I am sure you can, Eadulf. You said that you knew the countryside here like the back of your hand.'

Just then Garb entered and greeted them gruffly. He dropped to a bench and reached for the jug of mead that was still on the table, draining a beaker in one swift gulp.

'Any news?' asked Fidelma.

'There is still no sign that anyone from the abbey followed you, if that is what you mean,' replied Garb ungraciously.

'I was fairly certain that if we had been followed, we would have known about it before now,' agreed Fidelma, keeping her tone pleasant. 'What I was wondering about was whether you had heard any word of raids along the coast?'

Garb shook his head. 'The countryside is quiet enough. I think you may rest assured that the only dangers that threaten lurk within the walls of the abbey.'

'You are doubtless correct,' she replied. 'Tell me, Garb, is it possible to obtain two horses here? Brother Eadulf and I need to make some short journeys which we can do better and more quickly on horseback than on foot.'

Garb regarded her speculatively.

'If you can ride the tiny wild ponies that are bred in this country, then we have some to spare. We could not bring our own horses with us and so we purchased several of the native ponies, short-legged and broad-chested and not high at all.'

'If it resembles a horse, then I can ride it,' Fidelma replied determinedly.

Garb seemed amused. 'These are not fast mounts but sturdy little animals just right for this weather, with a thick wiry coat that insulates them. I can certainly give you the loan of two of them.'

'That is excellent.' She hesitated and added, 'How is your father today?'

Garb regarded her for a moment with interrogation in his eyes.

'If you mean, is he still determined to carry through the ritual, then – he is so determined.'

Fidelma sighed softly. 'I supposed that I had little doubt of it.'

'A chieftain's word is the binding of his honour. It is not made lightly. As his *tánaiste*, his heir-apparent, my sad duty is to ensure that he carries out his intention or be dishonoured in Maigh Eo and beyond.'

Fidelma frowned abruptly. 'I had forgotten that part of the ritual, that the heir-apparent needs to be present at a chieftain's *troscud*. Tell me, who governs in Maigh Eo while you and your father are here?'

'My younger brother.'

'Do you have a large family?'

'My father bore three sons and three daughters.'

'And with the exception of Gélgeis, are all living?'

Garb shook his head. 'One son died in the war against the Uí Néill of the north and my sister Mella was taken in a Saxon slave raid.'

Eadulf coughed, shuffling his feet uncomfortably. Fidelma ignored him.

'Mella?' She was thoughtful. 'Wasn't she the sister who tried to persuade Gélgeis not to marry Cild?'

'She was indeed. You have a good memory, Sister. Mella was a few hours younger than Gélgeis, and—'

Fidelma's eyes widened.

'A few *hours*? You mean that Mella and Gélgeis are twins?'

Garb nodded briefly.

'They were so.'

'Tell me what happened to Mella,' Fidelma pressed.

'A sad story but one that becomes common among the communities that dwell by the sea these days. There was

216

a raid by a Saxon longship and a dozen young women were carried off that day. Mella was among them.'

'Did you make an attempt to discover where this Saxon slave ship came from?' demanded Eadulf.

Garb turned to him. 'That we did. It was a ship from Mercia.'

'And did you attempt to discover her fate?'

'Merchants trading with Mercia were asked to make inquiries and it was put about that Gadra, as chieftain of Maigh Eo, would pay the honour price for the return of his daughter unharmed. Alas, we learnt nothing.'

'When did this happen?' asked Fidelma, thoughtfully.

'About the same time as we heard of the death of Gélgeis, perhaps a little before.'

'And you have heard no more of her?'

'We did. The captain of the ship bringing us hither reported the gossip of the ports of Mercia. This slave ship, which was apparently identified by its sail markings, was claimed to be the ship of Octha. It was reported to have foundered on the journey back from Éireann and everyone lost.'

Fidelma was quiet for a moment and then she asked: 'Was that ever confirmed?'

Garb shrugged. 'There would be little point in making the story up. If this Octha were alive, then he would have learnt that my father was offering ransom for the return of Mella. It would have been worth his while to return her for her honour price. But the only word we ever had was that Octha and his men, and all the prisoners he had taken, went down in the cruel seas.' He sighed. 'So we lamented and mourned poor Mella. It reinforced my father's determination to seek reparation for the death of Gélgeis.'

'Have you mentioned the story of Mella's fate to anyone since arriving here?'

'Botulf actually raised it with us.'

'How did Botulf know about Mella?'

'He said that on the night Gélgeis died, he met her outside the abbey looking pale. She said that she had just met a wandering religieux who had told her what had happened. She went off into the night and Botulf never saw her again.'

'So Gélgeis knew about Mella before she disappeared?' pressed Fidelma. 'Did you ask Botulf if he had mentioned this news to anyone else?'

Garb gestured negatively. 'Botulf told us that with Gélgeis's death, he had forgotten the story of her sister until we arrived. Only then did he remember it.'

'I see.' Fidelma was still thoughtful. 'Were your sisters much alike? Being twins, I mean?'

There was a faraway smile on Garb's features.

'Some people could not tell them apart. They were like two peas from the same pod. Only close family could tell which was which.'

'I understand. It seems that your family has suffered much hardship and grief.'

'It may be so. Yet there is a saying in our country that the wood will renew the foliage that it sheds.'

'There is wisdom in that, Garb. One must not give way to despair for after every tempest comes sunshine.'

They had been speaking in their common language and Eadulf, following the conversation, for he was, of course, fluent in the language of Éireann, fell to reflecting that there was more hyperbole and embellishment to their speech than the basic forms of expression in his own language.

They were silent for the moment before Fidelma slowly rose and looked meaningfully at Eadulf. Then she turned back to Garb.

'There are now five nights until Gadra begins his ritual fast. This does not give us long.'

Garb sat back, shaking his head.

'Do you really mean to make Cild admit his guilt and recompense my father?'

'Only if Cild is guilty,' replied Fidelma.

'And how could you prove that he is not guilty?'

'That is a question that cannot be answered until it is answered,' Fidelma remarked without humour. 'Now, let us examine these ponies of which you spoke. The sooner we start out, the sooner we shall return.'

Outside, with the sun having risen, though still extremely pale and almost translucent in the pastel skies, Fidelma and Eadulf were able to take in their surroundings for the first time. They had arrived at dusk on the previous day and had seen little before nightfall.

Tunstall lay in a large clearing amidst a forest that many years had done little to disturb. Even in their winter guise the trees grew thick and close together and being mainly evergreens they formed a bulwark against the outside world which was even more impenetrable than the stone blocks of Aldred's Abbey.

There were half a dozen buildings in the clearing, large wooden constructions similar to those Fidelma knew in Éireann and therefore, she estimated, built by the religious of her own land. Living quarters, a refectory and store houses, a chapel, more store houses and barns for the livestock which she could see grazing around them.

Apart from the central area where the activities of men and beasts had ground the snow and earth into mud, a thick covering of snow still lay across the buildings and the clearing. In spite of the pale sun and sky it was not warm enough to melt the snow which lay crisp on the ground. Indeed, everywhere men and beasts were, great clouds of warm breath appeared like clouds of steam; they stood out momentarily before evaporating into the cold morning air.

She estimated, from what she had seen at the midnight Offering and now that she was able to view the settlement, that there must be a dozen religious and half a dozen warriors now comprising the community.

'There is not much of a defence here, if this place was attacked,' she murmured.

'You have an eye for such things, Sister?' asked Garb.

'I am not without some knowledge,' she replied shortly without expanding further. 'Just remember that Abbot Cild could track you down if we have been able to do so with such ease.'

'This is true,' agreed Garb. 'Brother Laisre, however, has lived under such a threat ever since the decision at Whitby was endorsed by King Ealdwulf of East Anglia. Ealdwulf went further and ordered all the religious who held to the Rule of Colmcille to quit his kingdom. Brother Laisre and his small band have survived in spite of all attempts to eliminate them.'

'But now the stakes are higher,' pointed out Fidelma. 'Cild must know that you and your father would be hiding with Laisre.'

Garb gestured with one arm sweeping the clearing.

'Observe the trees, Sister. They are good sentinels.'

'I have already done so. Good as they are, there are paths through them and along paths men and arms may travel.'

'That is why Laisre has a series of lookouts along the trails and why there are escape routes already planned. Do not worry, Sister. This is not an easy encampment to take by surprise. Now, let me show you these ponies.'

He led the way to one of the barns where there were several native ponies of the type she knew well. Sturdy, short little animals. She eyed them professionally, having grown up with horses and ridden almost before she could walk.

'I'll take the dun-coloured one, that one with the oatmeal-coloured muzzle.'

Garb nodded approvingly. 'A good choice. She is strong and will not tire easily. And you, Brother? What is your choice?'

Eadulf looked uncomfortable for he was no horseman.

'I see you looking at the bay,' intervened Fidelma diplomatically. 'I think you have made a good choice there.'

Eadulf expressed his gratitude in a swift smile. He knew almost nothing about horses and was not a brilliant rider.

Garb had turned to one of his men and ordered him to saddle the two ponies.

'How long will you be away? Will you need provisions?'

'It may be best to take some although I am not intending to be away more than a few days. I will be back here long before the *troscud* is due to start.'

Garb appeared to be in charge in spite of Brother Laisre, issuing orders without deferring to the leader of the community. One of the brethren went hurrying to oversee the task of preparing some provisions for the journey without questioning Garb's authority.

Fidelma made a point of seeking out Brother Laisre and paying her respects as one religious leaving the hospitality of another. Brother Laisre appeared to have overcome his irritation of earlier that morning and was polite enough in accepting her assurances that she and Eadulf would return soon.

A little while later, astride their sturdy little ponies, Fidelma and Eadulf left the clearing and the community of the religious of Tunstall, and began to trek eastward through the forest. The woods immediately enshrouded them, almost as if a dark veil had been drawn around them. There was only room for one horse to move at a time along the path and because of this, Fidelma had let Eadulf take the lead for the obvious reason that he knew the country.

'I presume that we should head for Aldhere's encampment?' Eadulf called over his shoulder as soon as they left the community.

'That is the intention,' agreed Fidelma.

'Then we will strike east through these woods. The sea is no more than four or five miles away but before that there is a little settlement which lies by a stream. It used to be called the South Stream. Beyond it is an easy path which may lead us north, via a ford across the river, working our way around the abbey without having to go near it.'

'I leave the choice of path to you, Eadulf. It is your country,' she replied gravely.

They continued on in silence for a while. It was still fairly cold and Fidelma thanked the foresight she had in borrowing an extra cloak from Brother Laisre before setting out. She realised that in spite of her recovery, she was still weak.

She decided to let her pony have its head, following Eadulf, and sat easily in the saddle, letting her thoughts formulate into the *dercad*, the act of meditation which was both restful and less stressful than trying to dwell on the problems that faced them. It was almost like dozing, falling gradually asleep, until . . .

She found herself slipping and caught herself just in time to prevent herself from falling from her pony. It snorted in protest as she snatched at its mane.

Eadulf glanced back.

'Are you all right?' he asked solicitously.

'Of course!' she snapped back in irritation. Her bad temper was merely to hide her feeling of anger with herself. She had been falling asleep. That was not what the act of meditation was about; it was to refresh the mind without plunging it into sleep where dreams might equally destroy its equilibrium. She had never done that before. Perhaps it was a sign that her illness had weakened her. She felt contrite about her response to Eadulf's concern.

'I am sorry,' she called to Eadulf.

Eadulf half turned in his saddle.

'For what?' he asked blandly. He knew her too well to take exception to her irritation.

She did not reply for the moment and then said: 'I did not mean to snap at you.'

He shrugged and turned back. Ahead of them, she could hear a rushing sound of water, water gushing over rocks.

'Is that the South Stream of which you spoke?' she demanded.

'It is and soon we shall come to a clearing where we will find a few houses clustered together. If I remember correctly, there is a farm there. Do you want to skirt round it? Do you want to avoid it?'

'Might we be able to get a hot drink there without encountering trouble?' she asked.

She felt thirsty, but the chill of the winter morning was penetrating and she wanted to ensure that she did not sicken again. Cold water would not suffice for her needs.

'I am sure that the farmer will provide hospitality,' replied Eadulf.

'Let's go there then.'

Eadulf continued to lead the way through the woods in the direction of the sound of the gushing torrent.

Within a few moments they had reached the bank of a moderate-sized stream, bubbling and hissing over stones and pebbles, and the woods suddenly gave way to strips of undulating cultivated farmland. There was the distant glimpse of the sea some way beyond to be had from the elevation on which they emerged.

Not far away, in the cleft of the hills, was a curl of smoke and soon they could see the roofs of buildings.

'That's the farm,' called Eadulf.

Suddenly the sound of people shouting came to their ears and figures began to run here and there.

'What's up?' demanded Fidelma.

Eadulf pulled a face.

'They have seen us, that is all,' he replied. 'We are near the coast and if the East Saxons do raid the land from time to time, then these people are right to be wary of approaching strangers.'

A thick-set man was striding down the path towards them.

'Halt, strangers, and identify yourselves!' demanded a gravel voice as the man suddenly stopped and stood, feet apart, hands on hips, although one of the gigantic hands gripped a long-hafted hammer.

'Peace, my friend,' cried Eadulf, pulling up his pony. 'I am Brother Eadulf of Seaxmund's Ham, travelling with my companion. We bring you blessings of Christ on this holy day.'

Fidelma noticed that Eadulf did not identify her. Maybe it was best not to let on that she was a foreigner.

The attitude of the man seemed to unbend a little.

'Of Seaxmund's Ham, you say?'

'I do.'

'Whither do you go now?'

'We come merely to ask for some hot drink to refresh

ourselves this winter day and then we will be on our way north again.'

The burly man's eyes glanced from Eadulf to Fidelma and back again.

'Then we return your blessings on this feast of our Saviour. Forgive us our wariness, Brother Eadulf, but, as you know, we live in troubled times.'

'You mean raids from Sigehere?'

'That I do. There are constant rumours that his warbands raid along the coast. But, come. Come and betake yourselves of our hospitality and welcome.'

The man turned and waved to the group of people who had gathered some way off and, at his signal, they seemed to break up and go in different directions. The man led the way to the farmhouse.

'Wife,' he called to the large, homely woman who stood at the door, 'two religious, on their journey back to Seaxmund's Ham. A beaker of mulled mead will refresh and help them on their way.'

'That it will,' agreed Eadulf, dismounting. 'My companion has lost her voice and the mead will help ease her throat.'

Fidelma realised that he had said this so that she would arouse no suspicion by speaking in an accent that they would identify as foreign. She merely smiled and nodded at the farmer while the farmer's wife, clucking a little like a mother hen, came bustling forward to help her from her horse.

'Ah, poor dear. We shall soon see what we can do about that. A bad throat? Poor dear. Come into the house and I'll heat a beaker of mead for you right away. It is auspicious to have religious call at our door on this day of all days.'

Fidelma grunted and nodded and dutifully followed the woman into the kitchen.

The farmer ushered Eadulf after them.

'Are you heading to Seaxmund's Ham now, Brother?' he asked.

Eadulf nodded.

'Why do you ask?' he said, watching the farmer's wife pour two beakers of mead and then, taking a red-hot poker from the fire, plunge it first in one beaker and then the other, causing the mead to sizzle and bubble.

'Have you noticed the sky from the west, Brother?'

Eadulf might have confessed that, riding through the forest, he had seen precious little of the sky in any direction. He answered, however, with a simple negative.

'There are heavy grey clouds bunching up from the west. I fear that we will be having another blanketing of snow within the next few hours. Certainly before dusk.'

'We should be able to make it across the Alde by then.'

'Aye, if you do not tarry long.'

Eadulf lifted his beaker and took a swallow.

'Then as soon as we have downed this delicious nectar and said a blessing on this house we shall be on our way.'

The farmer grinned appreciatively.

'God grant a clear road to you, Brother. May He keep you safe from the outlaws who dwell in the marshes and from Sigehere's raiders.'

'Amen to that,' Eadulf replied fervently.

Chapter Thirteen

It had been snowing for more than an hour and it was very cold and damp. In spite of her double cloaks, Fidelma was still feeling the chill and her chest and throat were hurting again. The snow was slanting downwards once again like hard ice pellets, thick and heavy, almost obscuring Eadulf and his pony even though they were only a few yards ahead of her.

Half an hour ago they had crossed a river which Eadulf had told her was the Alde. Upstream lay Aldred's Abbey where the crossing was made by the bridge but here there was a ford which, although it was deep, was shallow enough to allow them to make it on horseback to the northern bank without wetting more than their lower legs.

Fidelma coughed wheezily and shivered.

'Eadulf?' she called uncertainly into the snow blanket that separated them.

His figure suddenly emerged out of the snow for he had halted his pony and waited for her to come alongside him.

'Are you all right?' he asked in concern.

'I think I need a rest. Is there any shelter along this path?'

Eadulf shook his head.

'It will take us some time to reach Aldhere's encampment,' he said. 'I doubt if I can find it until this snow lifts. We will find some place to shelter until it passes.'

She coughed again and the worried lines deepened in Eadulf's forehead. He had to admit to himself, if not to Fidelma, that he had no idea where they might rest.

'Don't worry. I will find a place,' he assured her. He urged his pony onwards and, automatically, she followed. Her illness was debilitating her, she knew. She was probably a fool to have insisted on leaving Tunstall before she had fully recovered. But she also knew that other lives hung in the balance. She could not help herself. Unsolved mysteries were like some terrible narcotic to her. She could not let go while there were still questions which needed answers.

Eadulf suddenly exclaimed out of the white gloom.

'What is it?' she called anxiously.

'It is all right,' he called back. His voice mirrored his relief. 'I've discovered exactly where we are.'

'I thought you already knew that?' she observed with scarcely veiled sarcasm.

'I think so. We are at Frig's Tun.'

'What is that?'

'Remember our mad farmer? The one who took us to the abbey on that first night? Well, that is his farm.'

'Because of that drive I . . .' she began and then turned to hide a wheeze, muttering something which Eadulf did not hear. He pretended not to notice her irritation.

'His name was Mul,' he went on. 'His farm is not far from this point. We will find warmth, food and shelter there. It is no use going on today with this blizzard.'

Fidelma did not respond. Eadulf was absolutely right, of course. If she attempted to go further in this snowstorm she might wind up with another bout of illness and perhaps a fatal one. But it also meant that another day would pass. Only a few days would then be left until the start of Gadra's *troscud*. She knew that prevention was easier than stopping things once they had begun.

'Keep close!' called Eadulf, turning once more and nearly being swallowed by the sheeting snow.

Fidelma screwed her eyes against the sleeting cold as she made an effort to keep up with Eadulf. She was unaware of her surroundings for they were entirely shrouded in the white gloom. But it was not long before she realised that Eadulf had halted and slid from his horse. He was standing looking up at her.

'Here we are,' he called.

She glanced up, trying to focus through the icy pellets.

The vague outline of a building emerged through the snow in front of her. And she could hear the sound of a dog barking.

Eadulf held her pony's head while she dismounted and then he hitched the reins to a post before going to the door. Before he could knock on it, the door swung open and a burly figure stood framed in it, one hand holding the collar of a straining hound who barked and snarled at them. Behind them shone the faint illumination of a welcoming fire.

'Who are you and what do you seek?' demanded a familiar rasping voice.

'Peace on your house, Mul,' replied Eadulf. 'You remember us? The travellers whom you took to Aldred's Abbey.'

Mul stepped forward and examined him and then glanced at Fidelma.

'I remember you well enough, *gerefa*, though I did not expect to see you again after you entered the portals of that accursed place!' He turned to his hound and struck it sharply on the nose. 'Peace, Bragi, peace! Go to your spot!'

The hound gave a soft growl but Mul tapped him sharply on the nose again and he put his head down and went inside.

Mul turned to them.

'What do you seek here?' he demanded again.

'Shelter from the elements,' replied Eadulf.

'I see you have acquired ponies since last we met. Take them into the barn. There is fodder and water inside.' He indicated a building close by and, as Eadulf obeyed the instruction, Mul turned to Fidelma. 'Come inside and warm yourself by the fire. These blizzards are as bad as any I have seen.'

Fidelma followed the farmer inside and Mul closed the door behind her. The hound glanced up and growled softly but made no move.

'Bragi will not harm you while he sees that you are no enemy to me.'

Fidelma smiled softly and removed her double-cloak before edging near the fire and bathing in its warmth.

There was a big metal cauldron hanging from a spit over the leaping flames filled with some aromatic stew. Its fragrance permeated the tiny two-roomed stone farmhouse. Mul moved to it and took down a ladle, stirring it and examining the contents.

'Pork stew,' he said by way of explanation. 'It will be ready soon.'

Mul was as she remembered him, with thick-set shoulders, a muscular torso, a coarse ruddy face and a thick pug nose. He was, in a word, ugly, but even with his close-set eyes and beak of a nose, and the glimpse of broken, yellowing teeth, there was something amiable about his attitude.

She glanced round the room. It was the usual living room with a central hearth for cooking. It was grey and smoky from the fire but the warmth was welcome even though the smoke tickled her sore throat. The second room bespoke a wealth not many such farmers had. This second room did not extend all the way to the roof but was capped by boards creating a third room, open on one side to the main living room from which a ladder gave access.

It seemed clear that Mul used neither this loft room nor the second room for there was a wooden cot on the far side of the hearth which appeared to be his bed. Most people would sleep next to the hearth during the winter months for it was the logical place to keep warm. It was gloomy, for the place was only lit by the light of the fire. As if reading her thoughts, Mul bent to the fire and lit a taper. Then he moved to a lamp and set its wick alight.

'A cup of cider to warm the spirit?' he inquired, setting the lamp on the table.

She nodded silently as she rubbed her arms to restore the circulation.

Mul went to a wooden cupboard and took out some clay beakers which he filled from a flagon.

'The God of the Christians could only create water,' he smiled as he handed her a beaker, 'but Aegir, the god of the Saxons, created cider, and provided the Aesir with their sacred drink at the autumnal equinox.'

Fidelma frowned. She had forgotten that Mul was a pagan. No wonder she saw none of the symbols with which a Christian would usually festoon the house to mark this day. She still had to remind herself that this was the day of the birth of Christ.

'So you still believe in your old gods, Mul?'

Mul grinned broadly. 'When I have need to, woman.'

She paused for a moment and took a sip at the cider that he had given her. It was sweet, strong and good in her aching throat.

'You have a large house, Mul.' She decided to ignore

his implied invitation to engage in an argument on religion. She noticed a shadow cross his face.

'Aye,' he said shortly.

'You have not married?'

Mul shifted his weight from one foot to another.

'I was married . . . once.'

'What happened?'

'You ask many questions for a woman,' snapped Mul.

'I am of an inquisitive nature,' replied Fidelma solemnly. Then she suddenly remembered. 'Ah, but I recall now. In your culture, you do not think it is fitting that women assert themselves as equals to men and ask questions.'

Mul glowered a little and it was clear that he was somewhat at a loss to know how to deal with her self-assertive and assured manner.

'I have come across religieuses of your nation before. I find it strange that your menfolk have allowed you this much freedom.'

The door opened suddenly. The hound leapt up and only a sharp command from Mul stopped it from springing forward. Eadulf stood in a flurry of snow before turning and pressing the door closed behind him.

'Sit, Bragi! Sit!' ordered Mul. Then he turned to Eadulf with a scowl. 'You had best be more cautious, *gerefa*,' he admonished. 'I do not keep the hound as a pet. Bragi is a guard dog.'

Eadulf replied with a noncommittal grunt, removed his cloak and sat down.

'The weather seems to be worsening,' he said, after accepting a cup of cider from Mul.

The farmer sat by the fire and the hound placed its head on one of his feet.

'You are right, *gerefa*. This winter has seen more

blizzards than I recall. Many beasts have perished around these parts. We poor farmers suffer as always, and when the King's men come to demand the King's taxes, it will be spring and the winter damage will be forgotten. We will have to pay or suffer confiscation. But that is the way of things. They will not alter. The King's men come down like thieves and take almost everything apart from that which allows us to survive until the next time of shearing.'

Fidelma smiled sympathetically.

'A learned man called Suetonius wrote that it is the part of the good shepherd to shear his flock, not to flay it.'

Mul glanced at her with sudden appreciation.

'Your woman has a good mind,' he confessed to Eadulf, 'but she does not know the King's tax gatherings. They would, indeed, remove the skin from the body if it was worth anything to them.'

'But, surely, such a winter as this would be borne in mind?' Eadulf argued.

'We have had bad winters but this is the worst I recall. You are from these parts, *gerefa*. You must bear witness to what I am saying.'

'You are right that I cannot recall a winter so cold and foul, and for giving us hospitality from the inclement elements we must thank you,' Eadulf replied.

Mul put his head back and roared with laughter.

Eadulf exchanged a glance with Fidelma and frowned.

'What amuses you?'

'That you presume that I am *giving* you hospitality.' He emphasised the word 'giving'.

'I do not understand,' Eadulf rejoined.

'I'll give you shelter and food but for a price.'

Eadulf's features tightened in annoyance.

'I remember that you charged to drive us to the abbey. I should have suspected that you would not bring people out of a blizzard and allow them to share your home for nothing.'

Mul was grinning. 'As a farmer I have learnt that money is like dung. It does no good unless it is spread, *gerefa*. I perceive that you have some to spread and that will help me survive the losses I will endure this winter.'

'That is not a Christian idea of charity . . .' protested Eadulf.

'As the woman will remind you,' returned Mul, 'I am not a Christian.'

'Eadulf,' Fidelma interrupted softly, 'the man has a point. A *quid pro quo* – something for something.'

Mul nodded towards her.

'A good philosophy, woman. Two things that are important, a good mind and the ability to use it. I am sure that you will not begrudge me a penny for this night's lodging, for the blizzard is set in now. You will not be able to leave here until tomorrow morning.'

Eadulf was disapproving.

'I fear that you have many faults, Mul.'

Mul grinned back.

'Is it not said that money will hide many faults?' he countered.

'Very well, Mul,' sighed Eadulf. 'But as you did not receive your fee until you had delivered us to the abbey, nor shall you receive your fee until we are about to depart.'

Mul grinned without rancour.

'It is agreed, *gerefa*. And now I think my stew is ready. It is a sparse meal, for I was not expecting guests, but there is plenty of cheese and bread to follow. Seat yourselves,' he added, indicating the table.

'Can we do anything?' inquired Fidelma politely.

Mul hesitated and then grimaced.

'No, thank you, woman. I have grown used to my own company and way of doing things.'

He fetched platters and spoons and soon set before them wooden bowls of the steaming pork to which some root vegetables had been added. Bread and cheese were also placed on the table along with more cider.

The hound gave the appearance of sleeping by the fire but once, when Eadulf moved too quickly, the eyelids flickered open. The lips of the animal drew back across the teeth in a silent growl.

Mul snapped an order and the dog closed its eyes again.

Fidelma waited until the remains of the stew had been cleared away before turning to the subject that had been in her mind ever since Eadulf had told her that they were at the farmhouse of Mul.

'I recall, Mul, that on the night you left us at Aldred's Abbey, you had little good to say about it. Was that a general indictment of Christians or specific to the inhabitants of the abbey?'

Mul fixed her with his piercing bright eyes.

'You will find few in these parts who have anything good to say about that place,' he replied.

'If I recall,' Fidelma pressed, 'you felt that the devil dwelt in that place.'

'You have a good memory, woman,' the farmer said, helping himself to more cider. 'I said that the devil had cast his shadow over Aldred's Abbey. I still say it.'

'What makes you say that?'

'You have met the abbot?'

'Abbot Cild. I did not see him, for I fell ill when we arrived, but Eadulf met him several times.'

Eadulf nodded.

'I would say that he might be described as a devil but not *the* devil,' he affirmed, taking another piece of cheese.

Mul looked at him wryly.

'Even though you be Christians, I would not have thought that either of you would have had much good to say about Abbot Cild.'

Fidelma heard some underlying meaning in his tone. She stared at him, trying to get beyond his bright, piercing gaze.

'Why would that be, Mul?' she asked softly.

Mul leant back smiling.

'Your companion, the *gerefa* Eadulf, is a person who reacts first and thinks afterwards,' he said. 'I have noticed it and so has Bragi there.'

The hound raised his head at the sound of its name.

Eadulf had stiffened slightly.

'Explain yourself, Mul,' he snapped.

'I just want to warn you not to move suddenly.' Mul continued to smile. 'Bragi does not like it. He also reacts and, poor animal, has no mind to reason whether the movement has an evil intent or not. I would not like you to respond physically to what I am about to say.

Eadulf's scowl deepened.

'Go on,' demanded Fidelma. 'What do you want to tell us that may cause consternation?'

'A rider from the abbey has been going around the surrounding farms and villages announcing that the abbot has placed a reward of three gold pieces on your heads. He urges anyone who encounters you to either take you captive or send to the abbey to report your whereabouts. Three gold pieces seems a great fortune. Especially to the poor farmers of this area.'

Fidelma glanced anxiously at Eadulf. He had gripped the edge of the table with his hands. His jaw was clenched but he did not otherwise move.

'And what reason does Abbot Cild give for announcing this reward?' Fidelma asked evenly.

Mul returned her composed stare.

'You probably know that well enough, woman. You are accused of witchcraft and the *gerefa* here is accused of aiding and abetting you.'

Eadulf had still not moved but now he said quietly, 'As you say, Mul, three gold pieces is a lot of money.'

The farmer nodded complacently. 'More than I will earn this year and even next year put together with this year. Aye, it is indeed a lot of money. More than I could ever hope to have at one time.'

'And we know how you like money,' muttered Eadulf, his eyes darting here and there in search of some means of self-defence.

The hound's head had risen and its eyes were wide open and alert. It had that amazing canine ability to detect atmosphere in the slight nuances of the human voice.

Mul was sitting back in his chair, a slight smile on his face, the cup of cider in his hand.

'You appear to be very much alarmed, *gerefa*,' he said mildly.

'Alarm is a reasonable reaction when you have confessed that your main interest is money and that you are in dire financial straits because of this winter,' replied Eadulf. 'Let me tell you why you should shun this gold . . .'

Fidelma reached forward in an easy manner and laid her hand on his arm.

'I do not think any eloquence will alter the intention of Mul. Publilius Syrus once wrote that when gold argues the cause, eloquence is impotent.'

Mul chuckled in appreciation.

'You have intelligence and wit, woman. The trouble with the religious is that they attempt to preach morality to the starving. Give a man an eloquent lecture on good and evil and give another man a penny and you will see which one of them will respect you the more.'

There was a silence and then Fidelma asked quietly: 'So what do you intend to do, Mul?'

The farmer poured another beaker of cider.

'Do? Nothing.'

For a moment neither Eadulf nor Fidelma replied.

'I don't understand,' Fidelma said after a while. 'Are you saying that the three gold pieces are not a temptation to you?'

'Oh, they are a temptation right enough. But I would not trust Abbot Cild to pay them after he has secured what he wants. I denounce him as the devil. I would rather freeze to death than deal with him.'

Eadulf sat back, relaxing slowly.

'Are you playing games with us, Mul?'

'You, *gerefa*, leapt to your own conclusion. You believed that I cared more for gold than for my own principles. Who am I to correct your errors?'

'Well, now that you have corrected our errors,' interposed Fidelma, 'perhaps I should explain that the abbot's accusations are false.'

Mul shrugged. 'I would not care one way or another. There was evil in that abbey before you went there and doubtless it will be there after you are gone.'

'Have you farmed long here, Mul?' Fidelma asked, causing Eadulf to look at her in surprise at what seemed an abrupt change of topic.

'All my life. Ask your companion, the young *gerefa* here.' He motioned humorously to Eadulf. 'My father and his father once went on a hosting together.'

'So you have seen many changes at the abbey?' asked Fidelma.

'Not that many,' replied Mul. 'I was a boy when the Irish missionaries came to this land, converting people to the new faith. I saw the building of the abbey rise on the walls of the old fortress that was there.'

'And you knew the religious that were there before Cild came along, men like Botulf?'

Mul blinked for a moment.

'Most people in the area knew Botulf.' He looked at Eadulf. 'You knew him better than most. I remember that you were boys together, though you probably don't remember me from those days.'

Fidelma leaned forward.

'You see, Mul, I would like to know a little more about this man Cild and his brother, Aldhere, as well. I want to know what the evil is that permeates this area.'

Mul grimaced in disgust.

'Each is doubtless as evil as the other. One is an outlaw, murdering and thieving outside the law. The other is a tyrant, murdering and thieving within the law. A curse on them both.'

Eadulf was about to open his mouth when he was stayed by a glance from Fidelma.

'I think that you should tell us your story, Mul, for I feel that you have one to tell.'

Mul regarded her keenly for a moment, then he shrugged.

'You are discerning, as I said before. I inherited this farm from my father. When he died a few years ago, I was married with two fine sons. It was a good farm and life was good even though the elements were often harsh. Then it all changed.'

'How did it change?' asked Fidelma when he paused.

'How? Cild arrived. I had never heard of Cild before, but when I visited the market in Seaxmund's Ham, not long afterwards, someone told me that he had once been a warlord on the borders with Mercia. They told me that

his father had disinherited him and so he had gone to
a land called Connacht beyond the western sea. He had
returned with a wife, a woman of your race.' He nodded
towards Fidelma.

'You refer to Gélgeis?'

'That was her name. Cild and Gélgeis came to the
abbey when Cild became its abbot. Then I heard that
Cild's brother, a thane, had been disgraced. It was said
that King Ealdwulf had refused to return Cild's father's
titles and lands to the abbot.'

'Go on.'

'For a few months all was quiet and then I heard that
Gélgeis had perished in the marshes near the abbey . . .'

'Did you find out how?'

'How?' Mul was bemused for a moment. Then he
shook his head. 'I heard that Cild had become like a
man possessed, driving out the religious who believed in
the original rules of their Order and welcoming these new
ideas from the Roman Rule of Canterbury. He slaughtered
many who would not change their ways. He separated
married clergy and sold the women into slavery. The
abbey became closed to all women.'

'You could have warned us about that,' intervened
Eadulf. 'The night you drove us to the abbey, you could
have warned us.'

'You were religious intent on going to the abbey,'
replied Mul. 'Why should I warn you? I am not a
Christian nor have I any desire to become one if all
you do is fight and argue among yourselves. Anyway,
as I was saying, Cild showed that he was still a warlord.
A few months ago he enticed into the abbey a band of
young warriors who, dressed in the holy robes which you
Christians adopt, would scour the countryside in search
of loot. They raided this farm and it was then that I knew
evil stalked the abbey.'

He fell silent for a moment or two as if contemplating the memory.

'What happened?' encouraged Fidelma softly.

Mul resumed his story, speaking in a studied voice as if to control his emotions.

'I was away at market when they came. They came to loot. My wife and two young boys were here. In trying to protect what little I had, my wife was slain and the two children with her. I found their bodies outside when I returned. They are buried just beyond the barn.'

Eadulf coughed awkwardly. 'How did you know that they were slain by the abbot's men?'

Mul rose and turned to a cupboard. He opened it and took something from it, then returned to the table. He hesitated a moment and set it down on the board. It was a piece of bloodstained woollen cloth and a small metal crucifix on a silver chain.

'That was clutched in my wife's hand where she had ripped it from her assailant,' Mul said quietly. 'I knew then that it was the religious from Aldred's Abbey who had paid me a visit that day. I will have my revenge on Cild, even if I have to wait ten years or ten times ten years. I have sworn this by the sword of Woden.'

'When did this happen?' Eadulf demanded.

'Less than six months ago. Just at the time the young men appeared in the abbey, young fighting men.'

Fidelma had picked up the small crucifix, turning it over in her hands with her brows drawn together.

'This is of Irish workmanship, not Saxon,' she said softly after a moment or two.

Mul shrugged. 'Many of the Christians are trained by your race, woman. Cild had been in this kingdom of Connacht. The provenance of the cross merely confirms what I say.'

She handed the cross to Eadulf without making further

comment. It was a small, richly enamelled ornament on silver. It was, he observed, the type of rich jewel affected by the female laity rather than any member of the religious.

'You say that this happened about six months ago?' Fidelma was asking.

'At the time of the summer solstice feasting,' Mul muttered.

'Tell me,' Fidelma continued and again it seemed that she was changing the subject, 'did you ever see Gélgeis, the abbot's wife?'

He shook his head. 'Not so far as I remember. I might have seen her from afar. I would not have known her to see, face to face. I was told once that she was pretty, with fair hair and features.'

'Did you ever hear what manner of woman she was?'

'What manner . . . ?' He paused and then grimaced dismissively. 'She was married to Cild. Isn't that enough? You are known by the company you keep and that goes for the partner you marry.'

'You are a man of hard judgment, Mul,' Eadulf sighed. 'Sometimes it is only after marriage that you get to know a person.'

'Did you ever hear a rumour that Cild murdered his wife?' asked Fidelma.

Mul's eyes widened a little and then he shook his head.

'I only heard that she had wandered into Hob's Mire. Many animals and several people have strayed into that bog and never returned. Perhaps her fate was a blessing for her.'

'You said that you knew Brother Botulf?' Fidelma pressed, ignoring his comment.

'I did.'

'Did you ever speak to him about Cild?'

'After he was sent back to the abbey in disgrace, I hardly ever saw him. He was not allowed to go far from the abbey walls.'

'What was this disgrace?' asked Eadulf.

'He supported Aldhere against the King.'

'Why was that?'

'I don't know. Aldhere was of the same poisonous root as his brother. I heard that he sacrificed the King's cousin during a battle when the Mercians invaded. Through his cowardice, King Ealdwulf's cousin died. Botulf defended Aldhere for which stand the King ordered that he should return to Aldred's Abbey, where he had been one of the brethren in the early days, and remain there, not leaving on pain of death.'

'You imply that Aldhere was guilty. Does that mean that you thought Botulf was a liar?' demanded Eadulf sullenly.

'I would not know his reasons for defending Aldhere. Botulf was a good man, so far as I knew. Perhaps he was simply misguided. But I never had time to speak to him about the matter.'

'Then how do you know that Aldhere is guilty?' Eadulf asked.

'Deeds not words!' snapped Mul.

'Explain that,' Fidelma invited.

'Simple enough. Ask anyone. Aldhere and his men are a band of robbers. They steal from everyone. They have also terrified and burnt the homes of many innocent people. Are these the actions of a good man who was not guilty of the accusation made against him?'

Fidelma sat back and sighed.

'Well, it might be the actions of a man driven to find a means of survival. But burning the homes of the innocent is certainly not in keeping with the character of a man of principle.'

'I say, a curse on both of them,' Mul growled. 'Religious brother or warrior brother; white dog, black dog, both are dogs.'

'You may well be right. It does not help us get closer to the truth,' Eadulf said in exasperation.

Mul turned to him with curiosity.

'What truth are you seeking, *gerefa*?'

'The truth of who killed my friend Botulf.'

Mul sat back with a look of astonishment.

'You did not tell me that Botulf was dead!'

Of course, Eadulf realised that Botulf had only been killed on the day Mul had dropped them at the abbey.

'I'm sorry. He was bludgeoned to death in the abbey.'

'I suppose the abbot was responsible,' Mul muttered bitterly. 'I felt that it was like putting a rabbit in with a run of ferrets . . . I mean, putting Botulf in Cild's abbey when Botulf had defended his brother. Cild would obviously resent that.'

'There is a logic in what you say,' agreed Fidelma. 'Do you know anything of the Irish religious in this area?'

Mul shook his head.

'I know that there are some who are in hiding. They refuse to accept the decisions made at Whitby and obey Canterbury. Rules! Christian rules!' He made a gesture like spitting. 'Who cares? In this land we will continue to call the vernal equinox by the name of the goddess Eostre; others may celebrate it as Pascha, the resurrection of the new god, Christ, or even as Pésah, the Jewish Passover feast . . . but it is still the vernal equinox.'

He saw Fidelma studying him in surprise and smiled disarmingly.

'Just because I am a farmer, you need not think that I have no knowledge. I have been to the coastal ports and spoken with Phoenician traders. I know all about Pésah and the like. All farmers know and name the seasons – seasons are seasons however you want to name them.'

'Do you know of a young woman of Éireann with red-gold hair who lives near the abbey?' interrupted Eadulf.

Mul was shaking his head when he suddenly smiled.

'Do you mean young Lioba? She is no woman of Éireann.'

Eadulf tried to recall if he had heard the name before. He thought he had but could not be sure.

'That's a Saxon name,' Fidelma pointed out, glancing at Eadulf.

'True enough,' agreed Mul. 'Her father was a farmer in the hills beyond the abbey. He is dead now. He died in the Yellow Plague. Her mother also died a year or so ago. But her mother had been a slave taken from a kingdom called Laigin. That's who you mean. Lioba.'

Laigin was one of the five kingdoms of Éireann, as well they knew.

Mul suddenly chuckled lewdly.

Eadulf frowned slightly. 'What does your humour imply, Mul?'

'That for all the piety at the abbey, Lioba seeks her pleasures there.'

'I am told that this Lioba bears a resemblance to Gélgeis,' hazarded Eadulf, pursuing a sudden train of thought.

Mul rubbed his chin. 'I would not know. Lioba must have been younger than the abbot's wife.'

'Let us return to the Irish religious in hiding. What do you know about them?' asked Fidelma.

'Little enough. As Christians, I do not care about them. I think it is said that they are down Tunstall way. They never bother me nor I them.'

He reached for more cider and grimaced with a bitter expression before sipping it.

'I want little to do with you Christians though I will go this far: all gods are the same when it comes to seeking their help. They are all united in ignoring your pleas and cries for help. I know that. There are three graves on the hill above the farmstead that bear me witness.'

'Christ was not responsible for the murder of your wife and children,' admonished Eadulf.

'No? If this Christ were an omnipotent deity he could have done something. Don't you teach that he is all powerful, all loving and ordains everything that happens? No, *gerefa*, all gods are alike. Silent to our suffering.'

Fidelma looked at Eadulf and shook her head quickly. It was not wise to pursue the argument further.

'Have you heard of any trouble between the abbey and those who adhere to the Rule of Colmcille . . . the blessed one whom you call Columba?' she asked.

'Trouble? Cild had two of them executed, I know that. The others he had driven out into the marshes. Perhaps they have returned to your land? Perhaps it is they who are hiding in Tunstall? There are so many deaths here, Sister, that I am surprised you bother to seek the reasons for one or two. The answer to all of them lies between two people – Cild and Aldhere.'

'It seems that there is no longer any law here,' muttered Eadulf. 'I would not believe it. I was brought up to believe that no one would dare to disobey the Law of the Wuffingas and a *gerefa*. Anarchy seems to reign in this land.'

Mul grinned cynically.

'Not anarchy, *gerefa*; but men who have swords and no compunction about using them. And, of course, such men have no loyalty to anyone other than themselves.'

Fidelma held her head to one side questioningly.

'Again you seem to imply something more than the words you use, Mul.'

The farmer nodded slowly.

'Speak to people in any market place and you will hear what they say.'

'We are not in a market place, so I would like to hear what *you* say. What have you heard?'

'I have heard that Aldhere would welcome a new King in this land. I have heard too that his brother, Cild, would also welcome a new King. Yet the word is that the brothers have different Kings in mind.'

'Can you explain further?' Fidelma pressed.

'This land is viewed with envy by Wulfhere of Mercia to the west and by Sigehere of the East Saxons to the south. Either King would be a fool not to take advantage of the conflict raging in this small corner of the kingdom.'

'Are you saying that you have definite word that either Cild or Aldhere is in league with Wulfhere or Sigehere?' Eadulf was aghast.

'Definite word? No, of course not. I tell you what I have heard in the market places.'

'Idle gossip. Speculation without facts!' suggested Eadulf. Fidelma noticed that even as he spoke Eadulf was less than confident and seemed preoccupied with his own thoughts.

'If the land of the South Folk fell, then the land of the North Folk would follow swiftly,' Mul snapped, undeterred.

'You might well be right,' conceded Fidelma. 'It seems that there is no peace between peoples anywhere in the world. There are plots and conspiracies between the five kingdoms of my own island. During our visit to the land of the Britons we found their kingdoms divided against each other. Why should the lands of the Angles and the Saxons be any different? However, that is not why we are here.'

Mul sniffed and once more reached for the cider jug. Finding it empty, he rose and went to the cupboard and drew out another flagon.

'No,' he said, 'you are here to find out how Cild murdered your friend Botulf.'

'We are here to find out first *if* Cild murdered Botulf,' corrected Eadulf. 'If he did so, then the "how" will follow.'

'And moreover whether he killed his wife, Gélgeis,' Fidelma added. 'We are here to prevent more tragedy and such an effusion of blood as this land has never seen before.'

Chapter Fourteen

The blizzard had passed on during the night. The morning, while still icy cold, was bright with the sky pastel blue and the sun almost white in its weakness. Fidelma and Eadulf had passed the night in the comfortable warmth of Mul's farmhouse. They had broken their fast with Mul but waited until he was out of earshot before they made their prayers to St Stephen, for it was his feast day – the feast of the first martyr for the new faith. Then, after paying Mul the promised coin for the night's lodging, they left on their journey northwards. The roads were filled with snow banks, crisp flakes that had drifted in the blizzard and piled against hedge and ditch. The journey was not going to be without hardship.

Fidelma, however, had slept well and felt much stronger than before. The ague that she had endured was now receding and she was more comfortable and relaxed.

Mul's smoking chimney had barely disappeared behind the hill when Eadulf turned to Fidelma. There were several questions that he had wanted to ask but had been unable to in the intimacy of the farmhouse in which Mul would hear even the whispered word.

'What did you mean by "preventing such an effusion of blood as this land has not seen before"?' Eadulf demanded.

Fidelma's expression was serious.

'Why am I so keen to prevent this ritual fast from taking place, Eadulf?'

'To prevent the death of Gadra . . . to find out the truth about the deaths of Gélgeis and Botulf . . .' Eadulf thought the reasons were surely obvious.

'There is one thing that you appear to have overlooked, or perhaps do not realise, about the *troscud*, the ritual fast. Gadra is a chieftain of Maigh Eo. He is a descendant of the Uí Briúin kings of Connacht, and they in turn are related to the Uí Néill High Kings. If Gadra dies, as it is like he will, and Cild does not compensate his family, as it is like he will not, then there will begin a blood feud which will encompass the Uí Briúin and perhaps the Uí Néill, which will spread from Cild to the whole kingdom of the East Angles, and soon, perhaps, every kingdom on these islands might be taking sides. From this incident, there might grow a terrible warfare.'

Eadulf was astounded. 'Do you really think that it could lead to that?'

Her features told him how earnest she was.

'As soon as I realised that Gadra was one of the Uí Briúin I knew that we were not dealing with some petty chieftain but one with powerful connections. That is what stirs me to find a solution to this matter.' She paused and added: 'What were the thoughts that occupied you when Mul suggested that Aldhere or Cild might be in league with neighbouring kings for their own aggrandisement?'

Eadulf grimaced. He had thought she had not noticed his apprehension when Mul spoke of the gossip in the market places. In fact, he had almost forgotten the subject now that they had left Mul's farmstead.

'I was merely thinking that Cild was once a warlord in this land. I remembered how strange it was, the morning after we arrived here, that he and some of the brethren rode out in search of Aldhere almost as if they were warriors in battle array rather than religious.'

'I recall that you told me about that,' agreed Fidelma. 'However, as you said, he was once a warrior and warriors' traits never leave them.'

'That was my reasoning.'

'There is something else worrying you?'

'Not worrying me, just irritating me. On our way out from the abbey, we passed a room full of warriors' equipment. Remember?'

Fidelma pursed her lips. She had forgotten.

'I confess that I was not feeling well enough to take that in. Perhaps Cild likes to retain that link with his past life.'

'If it is truly past. It was what Mul said that makes me think that it is not.'

'I don't follow.'

'Maybe the rumours are true. Cild might well be in league with Wulfhere of Mercia – involved in some plot to betray the South Folk to his kingdom.'

'Why Mercia?'

'Because the thing that has been worrying me is that the shields in that chamber each bore the battle emblem of the Iclingas. I had started to mention it to you when we found Botulf's purse and the discovery drove it from my mind.'

'Iclingas? What might that be?'

'The Iclingas are Kings of Mercia.'

They rode on in silence for a while, allowing the ponies their heads to find their own way through the snowdrifts – a task for which the animals' natural senses were far better fitted than the guidance of their riders.

'We should be at Aldhere's camp within the hour.' Eadulf eventually broke the silence.

'I shall look forward to meeting him after the conflicting reports of his character given by you and Mul.'

Eadulf snorted indignantly. 'What does Mul know? Yet again, he repeats only the local gossip. I simply say that I prefer Aldhere to his dour brother Cild.'

'There is often some truth to be found in gossip. Not so much fact but attitudes. I have known many ruthless men and women who are possessed of the sweetest temperaments until their plans are thwarted. It is often enlightening to listen to gossip.'

Eadulf looked disapproving.

'You are fond of quoting Publilius Syrus,' he rebuked her. 'Did you not once quote him, and quote him approvingly, that it was wrong to take notice of gossip?'

Fidelma smiled. 'You did not quote the exact words of Publilius Syrus, Eadulf, but the meaning is probably the same. However, what I said was to listen to gossip for attitudes and not for facts. In this instance the importance of the gossip lies in the context.'

'And have you been led to any conclusion?' Eadulf asked. He could not restrain the note of irony in his question.

Fidelma's features grew serious.

'I will admit to you, Eadulf, that nothing I have heard so far makes me see any solutions. In fact, this is the most frustrating conundrum I have ever encountered. We only know for certain of one crime. The death of your friend Botulf. We hear accusations of another crime . . . the abbot's wife . . . but is it a crime? We do not know, for accusations do not constitute facts, as you endeavoured to point out at Tunstall. But how are we to proceed? There are no witnesses to these events, only rumours and gossip.'

'There is another point to be considered.'

252

Fidelma glanced across at him, frowning at his doleful tone. 'Which is?'

'That even if we could miraculously find the truth of what is happening, through what means could we reveal it and force a mediation on those concerned? You have no legal authority in this land. At least in Dyfed, the Welisc king gave you an authority. But here among the Angles and the Saxons, you have none. No authority at all.'

'That is true,' she agreed gravely. 'But this is your country, Eadulf. These are your people. You are a *gerefa* here.'

Eadulf shook his head.

'I was a *gerefa* here, extolling the laws of the Wuffingas. Once I went into the religious my authority as a *gerefa* ceased to be.'

Fidelma's eyes narrowed slightly.

'Do you mean that a religious in this land cannot be an advocate of the law?'

Eadulf shook his head.

'It is with irony that Mul addresses me as *gerefa*. It is because as a non-Christian he refuses to call me Brother. Neither, if you noticed, does he call you Sister. I have found many in the religious who have sought my advice because of my legal background but, in truth, I no longer have authority in this kingdom and these people know it.'

Fidelma reflected for a moment. Somewhere in her memory she must have known. It must have been explained to her when she had first met Eadulf at the great council at Whitby. Yet she had in recent times emphasised his legal standing to her people as it gave him a moral authority to help her in her own investigations.

'Well, we will have to find some other way of exerting influence on matters,' she said. 'I believe Gadra and Garb will take notice if I can demonstrate that there is no need to undertake the ritual fast.'

'But in the meantime,' Eadulf sighed, 'we have to keep out of the hands of Abbot Cild. I wonder how he can afford three gold pieces for our capture? It is a large sum to offer and you cannot doubt that many will be tempted by it.'

Certainly Fidelma did not doubt it.

'More to the point, why is he so concerned to have us caught and silenced?' she said. 'He must surely know, as we do, that there is no way we can prove anything against him . . .'

'Unless we are overlooking the obvious,' muttered Eadulf.

Fidelma examined him thoughtfully. She could see his brows drawn together, his lips compressed, as if he were struggling to remember some forgotten information or event that had happened during the time that she lay in her fever.

'You noticed that the crucifix Mul found was not one usually worn by a religious?' she asked, after a while.

Eadulf nodded.

'It was made for a person of wealth, doubtless a woman,' he replied. 'It seems logical that it was Gélgeis's cross.'

'Logical, but its ownership is not certain, nor is the reason why it came to be at Mul's farmstead.'

A silence fell between them again before Fidelma broke it once more: 'You have had conversation with Cild. Tell me, is he truly unbalanced in the mind? If so, have you learnt the cause of it?'

Eadulf shrugged. 'I would say that Cild is unstable to the point of being deranged. What caused his dementia? I do not know.'

'The death of his wife and the strange apparitions at the abbey?'

To her surprise, Eadulf shook his head.

'I think there is more to it than that. Aldhere claims his brother was demented and cruel from childhood and this was why he was disinherited. Perhaps he was born evil.'

Fidelma made a face.

'Children are not born evil, Eadulf. They are usually created so.'

They had been travelling through a stretch of woodland, mainly of bare, gaunt trees with a few clumps of evergreens here and there. It was flat country close to the sea, so close that they could hear the distant whisper of the waves sliding towards the shore and then receding. Now came the sound of something else.

Fidelma drew rein and reached out a hand to touch Eadulf upon the arm. He glanced up from his reverie and halted too.

It had been the crack of a whip that had warned her and now came two more cracks in sharp succession. There was a soft rumbling sound and the clink of metal upon metal. A nearby voice shouted.

Fidelma looked quickly towards the direction of the sounds. They were coming from the track ahead, which seemed to twist out of sight through the woods.

Eadulf was examining the landscape in order to identify some place of concealment.

He nudged her arm and pointed inland beyond the tall sessile oaks which bordered the path to a nearby clump of evergreen trees and bushes, perhaps holly and polypody ferns, he was not sure. All he knew was that in this wilderness they offered the only hope of cover. There was no time to question the decision. They turned from the path and urged their ponies swiftly through the trees to ride around the meagre protection offered by the evergreens. As soon as they were behind the shelter, they both dismounted and held tight to their ponies' reins. Only then did Eadulf realise that in the snow that lay about, their tracks could plainly be seen.

It was too late, however. Around the corner, along the track, swung a light carriage drawn by two strong mares. It was a rich, ornate carriage, and highly decorated. A symbol was painted on the door but they could not discern what it was. Curtains at the window of the carriage flapped in the breeze caused by its momentum. Someone of substance was seated inside. But what astonished them both was the driver.

He was a young man, obviously used to driving a carriage and pair. He held the reins effortlessly in one hand, striking the air with a whip held in the other and crying encouragement to the beasts in their mad headlong plunge through the woods. What astonished them was that he was clad in the robes of a religieux.

Within one horse's space behind the carriage came four mounted warriors, one carrying a square of silk on a lance which flapped in the wind. They were all well dressed and well armed and were clearly the escort to the carriage.

Such was their momentum that no one noticed the disturbed snow where Eadulf and Fidelma had turned from the path. The carriage and its escort thundered on through the wood and they could hear the sound of its passing diminishing in the distance.

Eadulf straightened up with an exhalation of relief.

'Did you recognise the emblem on that coach?' Fidelma asked as she also straightened up and patted the muzzle of her pony in gratitude for its silence.

'Not on the coach,' admitted Eadulf. 'But the symbol on the flag carried by the escort was plain to see.'

'Which was?' prompted Fidelma, climbing back onto her mount.

'That was the wolf-symbol of the Wuffingas, the kings of the East Angles. Only the King's elite bodyguard may use it.'

Fidelma digested this in silence while he remounted his pony and they set off again slowly, retracing their path back to the main track.

'Are you saying that it was probably the King of the East Angles who passed us just now?' she finally asked. She suddenly smiled. 'Maybe there was truth after all in the gossip about your King journeying southwards.'

'Perhaps.' But Eadulf seemed reluctant and when she pressed him he added: 'I did not recognise the same symbol on the coach, nor do I understand why King Ealdwulf would be driven by a religieux. It is unusual.'

She was inclined to agree.

'And with only four warriors to protect him, it would seem strange that this King would ride into the territory of your friend Aldhere?' Fidelma pointed out.

Eadulf shook his head in bewilderment.

'Yet another mystery along the road to truth.'

'If truth can be found along any road here,' muttered Fidelma.

They rode on for a further hour or more before Eadulf spotted some familiar landmarks.

'I think we are near Aldhere's lair,' he said, sounding more cheerful than he had in a while. 'Perhaps we will be able to begin to clear up some of these matters.'

Fidelma did not reply and together they continued silently on in the direction he had indicated.

The sound of a ram's horn wailing nearby made them halt their ponies in momentary confusion.

There came a movement along the edges of the path and abruptly a half-dozen warriors appeared at their sides with weapons ready. At their head, Eadulf immediately recognised Wiglaf. He saw Eadulf and grinned broadly, telling the others to put up their weapons.

'Two more outlaws come to join us, eh, *gerefa*?' he greeted them. And when Eadulf replied with a puzzled expression he chuckled. 'Everyone has heard of the reward that the abbot has set on your heads so I suppose that you have come to take shelter with us. You should have tried to meet me as we arranged and we might have made your journey easier.'

Eadulf had forgotten that he had arranged to meet Wiglaf outside the abbey, as Botulf had done before him, if there was any urgency.

He was introducing Wiglaf to Fidelma when another rider came cantering along the path. It was a slim figure with a heavy cloak and hood drawn so well around it that they had no glimpse of the person's features. Eadulf had the impression of a youth or a woman. The outlaw band must have known who it was for they drew their horses to the side of the track to allow an unimpeded passage for the rider.

Wiglaf noticed Eadulf's curiousity and chuckled lewdly.

'That's an old friend. Lioba often comes for a visit to our camp. And now . . .' He jerked his head in the direction the rider had come from. 'I'll escort you there. Come, I will lead the way.'

He turned his horse, issuing orders to his men to take up their positions again. They were clearing sentinels, lookouts protecting the outlaw camp.

As they rode along Fidelma said: 'I understand that you were Botulf's cousin and in contact with him at the abbey?'

'That I was, Sister,' Wiglaf replied solemnly.

'I would like to ask you some questions.'

'Those must wait, then, for Aldhere's camp is just ahead and I have to return immediately to my men. I will come back to the camp for the midday meal, then you may ask of me what you will.'

The encampment was but minutes away and Aldhere had already been warned of their coming, for Wiglaf had taken out his ram's horn and blown another short, sharp blast on it. Aldhere stood before his hut, hands on hips, smiling slightly. As they halted their ponies and began to dismount, he came forward with an outstretched hand.

'Greetings, holy *gerefa*! I did not doubt that I would see your face again. And this time you have brought the Irish witch?'

He roared with laughter at Fidelma's disapproving features.

'Have no fear, good Sister, for my humour is unlike that of my brother. I doubt not your piety. I am Aldhere, sometime thane of Bretta's Ham, but now a simple outlaw. You are welcome to my encampment. Come away into my hut. It is a poor inhospitable place but it will shelter you from our fierce winter.'

Like Eadulf before her, Fidelma found herself swept along by his mixture of joviality and domineering. She followed the large man almost meekly, without saying anything, but her eyes swiftly took in the surroundings; the men, the women and the children who populated this small forest glade. Wiglaf had apparently gone back to his duties as lookout but she saw that there were plenty more armed warriors about the place.

'And do you approve, good Sister?' Aldhere asked, pushing the hut door open with one hand while standing back to allow her to enter first. His keen eyes had not missed her appraisal of the camp.

'Approve?' She was caught off guard.

'Of my camp, of course. My men bring their women

259

and children for safe-keeping here. We are not expecting an attack from King Ealdwulf until the thaw comes. If this winter continues as it has, that might not be until the spring, please God. Ealdwulf does not like to fight with mud on his boots. He'll wait until there is dry weather.'

He motioned them to the stools. The room had not changed since Eadulf's visit a few days ago. He looked round for the Frankish woman, Bertha, but there was no sign of her. Aldhere caught his glance and smiled again.

'My woman, Bertha, has gone with one of my men to get provisions at the market at Seaxmund's Ham. You see, we do not rob and steal but purchase goods from the traders.'

'And where does the money come from to pay the traders for those goods?' queried Eadulf innocently.

'By the holy wounds of Christ!' cried Aldhere with a bark of laughter. 'You are possessed of a sharp mind, holy *gerefa*.'

Fidelma had seated herself.

'So you do expect an attack from King Ealdwulf?' she asked abruptly, picking up on Aldhere's previous statement.

Aldhere was not put out by the question.

'Naturally,' he replied. 'He is not going to leave me as a thorn irritating this land of the South Folk.'

'Why do you stay here, then? If you expect an attack, I would have thought you might move to any of the other kingdoms and sell your swords to – say, Sigehere?'

'You shock me by your mercenary attitude, good Sister,' grinned the outlaw. 'I think some mead is called for.'

He turned and brought a flagon to the table and poured the drinks.

Fidelma suppressed a sigh of resignation. She realised

that the provision of strong drink was an essential part of the ritual of hospitality to strangers.

'Since I have been in your country, I have come to the conclusion that drinking is a main pursuit of your people, Aldhere.'

Eadulf was looking uncomfortable and he cleared his throat noisily.

'Perhaps it is best if I ask the questions . . .' he said with a meaningful look at Fidelma. When she stared in annoyance at his intervention, he said softly: 'I have mentioned before that the people of this land are unused to what is seen as forwardness in women. The role of women among the South Folk is very different from the benefits that you enjoy . . .'

Aldhere interrupted him with a disapproving glance.

'Tush, holy *gerefa*! Would you make me out to be a barbarian? I have mixed with the Irish missionaries and know the different ways they have. They might not be our ways nor do we need approve of them. But one of the missionaries instructed me in the words of the Blessed Ambrose: *Quando hic sum, non jeiuno Sabbato; quando Romae sum, jeiuno Sabbato.*'

'When I'm here, I do not fast on the sabbath, when I am in Rome, I fast on the sabbath,' muttered Eadulf.

'Perhaps it is badly expressed,' apologised Aldhere, 'but what I am saying is that since you are used to being treated equally, then I shall treat you equally. Now what were you saying . . . ?' Abruptly, the erstwhile thane of Bretta's Ham slapped a hand against his thigh and uttered a bellow of laughter.

'By God! Yes! Drink. In you, Sister, I find not only a pious religieuse but one with a sense of humour. Indeed, much is accomplished by drinking here for drink unlocks secrets, it confirms our hopes, lifts burdens from anxious minds, teaches us new arts and urges the timorous into battle. For a bad night, there is always the soft mattress of mead, and many a friend and many a lover have met over a jug.'

Fidelma was amused by his response.

'You sound like a philosopher, Aldhere.'

The outlaw put his head to one side and winked.

'Only one who has borrowed his learning.'

'Yet we have a saying in my country – when the cock is drunk, he forgets about the hawk.'

Aldhere shook his head. 'I do not forget about my brother, Cild, nor about King Ealdwulf. My lookouts keep me posted.'

'And did they keep you posted about the passage of warriors of Ealdwulf's bodyguard through your forests?' asked Eadulf cynically.

To their surprise, Aldhere nodded.

'Escorting a coach? Oh yes, we knew about them.'

Eadulf shook his head disbelievingly. 'If you knew that, why did you not stop it?'

'For what reason, holy *gerefa*?' he asked as if amused. 'It was only the lord Sigeric, who was being escorted to Aldred's Abbey. He is too elderly to be a threat to anyone. And, really, holy *gerefa*, why would I want to attack him or his escort? Do you think I am as black as my brother Cild paints me?'

'Lord Sigeric?' Eadulf was astonished. 'He is the high steward to King Ealdwulf,' he explained quickly to Fidelma.

'Then you have good reason to attack him,' Fidelma pointed out.

'He would have advised on the matter of your outlawry,' Eadulf agreed. 'One might think that you would enjoy visiting vengeance on him.'

Aldhere shook his head. 'Did I not tell you that Botulf was going to send an appeal to him about my sentence of outlawry? It may well be that he has come to hear the matter,' he told them.

'I recall that you did say that,' confessed Eadulf almost reluctantly.

'It seems, holy *gerefa*, that you do not accept my good faith. Why should you be so sceptical of my intentions?'

'There are some people who think you are just as bad as your brother,' intervened Fidelma as Eadulf hesitated, not knowing how to answer.

Aldhere swung back to her, favouring her with a swift scrutiny although his expression was still one of humour.

'I don't doubt it. There are many who would take the word of Cild and paint me as black as Satan. Some more mead?'

'You did not finish answering my question,' Fidelma responded.

'Finish?'

'I asked you why it was that you remain in this country and so near Aldred's Abbey when it endangers you and your followers and you could easily find a safer haven elsewhere.'

Aldhere sat down for the first time, poured a large measure into his goblet and sipped it thoughtfully.

'It is a good question,' he mused.

'And does it have a good answer?' Fidelma pressed.

Aldhere returned her gaze, his face wreathed in a smile.

'Oh, I believe so. I am here searching for justice.'

Fidelma inclined her head in acknowledgment.

'Eadulf has told me of your story. Falsely accused of cowardice. An elder brother who wishes to see you destroyed for disinheriting him. But why remain here? How will that achieve justice?'

Aldhere leaned forward, suddenly serious.

'It is because I have faith, Sister.'

'Scripture says that faith is the substance of things hoped for without evidence. What is it that you hope for?'

'I have been robbed of my property. My character has been ruined. My reputation tainted. Yet I have faith that my character may be vindicated and my property restored; that my persecutors may be brought to justice. That is my faith, Sister, and that is why I and my followers will not be driven forth from this land of the South Folk, which is our land by right of birth and sword. We came here four generations ago and drove the Welisc from this land, where they had grown indolent and degenerate. We are of the Wuffingas, descendants of Woden, and what we take we will not give back.'

Fidelma sat back with lips pursed in disapproval.

Eadulf glanced at her nervously but she did not say anything for a moment or two.

'You have explained your philosophy well, Aldhere,' she said quietly. 'Now, what can you tell me about your brother? I presume that he would share your principles?'

Aldhere looked uncertain. 'What do you want to know about Cild?'

'You have given Brother Eadulf here the impresson that Cild was always unbalanced.'

Aldhere shrugged. 'He had strange moods and sometimes he would do things which were not driven by logic. He loved power, he loved wealth. Those were the only two things he ever loved.'

'He did not love Gélgeis?'

'She was a chieftain's daughter. He probably loved the power and wealth he thought he would inherit.'

'But these strange moods – you say he had them from a child? Do you know when they became manifest?'

'He was not liked by my father,' Aldhere said. 'I told the holy *gerefa* here. Before Cild grew too strong, my father often beat him and used to lock him up as punishment.'

'Was your father justified in this?'

Aldhere shook his head. 'I think the rogue moods that Cild displays were inherited from my father, who was a difficult man.'

'Your father never punished you in the same manner as Cild.'

'Never.' Aldhere smiled grimly. 'Cild was always singled out by him.'

'And your mother? What role did she play in this?'

Aldhere sniffed. 'My mother died when we were young and my father's mistresses did not enter our lives. We were left to ourselves and Cild had his own world to retreat into. But why do you ask these questions?'

'I am a little confused as to when Cild came back from the kingdom of Connacht. Was that before or after you had been outlawed?'

'Before.'

'Did he come back to Bretta's Ham when he arrived from Maigh Eo?'

'No. He went straight to the abbey of Aldred. He had managed to be appointed abbot there.'

'He took his wife with him?'

'He did. She was not a religieuse but went to live with him.'

'When did you first meet her?' asked Fidelma.

'I told the *gerefa* here.'

'Tell me.'

'It was when I first went to the abbey, after which it was clear that my brother and I would never agree. Then, after I was outlawed, I saw her again.'

'And what was your opinion of his wife?'

Aldhere rubbed his chin thoughtfully. 'As I told the *gerefa*, she was a sweet girl, innocent. How she had been persuaded to marry Cild, I do not know. She was the opposite to everything I saw in my brother. He was immoral, ambitious, thinking with his sword arm before his mind.'

'It sounds as if you liked the girl,' Fidelma observed.

Aldhere flushed slightly. 'I did not dislike her. She was Cild's wife. She came to see me here in this encampment simply because I was the brother of her husband. She wanted to help.'

'Remind me, what happened after you were outlawed?'

'Cild claimed my title and lands. Ealdwulf only compensated him with a small share and told him that he should remain as a religious. He affirmed Cild as abbot over the community at Aldred. I believe Ealdwulf was already anticipating the decision at Whitby, for the moment that decision was made he issued a decree that all those religious holding to the Columban order should be expelled from the kingdom.'

'Yet at that time Cild and Gélgeis were living happily together at Aldred's Abbey?'

'Happily?' There was a note of derision in Aldhere's voice.

'You question that?'

'Such an innocent young girl could not have been happy with Cild,' he replied sharply.

'You may well be right. On the other hand, it is amazing in life how couples we believe are mismatched are completely compatible,' reflected Fidelma. 'I am more interested in whether you knew of any reason for discord between them? I mean, to your personal knowledge.'

Aldhere say back and gazed moodily at his mead as if an answer lay in the clay pot.

'I had the impression that she was unhappy,' he said.

'Did she tell you as much?' pressed Fidelma.

'Yes, she did.'

'When was that?'

'When I met her.'

Fidelma frowned. 'She said this on her first meeting with you at the abbey, before you were outlawed?'

He shook his head. 'No, this was afterwards, when . . .'

'How many times did you see her after you came here?'

'I saw the girl a few times for she used to go walking near the abbey. The river stretches nearby and there are woods there.'

'What did she tell you?'

'That since Cild had not been able to get his own way about his claim to be thane of Bretta's Ham, he had become morose and restless. He displayed a cruelty that she had not thought possible in one who claimed to follow the religious life.'

'Did she say that Cild was cruel to her?'

Aldhere's lips thinned. 'She did.'

'Why do you think that she felt able to confess this to you?' asked Eadulf thoughtfully. 'You were, after all, a stranger even though you were Cild's brother. And the very fact that you were Cild's brother would surely not be conducive to an exchange of confidences.'

'I don't see why not. She knew that Cild had treated me as cruelly as he treated her. She was alone. She wanted someone to talk to. Someone to share her desolation with. I think it is natural.'

'What do you know of the circumstances of Gélgeis's death?'

Aldhere glanced at her suspiciously. 'What should I know of it?'

'I ask what you know, not what you should know.' Her reply was so tart that he blinked rapidly for a moment.

'Only the story that she had wandered into Hob's Mire near the abbey and been sucked under its treacherous bog,' he said, regaining his easy manner.

'And this was a year ago?'

'About that. Yes.'

'When was the last time you saw Gélgeis before that?'

'Two days before she died,' replied Aldhere.

'Two days?' queried Fidelma. 'You are absolutely sure of that?'

Aldhere grinned. 'Absolutely sure.'

'Were you having an affair with your brother's wife?' Fidelma asked abruptly.

'An affair? Not as such,' came the reluctant response.

Fidelma smiled sceptically. 'What would be your interpretation of your relationship with your brother's wife? I am intrigued to know that there is a relationship which can be described as not an affair as such.'

Aldhere actually looked uncomfortable for a moment. He knew that Fidelma was making fun of him.

'I was the friend she needed, the person she needed to confess her anguish and fears to. There was nothing else in it.'

'Accepting that,' agreed Fidelma, 'you say that you did have an assignation with her two days before she died?'

'We had arranged to meet – yes. We met in the woods along the river near the abbey. We went for a walk and she told me how bad the situation had become with Cild. She had been in touch with her family through the intermediacy of a religieux named Pol. Cild had found out and lost his temper and had Pol hanged out of hand. His excuse was that Pol was a heretic. Gélgeis said she was fearful and wanted me to put her in touch with some Columban religious who might help her to return to her father's estates.'

'What did you say?'

'I said that I would do my best to help her.'

'Then?'

'Then she left me.'

'Having heard what she had to say, you let her return to the abbey?' queried Eadulf incredulously.

'It was her decision,' replied Aldhere defensively. 'She could have come with me there and then and I would have protected her, but . . .' He shrugged.

'When did you hear that she was dead?' Fidelma asked.

'The news came the day after she had wandered into the mire.'

'Would her route to come to see you lie through the marshes? Through this place called Hob's Mire?'

'Not really. When she came to see me we usually met at the little copse near the abbey. I know what you are thinking. She did know the marsh.'

'Did she know it well?'

Aldhere was looking at her curiously.

'I would say she knew it very well,' he said at last.

'She knew about the dangers of Hob's Mire?'

'Most people know about the mire. It is notorious.' He hesitated and anticipating a demand for specifics added: 'Yes; she did know of it.'

'So why do you think that she would have departed from the known and safe route to go through the bog?'

'I do not think so and I know what you are suggesting.'

'Suggesting? I am merely seeking the answers to some questions. I just find it curious that if she knew the dangers of the marshes, she would have gone out of her way on that particular occasion to court them.'

Aldhere fell silent.

'Did you not attempt to make some inquiries when you heard of her death?' Fidelma asked.

'She was dead. Why would I need to know the reason why she wandered into the mire?'

'To ascertain if she was assisted in wandering into that mire.'

Aldhere was silent for a moment or two before he replied.

'The idea only occurred to me months later when it was too late. Indeed, I scarcely thought more of it until the other day when the holy *gerefa* here came wandering out of the marshes and had to be rescued from East Saxon raiders. He told me that Gélgeis's father and brother had arrived here in some vain attempt to force Cild to confess to her murder.

'I said then, and I say it to you now, Sister, that they have no hope. Only Cild's conscience would force him to admit his guilt – if, indeed, he is guilty – and the fact is that my brother has no conscience. So there is little hope of achieving anything by that means.'

Fidelma sighed softly. 'Rumours, surmises – I have not one hard fact to prevent the tragedy that will soon overtake us.' She stared abruptly into the eyes of Aldhere. 'Did you ever meet Mella?'

The outlaw's eyes widened a little.

'Mella?' he muttered.

'Gélgeis's twin sister. They were so alike that only the close family could tell them apart.'

'Of course not. What makes you ask if I met her?'

'She tried to dissuade Gélgeis from marriage to Cild. It was said that she was brought to this land.'

'But Mella—' began Aldhere. He stopped suddenly.

'Yes? Mella . . . what?' snapped Fidelma.

'Mella was taken in a slave raid and perished at sea.'

'How do you know that?'

Aldhere raised his hands helplessly. 'Gélgeis must have told me.'

'But this happened *after* Gélgeis came to the land of the South Folk. How did she know?'

'I don't know. She told me. She knew.'

'When did she tell you?'

'I can't remember. On one of our walks, I suppose.'

'And what did she say exactly?'

'About Mella?' countered Aldhere.

'About Mella,' repeated Fidelma solemnly.

'That her sister had been reported taken by slavers and that the slave ship was lost at sea. I know no more than that.'

It was clear that Aldhere was lying. But why was he doing so?

He was rising.

'Enough of this talk,' he said brusquely, 'I have duties to see to. Stay here and rest until I return.'

He went out, leaving them alone in the hut.

Eadulf turned to Fidelma but she raised a hand and placed a finger to her lips, gesturing with her head towards the door.

'Tell me about this man Sigeric,' she commanded in a slightly raised voice.

Eadulf was disappointed.

'As I said, he is high steward to the King and was high steward to King Athelwold before him. He is said to be a bastard son of Ricbert who ruled here for about three years. Ricbert was a pagan who assassinated Eorpwald who had converted to Christianity.'

Fidelma raised her hands in protest.

'Truly, I cannot get my tongue around these Anglo-Saxon names. You say that Sigeric is high steward? Is he a bishop?'

'No, he is still a pagan. Our kings have found him an

excellent adviser and chief judge. There is no one who knows more of the laws of the Wuffingas. That is the law which we hold here—'

'I did gather that,' Fidelma said waspishly. Then she relaxed a little. 'What I am interested in is why would Sigeric, your chief Brehon, be sent to Aldred's Abbey? Is it truly to announce a pardon for Aldhere or is there some other purpose?'

Eadulf realised what Fidelma was thinking.

'Do you think that it has something to do with the accusation against Cild? Perhaps Gadra or his son contacted him. Perhaps Sigeric is here to forestall the same tragedy that you are seeking to prevent?'

'I wish I could believe that,' Fidelma said. 'I don't think your King Ealdwulf would know anything about the problems that would arise from the *troscud* of Gadra. But what is his purpose? The trouble is that the answer to that question is back at Aldred's Abbey.'

Chapter Fifteen

Eadulf regarded her with some nervousness.

'Are you really serious about going back to the abbey? The idea is fraught with danger.'

Fidelma grimaced indifferently.

'Name me another method of finding the truth other than going back. It is in Aldred's Abbey that the strands of this mystery entwine. It might well be a godsend that this lawyer or judge of your people has gone there. If he is an honest man then he may well be our salvation.'

'But if he prefers to take the side of Abbot Cild, then where will we be?' protested Eadulf.

'At least we have an advantage – we can get into the abbey without anyone observing us and perhaps we can get to the guests' quarters and find this old judge before Abbot Cild is alerted.'

'That is something of a desperate measure,' observed Eadulf. 'Most likely we would be seized by Cild or even Sigeric's bodyguard and would then be unable to help ourselves, let alone help anyone else or solve the mystery.'

There came the sound of raised voices outside. Eadulf went to the door of the hut and looked out.

'It's Aldhere's woman . . . the Frankish woman of whom I spoke to you.'

Fidelma joined him at the door.

Outside, the flaxen-haired woman had dismounted from a horse and was speaking rapidly to Aldhere. Another man was just dismounting and unloading some panniers of items which seemed to be foodstuffs. It seemed to confirm Aldhere's story that they had been to the neighbouring town to purchase goods. Aldhere was replying to Bertha quietly and also with rapidity. Bertha intervened and as she spoke she punched the air with her fist to emphasise whatever point she was making. She turned abruptly, remounted her horse and rode away. They had been too far away for Eadulf and Fidelma to hear any of what was said.

Fidelma shrugged and returned to her seat.

'It seems not all Saxon women are quiescent in front of their menfolk.' She smiled thinly.

'Bertha is a Frank,' pointed out Eadulf.

'A fine distinction. Anyway, I need to question our friend Wiglaf before we leave here,' she said as Eadulf turned back into the room.

'He said he would be returning to the camp by now,' replied Eadulf with a frown. 'I wonder where he is?'

'Where who is?' came Aldhere's voice. He had come through the door behind Eadulf unobserved.

Fidelma was not perturbed.

'Wiglaf. The man who brought us here.'

Aldhere's eyes narrowed for a moment.

'What can he tell you that I can't?' he demanded suspiciously.

'Perhaps nothing. None the less, he was in personal touch with Brother Botulf at the monastery until the other night when Botulf asked to meet you.'

Aldhere nodded slowly. 'That is correct.'

'So he might have something to add which may be useful.'

'Well, as you know, he is posted as a lookout but he

should be returning to camp shortly. I trust you will join us in the midday meal?'

'It will be a pleasure.' Fidelma smiled. 'Will your Frankish friend be joining us?'

Aldhere hesitated for a moment and then smiled back.

'Bertha has other matters to attend to for the moment, Sister. Perhaps she will join us later.'

'And Lioba?' asked Eadulf, with a sudden burst of mischievousness. 'Is she often a guest here?'

Aldhere's face reddened a little. His jaw came up defensively.

'What do you know of Lioba?'

'I am told that she is rather a wilful girl, well known at the abbey . . . and at your camp.'

Aldhere thought for a moment and then he shrugged.

'You have a good ear for gossip, holy *gerefa*. The girl is a local peasant's daughter who needs must make a living. She has contacts at the abbey and so she comes to my camp to supply me with news that I might not be able to gather in other ways.'

It was clear that Aldhere was not interested in amplifying the subject. Fidelma changed it, for there was something else on her mind.

'Have you heard of rumours of attacks made by East Saxon warbands recently?' she asked abruptly.

Aldhere smiled and looked at Eadulf.

'Your friend, the holy *gerefa*, should be able to give you information on that. He was nearly killed by an East Saxon longship's crew the other day.'

'Ah, that I know about. I meant a major attack by several ships.'

Aldhere expression was one of derision.

'Are you talking about Sigehere and his warbands? They have not the capability to invade in force. The kingdom of the East Saxons is too divided. Sigehere and

Sebbi are at each other's throats. Individual longboats may strike here and there from time to time and there have been a few attacks along the border but never a major attack. The men of Sigehere are like gnats, darting over a summer's marshland. Pinpricks of irritation but no more. What makes you ask such a question?'

It was what she had expected to hear.

'Someone said that there had been such an attack two days ago. I suppose they were mistaken?'

Aldhere nodded emphatically. 'When people are fearful they imagine all manner of things. I would know of such an attack.'

'I was wondering,' Fidelma adopted a musing tone, 'as you are in enmity with your own King, whether you might welcome the King of the East Saxons in this land?'

Aldhere drew himself up with an angry scowl.

'I might be an outlaw but no traitor am I,' he snapped. 'From a man, those words would invite me to draw my sword.'

'Then it is lucky that I am merely a woman,' replied Fidelma without contriteness. 'You see, there are those who would say it would be logical that in your anger against Ealdwulf you might turn to Sigehere.'

'Show them to me and I will test their truth against mine with a sword blade,' growled Aldhere.

Fidelma smiled faintly. 'All that you would test would be who is the better swordsman. Why do you think that such stories circulate about you?'

'I presume that such evil tales circulate because my brother spreads them. Who else would do so?'

'So they are malicious and entirely without foundation?'

'You are lucky that I am of a tranquil nature, Sister,' smiled Aldhere, without any humour in his features. 'I have told you that I would not sell my people. Ealdwulf may one day regret that he listened to prejudice in order to outlaw me. But he is the King and my quarrel is with him within the confines of this kingdom. I might raise a body from within this land to force him to see my viewpoint but I would not consort with any outside enemy to overthrow him.' He paused and then said: 'Now I fear your questions have come to an end. There is bread, meat and mead. We will eat and await the coming of Wiglaf.'

Fidelma accepted this curtailment to her inquiries and they fell to a meal which was spent by Aldhere in asking questions about the countries they had seen and the attitudes of the people there. He was particularly interested about the pilgrimage Fidelma and Eadulf had made to Rome. His questions were posed with wit and acumen.

Some time passed and they realised that there was no sign of the return of Wiglaf and his men. Fidelma could see that Aldhere, in spite of his bland and genial exterior, was growing concerned. It was long past the time when Wiglaf had been expected back and finally Aldhere could no longer conceal his anxiety. He stood up and apologised to them: 'If you will permit, I shall take a couple of my men and go in search of Wiglaf.'

Fidelma rose at once.

'In that case, we will ride with you. The hour grows late and we have much to do also. With luck, we may meet Wiglaf on the way and I can put my few questions to him then.'

Aldhere did not object and within a short time he and two of his men, along with Fidelma and Eadulf, were striking south on horseback along the woodland trail.

They had not gone far when one of the men raised a cry.

They did not have to look hard to see the reason.

A body was stretched on the ground before them. They

swiftly ascertained that it was one of Wiglaf's men. There were two arrows embedded in the man's chest and blood was staining the snow around him.

Another cry.

Through the trees a few yards away two more bodies were revealed. Once again, arrows showed the means of their death.

Aldhere and his men had unslung their shields and carried their swords in their hands, glancing around nervously at the surrounding woods.

A few yards more and they came across the body of Wiglaf. An arrow had transfixed his throat, another had penetrated under the breast bone. Eadulf looked down and sighed sadly.

'A man born to hang will never drown,' he whispered.

Fidelma looked at him in bewilderment. Eadulf shrugged. 'That was his philosophy,' he explained.

'Hey!'

They turned to where one of Aldhere's men had dismounted and was examining one of the other men.

'This man is still alive, thane of Bretta's Ham,' cried the man.

They dismounted and gathered round.

'I know something of medicine. Let me see,' insisted Eadulf, pushing them gently aside. One swift glance at the arrow wounds and he turned back with a quick shake of his head. The man was beyond help.

'Who did this?' called Aldhere softly, bending down to the man. 'Did you see who it was?'

The dying man looked up, eyes vacant, not really seeing those bending over him. His lips were dried and bloodied. They quivered a little. No sound came.

'Who was responsible?' cried Aldhere, bending down close to the man's ear. 'Speak. Try to speak.'

The lips trembled again.

'The . . . the abbot . . .'

There was a sigh and the man fell back.

Aldhere stood up and his face was full of anger.

'Cild!' he muttered.

'Lord!' cried one of his men, who had been examining the other bodies. He came forward and held something out.

Adhere took the object and turned it over in his hands, and then he showed Fidelma and Eadulf.

'There is no doubt about it,' he said softly.

The object that he held was a crucifix on a leather thong which had been snapped off.

'Cild is responsible for this atrocity.'

Fidelma was surprised at the bitterness in his voice.

'This hatred between you and your brother seems to run deep. More deeply than I think you are telling me.'

Aldhere's eyes narrowed. 'What do you mean?'

'I speak of the fact that the abbot, Abbot Cild, leads his religious brethren out, armed, in order to attack you and your followers. He slays your men without compunction. You ask me to believe that it is an enmity born of the fact that your father disinherited him in favour of you. I find it hard to understand the depth of hatred that he must feel to do this simply because of a disinheritance.'

Aldhere's face was grim.

'You do not know the depth of my brother's soul, Sister. A soul filled with black hatred against everyone.' He pointed around at the bodies that lay in the woods. 'Do you need further evidence of his evil?'

He turned and began to issue instructions to his men to gather the bodies ready for transportation back to the encampment.

'What will you do now?' he demanded, turning back

to Fidelma and Eadulf. 'Do you want to stay within the protection of my camp?'

'There is little to be done,' muttered Fidelma with a shake of her head. 'Wiglaf was the last person to speak with Botulf and Botulf was probably the only lead we had to discover what is really going in Aldred's Abbey. We will press on. There is little point in remaining here with you.'

'Do you mean that you will return to Canterbury?' demanded Aldhere in surprise.

'Perhaps,' replied Fidelma shortly.

They mounted their ponies and left Aldhere and his men to their gruesome task.

They were some distance away when Eadulf said: 'I know you, Fidelma. I am sure that you do not mean to go back to Canterbury yet.'

Fidelma grimaced.

'Of course not,' she pouted.

'Then you still mean to go back to the abbey? Even after this example of Cild's brutality?'

'Had you any doubt of that?'

Eadulf was silent for a moment and then he shrugged. 'I suppose not.' He hesitated and then added: 'You really mean to appeal for assistance to Lord Sigeric?'

'It seems as if that is our only hope of preventing the *troscud*. If we cannot discover what happened to Gelgéis and Botulf then we must find another way of preventing Gadra's ritual fast.'

'Would the consequences really be as serious as you say they would?'

Fidelma looked at him and he read the answer in her face.

'If they were not,' she said, 'then I would be on the road to a port looking for a ship bound for home and not spending one hour more in this wilderness of hate and war.'

Eadulf blinked at the brutality of her words. She saw his reaction and immediately felt contrite.

'It is no good my pretending that I like this country with its customs, Eadulf. I find it a place of violent and intemperate nature. A place of extremes, aggressive, presumptuous and inconsiderate of others.'

Eadulf looked shocked. 'You have hardly seen enough to come to that decision.'

'Have I not?'

'These are my people, Fidelma. Yes, they are sprung from a tradition more used to handling a sword than a plough but I know my people to be straightforward, ingenious and disposed to leadership in enterprises of danger. We are a combative people, that is true, but we are enthusiastic in our religion and our politics and at all times we are determined.'

Fidelma looked at him in amusement.

'You are fiercely defendant of your people, Eadulf.' She smiled.

'I fear that you do them an injustice.'

'I have to comment as I find.'

'Comment on the likes of Cild and Aldhere? They are not typical of my people.'

'They are not the shapers of my thoughts here. I observe your customs and your laws. Withal your people seem brash and inexperienced in civilised ways of living. Perhaps the disposition to leadership you mention ought to be balanced by the desire among individuals to grow more.'

Eadulf flushed in annoyance.

'I do not find this worthy of you, Fidelma,' he said sulkily. 'There is war, murder, hate and jealousy in your own land, yet you do not condemn it as barbaric.'

'Because we have evolved a law system, a social system, in which such things are not the normal way

281

of life. I fear that in your land, Eadulf, even the law seems entrenched in the brutality of life.'

Eadulf did not respond. It was clear that he was deeply annoyed. Fidelma suppressed a sigh of irritation as she saw the anger which she had provoked in Eadulf. But she knew that his temper, though quick and fretful, was all flame, burning with a sudden brightness, and dying out just as quickly, capricious and soon pacified. Eadulf was not one to bear resentment for long.

They had ridden in silence for a while when her estimation of his character was proved.

It was growing dark, even though the hour was not far advanced, for the day always darkened early in winter. So far as Eadulf could estimate they were approaching the area known as Hob's Mire and he was feeling some trepidation. He attuned his eyes to watching for the wisp of blue flame. While the logical part of his mind knew the explanation behind firedrake, the *ignis fatuus*, he also recalled the legends of the 'corpse fire' as his people called it.

'Beyond those trees ahead,' he warned softly, 'is the abbey. We must go carefully from here.'

She nodded. 'I think that the best way in will be to enter as we came out.'

'I wish we had some daylight to see by,' he muttered. 'It will be difficult finding the entrance passage without a light.'

He paused, concentrating his gaze into the gloom ahead and then suddenly he reached forward and touched her arm. She turned to question him but saw that he had placed a finger against his lips. She waited and then he indicated ahead.

'I think I saw movement there,' he whispered. 'There are some horsemen by the trees.'

'Horsemen?' she replied softly. 'Can you see what manner of men they are?'

'Not from here.'

'A strange place for a gathering.' Suddenly she was dismounting. 'Let's leave our ponies here, behind those trees, well out of sight of the track. Then we can move up towards them in order to find out more.'

'Is that wise?' Eadulf questioned. 'There are several men who may be armed.'

Fidelma grinned in the gloom. 'I deem it wise and, as Phaedrus says, "wisdom is ever stronger than mere force". Come.'

Eadulf climbed down reluctantly, led the ponies to the shelter of the trees and secured the reins to some strong bushes. He rejoined her and together they crept cautiously forward along the track.

'We should move more into the wood,' he suggested nervously after they had progressed several yards. 'Even though it is dusk, the snow gives us no cover.'

She nodded quickly, appreciating the logic, and moved off the track to the right where the trees rose on the incline of a small knoll that would bring them in a position overlooking the gathering. They found shelter behind some rocks no more than five paces away from the group, from where it was easy to make out the half-dozen riders muffled against the coldness of the weather.

The first voice they heard made Eadulf shiver. He knew the voice even though Fidelma did not recognise it.

'Well, Brother Willibrod? How much longer?'

It was Abbot Cild himself.

Fidelma certainly recognised the voice which answered him.

'They should not be long now,' came the voice of the one-eyed *dominus* of the abbey.

Eadulf leaned forward and placed his lips against Fidelma's ear.

'Cild was the first speaker,' he whispered, so that she would understand who it was whom Brother Willibrod was addressing.

'If Brother Higbald is not here within a few minutes, then I am returning to the abbey. It is cold and it is dark and we have an important guest to attend to.'

'Do not concern yourself. The lord Sigeric will be resting from his journey for a while longer.'

'He is the King's envoy. We must see that he is treated with all courtesy.'

'It will be done,' came the assurance of the *dominus*.

'Are you sure that this is the right spot?'

'Brother Higbald was most specific. He sent one of the brethren to—'

'I know, I know,' interrupted Abbot Cild irritably. 'Though why he could not tell me this important news on returning to the abbey, I don't know. Are you sure that he said it was to do with Gadra and his claims?'

'You know all that his messenger told me.'

'I do not understand it. Who gave Brother Higbald permission to leave the abbey and go traversing the countryside?'

'All should be explained when he arrives. I am sure it will,' Brother Willibrod assured him.

There came a startled exclamation from one of the figures below.

'Christ and His Apostles protect us!' was the hoarse shout. 'Look!'

One of the riders had raised an arm to point across the marshes on the far side of the track.

Fidelma and Eadulf raised their heads to see what was causing the alarm. Out on the marshes they could see a flickering blue light. Eadulf shivered slightly.

'Corpse fire,' he whispered to Fidelma.

'*Ignis fatuus*,' she responded in the same tone. 'A natural phenomenon. Why does it cause such distress among them?'

Abbot Cild's sharp cry drowned her out.

'God protect me!'

He had turned and was urging his horse back along the track towards the abbey. Brother Willibrod and his companions were hard on his heels.

It was then that Eadulf placed a hand on Fidelma's arm and pointed in the direction of the flickering blue flame. A shape seemed to be actually glowing there. Fidelma's eyes narrowed as she sought to make it out. It was a figure. A figure on horseback. She exhaled sharply. It was the figure of a woman.

Eadulf, at her side, groaned softly.

'It is the woman I saw in the abbey on that first night.' His voice was edged in horror. 'It is the ghost of Gelgéis!'

Chapter Sixteen

Eadulf was frozen for the moment by the sheer horror of what he thought he was seeing. Then he was aware that Fidelma was on her feet and moving rapidly down the knoll to the now deserted track before them. For a second he was undecided what to do, then he gave a cry of alarm and started chasing her.

'What are you doing?' he gasped as he attempted to reach her and halt her rapid advance.

'I'm going to get closer to whatever that is,' replied Fidelma as she darted across the track and went plunging into the darkness beyond, heading towards the distant flickering blue light.

'Stop! For heaven's sake, stop! This is Hob's Mire,' cried Eadulf in desperation.

She did not heed his warning cry and, oblivious of the dangers, she plunged on with Eadulf in hot pursuit. They heard the startled whinny of a horse and then the curiously glowing figure seemed to disappear abruptly. Fidelma did not pause but continued to press forward. Behind her, Eadulf, trying to keep up, slipped and found himself sinking into the mud which lay just below the surface snow.

'Help me!' he cried in panic as he felt himself slipping.

Fidelma hesitated, glanced behind, saw him struggling in the gloom and grabbed at his arm. He had only sunk up to the calves and it was easy to pull him back onto the path. He accomplished the feat more by his own strength than Fidelma's; but she gave him the impetus to do so, steadying his panic. However, the incident made Fidelma realise that she had let her determination to close on the ghost-like figure overturn her sense of danger. She silently cursed herself for a fool.

'Are you all right, Eadulf?' she asked with concern as he sat on the firm strip of pathway breathing heavily from his exertion.

'I think I might be,' he confessed uncertainly.

'I am sorry. I behaved foolishly. There is nothing for it but to make our way back to the track. It is no use trying to pursue whoever it was tonight.'

Eadulf gazed up in the darkness but she could not see his bewildered expression.

'*Whoever*?' he demanded. 'Don't you mean *whatever* it was?'

'I mean whoever. If only there was some means of lighting a path to that spot. I wonder if we could find our way to the *ignis fatuus* in daylight. I'd like to examine the ground.'

Eadulf rose and shook his head slowly.

'Right now, I would settle on finding my way back out of this mire safely rather than go forward in search of a will o' the wisp.' He looked around, shivering.

Dusk had given way to darkness and the countryside seemed to coalesce into an unfriendly backdrop of threatening shadows. There were few points of reference to guide them back. The path on which they had entered the mire had not been a straight one.

Eadulf led the way, treading slowly and cautiously from one position to another, testing the firmness of the ground before each guarded step. It was some time before they came back to the main track. They were just about to collapse and rest on the firm ground when the sound of horses came to their ears.

'It may be Cild returning,' whispered Eadulf. 'Quick! Let's get back in the trees, behind the rocks.'

Fidelma obeyed, but she realised that the horses were coming in the opposite direction from the abbey.

They plunged breathlessly up the knoll through the trees and flung themselves behind the cover of the rocks. They had barely reached them when a half-dozen horsemen came to a noisy halt below. One of them held aloft a brand torch but it did not throw out sufficient light to illuminate their faces.

'Not here!' cried a female voice. 'Are you sure this is the place you told them to be?'

'Of course,' came Brother Higbald's voice out of the gloom. 'Are you sure that you delivered the message correctly, Arwald?'

A male voice rose indignantly. 'Word for word as you gave it to me, my lord Higbald. I gave it word for word to Brother Willibrod.'

Lord Higbald! Eadulf's eyebrows rose in the darkness.

'He did not suspect?' came Higbald's voice again. But the female voice interrupted with a licentious chuckle.

'That old idiot? He would not be suspicious about anything. He thinks only of one thing.'

'Nevertheless, was he suspicious when you gave him the message, Arwald?' insisted Higbald.

'Not at all,' came the response.

'Then God rot them! They may have gone back to the abbey instead of waiting for us.'

'More than likely, Higbald.' It was the female speaker again, a firm assured voice.

'Then God rot them!' Higbald repeated.

The woman chuckled again. 'That's no way for a pious

brother to behave, Higbald. Try to maintain your holy
orders a little longer. Anyway, there is no cause to fret. I
think we have done enough to set the wheels in motion.'

'But if I return to the abbey now, Lioba, then I will
have to make some excuse about Gadra.'

'Easy enough,' declared Lioba. 'Anyway, perhaps
tonight might have oversalted the dish.'

'Very well,' came Higbald's voice again. 'I will return
to the abbey and make my excuses. We'll see if this old
man, Sigeric, is as astute as he is reputed to be. We will
meet tomorrow evening in the chapel.'

'Is that wise?'

'No one is suspicious. Let us give the pot one more
stir and then I am sure King Ealdwulf will be forced to
march against Aldhere.'

The band of horsemen moved on, sliding rapidly
into a canter and disappearing down the track towards
the abbey.

Eadulf rose to his feet and helped Fidelma up.

'What do you make of that? This grows more mysterious by the hour.'

'On the contrary, Eadulf, I am beginning to see some
light for the first time. We have another call to make
before going back to the abbey. How far is Mul's farmhouse from here?'

'Mul's farmhouse?' Eadulf was surprised. 'Why . . . ?'
He paused. Although he could not see Fidelma's face
in the darkness he realised that it would be registering
irritation at his half-finished question. 'It is under an
hour's ride. Less, if those clouds pull away from the
moon and we are able to see the path more clearly. I
know the way to Frig's Tun well from here.'

'That is good,' said Fidelma. 'Do you think Mul would
know the paths through Hob's Mire well enough to guide
us in daylight?'

'I don't know. I suppose that he would know ways through the mire. Why do you want him to guide you?'

'I have already told you. I want to examine the area where we saw the *ignis fatuus*. I am beginning to piece things together and if I am right about that particular piece . . . well, I think that I will have the whole picture of what is happening in this place.'

'Truly?' Eadulf was astounded.

'Truly,' Fidelma responded firmly. 'But first we will have to persuade Mul to give us hospitality for one more night.'

'Mul can probably be persuaded to do anything for a coin,' replied Eadulf cynically. 'So you do not plan to go on to the abbey and speak with Sigeric?'

'Not yet. I think what has happened here in the last hour or so has given a new dimension to this problem and I need that final piece of information before I can present a believable case to Sigeric.'

'Should we not discuss it first?' Eadulf sounded almost petulant at her mystifying pronouncement.

'When would I not discuss any matter with you?' she countered irritably. 'Of course we'll discuss it. But let us start out for Mul's farmhouse rather than stand here wasting time.'

Although dawn had come an hour before, the day was grey and gloomy, almost like dusk. White clouds edged with grey hung low and almost motionless in the sky. There was no hope that the pale winter sun would ever penetrate the overcast that seemed at one with the grey snow-covering that spread across the landscape. It was a melancholy vista.

Mul was leading the way on one of his mules, sitting easily astride it without benefit of saddle. Behind him came Fidelma and Eadulf on their borrowed ponies. The countryside through which they moved was like some fantastic dream landscape. The snow-covered panorama was mainly flat with little dark patches of evergreen woodland here and there and a distant grey, jagged rock summit poking sharply up in the evenness of the place, like a huge stone thrown down in the middle of the plain by the giant hand of some god. It was a bleak and wild vista and the only movement was the gush of an occasional stream across their tracks, fed by gently melting snow. The gaunt leafless trees were almost sinister as they rose in the gloomy landscape. There seemed little to distinguish the flat stretch of marshland. Apart from the occasional dark shadow of a flitting unidentifiable bird in the sky, there seemed no other animals abroad, nor any sound to distinguish them.

Mul halted his mule and swung round to watch Fidelma and Eadulf come up to him and halt.

'Well, there is Hob's Mire.' He gestured with an outstretched arm. 'You can see the lines of trees ahead. Those run by the river. That is the River Alde ahead and about a mile over there, beyond that tree-covered hill, is Aldred's Abbey.'

Eadulf frowned slightly.

'We are approaching the mire from the wrong direction,' he complained. 'I cannot estimate where the *ignis fatuus* was situated.'

Mul grimaced cynically. 'I am taking you the safest way into the mire, *gerefa*. If you want to kill yourselves, then that is your concern. You asked me to show you into the mire and that I will, but do not ask me to put myself in danger.'

Fidelma smiled in reassurance. 'We would not ask you to do that. However, we do need to get our bearings. It is important that we find the exact place.'

Mul sniffed in disgust and pointed with his finger towards a bank of trees in the distance.

'See that line? That is where a track runs which would lead you to the river bank and then along to the wooden bridge across the Alde and to the abbey. I think that is the road you say you were on last night.'

Eadulf screwed up his eyes to examine the distant terrain.

'I think I have the position now,' he admitted slowly. 'See that small hill covered in trees? That is where we were last night.'

Fidelma followed his gaze.

'So we must aim our steps in that direction. Mul, is there a path from here which would cross towards that point?'

'Not directly, but I can take you across. It will be a tight path, though. Only room for one horse at a time. Are you willing to try it?'

She inclined her head in confirmation.

'That, after all, is why we came to you,' she answered gravely.

The farmer pulled a face. He glanced to Eadulf.

'Are you ready, *gerefa*?'

'Of course,' Eadulf almost snapped.

'Then follow me in single file and do not stray from where I lead with my horse. One false step and you and the horse will disappear in these treacherous mud flats. Do you understand?'

He turned his mount and set off into the white landscape. Fidelma realised that under that coating of snow lay the soft green sedges and bog holes that waited eagerly to clutch their victims and drag them down to oblivion. She leaned forward over her pony's shoulder and kept a careful eye on the pathway which the farmer's mule picked out for them.

Here and there, poking through the snow, were thin spikes of dying rushes, and now and then there was a strange plopping sound as a bubble of air burst through the mud from some indescribable depth, pushing upwards perhaps from the rotting remains of some animal that had been dragged under.

There was a sudden movement and something took off from a clump of reeds in front of her. She thought for a moment that it was an owl, but then she saw the brown and black streaked plumage and the green legs which were usually an effective means of camouflage to eyes less sharp than Fidelma's. Then came a resonant booming sound.

'A bittern!' she exclaimed.

'You have a good eye, Sister,' called Mul appreciatively.

'Do you know anything about *ignis fatuus*, Mul?' she called back.

'What?'

'She means firedrake,' called Eadulf.

'Oh, that.' Mul shrugged carelessly. 'You can see firedrake quite regularly in these marshlands. Corpse fire, it is called in these parts. It's a pale flickering light that appears on the marshland. A lot of people don't like it but I've grown up on the marshes. There's no call to be alarmed by it. You saw it last night?'

'We did indeed,' replied Fidelma.

'You should have told me. If you wanted to know what it is I could have told you. No need to come all the way out here into the marsh.'

Fidelma shook her head. 'No, it was not just the *ignis fatuus* that I wanted to see—'

Mul interrupted her. 'You really only see it in the dark because the flame is too light to see in daylight. This will be a wasted journey.'

'No; I need to see the ground nearby,' insisted Fidelma. 'But tell us, what causes it?'

'What causes corpse fire? You know of the gases given off by animal corpses . . . in fact, the smell both plant and animal corpses give off when they disintegrate? The smell is the gas. Sometimes there is a spontaneous ignition and that's when you see the light. It is the gas burning. It's eerie and you can understand why people are sometimes afraid of it.' He waved his hand across the flat marshes. 'Plenty of animals have been sucked down into this mire so there are plenty of rotting corpses underneath it to create the corpse fire. Do you still want to go on?'

Fidelma looked up and measured the distance to the track which she could see they were now nearing.

'Is it possible to work our way a little to the right?' she asked, not answering the question directly.

Mul glanced in the direction she indicated and shrugged.

'Yes, but stay close,' he advised.

They moved on for a while and when Mul halted they found themselves on a large island of firm ground, a slight rise which was surrounded by the level flat area of the mire. The layer of snow barely covered the surrounding area and they could see the dark threatening mud beneath.

'Stop!' cried Fidelma, suddenly sliding from her pony. 'Don't move further.'

Mul looked at her as if she were mad.

'It's all right,' he said, 'this place is as firm as anywhere . . .'

But that was not what Fidelma had meant.

She walked quickly forward and went down on one knee. The area of snow, lying more thickly here on firm ground than on the warmer mud flats, was churned up. There were prints in the hardened snow which were only just beginning to melt in the warmer air of morning.

Eadulf had dismounted and come up behind her.

'What is it?' he demanded.

She pointed downwards.

'Someone stood here both on foot and then on horse-back. One horse . . . see the prints. One person. Small footprints. What does that tell you?'

'A small man or . . .'

'A woman. They stood near the edge of the mire here. They must have known what they were doing. A false step and there would have been another corpse rotting in the mire.'

Mul was standing patiently holding the reins of their mounts.

'I don't understand. What are you looking for?' he demanded.

'I have found it,' replied Fidelma with satisfaction, turning slightly towards him. Then to Eadulf she said: 'This is the mystery of the so-called ghost that appeared last night. Someone obviously navigated their way here by horseback. That was the figure we all saw.'

Eadulf glanced across the mire to the knoll on which they had stayed hidden on the previous night watching Abbot Cild.

'But how did she appear in that shimmering light? What about the firedrake? It is hard to manipulate that.'

Fidelma sniffed the air. 'Smell that?'

Eadulf cautiously sniffed and caught a malodorous reek. He had been among the dead often enough to know the signs.

'That is a gaseous smell of rotting corpses,' he admitted.

Fidelma glanced at Mul. 'What do you say, Mul? Is he right?'

The farmer looked confused by their comments.

'There's plenty of fuel here for the firedrake,' he said.

'And your sharp eyes should have picked out the flame already. See?'

He pointed in front of them.

Some way away they saw a curious shimmering against the white snowy background, something like a heat haze. That, in fact, was exactly what it was.

'If you were able to put your hand in that,' observed Mul, 'you would be burnt. That's a flame, but it's so faint that you can't really see it until night falls and then you get the eerie blue light which people call corpse fire.'

Fidelma breathed out gently.

'So these lights burn both by day and by night and we don't really see them until there is darkness enough to give the contrast?'

'Exactly so.'

Eadulf stood up and glanced around with hands on hips.

'I see your reasoning, Fidelma. But there is still an explanation needed.'

'Which is?' asked Fidelma.

'You told me last night that you felt that the figure we saw was no ghostly apparition, but a real woman. You have now demonstrated that the firedrake was simply a natural phenomenon. Fine. But how can you explain that as well as the firedrake we saw the outline of the woman glowing? That she – not merely the firedrake flame – had a ghostly appearance? That is what scared Abbot Cild and his men – not anything else.'

Fidelma had also risen and walked back to her pony. She stroked its muzzle for a few moments before speaking.

'A few years ago, Eadulf, it was a midwinter much like this, and I was on my way home to Cashel. I was coming through the snowbound mountains and was forced to stop the night at an inn. The innkeeper and his wife thought they were being haunted. They had seen this vision. It turned out to be someone trying to scare them. That person was also able to give himself a curious glowing aura.'

'How?' demanded Eadulf. 'How did they do it?'

'In my country there is a yellow clay-like substance that gives off a curious luminosity. It is scooped from the walls of caves. We call it *mearnáil*. It glows in the gloom. I don't know what it might be called here. But I believe the woman who came here had it smeared on her clothing and with the flickering flame of the firedrake before her, it reflected on the clay she had smeared on herself and that is why we saw the ghostly image.'

Eadulf pursed his lips in a soundless whistle.

'You mean this "haunting" of Cild is some strange conspiracy?'

'I think so.'

'And Botulf knew about it? He had discovered who was behind it? That is what led to his death?'

'It will take a little time to work out,' cautioned Fidelma.

Mul had been standing watching them with a look of incomprehension on his features. Fidelma turned to him with a smile.

'You have been a great help, Mul. It may well be that we shall be able to procure a larger sum in recompense than the few coins we have been able to give you. If my idea works out correctly, I think you will also be avenged for the murder of your wife and children.'

Mul returned her smile grimly.

'For the avenging of my family, I am prepared to give what little I own in the world,' he said quietly.

'Then I would ask you to indulge us further, Mul. We are going to the abbey to find this man . . .' She glanced at Eadulf in interrogation.

'The lord Sigeric,' he supplied.

'Sigeric. He went to the abbey yesterday and, if Brother Eadulf is correct, then he is the one person who will help us. If he is willing, we might need your help further. Is there anywhere in the vicinity of the abbey where you can wait until we contact you?'

'Aye,' he agreed. 'There is a smithy just south of the bridge. I'll wait there for word from you. If it means the destruction of Cild I am prepared to wait until the crack of doom. You may find me there.'

Fidelma glanced up at the sky. There was still no sun to regulate the day but she guessed that it lacked only a couple of hours until noon.

'If you do not hear from us by mid-afternoon, then I think you can conclude that we have not been able to persuade Sigeric to help us.' She paused and grimaced. 'Now, Mul, you can lead us out of this mire and set us on the right path to the abbey.'

Having left Mul to continue on to the bridge, Fidelma and Eadulf turned off through the woods behind the abbey buildings. They found the path they had taken on their escape from the abbey and now discovered a little copse where they decided to leave the ponies, tethered in case they needed to reclaim them in a hurry.

Eadulf led the way back to the tunnel entrance. He remembered the route better than Fidelma, for she had not been entirely well when they had left by that means. The entrance, despite being overgrown with evergreens, was not too difficult for Eadulf to find.

Fidelma was surprised when Eadulf halted outside it and from his *marsupium* brought forth a piece of candle which he proceeded to light from his flint and tinder box. He looked up and grinned.

'I had a feeling that we might be returning by this

tunnel and so took the opportunity to appropriate a piece of candle from Mul's farmhouse.'

He turned and pushed into the tunnel, dank and chill. The darkness closed in oppressively as soon as they were a few paces along the tunnel. The candle did not throw out much of a light and what it did was flickering and unstable, not enough to see far ahead.

'Strange,' Fidelma said after a while, 'I imagined that we would have passed that chamber filled with weapons before now. I wanted to examine that place again.'

'We have passed a few darkened entrances,' came Eadulf's voice in front of her. 'Perhaps the lights in that chamber have been doused and we have already passed it.'

Fidelma admitted that his suggestion was probably the right one.

'Can you find your way back to the guests' chambers? I think that is where we should find this Sigeric.'

Eadulf acknowledged her question with an affirmative grunt. He moved slowly, trying to remember the turns he had taken but reversing them. After a short while, as he turned a corner, he saw a faint light ahead, permeating through a hanging cloth. It was a tapestry.

He halted and turned to Fidelma with a whisper.

'I think I might have reached the guests' chamber where we were. It should be beyond that tapestry.'

'You have done well, Eadulf,' she said, moving forward to join him.

He put a restraining hand on her arm.

'When we left the chamber,' he whispered, 'I remember closing the door behind the tapestry. Someone must have opened it.'

She was not worried. 'Brother Higbald doubtless checked our escape route after we had left.'

'Perhaps,' he replied reluctantly.

'Are you ready, then?'

'I suppose so.'

'Then let us proceed!'

Eadulf moved forward along the tunnel to the tapestry. He could not see through it but was aware that there was a light filtering through the strands of the material. It could only come from candlelight beyond. He did not pause but reached forward, drew the cloth aside and stepped into the room behind. Fidelma followed him closely.

There was an elderly man seated in the chamber where Fidelma had been confined during her stay at Aldred's Abbey. He was seated with his bent back towards then, his head down as he appeared to be studying some sheets of vellum on the table before him. There were several candles lighting the room. The old man was making notes with a scratchy quill.

Perhaps it was the draught of air from the tunnel, a slight flickering of the candle on his desk, but the occupant of the room swung round in his chair and started up as his pale blue eyes fell upon them.

It was clear that in his youth he had been a handsome man. His features were strong. The jaw was still determined. His white hair grew thickly. He had the look of a man used to command; a warrior by build although age had caused his back to bend a little and his hand to tremble, although so slightly as to be not immediately noticeable until one examined it for a while.

He looked from one to another, his eyes now narrowing slightly.

'And who are you that creep up on me like thieves in the night?' he demanded. Then, without warning, he bellowed: 'Guards! To me!' His voice was still strong and resonant in spite of his age.

No sooner had he spoken than the door burst open. Two warriors rushed in with drawn swords. A moment later the muscular but mute Brother Beornwulf looked in and then disappeared. A bell began a clamour further down the corridor.

The old man slowly stood up and examined them.

'And who do we have here?' His voice was now soft but with a steely quality to it. 'Assassins? Thieves?'

Eadulf was about to speak when there came the sound of movement along the corridor.

Abbot Cild strode into the room, followed by an anxious-looking Brother Willibrod, his dark eye glinting. Behind them, Brother Beornwulf stood, still clutching the handbell by which he had summoned them.

Abbot Cild's features broke into a smile of triumph as he beheld them.

'Seize them!' he cried. 'Before they murder the lord Sigeric! No need for a trial now. We'll take them out and hang them immediately.'

Chapter Seventeen

'Wait!'

The old man spoke quietly, almost under his breath, but the word halted Abbot Cild and his companions. The abbot turned in protest to him.

'Lord Sigeric, they are foreigners who have come to our land spreading witchcraft and evil . . .'

Eadulf took a step forward.

'That is a lie. I am Eadulf of Seaxmund's Ham, one time *gerefa* of that place . . .'

'Silence!' roared Abbot Cild. 'How dare you address the high steward without permission?'

The old man examined Eadulf with bright grey eyes.

'And you are now a Christian?' He smiled thinly. 'Who is it that you travel with?' His eyes turned to Fidelma. 'She has the appearance of one of the Irish missionaries who have turned this land away from its old gods. Irish missionaries that King Ealdwulf has ordered to quit the kingdom.'

'It is true that Sister Fidelma is of the kingdom of Muman in the land of Éireann. Her brother reigns as King of that distant land. But she is no missionary here but a reputed advocate of the Irish laws.'

Sigeric sighed gently.

'I have heard of the kingdom of Muman. I have learnt much of that country from missionaries who have come to our land. Why did you sneak up on me like assassins? Is that what you are? Did you plan to kill me?'

Abbot Cild moved a step forward. His voice was loud and eager.

'Lord Sigeric, they clearly meant you harm, or they would not have come creeping up on you—'

'It is not so!' interrupted Eadulf. 'We needed to speak with you—'

Abbot Cild had nodded to Brother Beornwulf who took a step to Eadulf and, without warning, slapped him hard across the mouth, sending him staggering back against Fidelma. He lost his footing and stumbled to the ground. Blood appeared from his mouth. Fidelma bent to help him back on his feet.

'These are the evil pair that I warned you about, lord Sigeric,' Abbot Cild continued in his rage. 'The woman who conjures spirits. They escaped from my justice a few days ago. Search them and they will have weapons on them. They meant to kill you. I have no doubt about it.'

Sigeric's face, however, wore an expression of disapproval.

'You have no doubt? Well, perhaps I should be the best judge of their intentions, Cild. There is no need to ill-treat them. The laws of the Wuffingas say that each is allowed to speak in their defence. Would you deny the law?'

'My lord Sigeric, I say—'

'I will deal with this matter,' he said sharply. 'Now, Cild, you may take your people and leave this to me.'

The abbot hesitated a moment more. His features were still inflamed and for a moment it seemed that he would argue with Sigeric. Then he turned, still angry, and left without another word. He was followed by Brother Willibrod and the mute Brother Beornwulf.

Fidelma was still dabbing at Eadulf's bloodied mouth

with a cloth which she had damped from a jug of water. She turned to Sigeric.

'I thank you for your intervention.'

Sigeric sat back and there was no humour in his face.

'You may soon have no cause to thank me, Sister Fidelma. I am merciless to those who transgress our laws be they high born or low born, native or foreign.'

'Yet I have heard that you are a judge of sound qualities who seeks truth and justice for all, be they high born or low born, native or foreign,' replied Fidelma with a faint smile.

'And I am not susceptible to flattery, especially from a pretty woman,' snapped Sigeric. He turned to Eadulf. 'Well, Eadulf of Seaxmund's Ham – are you able to answer my questions?'

Eadulf took the cloth from Fidelma's hands and straightened up before the high steward of the King of the East Angles. He dabbed gently at his still bloodied mouth.

'I can only tell you the truth as I know it, lord Sigeric.'

'That is all anyone can do,' agreed Sigeric gravely. He sat back in his chair, his hands before him, fingertips pressing fingertips, and gazed from one to the other. 'What purpose brought you hither?'

'To appeal to you,' replied Eadulf. 'You are our only hope in our search for the truth in this place.'

'I have heard strange stories about you from Abbot Cild,' replied Sigeric. 'I have heard that you both forced your way into this abbey, and from that moment many evil portents appeared. The abbot says that the Irish woman conjured a spirit to haunt him. That when he charged her with witchcraft you both fled from the abbey, escaping his custody. Now you suddenly appear from I know not where and sneak into my chamber. Your purpose –

according to the abbot – is to kill me. You deny it. Very well. What have you to say?'

'It is not true,' replied Eadulf simply.

Sigeric sighed and nodded slowly.

'Of course it is not true.' He smiled thinly, sarcastically. 'No charge is ever true according to the person being charged. However, you must convince me that it is not so.'

'Let me explain,' began Fidelma, but Sigeric held up a hand.

'I am told that in your culture, Sister Fidelma, women have equal rights to be heard with men. That is not so among our people. I will listen only to Eadulf of Seaxmund's Ham.' He turned to Eadulf, who had flushed nervously at the expression on Fidelma's face.

'Lord Sigeric,' he began hesitantly, 'as I have said, Sister Fidelma is a learned judge in her own land. She has been asked by King Oswy of Northumberland to act in a legal capacity at Whitby and, indeed, by the Holy Father when she was in Rome . . .'

Sigeric shook his head. 'I do not doubt your good intentions, Eadulf, but those are foreign places. We are here in the kingdom of the East Angles and should I not follow our laws and customs? Let me remind you that those laws are the laws of the Wuffingas. Come, spare my impatience and let us proceed. Do you deny the charges of Abbot Cild?'

'We do,' Eadulf said with emphasis. 'There was evil in this abbey before we arrived.'

'Evil? Much power in that word "evil". Yet it is the individual who interprets what evil is and that interpretation varies from individual to individual,' Sigeric replied. 'Perhaps it is better to proceed with the story of how you came to this place, what you found and how matters unfolded.'

'It began, lord Sigeric, when Sister Fidelma and I

were in Canterbury. I was emissary of the Archbishop Theodore and had been on my embassy to King Colgú of Cashel, who is the brother of Sister Fidelma.'

Sigeric nodded slowly.

'So you move in illustrious circles, Eadulf?' he said in a dismissive tone. 'And so?'

'I was not meaning to impress you, lord Sigeric. It is a fact that I was at Canterbury and while there received a message from my old fried Brother Botulf, who was steward at this abbey.'

The name seemed to have an impact on the old man.

'Botulf? Botulf of Seaxmund . . . ? Of course you would know him. He was your friend? I knew him also for he tried to protect a coward who was outlawed. Botulf was sent to this abbey as a punishment.'

'So I have heard. But he was a moral man. When I was at Canterbury, I received a message requesting that I come to this abbey by a certain hour on a certain day as it was important. I did so, and Sister Fidelma accompanied me.'

Slowly, step by step, Eadulf began to trace the events of the last few days.

Sigeric sat quietly. He did not intervene further but sat, head bowed, nodding as if he were asleep.

When Eadulf finished, he glanced quickly at Fidelma, who smiled her approval at his recital. He had not left out any significant point.

Sigeric was drumming his fingers on the arm of his chair.

'You make claims that appear incredible and yet you present me with no solutions.'

'If Sister Fidelma were allowed to conduct—'

Sigeric interrupted with a sniff of disdain.

'I have told you of my decision on the matter of keeping to our customs. I do not like words like "if", either.'

Eadulf was outraged. 'Your reputation is great, lord

Sigeric, but how can you justify shutting your ears to the truth simply because it comes from the mouth of a woman?'

'You are impertinent, Eadulf of Seaxmund's Ham.' The high steward glowered. 'Perhaps you have dwelt too long among foreigners to recall your own cultural values?'

'The values that concern me are beyond cultures. They are intrinsic to all peoples,' snapped Eadulf, causing Fidelma to look at him in surprise. She had hardly seen him so angry before.

Sigeric's bodyguards moved uneasily forward but the old man motioned them back.

'Your concern to speak up for your companion is laudable, Eadulf . . .'

'My concern is to speak up for truth and justice,' replied Eadulf sharply.

'Whatever the purpose, there is a way of proceeding. In the first place, I need to put your version of the events to those who are concerned with them. You will be held until such time as I have done so.'

'Held?' demanded Eadulf, anger once more flushing his features.

This time Sigeric did not stop the two warriors moving forward and interposing themselves between Fidelma and Eadulf.

'No harm will come to either of you – neither from Abbot Cild nor anyone else. You have nothing to fear from that quarter until such time as I decide whether you are telling the truth or whether there is some other motive behind your actions.'

He reached forward and picked up a silver handbell from the table and rang it.

Almost at once the one-eyed Brother Willibrod came hurrying in.

'Does this abbey possess some secure chambers?' Sigeric demanded.

'Secure chambers?' The *dominus*'s eyes widened a little.

'That is what I asked,' Sigeric said patiently. 'I want this man and woman placed in a chamber under lock and key and held there until I say otherwise. They are to be treated well and not to be harmed. Anyone who transgresses that order will be answerable directly to me. Now, a secure chamber . . . and one which has no secret tunnels by which they may escape.'

'There is a chamber close to this one,' Brother Willibrod reflected. 'There is one door and a small window in it but the window is barred.'

'And you are sure that there are no passageways behind tapestries or moving masonry?' Sigeric demanded sarcastically. 'After all, you did not seem aware of the tunnel that leads into this room.'

Brother Willibrod spread his hands helplessly.

'This is an old building, my lord, built on an ancient Welisc fortress . . .'

'I do not want a history lesson, just an assurance that there is no exit apart from the one door which my men will guard.'

'I will swear an oath on it,' stuttered Brother Willibrod.

'Good,' replied the old man. His voice held a malicious quality. 'No one from this abbey, not even the abbot, will be permitted to see them. Werferth,' he turned to one of the two warriors, who was obviously the commander of his guards, 'you have heard my orders? Admit no one to their presence.'

'It shall be done, lord . . .' replied the warrior called Werferth, 'but what of food and drink?'

Sigeric considered the question with seriousness.

'I would not deny them that. You will see to that,

Willibrod. Meals will be handed to Werferth here who will then see that they are fed. Now, let it be done.'

Eadulf moved to protest.

'This will not solve the matter, lord Sigeric,' he stated coldly. He was now in control of his temper. 'Nor will imprisoning us prevent the effusion of blood that is coming because of this *troscud* which will, as I have explained, by its nature, plunge the kingdoms into war.'

The lord Sigeric rose, hands on hips.

'I am too old a dog to be taught new tricks, Eadulf. I will do things my way and that is the way of the Wuffingas. I have heard all that you have had to say. Now I shall consider it and form my judgments.' He signalled their dismissal.

His men pushed Fidelma and Eadulf outside, although it was not done roughly. Brother Willibrod preceded them to show them to the chamber that he had selected as their prison.

When the door slammed behind them they stood examining the tiny room into which they had been pushed. It was no more than two paces wide by three paces in depth and only just large enough to stand up in. At one end was a small barred window which looked out to nothing but sky. A bed and a stool comprised the only pieces of furniture. It was freezing cold.

'Well,' sighed Eadulf as he slumped to the stool, 'that effort was of little use to anyone.' His tone was bitter.

Fidelma was not one to spend much time lamenting on ill fortune. She went directly to the window and stared out.

'Time has passed swiftly,' she muttered. 'Mul must have given us up long ago. I see the dusk already coming down.'

'My stomach has already told me it is late,' complained Eadulf.

310

Fidelma turned back and examined the tiny chamber.

'I presume that this was once the cell of a brother. There is hardly room for two and that bed is very narrow.' She bent down and peered under it and uttered an expression of disgust. 'I hope we are not incarcerated in here long.'

Eadulf watched her mournfully.

'Sigeric was our only chance,' he said angrily, 'and he wouldn't even listen to you. Blind prejudice, I shall call it.'

To his surprise, Fidelma shook her head.

'He acted according to his conscience. You cannot argue that he could do more,' she replied. She was not upset.

'You surely can't say that you support his actions?' Eadulf was aghast at her apparent passivity.

'Put yourself in his place, Eadulf. What would you have done differently?'

'I cannot put myself in his place. I am not Sigeric.'

'Exactly. Nor is Sigeric you. He acts according to what he knows.'

'Then just how are we to get out of this place now? Abbot Cild is not going to allow us to escape a second time. He is already baying for our blood.'

She sat down on the bed. 'At least Sigeric seems sceptical about his charge of witchcraft,' she pointed out as she relaxed. Then she started forward and exclaimed: 'Oh!'

Eadulf flinched nervously and glanced round.

'What is it?' he demanded.

'I should tell someone where we left the ponies. It will be a cold night and they might freeze.'

Eadulf sighed. It was so like Fidelma to think of the welfare of animals even in this predicament.

She stood up and glanced around again.

'Well, I do not think we will be escaping from here

before Sigeric is ready to allow us out, so there is no need to have the ponies hidden ready, and by morning, well . . .'

She went to the door and called for the guards.

The bolts scraped and the tall warrior, Werferth, stood framed in the door, sword in hand.

'Speak, woman,' he snapped.

Fidelma returned his bleak look with a smile and told him where their ponies were tethered.

'Send someone to bring them into the abbey for warmth and fodder,' she instructed. 'Otherwise they will freeze outside during the night.'

The warrior stared at her in surprise, possibly sharing Eadulf's astonishment that she could think of the welfare of ponies at a time like this.

'It shall be done, woman,' Werferth said finally. 'Is that all?'

'It is all, except my friend here would welcome something to stay his hunger.'

'Food will be brought to you soon,' Werferth replied brusquely and closed the door. They heard the bolts rasping shut.

Fidelma returned and sat down on the bed again.

The time dragged and finally a meal was brought to them by Werferth. He was dour and professional, and there was no chance of opening any conversation with him. His companion stood at the door with drawn sword while he placed the tray on the stool before them. Then he exited without a word.

They ate in silence.

It was as they were finishing that they heard the sound of distant shouting. Then silence.

'What do you think that was?' asked Eadulf.

Fidelma shook her head. She did not reply. Quiet descended. Time passed. Finally, realising that they would probably be incarcerated overnight, they squeezed together on the narrow bed and tried to sleep.

They had been dozing. Neither of them was certain whether it was before or after midnight. The darkness had been a long time in their cell and there was no means of alleviating its shroud for they had neither candle nor oil lamp. They had made themselves as comfortable as they could on the bed and, in this manner, a fitful slumber had eventually overtaken them.

It was the rasping of bolts and the snap of commands which startled them into wakefulness and gave them a bare few seconds' warning before the door crashed in.

Eadulf rolled from the bed first, blinking and trying to focus.

Werferth and his companion stood inside the door with drawn swords.

A moment later, Sigeric entered with a lamp held in his hand. His face was pale and he looked shocked.

He waited while Fidelma roused herself and stood, bleary-eyed, trying to gather her wits.

'What is the matter?' Eadulf demanded, having recovered first.

Sigeric regarded him with his bright grey eyes for a moment and then said: 'Come with me. Both of you.' He turned abruptly.

Outside, the two warriors closed in behind Fidelma and Eadulf.

Eadulf instinctively reached for Fidelma's hand, found it and held it tight.

'Don't be afraid,' he whispered. 'If they mean to kill us, we will show that we care little for their pleasure in it.'

Fidelma's jaw tightened at his words but she said nothing.

Sigeric, his lamp held high, marched swiftly down the

corridors of the abbey – surprisingly swiftly for one of his advancing years.

He went directly towards the chapel of the abbey, through the cloisters and quadrangle, and entered through the main doors.

Groups of brethren were gathered in little knots here and there in the chapel. They turned as Sigeric came in. Fidelma and Eadulf noticed that, in the candlelight, their faces were frightened as they watched while the old man led his charges through their group towards the high altar.

Fidelma and Eadulf moved closer together, an instinctive form of self-protection, hands held even tighter. Was this to be some midnight trial at which they were already condemned?

As they drew nearer the altar, Eadulf caught sight of Brother Willibrod collapsed in a seat nearby. His shoulders were shaking uncontrollably and, to his surprise, Eadulf saw that the *dominus* was sobbing in an inconsolable manner. Eadulf exchanged an astonished glance with Fidelma. Sigeric took no notice of the *dominus*. He guided them towards another small group before the high altar.

Fidelma and Eadulf were aware of Brother Higbald bending over something which lay near the altar. Brother Beornwulf was also there, standing behind him with a scowl on his features.

To one side yet another figure sat surrounded by some of the brethren. One of Sigeric's warriors stood nearby. As they approached, those around the figure parted slightly as they turned towards them. The figure seated in their midst was revealed as Abbot Cild.

Sigeric halted before him. Fidelma and Eadulf drew up at his shoulder.

Abbot Cild looked up at them. His usually grim face

was wreathed in an inane smile. In fact, he was giggling like a child. Eadulf had never seen anything so alarming to the senses. It was a frightening, unpleasant sight, to see the strange, vacuous expression on the abbot's face.

They became aware that blood saturated the abbot's clothing; literally saturated it. Blood stained his hands which he held before him, twisting and wringing them together.

The abbot's eyes were vacant and, while he seemed aware of their presence as they stood before him, he did not appear to see them as individuals. He knew that they were there and he smiled up at them.

'I am free.' The words came out in between the giggles. 'I have rid myself of the ghost that has haunted me.'

Eadulf looked towards Sigeric but the old man was impassive.

'The demon, the wraith, that was conjured up to persecute me,' the abbot was continuing. 'I have destroyed it. Destroyed it. So easy. I am free.'

Eadulf was aware that Brother Redwald was one of the religious standing around the abbot. He looked towards the shocked face of the boy. Redwald met his gaze. His face was deathly white and his lip was trembling as his eyes went to where Brother Higbald was bending down. Both Eadulf and Fidelma turned and stared at what lay on the floor there. It was a slim body. The body of a girl with red-gold hair.

'It is Gélgeis.' Brother Redwald's hysterical cry suddenly resounded through the chapel. 'She is dead. Yet she was dead before. But now she is dead again. The abbot has killed the ghost of Gélgeis!'

Chapter Eighteen

Eadulf let go of Fidelma's hand and strode forward to where Brother Higbald was still bending over the body. The apothecary glanced up. Eadulf was surprised at the anger in the man's face. Higbald seemed about to say something to him but then he looked quickly away. Eadulf glanced down, peering closely at the features of the dead girl. Then he turned towards the sobbing Brother Redwald, who was trying to control an emotion that Eadulf realised was not grief.

'Come here,' Eadulf ordered in a sharp, imperative voice that surprised those about him.

The young boy moved automatically in response to his command. He shuffled forward to stand by Eadulf, his face twitching nervously.

'Don't be afraid, son.' Eadulf was suddenly gentle but firm. 'This body is bleeding too profusely to be a ghost. I want you to look down upon her face.'

Brother Redwald stared back at him, eyes wide, almost pleading.

'I cannot, Brother . . .'

'Look down!' snapped Eadulf.

The boy unwillingly lowered his gaze to the corpse.

'Tell us now, is that Gélgeis? You said that you knew her well. Is it she?'

Brother Redwald closed his eyes, not really looking, and merely nodded vigorously before backing quickly away.

'Do you say that this is a woman who has been dead for over a year?' growled Sigeric angrily. 'Think, boy. This is a substantial body and no ghost.'

The boy was crying, frightened and incoherent.

'The boy is useless as a witness,' admonished Fidelma, moving forward. She glanced towards Brother Willibrod. 'Shall we explain the identity of this girl, *dominus*, or will you?'

Sigeric was surprised. 'You know the identity of this girl?'

Fidelma grimaced, still looking at Brother Willibrod. He was too immersed in grief to answer her.

'Then I shall explain,' Eadulf said. 'This is the girl known locally as Lioba.'

'You mean that Gélgeis has not been dead but was living under the name of Lioba?' Sigeric asked quickly. 'You told me that you suspected a girl Lioba as being involved in some conspiracy. Now I am confused. What has that to do with Willibrod?'

'I'd rather that Brother Willibrod answer that question,' replied Eadulf firmly.

'I am at a loss to understand what is happening here.' Sigeric sighed. Then he looked across at Fidelma. She was bent down to the body of the girl and seemed to be examining her clothing. She looked up at Eadulf and gave a quick shake of her head. A number of expressions chased themselves across Sigeric's features. Confusion. Annoyance. Finally, resignation.

'Let no one touch anything here,' he ordered sharply. 'Remove Abbot Cild to his chamber and let someone remain with him. Brother Willibrod, are you able to return to your own chambers?' The *dominus* seemed to pull himself together at the harsh tone of command. He rose, wiping his face on his sleeve, and inclined his head in supplication. 'Then do so. Also take that young boy away,' motioning to Redwald, 'and see to him.'

Sigeric issued a stream of orders, placing his warriors on guard around the chapel. Finally, he turned back to Fidelma and Eadulf. He now seemed to have difficulty in articulating his thoughts.

'I have, perhaps, made a mistake,' he began hesitantly. 'My questions throw up more questions and now it seems that the abbot has killed a woman in this chapel because he believed that she was the ghost of his dead wife. But you identify her as a local woman named Lioba. This is a matter beyond my understanding.'

They waited silently for him to finish.

Sigeric was a proud man and it was hard for him to come to the point.

'Perhaps I made a mistake in incarcerating you while I tried to substantiate your claims against Abbot Cild. It might be that we could have prevented an unnecessary death.'

Fidelma waited a moment before she made a response.

'You did what you considered the right thing. No blame on you for that.'

Sigeric continued to look awkward.

'What I am trying to say is, do you see any solution to this mystery, Fidelma of Cashel? I . . . I would appreciate your assistance.'

Fidelma regarded him thoughtfully. The man was trying his best to overcome a cultural prejudice. She finally smiled gently.

'I believe that I might see the solution to the tragedy that pervades this abbey.'

Sigeric regarded her, still with some embarrassment on his features.

'You believe you can solve the mystery?'

Fidelma nodded quickly. 'I am sure of it.'

'Then explain it to me.'

To Eadulf's surprise, Fidelma shook her head.

'I will do so only on certain conditions,' she announced confidently.

An angry expression immediately crossed Sigeric's features.

'Do you dare bargain with me?' he asked sharply.

'I am not bargaining,' she assured him. 'I am telling you what I need in order to bring this matter to a successful conclusion.'

Sigeric hesitated, controlling his irritation. His features mirrored an inward struggle and then he seemed to relax. His calm nature returned.

'And what is it that you need?' he asked softly.

'Complete freedom and authority to conduct the investigation in the manner I am used to. I do not ask that you set up a court of law as we do in the five kingdoms of Éireann, but allow me to gather those I would call as witnesses and question them, using your authority to force them to answer my questions if they attempt to take refuge in your customs which give no regard to women.'

Sigeric blinked rapidly. 'We regard women only . . .' He paused and shrugged. 'This is much to ask of my people.'

'When I have conducted the inquiry,' went on Fidelma as if he had not spoken, 'then and only then shall you seek to prosecute those who bear culpability. But I want people to come to this abbey freely and to go freely if they are not guilty of the matters into which we inquire.'

There was a silence while Sigeric considered the proposal.

'You intrigue me, Fidelma,' he finally said. 'You intimate that you will call people who might be guilty of other crimes.'

'Guilty of no crimes I know of but perhaps guilty of something in your eyes,' she explained.

'Such as what?'

'I was thinking of Aldhere.'

Sigeric was astonished. 'The former thane of Bretta's Ham? The outlaw? You would call him here? He is guilty enough to hang for his other deeds.'

'Nevertheless, I would want him here and under safe conduct. He and his woman, Bertha.'

Sigeric hesitated again. It was clear that he was having difficulty with the decision he was having to make. Then he raised his arms slightly in resignation.

'You have my word. I accept your conditions.'

'And, of course, we must ask Gadra and his followers to attend. That is essential. Your King may not welcome them into this kingdom. Yet here they are and they must also have safe conduct to come and go.'

'Is there anyone else whom you would like to bring here? Perhaps we should invite Sigehere of the East Saxons? Perhaps, Wulfhere of Mercia?' asked Sigeric sarcastically. 'I suppose safe conduct will apply to all who are guilty of anything.'

'I must tell everyone that they may come freely, but if murder and treasonable conspiracy against this kingdom can be charged at their door, then they may not go freely. If they do not come under those conditions, if they choose to stay away, then their absence may be interpreted to their detriment.'

Sigeric's eyes narrowed for a moment and then he suddenly burst out laughing.

'By Woden's sword, Fidelma, you are a clever woman. I am sorry that I did not listen to you sooner.'

'Do I have your agreement on this?'

'You do.'

'Then I shall want riders to go out to find Aldhere and Gadra.'

She glanced at the frowning face of the apothecary hovering in the background and called him forward.

'Brother Higbald, I want you to make contact with Brother Laisre's man outside the abbey . . .'

The apothecary's jaw dropped.

'You know?' he gasped.

'I know that you are the unwilling means of communication with Gadra, Garb and Brother Laisre. I want them to be here in the chapel at noon tomorrow. Tell them that I can assure their safe conduct.'

Brother Higbald stood hesitating.

Sigeric was undoubtedly full of questions but he merely gestured impatiently at Brother Higbald.

'Do as she says. You may add my guarantee of safe conduct to Sister Fidelma's.'

'Now if we could find Mul . . .' Fidelma said, as the apothecary hurried off.

'Mul the farmer? The one who is called, locally, Mad Mul?'

Fidelma turned to Sigeric in surprise. 'Do you know him?'

'My men picked him up at dusk trying to find a way into this abbey. I will have him released immediately.'

Fidelma glanced at Eadulf in bewilderment.

Sigeric was smiling. 'It seems that when you did not contact him at the appointed hour at the smithy, he felt that harm had befallen you and attempted to enter the abbey to rescue you. A foolhardy man. But one, it seems, who is loyal to you both. You may instruct him as you wish.'

'Mul's coming here is certainly fortuitous,' agreed Fidelma. 'Tomorrow at noon, we may gather everyone here in the chapel of the abbey and unravel a strange

mystery. But before we do so there is more one question
that I would like to ask you.'

The old man gave a little bark of laughter.

'How can I refuse you now? Ask away, Fidelma.'

'What is the purpose of your visit to this abbey? What
brings the high steward of the kingdom to this remote
corner of it?'

Sigeric grinned. 'A good question and one that I
expected to be asked.'

'And will it receive an answer?'

'It will. I came here in answer to Brother Botulf's pleas
to King Ealdwulf to hold a new inquiry into Aldhere's
sentence of outlawry.'

'And was there to be a new inquiry?'

Sigeric shook his head. 'The sentence was to stand.
Similarly, there were complaints by Abbot Cild who
argued that he should be made thane of Bretta's Ham.'

'And what were you to say to him?' asked Fidelma.

'I was to advise Cild to accept his King's justice. King
Ealdwulf was growing weary of his complaints.'

'He had refused to accept the King's original judgment,' Eadulf pointed out. 'Why would he accept it
now?'

'That is what probably drove the devils in him.' Sigeric
reflected for a moment. 'I am not a Christian but I am old
enough to see the devils in a man. I think the King made
a mistake in confirming him as abbot in this abbey. I shall
request that he discuss the matter with his bishop on my
return. Cild is not suited to remain here.'

'It seems strange that the King would send his high
steward all the way here to state this,' observed Eadulf.
'It could be done by a messenger of lesser rank.'

Sigeric smiled at him, his bright eyes sparkling.

'You are an observant fellow, Eadulf. It was not the
only reason I was sent. Very well, I will tell you. Brother

Botulf may have been mistaken in his support of Aldhere but he was a good man. He had reported that in the last few months there had been an increase in raids by warbands in this area which he believed were not to be blamed on Aldhere. He believed that Cild was responsible for them but could not prove it. I came here to make inquiries into this matter.'

'And what of Aldhere?' asked Fidelma.

'Aldhere? He is safe for tomorrow. Whether the raids and burnings are due to him or to his brother, and I will find out, as an outlaw, Aldhere is still beyond the King's pardon.'

'Do you think that his judgment was just?'

Again Sigeric smiled thinly. 'You have spoken to Aldhere, no doubt.'

'Of course.'

'He is a personable and persuasive man. But let us say that the King's judgment was just according to the facts placed before him. The King's justice will not change.'

Fidelma nodded thoughtfully. 'Well, now we can pursue the main purpose and attempt to resolve the evil that seems to permeate these walls.'

The chapel was packed to capacity not only with members of the abbey's religious community but with Gadra and Garb and their followers, with Brother Laisre and his co-religionists, and with the cynical Aldhere, his woman Bertha, and some members of his outlaw band, whom he insisted on including for his personal protection. The farmer, Mul, was also present, having acted as Fidelma's messenger that morning. The lord Sigeric had taken the abbot's usual seat before the congregation. He wore a chain of office and carried his official staff.

As Fidelma entered the chapel with Eadulf at her side, she had noticed that there was no sign of Abbot Cild and she had turned directly to Sigeric with the obvious question.

'The man is out of his mind, Sister. He is no longer in this world,' the high steward explained. 'The slaughter of what he deemed to be the ghost of the wife he thought long dead has unhinged his mind. He sits in his chambers mumbling and chuckling, shut in his own world. It would be pointless to bring him before this assembly.'

The news did not surprise her. She had seen the state of Abbot Cild when he had been led away to his chamber. It was a condition from which she felt that he would not recover immediately, if at all. It was justice in a sort of way, although it would have been better had he been able to answer before the assembly for his sins.

She glanced around the gathering and saw Brother Willibrod seated prominently. He was now composed and sitting straight-backed, his one restless dark eye red from weeping. Beside him was young Brother Redwald, still with drawn, white face and shivering now and then.

Sigeric cleared his throat to attract Fidelma's attention and whispered, 'Are you now ready to proceed to enlighten us about this matter, Sister?'

'I am,' she replied firmly.

Sigeric immediately rose from his seat and an expectant hush descended in the chapel. Although there was no need, he tapped the butt end of his staff of office on the ground.

'Most of you know me,' he began in a harsh tone which compelled their obedience. 'I am the lord Sigeric, high steward to Ealdwulf, King of the East Angles. I am come to this place to dispense the justice of the Wuffingas. You are all come safely here at my pleasure and will go safely unless there be any here that are guilty of the crimes connected with the deaths that have occurred in this abbey, or of treason against this kingdom. I trust that I have made myself clear on this matter?'

He paused and when no one answered him he indicated Fidelma with a motion of his hand.

'You may all know that this is Fidelma, sister to the King of Muman in the land of Éireann. I am told that she is a lawyer of some repute in her own land. Even beyond the boundaries of her own country, she has been consulted by King Oswy of Northumberland and by the head of your religion of Christ who dwells in far-off Rome. Though I represent the law of the Wuffingas which accords no place of authority to women, even though I be of the ancient faith, I have accepted that Fidelma of Cashel may have authority under me to pursue the truth of the events that have taken place here. Let none among you deny her authority, for in doing so you deny my authority and that of your King whom I represent. Is this understood?'

Again there was a silence, while the congregation looked at one another in surprise but said nothing. The Angles and Saxons were momentarily shocked at what Sigeric was suggesting. That a woman argue law before them was beyond their experience. Sigeric simply took their stunned silence as a sign of assent. He returned to his seat and motioned for Fidelma to take his place before them.

Fidelma had argued before bigger and grander gatherings and had no fears of addressing an assembly that was both surprised and hostile. It seemed that only Gadra's party and the Irish religious were not perturbed by Fidelma's being asked to officiate. Many of them were smiling, pleased that one representing their own legal system was to argue the case before them.

'There is a saying among my people,' Fidelma began, 'that evil enters like a needle and grows like an oak tree. Truly, there was a great evil within these walls.'

Her flat opening statement caught their attention and the whispering that had begun among the Angles and Saxons as she stepped forward to address them slowly faded. There followed a silence, broken only by the murmuring of Brother Laisre who had taken it on himself to interpret from Saxon into Irish for the benefit of Gadra. Garb seemed to have enough command of the language to follow the proceedings.

'It is appropriate that we are gathered here in this place today on the Feast of the Holy Innocents. This is the day when we remember the infants of Bethlehem who were killed by the order of King Herod in an attempt to be rid of the child Jesus. This is the day we commemorate the shedding of innocent blood. What better day to ask account of the innocent blood that has been shed here?'

She paused to gather her thoughts.

'There have been several killings within these walls and even emanating from these walls. Blood almost saturates them. That is not right for a house of religious devotion. Since coming here I have heard how the original brethren were chased out and some were executed. Brother Pol, for example, was hanged outside the gates as a heretic. We have heard that the abbot's wife, unhappy and alone, also met her death. Some claim she met that death by her husband's own hand, others say that she wandered into a nearby mire to meet her tragic end.

'We have heard that local people, during the last six months, have come to expect raids on their farms and homesteads. Mul, a local farmer who is present, lost his wife and two children to the swords of these raiders.

'Brother Eadulf's friend, Brother Botulf, asked us to come to this place because he needed help. The morning of the day we arrived, he was murdered. Two days ago, Botulf's cousin, one of Aldhere's outlaws, and several more of his men were slain. The evidence indicated that they were slain by the brethren of this abbey and, indeed, Mul will tell you that the evidence at his farmstead points to the raiders' being the religious of this abbey.'

This brought forth gasps of astonishment from many of the brethren, while the men of Aldhere and Gadra cast angry and threatening glances towards the abbey's religious.

Fidelma held up a hand to quiet them.

'Throughout all these troubles, the abbot claimed that he was haunted by the ghost of his wife, Gélgeis.'

'God's justice!' sang out Brother Tola from the ranks of the Irish religious. 'The shade of a wronged woman, murdered. May she haunt him to hell!'

An uneasy muttering broke out and Fidelma had to hold up her hands to still it once again.

'So obsessed was Abbot Cild that he even accused me of conjuring this wraith that seemed to haunt the abbey grounds. Last night he came across a young woman who he thought was that shade and in his madness he struck out with a knife and slew her.'

She saw Brother Redwald sitting shivering.

'It was her,' he whispered, loud enough to be heard. 'It was the lady Gélgeis. I saw her.'

Gadra had sprung up, his face contorted by anger, when the statement had been interpreted.

'What nonsense is this?' he demanded. 'My daughter was murdered by Cild months ago. Who says that she was slain last night?'

'Peace, Gadra of Maigh Eo,' instructed Fidelma. 'Things will be revealed but all in their time. This mystery has several strands – separate strands that, in some predestined pattern, seem to entwine and meet together in this gloomy spot. I will unravel each in turn, or make the best attempt I can. I have the word of the high steward Sigeric that no one need fear this process unless they are directly connected to treason or an unlawful death.'

Sigeric nodded from his chair.

'I have made clear my intentions,' he announced firmly. 'Continue.'

'Let us start firstly with an area in which I have some expertise. Gadra's *troscud*. Gadra.' She turned towards him.

The elderly chieftain from Maigh Eo rose again from his seat.

'You know well the conditions of the ritual fast, Sister Fidelma. You will not dissuade me from it.'

'Indeed. But you have heard that Abbot Cild is insane. The law in the text *Do Brethaibh Gaire*, which is designed to protect society from the insane, and likewise protects the insane from society, states that you cannot fast against someone who is insane.'

She had begun speaking to him in Irish while Eadulf interpreted for those who did not understand the language.

Gadra was not perturbed.

'Should it be that Cild is proved to have gone insane – and proof is required under the law – then it does not affect the outcome of my search for justice.'

'How so?' replied Fidelma, knowing full well but wishing him to explain the law to the assembly.

'Because the crime against my daughter, Gélgeis, was committed when he was sane. Therefore, he was still legally responsible and the matter of compensation for my daughter's death is still payable.'

'But a *dásachtarch*,' Fidelma resorted to the legal term for an insane person subject to violent and destructive moods, 'is not liable.'

'No, but his kin are,' replied the old chieftain sourly. 'In this case, as a religieux, the community of this abbey are his kin and must recompense me for the death of my daughter. If they do not, my ritual fast becomes a fast against this abbey and I will maintain it to the death.'

Fidelma shook her head sadly.

'Never have I seen a man pursue death so eagerly, Gadra,' she murmured.

Aldhere arose and was smiling his usual cynically amused expression.

'At least my brother, Cild, did one good thing, Sister. He went into the church and the church became his family. So I am absolved, under your laws, from paying compensation for his deeds.'

'The law is as Gadra says,' she agreed. 'So, Gadra, you are determined to continue with the *troscud* and all that will come of it?'

Garb was on his feet in support of his father.

'My father has said so,' he snapped. 'Just because the murderer now seeks asylum in the dark reaches of his mind it does not abrogate his responsibility.'

'But what if the girl whom the abbot stabbed to death in his torment last night was Gélgeis, what then?' Eadulf intervened, much to Fidelma's disapproval. 'That would mean that Gélgeis had fabricated her death some months ago and was playing some game of her own devising.'

There was a shocked silence for a moment. Then Garb chuckled.

'If such a ridiculous claim were true, are you trying to tell us that Cild would not be responsible under law?'

Before Fidelma could intervene, Eadulf spoke again, having caught sight of her disapproving features.

'I was hypothesising, Garb.'

An angry murmur began but Garb's voice rang out: 'A cruel hypothesis, when we know the facts! But I will answer. It would still mean that Cild murdered my

330

sister whether that act took place last year or last night! Recompense would still be due.'

There was a growing unrest.

'Is this your argument?' intervened Sigeric. 'Are you claiming that Gélgeis was still alive until last night and part of some plot? What was its purpose? To drive Cild insane?'

'I intend to prove that a real person was haunting this abbey and not a ghost,' replied Fidelma calmly. 'What I cannot yet prove is who this person was. I believe that Cild, whether in his madness or in reality, thought that it was his wife. The next step in the process is to find out who the dead girl was.'

Sigeric looked bewildered. Fidelma continued.

'Certainly, the abbot was seeing a person who he thought was the ghost of his wife and that encouraged his dementia,' she explained. 'Cild was of an abnormal mentality right from the start of his life. Aldhere was telling the truth about his brother's fits and rages as a young man, which was why his father dispossessed him. He knew that his eldest son was insane. How that insanity began I do not know. What evil possessed him is difficult to say. A single leaf of the oak does not go brown, wither and fall on its own account. It does so with the knowledge of the whole tree. In search of that reason, we should examine Cild's family.'

Aldhere gave a bark of laughter. 'You'll not find insanity in me, Sister.'

'We will accept your word for it . . . for the time being.' Fidelma smiled icily. 'However, that does not immediately concern us. We are concerned with Cild's behaviour. It was growing more aberrant as time went by. When he started to see what he thought was the apparition of his wife, it merely pushed him further, more quickly, into the abyss of insanity.'

331

Sigeric nodded appreciatively. 'And then, when he had the opportunity, he struck out at the girl?'

'That is so. He came across Lioba in the chapel and, in the darkness, unreason overtook him and in his fear and rage he struck her down.' She looked around at the assembly. 'There is one thing, however, which is the most important point.'

'What is that?' demanded Sigeric, when Fidelma paused.

'Someone instigated the appearance of these apparitions. I am told that during this particular time of year, what you called Yuletide before the coming of the Christian celebrations, the dead could seek vengeance on the living. I believe that these apparitions were timed to this period. Someone meant to drive Cild insane.'

There was a sudden hush.

Slowly, Fidelma turned to where Brother Higbald was sitting. He saw her eyes resting on him, saw a faint smile at the corner of her mouth, and he returned her gaze with a frown crossing his features. After a few minutes he coughed nervously.

'Why do you stare at me so, Sister?' he demanded in a tight voice.

'Lioba came into the abbey last night to meet someone by the chapel,' she said. 'She came to meet you, Brother Higbald.'

The apothecary's eyes narrowed slightly. 'What makes you think that?'

'I do not think it, Higbald. I know it to be so. You knew Lioba well—'

'So did many people,' snapped the apothecary. 'Many knew her very well. She sold her body for what she could get—'

Brother Willibrod moved with such alacrity for one of his girth and visual handicap that most people were surprised. Only Eadulf managed to reach him before the *dominus* made contact with the apothecary. He twisted his arm in a tight hold and pushed him back towards his seat.

'Control yourself, Willibrod,' he hissed. 'Our aim is to get to the truth, unpalatable or not. Sit and control yourself otherwise I must eject you from these proceedings.'

When order had been restored, Fidelma resumed: 'Lioba may well have sold her body but not to you, Higbald. With you she seemed to have a different relationship. Why was that?'

The apothecary shrugged in feigned indifference. 'I don't know what you mean.'

'Let me enlighten you. You persuaded Eadulf and myself to escape from the abbey by telling us a warband was marching on the abbey. It was not true. Lioba and a band of warriors were waiting at the spot where they thought we would emerge from the tunnels. You had carefully directed us. It was thanks to Eadulf's confusion that we emerged at another place.'

Higbald did not answer but sat scowling at her.

'Lioba was also in your band of warriors when you came to what you thought was a rendezvous with Cild and Willibrod the other night. Cild had already left the appointed place. That was when you made the arrangement to meet Lioba in the abbey last night.'

Sigeric started forward in his chair. 'You will have to explain this, Fidelma, because it has gone far beyond my understanding. I am not following this at all.'

'I will now explain very clearly,' Fidelma assured him.

At that moment the doors of the chapel crashed open and one of the brethren of the abbey came rushing in breathlessly. He was wringing his hands in an almost comical fashion.

'It's the abbot! The abbot has fled his chamber!'

Chapter Nineteen

As Sigeric struggled to call for order as the babble of reaction greeted the news, a new chaos ensued when Garb leapt from his seat shouting: 'The beast is escaping! He shall not elude his responsibility so easily!' Then, with several of his warriors at his heels, the young man hurried from the chapel, ignoring calls from Sigeric to stay where he was. Behind him, the religious and warriors were in disarray.

Eadulf was conscious of Fidelma's frustration. She barely concealed her anger at the turn of events as the assembly arose beyond control. Sigeric gave up the task. With Fidelma and Eadulf following, he hurried towards the religieux standing by the chapel doors.

'What happened?' demanded Sigeric loudly, trying to make himself heard above the noise.

The religieux waved his hands in a fluttering, helpless gesture.

'I am not at fault, lord . . .'

'What happened?' Sigeric thundered again in a tone that seemed to reverberate around him.

'I was tricked,' the man complained, in a whining voice. 'I thought Abbot Cild had fallen asleep and so I took the opportunity to go to the *defaecatorum* but when I returned he had gone. I rushed to the gates and saw him heading off along the road on horse-back.'

'By the wounds of Thunor!' cried Sigeric. 'He will be well away by now. Which way did he go?'

'Towards Hob's Mire.'

They rushed into the main courtyard of the chapel to see a group of Irish warriors clattering out of the courtyard on horseback, led by Garb.

Sigeric turned to Werferth, who had kept close to his side.

'Go after them,' he instructed sharply. 'See that they inflict no harm on the abbot if they retake him.'

Gadra, who had joined them unnoticed with Brother Laisre, said softly: 'My son will not inflict harm on Cild. He is under the constraint of the *troscud*. To inflict injury on the abbot now is prohibited. Sister Fidelma, tell the Saxon that what I say is true.'

'Gadra is correct,' she said at once. 'Once the *troscud* is announced, no harm may be inflicted by either party until they are come to arbitration.'

Werferth had already left, urging his horse out of the abbey gates after the others.

Fidelma was shaking her head in frustration.

'This is most vexing,' she breathed.

Sigeric was in agreement.

'If I remember correctly, you were about to accuse one of the brethren here . . .'

'Brother Higbald, the apothecary,' pointed out Eadulf in excitement. 'He was involved in a conspiracy with Lioba.'

Fidelma suddenly turned round with a startled expression. She raced back into the chapel, the others on her heels. As she suspected, there was no sign of Higbald, nor of Beornwulf and a half-dozen other of the younger religious. She stamped her foot and turned quickly to Sigeric.

'How many warriors do you have left here to rely on?'

Sigeric was startled.

'Werferth has just gone after the Irish. I only have three men left and my coachman, who is no warrior. What danger is there that you need warriors?'

She ignored the question and turned to Gadra.

'And you? How many warriors?'

'Two men, my personal bodyguard. My son has taken the rest. What troubles you, Sister Fidelma?'

'Higbald,' replied Fidelma. 'He intends to trouble all of us. He is a warrior of Mercia and so are six, at least, of the young men who have gone with him, including Beornwulf.'

Sigeric was bewildered.

'I don't understand. What are Mercian warriors doing in this abbey?'

Fidelma compressed her lips momentarily.

'It is easy to explain. Your neighbour, Wulfhere of Mercia, is trying to reassert the power of his kingdom. Higbald was sent here with some of his warriors because Mercia had heard of the dissensions between Cild and Aldhere. He came here to incite violence and increase the tension so that King Ealdwulf would have to intervene with force . . .'

'Which is precisely what he is thinking of doing,' agreed Sigeric. 'That is why I was sent here, to answer Botulf and give Cild and Aldhere warning that if the violence did not end then Ealdwulf would end it.'

'Higbald and his men came to this abbey pretending to be religious. It was a good disguise and the abbey a good base from which to stir up unrest. As it is an old fortress, they were able to keep their weapons in one of the disused chambers below the abbey. There are several chambers and passageways there. Botulf had discovered this but he was killed by Higbald or one of his men before he could reveal it. His body was found outside the crypt door.'

Sigeric was still puzzled.

'Are you saying that Botulf brought you to the abbey because of this?'

'His discovery of Higbald's hidden armoury was coincidental,' explained Fidelma. 'He had called Eadulf here simply because of the *troscud*.'

'So when you were about to accuse Higbald of conspiracy with Lioba, this was where your accusations were leading?' asked Sigeric.

'I was hoping to make Higbald admit the conspiracy,' agreed Fidelma. 'The proof seems to be in his flight. When several of Aldhere's men were slaughtered two days ago, evidence was planted with the bodies to show that it was the religious of this abbey who were responsible. Higbald had conducted several raids in the surrounding area, each time leaving evidence to incriminate either Cild and his men or Aldhere and his men. Finally, in one last act to incite King Ealdwulf to march to this region with a small force to attack Aldhere, Higbald planned to slaughter Abbot Cild and some of the brethren. He lured them with a message to a spot near here, where he intended to ambush them. As fortune had it, Abbot Cild thought he saw the ghost of his wife on the marsh and fled before Higbald came along. When Higbald arrived, Lioba was riding with him.'

'How do you know this?' asked Sigeric.

'Because we were there, under cover, watching the event transpire.'

'And what are you saying that the purpose of these slaughters was?'

'To ensure that the people remained at each other's throats. Above all, as I said, to entice King Ealdwulf to come to this area with a small force, large enough to attack Aldhere but not large enough to withstand an ambush which would have been prepared using Wulfhere's main army from Mercia. King Ealdwulf would have been killed and Mercia would have taken over the kingdom.'

'You will have to prove this,' Sigeric said heavily.

'I will. But now Higbald and his men have gone for their arms, we might be in danger.'

Sigeric realised why Fidelma was now anxious about the number of warriors they could rely on. He glanced quickly across to Gadra.

'Well, Gadra, will your men join me in defending this place against Higbald?'

The old chieftain shook his head when Brother Laisre interpreted the request. His face wore a stubborn expression.

'This quarrel with Mercia is no quarrel of mine. My quarrel is with Abbot Cild.'

Sigeric's face fell.

'I am with you!' cried Mul the farmer, who was now brandishing a wicked-looking sickle.

'You have not asked me,' intervened Aldhere, who had been standing nearby. 'I have half a dozen men with me. If it was Higbald who slaughtered Wiglaf and my men the other day then I owe him a debt that must be settled in blood.'

'I cannot use outlaws . . .' protested Sigeric.

'There is no time to quibble, Sigeric,' Fidelma advised sharply. 'We must find Higbald before he finds us.'

The old man hesitated a moment and then shrugged.

'Needs must when the devil drives,' he muttered. 'We'll search the abbey. Where first?'

'The chamber where they hid their weapons,' Eadulf suggested immediately. 'They will have gone there to get their armour.'

Gadra and his followers, with the rest of the religious, remained in the chapel. Fidelma and Eadulf led the way to the guests' chambers and through the tunnel. They realised that there must be an entrance through the crypt but Higbald might have prepared an ambush for them on that direct route. With Sigeric and his men, and Aldhere and some of his warriors, pressing after them, they made their way cautiously along the tunnels. The chamber was lit but empty. However, it was clear that Higbald and his men had been there and taken what equipment they could. Discarded items lay scattered on the floor. Eadulf pointed out the Mercian emblems to Sigeric.

'Have they gone back to attack the abbey?' Aldhere asked.

'I don't think so, at least not yet,' Fidelma said. 'Higbald has only half a dozen men and he is probably not sure how many we can rely on. I think he will withdraw to consider his next move.'

Aldhere laughed grimly.

'Then I'll go after him. He'll not get far.'

Fidelma surprised him by firmly shaking her head.

'Not yet, Aldhere. He might have anticipated that and be waiting in ambush. From what I've seen, he had good archers among his men. Wiglaf found that out the hard way. We should make ourselves secure, that is all. Besides, we are still in the middle of bringing the story of these mysteries at Aldred's Abbey to a conclusion. If we defend ourselves from a surprise attack we may then conclude our deliberations in the chapel.'

The outlaw shrugged nonchalantly.

'Whatever you say, Sister. The sooner this charade is ended the better. From what Sigeric has already said, it will do me no good. I am judged guilty no matter how this affair turns out.'

Sigeric did not respond to his gibe. They made their way back to the main quadrangle of the abbey in silence. As they reached it, Garb and his men, together with Werferth, came riding back through the gate. Their faces were grim and there was no sign of Abbot Cild, only a single riderless horse.

Garb addressed himself directly to Fidelma.

'The abbot is dead,' he said flatly.

When Fidelma translated, Aldhere gave a strange sound, like a sharp bark. But he said no more.

'What happened?' demanded Sigeric threateningly. 'Did any of your men lay a hand on him? I thought you said that such a thing would not happen under your law?'

'My men laid no hand on him,' snapped Garb.

Werferth had dismounted and came with confirmation of the facts.

'Lord Sigeric,' he said, 'we rode after the abbot, who made for the marshlands near here. We had no chance of catching up with him. He came to the marsh, flung himself from his horse and leapt into a bog.' The man shrugged. 'He had gone under by the time we reached it. There was nothing we could do.'

Sigeric exhaled in a long, deep sigh.

'Then Abbot Cild is dead by his own hand?'

'Sunk into the bog, lord. No other man was involved in his death.'

'Exactly as Gélgeis met her end,' said Garb. 'He has gone to join her in the shifting mud of the marsh.'

'Hob's Mire. A fitting end. A fitting end.' It was the mournful voice of the *dominus*, Brother Willibrod, who had joined them unnoticed.

'An end too easy for a murderer,' replied Garb. 'I will report this to my father.'

He turned and strode into the chapel, followed by his companions.

Fidelma turned to Werferth.

'Are you sure that Cild has met his end in the marsh-lands? There is no possibility that he could have escaped from the bog?'

The warrior glanced nervously at Sigeric, as if waiting for his permission to respond to her. Then he inclined his head.

'I swear to it. I was a witness. There was nothing that could be done. I saw him jump into the mire and by the time the foreigner and I reached the spot there were but bubbles on the surface.'

'Very well,' said Sigeric. 'You are a good tracker, Werferth. The men will remain here, but see if you can follow the tracks of half a dozen riders who have recently left here. You should pick up their trail from the back of the abbey. They are Mercian warriors. Higbald leads them. I want to know where they are or in what direction they have gone. Be absolutely vigilant. They might be waiting in ambush or they might be planning an attack on the abbey.'

If Werferth was surprised, he did not show it, but went quickly to his horse and left through the abbey gates.

Aldhere was now standing with a forced smile on his lips. He seemed to have made a quick recovery from the news of his brother's suicide.

'So Cild has met a fitting end, eh? In which case, there is no need for my men and me to stay.'

Fidelma eyed him coldly. 'On the contrary, as I said before, there is every need. We have yet to finish summing up this mystery. Please, go back to the chapel.'

He shrugged but did not argue with her orders.

Fidelma, Eadulf and Sigeric walked slowly after him.

'Does Cild's death end the threat of this *troscud* by Gadra?' asked Eadulf.

'No. But the truth must come out even though it is unpalatable to him,' replied Fidelma inscrutably.

They entered the chapel and took up their positions. There was a restlessness among the assembly that had not been there before. Gadra and his followers were talking among themselves.

'Gadra!' cried Fidelma, stilling their murmurs. 'You have heard that Abbot Cild has taken his own life, plunging into the bog in his insanity. Do you now call off your *troscud*?'

Gadra stood up. 'While the news is greeted as a just and fitting end to a base and evil life, I am still left without a daughter. I have told you before that if Cild was unable to compensate me for her honour price then his family, that is this abbey, is responsible. The *troscud* goes on until I am recompensed for the loss of my daughter.'

Fidelma sighed softly.

'You are a hard man, Gadra.'

'I am Gadra of the Uí Briúin, chieftain of Maigh Eo!' he replied with dignity.

'So be it.' Fidelma paused. 'I said, when I started, that I would take matters step by step. Lord Sigeric, will you lead the way to the crypt where the body of the girl slaughtered by Abbot Cild has been laid out?'

The old man rose, his features expressing his perplexity, but he had long since given up any hope of following Fidelma's argument.

'Gadra, Garb – I want you both to accompany us. Also, I want you, Brother Willibrod, and you, Brother Redwald, to come. You all knew Gélgeis and the girl called Lioba.'

Eadulf was instructed to see that no one left the chapel in their absence.

In grim procession they proceeded down the short flight of steps to the crypt. On a stone slab, the girl's body had been laid out ready for burial.

Gadra and Garb gave a gasp as they saw her red hair and slim pale figure.

'By the . . .' began Gadra, moving quickly forward,

and then he sighed, shaking his head. 'There is a super-ficial resemblance, Fidelma, but you are wrong if you thought that this was my daughter. I do not know who this poor girl was but I know that it is not Gélgeis.'

Brother Redwald, at Fidelma's firm prompting, bent forward and his face was crimson.

'Well?' she pressed him. 'What have you to say?'

The boy look anguished.

'In the shadows, I swore . . . she does look so like. Maybe I imagined the likeness when she was leaning over you in the chamber.'

'But this is not Gélgeis as you remember her?'

The boy shook his head.

Fidelma swung round to Brother Willibrod.

'But you can confirm that it is Lioba, can't you?'

Brother Willibrod was doing his best to control his features and stop his lips trembling. He nodded. Then he gave a long sob.

'That is Lioba. There was never any question of its being Gélgeis. I loved Lioba. Now let us be gone from this place and I will tell you what you want to know.'

Back in the chapel, Fidelma explained.

'The girl is not Gélgeis but a local girl called Lioba who bears a superficial resemblance to Gélgeis,' she announced. She turned to Brother Willibrod. 'Do you confirm this?'

He stood with his head hung low as everyone resumed their seats.

'Several in this abbey knew Lioba. She was the daughter of a farmer up in the hills behind the abbey while her mother had been a slave taken in a raid on the shores of Éireann.'

'She spoke both languages?' queried Eadulf. 'Irish as well as Saxon?'

Brother Willibrod nodded.

'And you were her lover? You disobeyed the rule of celibacy that Abbot Cild was trying to enforce?'

Again the *dominus* hung his head and nodded.

'How often did Lioba come to the abbey?' went on Eadulf after Fidelma had indicated that he should continue with his questions.

'Come to the abbey?' Brother Willibrod shrugged. 'Now and again. Not often. But I used to meet her at her father's hut, some way from here in the woods.'

'Think about this question carefully, Brother Willibrod,' Eadulf urged. 'Let your mind and not your emotions answer it, for I think you had great emotions for this poor girl.'

Willibrod's eyes flashed a moment.

'I do,' he muttered.

'What sort of things did you discuss with Lioba? Was she interested in events at the abbey? Was she interested in anyone else here?'

'What are you saying?' cried Brother Willibrod, suddenly angry.

'What I am saying,' Eadulf calmly replied, 'is that some local people thought that Lioba sold her favours not merely to the brethren but to Aldhere's men.'

'It's a lie! A lie!' cried the outraged *dominus*. 'She loved me. True, I gave her little gifts. She was alone. She had to get the wherewithal to be able to live, but you are suggesting that she was . . . suggesting that she was a . . .' He broke down into outraged sobbing.

Eadulf was not deterred.

'Come, Brother Willibrod. Isn't it true that Lioba used to ask you many questions about what was happening within the abbey?'

Receiving no reply, Eadulf suddenly turned to Aldhere.

'You seem to offer a different picture of Lioba from Brother Willibrod's. Perhaps you might explain that?'

Aldhere stood up hesitantly.

'It is true that the girl appeared to make her living by visits to my men,' he said.

Brother Willibrod raised both fists to his forehead and gave forth a wretched cry. He collapsed in his seat and huddled there giving vent to long, inconsolable sobs.

'And was it noticed that Lioba liked to ask questions of your men?'

The look on Aldhere's face answered the question.

Fidelma now turned to the young, pale-featured Brother Redwald.

'You told Abbot Cild that when you entered my chamber as I lay ill you saw the figure of Gélgeis bending over me. You swore that you knew her because she had nursed you when you were sick. Was that figure, in reality, the girl Lioba?'

Brother Redwald stood up, looking around him nervously. He was embarrassed.

'I was mistaken in thinking this morning that Lioba was Gélgeis,' he said hesitantly.

'Think what I am asking you,' Fidelma pressed.

'I accept now that the person I saw must have been Lioba,' said the boy. 'At the time, I was sure that it was Gélgeis. But it was evening, the chamber was dark. I must have been wrong.'

Sigeric had sat back in his chair, rubbing his chin thoughtfully.

'So let us sum matters up. What are we saying? That this girl, who had a superficial resemblance to Gélgeis, the wife of the abbot, was seen at various times at the abbey. That Abbot Cild became demented and thought he was being haunted. In his madness, he killed her?'

Aldhere called out humorously: 'But since Cild is dead and the abbey has to pay this foreign prince to prevent war, there should be an end to this story. Surely there is no more to hear?'

'There are the evil deeds of Higbald,' Sigeric pointed out. 'We are told that he meant to create mayhem and bloodshed in this land.'

'He was responsible for many murders which have been ascribed to Abbot Cild,' agreed Fidelma.

'What?' It was Gadra's son rising to his feet, only just having heard what had happened in his absence from his father. 'You are not suggesting that it was this Higbald and not Cild who murdered my sister, Gélgeis?'

Fidelma shook her head sadly.

'I am not suggesting that, Garb. Cild was responsible for several deaths, such as that of Brother Pol and many other brothers and even sisters who followed the Rule of Columba. At first I suspected that Cild was responsible for Brother Botulf's death. Botulf knew all about Gadra's intended *troscud*. He became the intermediary after Brother Pol was killed and so knew when Garb would come to the abbey, the hour and the day when he would announce the *troscud*. That was why he sent a message to Brother Eadulf at Canterbury asking him to come to the abbey before that hour.'

'He had hoped that I could advise him and, indeed, the abbey, of the laws applying to the *troscud*,' added Eadulf unnecessarily.

'Yet it was not the forthcoming announcement of the *troscud* nor Botulf's liaison with Garb that led to his death,' Fidelma went on. 'Botulf had begun to suspect that Higbald was not what he appeared. The night before we arrived at the abbey, Botulf discovered where Higbald and his men kept their weapons. He was surprised by Higbald or one of his men who slew him and then removed his body to the courtyard outside this chapel.'

'How do you know this?' demanded Sigeric. 'Do you have a witness?'

'No,' replied Fidelma. 'But there are two pieces of evidence. Firstly, Eadulf found some writing in Brother Botulf's own hand.'

She gestured for him to produce it.

Eadulf held up the paper that he had discovered in his friend's cell. The paper that had been hidden in the book satchel.

'I am sure Brother Willibrod will remember when I searched that book satchel,' he said. 'And he will recognise the hand of Brother Botulf.'

'Botulf tells us several things in these encrypted notes,' Fidelma explained. 'In the last note, a quotation from Proverbs, he tells us that Bretta's son was going insane. It was Cild of whom we spoke. More importantly, he indicates that he was waiting for Eadulf to arrive.'

Eadulf handed Sigeric the papers.

Sigeric began to read the Latin with a fluency which surprised Fidelma. She had not thought a pagan would have a knowledge of the language.

'God willing, my friend will be here soon.' Sigeric frowned. 'This refers to Eadulf?'

Eadulf nodded. Sigeric continued: 'Is it not written that mercy is the support of justice? Not so in the man of Merce. We will be destroyed by the people . . .' Sigeric paused and frowned. 'How does this relate to this matter?'

'Eadulf and I were confused because the note is encrypted,' replied Fidelma. 'We thought it read "people of the marshes". What are those but Aldhere's outlaws? But that was not what Botulf was saying. We misread it. He wrote "We will be destroyed by the people of the march." The borderlands . . . and who are they?'

Sigeric's eyebrows rose a little.

'Not marsh but march, which is the meaning of the name of Mercia,' he said slowly.

'Indeed.' Fidelma smiled. 'What does he write, Eadulf?'

'It is written that mercy is the support of justice but not in Higbald, a man of Merce . . . Merce is the old form of the name Mercia.'

'Botulf has preceded this by hinting that outward appearances were not what they seemed. That Higbald was no more a religious than Aldhere was a saint.'

'If Higbald is taken captive, he shall be interrogated closely on this matter,' Sigeric said. 'But you said that you have further evidence?'

Fidelma nodded.

'I said that Botulf was slain in the underground chamber where Higbald and his men kept their weaponry. You will find bloodstains which lead from there into the crypt. Eadulf and I found Botulf's purse there. It had been ripped from his belt as he was killed or as he was removed to where his body was later found.'

'So Higbald's plot has been uncovered but is unrelated to the conflict between Abbot Cild and his brother Aldhere?' Sigeric asked.

'Only in that he was able to play on their quarrel,' confirmed Fidelma.

Gadra had risen, finally betraying his impatience.

'All this is no concern of mine. Once more I call upon the people of this abbey to recompense me for the murder of my daughter – murdered at the hands of its abbot. Without compensation, the *troscud* starts at the intended time and its result is the responsibility of everyone here.'

He rose and turned towards the doors. Garb and his followers began to move with him.

'Wait, Gadra of Maigh Eo!' Fidelma called.

The sharp command in her voice caused the old chieftain to turn, frowning at her.

'I did not want to do this, Gadra, but your determination thrusts this action upon me.'

She had their attention now. They turned to her expectantly.

'You were right, Gadra, when you said that your daughter Gélgeis made a mistake when she left Maigh Eo with Cild. She discovered that mistake soon afterwards and, as you said, she wrote to you about it. She was young, in a foreign land, and her husband abused her badly. All this you knew.'

'I am glad that you accept my word on this, Fidelma,' replied Gadra, frowning but clearly not understanding where Fidelma was leading.

'Gélgeis was reported dead in Hob's Mire, where Cild has now taken his own life. Cild had been of an unbalanced nature probably since childhood. On that I have said that we may accept the word of his brother Aldhere.'

The outlaw smiled thinly and gave a mocking bow in her direction.

'Again, as I have said, a woman was seen about the abbey. She resembled Gélgeis. Her form haunted Abbot Cild. There was the slaughter of the black cat on the high altar, recalling an incident from his youthful madness. This wraith pursued him, until it drove him completely out of his mind with the result that he killed Lioba and then took his own life.'

'We have heard about Lioba's movements in the abbey,' agreed Sigeric. 'So this spectre was one of flesh and blood?'

'Indeed, it was. There were several witnesses to this spectre, including myself. Yesterday morning, on the marshes with Eadulf and Mul, I found evidence of how one of the manifestations was done and traces of how a ghostly sheen was given to her appearance.'

'What purpose would this false haunting achieve?' demanded Gadra.

'The very thing it has achieved – to drive Cild insane.'

'Why?'

'An act of vengeance for the cruelty that he has inflicted.'

Sigeric leaned forward.

'And Lioba played this role? But what cruelty had the abbot done to her?' he demanded.

'The other evening, when Eadulf and I were watching Abbot Cild with Brother Willibrod and the others waiting by the marsh – you'll recall they had been asked to be there by Higbald who planned to kill them and lay the blame on Aldhere – just as he killed Wiglaf and his men and laid the blame on Abbot Cild . . . while we were watching, the image of Gélgeis on horseback appeared in the marsh . . .'

'That's right, that's right,' cried Brother Willibrod. 'But that was no ordinary person! It glowed! It was a ghost . . . !'

'It was not. As I have said, the next morning we went to the spot and found proof that a real person had been there on horseback. She had smeared herself with a special clay which glows and reflects near a light . . . the light supplied by the *ignis fatuus*.'

'Where are you leading us now, Fidelma?' demanded Sigeric.

'Shortly after the apparition put Cild to flight, Higbald and his men came along – and Lioba was with them. The apparition had not been Lioba. Young Brother Redwald was right when he pointed out that Lioba only bore a superficial resemblance to Gélgeis . . . and that he was absolutely certain that it was Gélgeis whom he saw bending over me when I was stricken with fever.'

There was a long silence.

Fidelma turned to Gadra. 'You see, Gélgeis did not perish in Hob's Mire. She is alive and sought vengeance on Cild – and was supported in that vengeance by the man who gave her comfort in her misery and with whom she went to live.'

Gadra was shaking his head as if unable to understand what she was saying.

'I don't understand.'

Fidelma turned to Aldhere. 'Tell me, Aldhere, did Botulf ever speak to you of Gélgeis's sister, Mella? Did he tell you the news that Gélgeis heard just before she left the abbey on the night she disappeared?'

'News?' Aldhere was bewildered.

'Did Botulf tell you that Mella had been taken by a Saxon slaver and had died?'

'No, why would—?' His jaw clamped shut suddenly.

Fidelma had turned to the woman at his side.

'Will you cast aside your veil now, Gélgeis?'

Bertha the Frank rose slowly to her feet. Then she drew her veil aside, along with a flaxen hair piece, and revealed a small, pale complexion surmounted by red hair. She smiled at Fidelma, but it was a smile filled with venom, and bowed her head slowly in her direction.

It took a long while for the hubbub to die down.

When it did, Gélgeis spoke, slowly and coldly.

'You are very clever, Fidelma of Cashel. How did you know?'

'I suspected when Brother Eadulf observed the scar on the arm of the woman known as Bertha and when Garb told us that Brother Pol had observed the scar on Gélgeis's arm caused by Cild's whip. If Bertha and Gélgeis were one and the same, then things began to fit into a pattern. Was it your intention to drive Cild insane when you began these appearances as the ghost of yourself?'

'I did not drive Cild insane – he was insane when I

married him, although I did not realise it. He wanted the money and position that he thought marriage to me would bring him. He did not realise that under our law, no such privileges come by right as they do under Saxon law. When he realised it he showed his true, evil self. He never loved me. His dementia became more extreme. It is a just retribution that he has taken his own life. My satisfaction is but a small token of the payment that I am owed. My life was a misery. Finally I wrote to my father and told him of my unhappiness.'

Gadra had sat down abruptly, pale and bewildered. There was no pity in her look when Gélgeis glanced at the shocked old man.

'I desperately wanted my father to come and rescue me from my misery. When I needed practical help, all that came back was a message via Brother Pol and that message was no more than a lecture on duty, obedience, law and the rituals of law. That is what he is pursuing now with his stupid *troscud*. What use is that? Ritual to hide the reality. There is no feeling in ritual.

'Each day I prayed that my father would come riding up to the abbey and take me away from the pain that my life had become. Yes, I made the choice to go with Cild. Must I suffer forever from a wrong choice? In my own land, I could have been divorced from him by law. Is that not so, *dálaigh*?'

Fidelma inclined her head.

'In our law, divorce is permitted for many reasons. There are several grounds for divorce and eleven circumstances for a separation without fine or penalty from either partner.'

Gélgeis chuckled without humour.

'And here, in this land, there is no right for women to divorce. And still my father spoke to me of obedience to law and ritual. Now he comes here with his law and ritual but without care for me.'

Perhaps only Fidelma heard the lonely wail of a lost child that lay behind the girl's coldness.

'And so you met Aldhere?' she prompted.

'Yes, I met Aldhere and we shared a hatred of Cild. I ran off with him and stayed with him in the guise of a badly treated Frankish slave woman, thus explaining my veil and accent. We managed to convince people that Gélgeis had perished in Hob's Mire. It was only when we heard recently from Wiglaf that his Cousin Botulf was increasingly concerned that Cild was growing more and more demented that we decided that we would help that beast suffer.'

'Did Botulf know that you were not dead?'

Aldhere intervened. 'Botulf, as I have said before, was an old friend of mine. He knew Gélgeis was unhappy. He knew that she had found happiness with me and had decided to leave Cild. Botulf knew our secret and kept it until death.'

'From Wiglaf I learnt the secret of the tunnels into the abbey,' went on Gélgeis, 'and using them I made the ghostly appearances.'

'Your purpose was to drive Cild into such insanity that he would take his own life?' Fidelma pressed.

'My purpose was to revenge myself on him,' Gélgeis said simply.

'Surely he had some feelings of love for you? He would not have been so emotionally disturbed by the appearance of a dead wife for whom he felt nothing.' Eadulf frowned.

Gélgeis laughed. It was not a humorous sound.

'He felt only fear and guilt and, in his madness, thought the spirits of the dark world were taking their vengeance on him.'

'Did Botulf approve of this?' Eadulf was incredulous.

Gélgeis shook her head. 'Your friend Botulf was a moral man, as Aldhere will confirm. No, he did not even know of my plan to revenge myself. But he did not betray me – even to my own brother, Garb, when he arrived with this ridiculous plan of a *troscud*.'

'Ridiculous? We came and placed ourselves in danger for you and yet you never thought of informing us, your family, that you were alive!' exploded Garb, staring angrily at his sister.

Gélgeis shook her head with a cynical smile.

'My family did not care about me until I was dead and then only because he' – she pointed to her father – 'wanted to act out his concern with ritual.'

Aldhere now rose and took Gélgeis's hand. His men rose too and gathered around him.

'As Gélgeis says, you are a clever woman, Fidelma. I am still not sure how you knew. It surely cannot have been that Bertha and Gélgeis shared a scar?'

Fidelma smiled briefly at him. 'You made a mistake. You spoke of your knowledge of Mella's death. You said that Gélgeis had told you. But the news of Mella's death was not known until after Gélgeis was supposed to have died in Hob's Mire. Unless you were communing with the dead, then Gélgeis was still alive. If she was still alive, and Lioba was not Gélgeis, then it was simple, when Eadulf mentioned the scar, to work out who she must be.'

Aldhere looked thoughtful for a moment and then he smiled thinly.

'As neither Gélgeis nor I have played any part in the bloodshed that has taken place here, we will take our leave.'

'Where will you go?' asked Eadulf in astonishment. He could not help liking the outlaw.

Aldhere smiled broadly. 'Back to the marshlands, holy *gerefa*, where else? There we will remain until King Ealdwulf changes his mind or has need of us. When the armies of Wulfhere of Mercia march across our borders King Ealdwulf will need us. I was thane of Bretta's Ham and will be so again. Tell him that from me, lord Sigeric.'

Sigeric went to say something, hesitated and then waved his hand in dismissal.

'One moment, Gélgeis!' Fidelma's voice stayed them and the girl looked around with a frown. 'There is one final question I would like to ask before you leave. When you manifested your ghostly appearance the other night before Cild in Hob's Mire, how did you know that Cild and some of the brethren would be there to see you?'

Gélgeis chuckled, this time with genuine humour.

'Do not tell me that the great *dálaigh* is not omniscient?' She smiled sarcastically. 'Is it not said that a person of learning should understand half a word?'

'It is also said that when you admit ignorance, then you obtain wisdom.'

Gélgeis pouted. 'Many events are not planned. I was on my way to the abbey to make another appearance to Cild. As I was crossing the marsh, I saw a band of riders by the trees. I seized the opportunity, not knowing it was Cild. When I saw the riders return to the abbey and saw two figures coming into the marsh towards me, I decided that it was manifestation enough for that night. So I departed home.'

'So it was mere coincidence?'

'Our fate is written more by coincidence than by careful planning.'

Fidelma inclined her head to the girl.

'You have become a philosopher, Gélgeis. May you find peace and contentment.'

There was a silence as Aldhere and Gélgeis, with Aldhere's men, walked out of the chapel. Gélgeis did not look once in the direction of her father and brother.

As they left, Eadulf turned quietly to Fidelma.

'I cannot make up my mind whether Gélgeis is possessed of a good or evil character.'

Fidelma smiled. 'As you will recall, neither could others. Some in the abbey thought of her as kindly and well loved while others did not like her. The fact is that no person is all good or all bad and can display both qualities at the same time to different people. I tend to the conclusion that the badness was brought out by circumstance.'

She glanced across to Gélgeis's family. She could not help a tinge of sympathy as they sat, pale and hunched. Brother Laisre was leaning forward and patting the old chieftain on the arm.

'And you, Gadra of Maigh Eo, will you depart now in peace and abandon this *troscud*?' Fidelma asked. 'Remember that I did not want to bring you to this realisation. Only your blind insistence to pursue . . .' She paused and lifted her shoulder slightly before letting it fall.

It was Garb who answered her on behalf of his father.

'The *troscud* is abandoned, Sister. If there is no cause then there can be no effect. We will return to Maigh Eo.'

They were leaving the chapel when Werferth, the commander of Sigeric's bodyguard, entered and came to Sigeric.

'I have followed the tracks of the Mercian Higbald and his men, lord Sigeric. They are heading directly to Mercia. They have fled from this place.'

Sigeric sighed in resignation.

'So it would seem that we cannot even punish Higbald

for the crimes here? There is one part of this sad tale that I do not understand. Why did Higbald want to lead you both into a trap? Cild was going to charge you with witchcraft. Why not let Cild judiciously murder you? Why go to the trouble?'

'Remember that Higbald was an agent of Mercia, sent here to cause the maximum dissension and trouble,' Eadulf pointed out. 'I realised, in retrospect, that when I rode out after Cild so that I would be with him when he caught up with Aldhere – that morning when Cild pretended to go in search of his brother – I was just saved from death at the hands of Higbald myself.'

Sigeric was puzzled and even Fidelma turned with interest.

'Remember that Garb told us that Higbald followed me from the abbey?' went on Eadulf. 'Had not Garb and his men waylaid Higbald, I believe it was Higbald's intention to kill me and blame that act on Aldhere. The spreading of dissonance, suspicion and discord was his primary aim. Garb probably saved my life. The same motivation applied when he made an elaborate plan to get Fidelma and me to escape. Had Cild executed Fidelma for witchcraft, insane as the act would be, it could be argued that it was done within the law. But if we were murdered outside the abbey, then there would be no excuse. More suspicion and alarm could be created. What a consummate liar Higbald proved to be.'

'Ah well, we may meet Higbald again one day,' Sigeric sighed. 'If Mercia does attack, let us hope our sword arms are stronger than Mercian intrigue.' The old man glanced around the chapel. Now all that was left of the assembly were the dozen or so religious with Brother Willibrod at their head. He was chastened, still red-eyed but now in doleful command. The high steward waved him forward.

'There is still a stench of evil in this abbey, Brother Willibrod,' Sigeric announced. 'I will apportion no blame here but I will report this to King Ealdwulf's bishop, who should take responsibility for this place. Woden's blessing that I am not Christian to upbraid you. Why were no reports sent to King Ealdwulf or to his bishop on the behaviour of your abbot?'

When Brother Willibrod opened his mouth, Sigeric held up his hand, palm outwards.

'No, I do not want to hear. Save your excuses for the bishop of your faith. I will merely report on what I have found. Meantime, you will remain here in charge of the brethren of this place until you hear from the bishop. It will be your task to set this abbey to rights.'

He rose from his seat and moved forward to Fidelma with his hand outstretched.

'I have learnt much in the last few hours, Fidelma of Cashel. I apologise for my cultural ignorance. I regret it. May your God be on all the roads you travel. You, too, Brother Eadulf. You have a companion whose beauty is matched by her wisdom.'

Signalling to Werferth to accompany him, the old man turned and left the chapel.

Brother Willibrod turned to his brethren and started to issue orders, leaving Fidelma and Eadulf to exit into the main quadrangle together. They emerged in the pale sunshine of the late winter afternoon. Another hour and it would be dark. Mul the farmer was waiting for them.

'Well,' the farmer smiled nervously, looking from one to the other, 'I presume that neither of you wants to stay another night in this evil place? There is always a warm bed in my farmhouse. A warm bed, good sweet cider and a wholesome meal.'

Fidelma exchanged a quick look with Eadulf and nodded slightly.

Mul grinned broadly. 'In that case, I'll go and find those ponies of yours. I don't think your countrymen will be wanting them back, Sister. They've all set out for Tunstall in a great hurry. I'll meet you back here in a moment.'

Fidelma sat down on the stone bench in the quadrangle and looked around at the oppressive dark walls of the abbey.

'A sad business, Eadulf. Truly sad.'

'Will you come on to Seaxmund's Ham, then?' Eadulf suddenly asked. 'You have not seen where I was born. Not that there is much to see. Poor Botulf is gone and he was the friend of my youth. Nor is there anyone left there whom I can call kin. Nevertheless, I would like to see the place as I am so close.'

Fidelma smiled softly at him.

'Indeed, since we are so close, I will not refuse to come with you, Eadulf,' she said quietly. 'After all, it is your birthplace.'

'And after that, what then?' he asked hesitantly.

'After that?' The corners of Fidelma's mouth turned downwards with a suggestion of her old humour. 'I want to return to my brother's kingdom. I want my baby to be born in Cashel.'